Lemonade Farm

by
Laura Cayouette

LA to NOLA Press

© 2014 Laura Cayouette

ISBN 978-1503264144

First Edition: December 2014

Back cover photo by Robert Larriviere.

For the people who taught me

that family takes many shapes.

Chapter One

Mommy kept talking the whole way there. I could see her Frost-N-Tip curls shaking from behind the headrest. The engine was so loud that sometimes it drowned out her voice and a wave of calm would wash over me for just one second. We were really nowhere now. Nothing looked familiar. Sometimes we'd pass a house but mostly it was just green with cows or horses.

Montgomery was sitting in the front seat looking through the glove box for something to play with. Mommy just kept talking. We turned right. A development of two-story houses with aluminum siding, yards and carports (just like at home) moved past my window like the backdrop outside the *Partridge Family*'s bus. Mommy was saying how we'd probably go to school with these kids. I pictured myself living in the blue one with the white trim. I pictured my husband, Tommy, pulling into the carport as I waved hello from the doorway. But Mommy just kept driving into the green.

It was a tunnel now, a tree tunnel. Nothing around but Mommy's bouncing curls, my brother rooting through trash and green so thick it stopped the sun. We could be anywhere. Anywhere but home.

Home was Mayfair Drive. Home had a poured concrete porch, scarred with white scrapes in circles from the metal wheels of my roller skates. It was where I knew the good hiding places and what part of the street was best for zone dodge. Home was where the molded-metal front door made that same old "crack-eeeek" it had since we moved in when I was five. It was where I knew which candy each house handed out for Halloween and who gave fruit. Home had a maple tree Daddy planted in the front yard to grow with me. It was still a sapling.

I lost my stomach on the last hill before the trees opened out to fields of grass and corn. My stomach thudded back down as the sun hit my face. Montgomery took pennies out of the glove box and stuffed them in his front pocket, looked around sneaky-like then closed the box. We turned right. Grey rocks spit out from under the tires and flew into bushes on either side of the driveway.

Mommy's voice was too high from nerves she hoped we wouldn't detect. "This is it! We're here! Isn't it beautiful? A whole mansion just for us."

It was truly huge if that's what makes a mansion. All bricks and windows, it seemed insurmountable. Mommy got out of the Mustang and pushed the seat forward for me. I stepped on her greying Keds as she loaded me up with bags from the backseat and handed her purse to Montgomery. He hopped on one foot toward the flagstone side porch with staircases on either end leading to doors.

"Take the staircase on the right, Honey." Mommy pointed with her hip while lifting another box. "The right one, honey. Other way, sweetie. That's it. Ariel, he's dropping things. Can you take that from him? Hold on for Mommy, honey. I'll get the door."

I trailed behind Montgomery picking up Mommy's lipstick and wallet. Mommy took the purse and pushed her hand around in it. "Oh dear." She ran back down to the car and leaned inside the open window. "Oh dear." She pulled the door open and leaned across the front seat. "Ariel, honey, knock on the door, please."

I knocked on peeling white paint.

"Knock loud, honey."

The pounding echoed inside. The cats had moved in yesterday and Pillows jumped to the window beside me. He pushed his grey cheek along the screen and rumbled. Mommy said the cats had to stay inside until they realized we lived here now. I stuck my finger on the screen for Pillows to rub and lick.

"No answer? Don't panic. Herbert has to be around here somewhere. See, this just builds the suspense of the moment you finally get to see inside."

Herbert Hobart had lived in the house behind us on Mayfair Drive but Janet took their three kids and moved out.

Through brown film on the little windows in the door, I could see some of the dark kitchen full of boxes. Mommy opened the other door a crack but a chain held it tight. Her yell bounced around inside. "Heeeerbert! Herbeeeert?"

"Mommy, I can do it." Pride pushed my chest out. "I can open the door." I thrust my arm through the opening. "Watch, Mommy." I closed the door on my arm as far as it would go, pressing the old wood on my bones. My fingers found the chain's end and slowly slid it down its metal track toward the bulb at the end. Almost. I pictured myself the hero. Almost. I saw Mommy bragging to the newspapers. Got it. The chain thudded against the molding when I pushed the door open.

"Home." Mommy took a step in then whirled around. "No, wait! Go back outside. I'll open the other door and we'll start from the back and work forward."

Montgomery stopped at each window to peek on his way to the kitchen door. Passing him, I lightly smacked his arm. "Hurry up, dummy. We can look at it from the inside."

He just kept stopping.

Mommy opened the kitchen door like it was the end of a magic trick. "Home."

Inside, beyond the boxes, all marked "KITCHEN" in black magic marker, was a white enamel sink and wash board with rust stains - tea on teeth. I ran my fingers along the rough surface of a red brick wall with a fireplace like the ones in Williamsburg. "Is this a pioneer house, Mommy?"

"No, sweetie. It was built in the late seventeen hundreds. I think the pioneers here were done by then."

"What kind of house is it?"

"A wonderful, old house."

I squatted in front of the fireplace. A black metal rod stuck out and a joint made it movable. Ashes filled the grooves between the bricks like dirty snow in roadside ditches. I pictured a black kettle full of some pioneer food bubbling over a fire. I pictured myself sitting by the fire in a long, plaid dress with a shawl over my shoulders. I was sewing homemade clothes. My husband would be home from hunting soon. The baby was asleep in the wooden cradle he built under the quilt I had sewn. It was a baby girl and we named her...

"Ariel, don't touch. Wait until we get unpacked and clean it up a little."

I followed Mommy into the dining room. Montgomery stayed behind disobediently touching the metal rod, then joined us, rubbing and pounding at soot on his Levi's.

"Okay kids, this is a very special doorway here. Come hold hands."

"Mommy, it's just a door." Sometimes, her enthusiasm felt like a burden, something for me to live up to.

"No, this is very special. This house was built in two halves one hundred years apart. When you step out of this part of the house, you're stepping forward in history. Hold on and we'll jump through the door together."

"Mommy." I pulled my hand from hers but she had that "don't spoil this" face on, and my heart hurt. I sighed and put my hand back up.

"One, two, three, jump!"

Our plastic soled shoes slapped down onto rich burgundy wood. The unchained door still hung open. We passed Anne's room without going in. Even though she wasn't moved in yet, we knew better than to invade her privacy. An old, tall trunk of a tree with no limbs and no leaves loomed outside the floor to ceiling windows in the living room. The fireplace mantle was as big as a railroad tie and the room was so long that there was a door at either end.

We passed a *Gone with the Wind* staircase, giant double doors that marked the front of the house and a room full of light with a plush, pale green carpet running from wall to wall with white flecks throughout like snow on grass. I followed Mommy up the showy staircase while Montgomery stayed behind to lick a distorted pane of glass.

Framed posters rested against walls in Mommy's room and pretty fabrics spilled out of boxes like paint flowing from toppled cans. Herbert's room was sparsely furnished with an early American dresser and a simple four poster bed. Isabelle's whimsical fairy-land of pottery and macramé and Merlin's eclectic gathering of kaleidoscopes, kites and geodes were upstairs in the attic.

Isabelle Busch used to live down the street at Mayfair Drive but she left Bentley and moved into a big house with lots of people where she met Merlin. They called it, "The Big House." Dad moved in with Bentley after they sent the girls to live with Nana and Grandy "until Isabelle and Bentley could figure things out." But they never did.

The playroom was in the older half of the house, a space full of nothing but the promise of children playing board games, watching cartoons and dressing dolls. It was big enough for forward rolls and maybe even a cartwheel.

Mom pointed to the door at the back. "That room is yours, Montgomery. In the back is the door to Rayne's room and through there is the door to the room you and Samantha will share, Ariel."

"All those people have to go through my room?" Montgomery's face was all sour and questioning.

"For now, honey, but we'll fix it. Don't worry."

I walked through the maze to the staircase, narrow and curved, that led to the loft I would share with Sammi. The tiny, hot A-framed room was five and a half feet, my height, at its apex. I kneeled on the short loops of kelly green indoor/outdoor carpeting to look out the two small windows near the floor. The backyard was giant with a Lincoln Log type pavilion and a tree-lined field.

"Look, Ariel." Mommy stood at the bottom of the stairs. "You two can close this door and stay private. There's a latch on the door."

"That latch works from Rayne's side." I descended the staircase and challenged her with my unsmiling eyes. Sometimes I felt so superior to her.

"Oh. Well, look, here's a hook-and-eye on your side and she probably can't reach that latch. Won't it be great to room with Samantha?"

Rayne's windows overlooked our very own pool and from here I could see the only water - a green slime in the diving well. Mommy's hand ran over the back of my head. "We're going to clean it and fill it. It's going to be a lot of fun, Ariel. You'll see. Just give it a chance."

Downstairs, a door opened and Mommy's hand jerked away.

"Madeleine, you here?" Merlin's voice had a tone that made everything he said sound like a joke. On Halloween, he had come to Isabelle's party wearing a bear head and kept it on all night so that I never knew what he looked like until we met again. He was sort of like a bear without the mask on too, all brown-haired and wet-eyed.

He helped Herbert and Isabelle unload groceries but stopped to toss me a Tootsie Roll. "Hey, how's it goin', Ariel? We got some food. Madeleine, you would have loved this store. Like something out of *The Twilight Zone*. It was called Pam Paw's Grocery and Feed. Can you believe it? Madeleine, these guys were wearing overalls. No shit. Real overalls. I'm talking' Osh Kosh B'Gosh. I bet they own cows. It was great. They didn't know what to make of us, they thought we were hippies. Next time, you have to come with us. We'll make it a field trip. Ariel, catch." He threw another Tootsie Roll. "Remind me I owe Montgomery two. Heck, we'll take the kids too. Let 'em see what it's like out here in the country."

The Busch's cats, Mehetabel and Uncha, ran through Mommy's legs as she grabbed a paper bag from Herbert whose dark hairy-knuckled hand continued moving and pushed grey and black plastic glasses into his head.

"I forgot to take a key with me today, Herbert. We have to get the copies soon. I thought we were locked out when I got here with the kids. If it hadn't been for---"

I felt my back get straight.

"I left the front door unlocked." Herbert returned to the car for another load, shoving the back of his button-down office shirt into belted shorts.

"You did? We didn't try that. Now, why didn't we try the front?"

My heart sank down into me like we'd just driven over a big bump on a winding road.

Montgomery looked down at me from his bedroom window, long blonde curls obscuring his eyes. I looked back until he finally walked away from the screen.

Everyone was busy unpacking paper bags when I put mine on the dirty linoleum floor. They were all laughing.

"Finish the story, Merlin." Mommy pulled her shirt down smooth over her breasts.

"Oh yeah. So I say to the guy, 'You know, bottled water,' and he says, `You mean distilled water?' I mean, he'd really never heard of it."

"I bet most people never heard of paying for drinking water, Merlin. I hope you didn't make him feel too stupid."

"No, I didn't, Mad. But what are we supposed to do 'til the pipes clear? Have you seen this water? It's like something out of a bad horror movie."

Mommy piled vegetables into the crisper. "Did you flush the system?"

"What's that?"

"That's what the guy said. He said to `flush the system.' I thought you'd know what it meant."

"That's when you run water through all the pipes in the house until the water comes clear." Herbert always knew what to do.

"No, we didn't do that yet. Sounds good. What say, guys? Why don't we try it after we eat?" One thing I knew about Merlin was that he always liked food and fun before chores, just like a kid.

Herbert stopped stacking boxes of cereal and used his man-in-charge voice. "It only takes about ten minutes. I'll take the bathroom down here."

Merlin lifted the lever on the double basin sink. Loud grumbling came from behind a wall and rust colored water spat from the faucet, splashed against the stained white enamel and flew back up onto Merlin's lavender Izod shirt. "Shit!"

He said the S-word.

Isabelle left the room so she wouldn't snicker in front of him. I heard her running up the stairs then more grumbling and creaking emanated from all around us as air bubbles pulsed the stream of water in the sink. Everyone silently stared waiting for it to turn colors.

I laid my head against Mommy's ribs. "I'm hungry, Mommy."

"We're eating later, honey. Why don't you unpack those two bags over there. I think they're all canned goods."

"Mommy, I'm hungry now."

"Look, it's getting clear." Merlin slapped his hand against his thigh like he was surprised.

I stuck my finger in the water, chilled from the ground. Peach tinted, it divided over my pointer and joined at the other side. Mommy lay salad fixings beside me and I smacked the lettuce against the sideboard. I dug my fingers through the layers and beneath the loosened core to pull it out, then poured now-clear water into the hole. Mommy dropped some carrots next to me. Isabelle and Herbert reentered, victorious.

"Did you all come up with a name while you were out?" Mommy grabbed a can of instant lemonade.

Isabelle handed her a scuffed Tupperware pitcher. "Merlin, you had one, didn't you?"

"Yeah, yeah. The Second Chance."

Mommy turned the hand wheel on the can opener. "Hey, that's nice. I like that. Didn't you think of one, Isabelle?" She rinsed newspaper ink from the pitcher. "What about Starting Over or something like that?"

"Mine was Warm Fuzzy Farm."

"Oh, how precious." Mommy's voice rose in timber. "Like in *T.A. for Tots*."

"How about The Nut House 'cause I'm not living anywhere named Warm Fuzzy Farm." I threw long, heavy hair over my shoulder.

Isabelle laughed. "What about The New Virgins?"

"I've got it." Mommy clapped her hands, applauding her own idea. "The New Family Farm."

"Wow, that's good." Isabelle nodded. "Or The Creative Living Farm."

Herbert methodically stacked canned goods. "Why not Crowsfoot Estates? That's what the sign says and I think it's a fine name."

"Why not Egghead Estates or Every Man Estates?" Merlin liked teasing.

"Okay, Shoestring Estates, you know, like our budgets," Isabelle dug through a box. "Or Friendly Neighbor Farm."

"I still like New Family Farm." Dust rose as Mommy poured lemonade powder into the water. "Or Creative Living."

Herbert smiled like he had a secret. "Why not call it what it really is?"

"Not Crowsfoot again."

"No, Divorce Court Farm."

"That's not funny." The wooden spoon clanged dully against the plastic pitcher while Mommy swirled the liquid solution. "We can't call it that. Why not something cheerful?"

"We'll call it Happy Farm." Isabelle let a low chuckle escape and passed out cups with no ice.

"No, Sneezy Farm or Dopey Farm."

"Freaky Farm."

"Far Out Farm."

"For Real Farm."

"Jonathan Livingston Seagull Farm!"

"No way."

"Rusty Waters Farm."

"Gravel Driveway Farm."

"Really Big Farm."

"Not Near Anything Farm."

"Fruit Tree Farm."

"Lemonade Farm!" I laughed with everyone and raised my cup so quickly that lemonade spilled down my arm.

"Lemonade Farm?"

"You know, 'cause we're all drinking lemonade."

Isabelle's large, deep-set eyes got wide. "Wait guys, when life gives you lemons? Well? Make lemonade! Haven't you seen the poster? When life gives you lemons, make lemonade. When things go bad, make do. It's perfect." She raised her cup. "To Lemonade Farm!"

Everyone toasted with her. "To Lemonade Farm!"

*   *   *

Each step into Mommy's room echoed. She was unfolding futons we'd gotten as kids in Japan while Montgomery was digging through a box marked "B.R. Etc."

"Ariel, honey, can you hand me those quilts? Isn't this exciting? Just like camping out."

"Just like it." The words tasted sour coming out.

Her palm ran over her grandmother's stitches, smoothing out wrinkles. She was still wearing her gold band and the princess ring Dad got her for an anniversary. She didn't look up. "Tomorrow, the Hobart kids will arrive and y'all will have so much fun living out here in the country. You'll have a pool and all this land and the barn and the trees. I envy you. To be a child in this environment, with all these people around you, what a time you'll have." She grabbed three throw pillows and put them on top of the futons. "And Ariel, you'll be living with your very best friend. It is truly a gift from heaven that you and Samantha will be together for this time in your lives."

"But Dad won't be here." I felt my eyes burning to cry and tilted my chin back to stop it.

"No, he won't. But think of this, Ariel." She folded back the quilts, climbing between them. "If you were with Dad, you wouldn't be living with Sammi and Anne and Rayne. And Herbert's kids will come visit. You like them. And you'll still see your Dad every other weekend." She motioned for us to lay on either side of her. "See, nothing's really changing. It's all just getting better."

But I could feel the earth moving beneath me and I knew nothing would ever be the same. I knew that I used to play with Sammi and live with Daddy. I knew I used see Tommy, Cory and Edwina Hobart in our adjoining back yards. I knew that there would be no more block parties or trick-or-treat-for-Unicef with the little orange boxes. I knew that someone had set dynamite in our old neighborhood and only one family survived. It wasn't mine.

Montgomery's eyes opened more and more slowly as Mommy's lullaby tone went through him and her hand stroked his long curls. "Do you hear the train?"

"Mommy, where am I going to go to school?"

"Shhhhh, Ariel. Everything's going to be fine. It's time to sleep now." Her slim fingers snapped off the table lamp sitting on the floor. "I love you, my heart."

"I love you too, Mommy."

*   *   *

Mommy smiled and nodded as the man in the yellow shirt pointed into the truck. "Now lady, this here's your shift. There's a diagram on top shows you where to put it. Right there's the manual but it's fairly standard. Leave the keys in the mail slot when you're done with the vehicle and we'll bill you if you owe us. Got it?" He jingled the keys then handed them to her.

Montgomery and I jumped into the cab and adjusted our little butts to share the front seat. Mommy pushed the stick around until she found a gear. "Off we go, kids."

We pulled out of the gas station and the truck vibrated. Montgomery and I opened our mouths and "aaaaaaaaahed" to hear the jumping in our throats. Air from the open window whipped my hair into his mouth. He wiped his face over and over and I snickered. We rolled past Sammi's old house with the vines climbing up the side, then past the field where Sammi and I played Indians and ground dried corn with rocks, past the Hobart's old house that was being painted a cheerful yellow by some new family then up Mayfair Drive. Mommy pulled past the driveway then fiddled with the stick. Push up, pull right, push down, pull left, jiggle, pull right. "Ariel, honey, read Mommy the part in the manual about reverse."

I turned page after page of cartoons of the truck, drawings of dials and gauges - nothing about reverse. Mommy kept pushing and pulling but we hadn't moved.

"I can't find it, Mommy."

She looked at me then took her foot from the brake. The truck slid slowly into the carport and slammed to a stop. My door hit the mod, angular mailbox my dad had built. "6906" ran down its side in black plastic. The grassy hill leading up to the house was just getting lush, perfect for rolling down.

The molded-metal front door made that same old "crack-eeeek." Rugs were lined up in cigar rolls, furniture was pushed together in the middle of the floor, curtains were folded on top of a pile of throw pillows in the living room and boxes were stacked throughout the kitchen and the dining room.

Herbert and Merlin were on their way so we only had a few minutes to check all the rooms and make sure they were empty. Montgomery started up the stairs and I ran past him to Mommy and Daddy's room. There wasn't even a hanger in the large closet. No cuff link box overflowing with pennies and the odd aroma of Japanese wood. No magazine basket full of Playboys in Dad's bathroom and no bottles of blue and green smells.

The guest room down the hall was white and sterile. The sewing machine, trundle bed - all gone. I passed Montgomery in his room before I stepped into the "Parfait Pink" of my own. The paint still looked new except for tiny holes from the tacks that used to hold my Donny Osmond posters. I sat in the corner on the hardwood floor and looked toward the door. I wanted a hot bath. I felt the hot water swooshing back and forth as I slid my bottom. I pictured washing Baby Tender Love's hair and dumping too much Mr. Bubble into the running water. My hair was piled high on my head under a rubber cap and Mommy scrubbed my arms with a soapy washcloth.

"Ariel, come on downstairs, honey. They're here."

We had even painted the ceiling pink.

"Coming."

Herbert stood with Cory at the bottom of the stairs. Cory's coarse hair was sandy blonde and always stuck up in the most unusual places and his skin was tan all year long so bruises never showed through on him. He looked like he was from some other blonder family than the Hobarts and always seemed just a little dirty. He was short for his age, Montgomery was at least half a head taller. All of his clothes were permanently stained. Mommy and Daddy called him "a rough and tumble" kid. We called him "Rock Head" because of the time, at church, he had run down the hall and hit me in the mouth like a ram. My lip was fat for two weeks.

Herbert and Merlin loaded the furniture onto the yield-sign-yellow truck while we kids stacked boxes in the carport. Mommy supervised. There was a loud and final "clack," like a jail cell slamming shut, when Herbert closed the back of the truck. "Son, you coming with us?"

Cory looked up from double-knotting his shoelace. "Huh? No. I'm going with Monty."

None of us ever called him that but Cory had trouble pronouncing Montgomery when they met at age three so Monty had just stuck for him.

Herbert and Merlin waved goodbye from the orange Gremlin.

"Goodbye guys. See you there." Mommy waved. "Goodbye house on Mayfair Drive."

Goodbye. Goodbye house. Goodbye bay window for sitting in. Goodbye backyard with the fort we built from Dad's scrap wood. Goodbye swinging basket chair on the sun deck. Goodbye avocado and goldenrod-yellow kitchen. Goodbye nook under the staircase. Goodbye downhill Mayfair Drive for sledding and skating and bike riding. Goodbye "Fat Allison" who lived next door. Goodbye. Goodbye.

"Everyone's so quiet." Mommy waited until after we left the old neighborhood. "Is it because you need some... ice cream to loosen your lips?"

"Yeah!"

We checked both sides of the road for a High's store. We searched for the cheerful, pink-and-white sign of Baskin and Robbins' thirty-one flavors. Montgomery finally jumped up. "Look, Mommy! Right there!"

At the top of a hill with a long driveway stood an ice cream and sundries store with a big "S" on top. It looked like a small, crappy plantation home with golden-framed photos and postcards of cows. A giant, plastic black-and-white cow had the prices of cones on its side. I got a single scoop chocolate on a sugar cone, as usual. Montgomery got his same old double scoop of French vanilla and Cory ordered bubble gum. Mommy licked her toasted almond fudge from the edge of the cone up as we sat on the front porch. Montgomery's elbow dripped. We stared at the big yellow truck sitting across the lot.

"Won't it be nice to have all your things unpacked?" Mommy licked the side of her cone and rotated it.

"It's okay." Montgomery didn't look at her for approval the way I would have.

"It'll be just like home once you get all of your stuff in there. It feels so good to have this move almost over, doesn't it?"

"Mommy?" I hated when the wheels in my head started spinning. "How are we going to get the truck out of here?"

"What honey?"

"The truck. How are we going to get it down from here?"

"The same way we came up, silly."

"No. I mean the reverse. Don't you have to go in reverse to get out of here?"

"Oh dear." Mommy licked again. "Well, I guess we should have parked on the road. And the manual didn't say anything, huh? Okay, now wait." Another lick. "Okay, someone here must know. Ariel, you go inside and... now wait. Okay. You three stay right here." Mommy walked inside and we licked our cones.

"Look." Cory used his cone to point at ours. "We got pink, white, and brown like the box that has three flavors."

"Montgomery's is yellow, dummy." I hated the sound of my voice the minute it came out like that, all mean and superior.

Mommy came back past us talking to a man in a baseball cap. She moved her hands a lot and the man nodded, then put his hand on her bare arm and nodded some more. He brayed and moved his hand onto her shoulder. Mommy pulled away and walked over to the truck then stood beside it moving her hands some more. High pitched beeps came from the truck while the man in the cap backed out of the spot and up to the top of the driveway. He started down the drive. Mommy yelled and we chased until the truck came to a stop at the bottom of the hill. The man pulled his jeans out of his crotch and walked past us to Mommy. He looked at her only and I could feel him trying to make her special.

"Those yours?" He touched both ends of his mustache with a u-shaped hand.

"Yes, yes they are. Thanks again." She pushed us into the front seat. "Really appreciate it." Her head hit the doorway when she climbed into the driver's side. Sandy curls fell over her eyes and she used her hand like a comb to push them back. "Thanks again." She rolled the window up and took a deep breath with her hands gripping the wheel before snatching another smile from thin air and slapping it on her face. "Off we go, kids!"

*   *   *

It was sticky-hot out though the sun was going down. I had gotten in the habit of holding my breath every time I walked into the house. It was a mental measure of protection against the constant barrage of newness and oddity. In the dim light, I clearly saw Oscar, Herbert's giant pet fish, slapping down the hallway. Pillows, our cat, bounded after him with Herbert and Isabelle chasing the convoy. No amount of breath was going to make that picture normal. Laughing and squealing, they caught the fish and put it in a bucket. I just kept walking.

The only completed room in the house was the dining room. Our super-long butcher block sat on top of Isabelle's table base. Tommy and Edwina helped Isabelle serve supper to "the hungry movers." I tried hard not to let Tommy hear my breathing getting faster around him.

Herbert bowed his head and extended his hands. "Our Heavenly Father, thank you for the meal before us. Bless it to the nourishment of our bodies. Thank you further, God, for this family. Bless my children; Tommy, Cory, and Edwina. Bless Madeleine, Ariel and Montgomery. Bless Merlin and Isabelle and bless Anne, Samantha, and Rayne who could not join us yet. Amen."

"Amen."

Everything on the table shuffled around.

"Herbert, why don't you give everyone the good news about the pool." Mommy threw him a smile he couldn't help but catch.

"Next Saturday, we're going to scrub out the pool because Sunday, they're going to fill it."

"Isn't that great, kids?" I saw chewed lettuce on Mommy's tongue when her teeth parted. "It'll be our first pool party!"

Tommy threw his hands up and said "hooray" along with the rest of us then caught me staring at him. His straight, brown hair fell across his mud-brown eyes and shook when he chuckled. He was wearing the blue-and-white plaid shirt I had helped his mom pick last Christmas. It wasn't buttoned to the top so I could see his skin, darker than mine though just as smooth. His sleeves were rolled to the elbow exposing black hair on his arms, not like my family. Eddy had the same dark hair and Mommy always said, "Poor Edwina, shaving will be her curse."

I looked down at my salad, embarrassed. Tommy always made me feel so obvious. I was sure that everyone had seen me looking at him, not chewing my food. Had my breathing always been this loud?

Mommy's best hostess voice snapped. "You know where everything is, Ariel, so after dinner, you'll show the Hobart kids around, right?"

"What? Oh, yes I do. I mean, I can. I mean..." Whatever.

"And tomorrow we'll all walk to town."

"Walk?" Montgomery's mouth stayed open.

"Yes, Honey. We're going to explore. Exploring is always better on foot. The road follows the Patapsco River and maybe we'll meet a neighbor."

Tommy was giving himself seconds of lasagna. His white plastic buttons clicked on the edge of his plate as he cut strings of mozzarella with the Tupperware spatula.

"Mommy?" I held my breath to make a wish. "Where is everyone sleeping?"

"I thought you and Montgomery would want to sleep in my room again. Why?"

"I just wondered." My stomach shrunk inward and my chest felt like someone was standing on it. "What if all us kids sleep in the playroom together?"

"That sounds like fun, don't you think, Herbert?"

"That's fine. There's not enough room for the kids in my room anyway."

"Do Cory and me have to stay with them?" Montgomery's voice had that pleading quality. "Can't he stay in my room? It's right next door. Please, Mom?"

"I don't see why not."

Isabelle smacked Merlin's hand when he reached for the bread basket again.

He playfully smacked her back. "There's more in the kitchen, Belle. Say, Tommy, don't you start high school next year? Pass that butter, Eddy, will you?"

"I was supposed to go to Montpelier Senior, but now Mom's moving us to Greenbelt or something."

"So this is your last year in junior high? That's great. This will be a good summer for you. Not a care in the world. No pressure. Then it's off to the big leagues. Girls, cars. Wow, do I remember those days. Enjoy, Tommy. Have people been saying it'll be the best time of your life? Sad if it's true, but it was a lot more fun than paying the mortgage."

"I hated high school." Mommy scooted a piece of rejected food to the edge of her plate. "I was so tall. I always stood out. College was much better. But all my life, the question I've gotten more than any other, more than 'Where are you from?' or 'What's your major?' is 'How tall are you?' Oh, and men are always looking at my feet!"

Merlin snickered with food in his mouth. "Your feet?"

"To see if you're wearing high heels. I was tall in school too, but not like you, Madeleine." Isabelle ate the last of her salad. "We called any girl in our school over five-seven 'bean pole.'"

My voice bubbled up out of me involuntarily. "That's what I have to look forward to?"

"Ariel." Mommy's eyes narrowed with disapproval. "Not at the table. Isabelle's just making a generalization. Besides, it's the seventies. People aren't the same now as they were in the fifties. They're more accepting."

Herbert looked at me and the left half of his bearded mouth lifted in a smile. "Besides, Ariel, you might not get much taller."

Everyone was staring at me. My fingers were wrapped around the seat of my chair. My ears burned. "I'm eleven years old. Of course I'm going to get taller. The worst is yet to come!" I jumped dramatically out of my chair, ran halfway up the steps and waited. Pillows bounded up to sit with me.

"It's not your fault, Isabelle." Mommy's voice carried up the walls. "She's been touchy lately. She says she feels different."

That was supposed to be a secret.

Isabelle sounded sad. "I didn't mean to say something like that. I wasn't thinking. Maybe I should go up and apologize."

"For what?" Merlin's voice was dancing on the edge of laughter. "She's not going to stop growing because you say you're sorry. Let her cry. She could probably use it."

I heard my mouth mutter. "Jerk." I trudged up to my room, Pillows' grey fur rubbing at my ankles. No one was ever going to like me. The least they could do was feel sorry for me.

"Ariel?"

"Eddy?"

"Are you up there?"

"Yes."

"Is it scary?"

"No, come up."

Her small brown head peeked in. "Are you sure?"

"It's quiet. You'll like it."

She put a tentative foot on the first step. "I'm coming up now. It's kinda dark in here. Don't you have windows? Are you coming downstairs again?"

"Later."

"Me and Tommy are putting our sleeping bags in the playroom. Do you want me to put yours in there?"

"Sure, Eddy. I said I'd sleep in there, didn't I? Do you think Tommy will want to look around?"

"Oh, I want to."

"Do you think he'll go with us? You guys don't know your way around yet so he should come with us." Was that too obvious?

Tommy noticed all the things I hadn't. He showed me the trees that were good for climbing, the grass patches tall enough to hide in, the rocks that were perfect for knocking cans off a fence. He liked the big hills and said sledding here would be great. He thought the barn was perfect for hide-and-seek and that we might find old horseshoes and stuff there. We walked until Eddy had to go to the bathroom so bad that she started to cry.

The sky was pink above the house and made the tin roof of the pavilion glow in the last bit of daylight. I brushed my hand against Tommy's when we came out of the daisy field and thought my heart would burst. Eddy walked ahead of us with her hands gripped between her legs. I pictured her as our daughter and we were walking to our mansion. I was in a beautiful pink dress with Tommy holding my hand.

The grown-ups were all in the living room when we got back. Montgomery and Cory were watching *Hogan's Heroes* in the green room. We went straight upstairs. Eddy ran to the bathroom and slammed the door shut. I wanted Tommy to turn around and look at me. I wanted him to touch my hand. I wanted. I wanted. I wanted.

"Is everything all right up there? What's going on, kids? Herbert's voice boomed from downstairs.

Tommy whirled around. "It was Eddy." He hung his head. "Now watch, he won't be mad."

"Okay. Let us know if you need anything, okay kids?"

"Yeah, Dad." He turned back to the window and looked down at parked cars. "See, if it had been me who slammed the door, he'd at least yell. Girls have it easy."

His melted face reflected in the warped glass. I wasn't sure if he was looking at me, talking to me. Maybe it was just a statement.

I breathed in and heard the air rush up my nostrils too loud. "No." More breath. "No, they don't. I think it's because she's the baby of the family. I think they're easier on the babies."

"Maybe." He walked to the next window and looked toward Patapsco Road. "We live in an apartment now."

"Really? Is it nice?"

"No, Stanley Towers. It's a dump."

"But you're moving soon, right?"

"To another dump." He leaned against the sill. "And Mike's going to move in."

"I can't believe your mom's with him." I wanted to put my hand on his shoulder but I sat on the trundle bed instead. "The only thing I remember is when he first joined the church, he was dancing and stepped on Mommy's foot and sprained it. She says he broke it but she never got a hard cast so I know it was just a sprain. But they say those are harder to heal."

"He's pretty fat. He could've broken it." His shoulders shook a little bit with laughter.

Eddy walked in. "Who broke what?"

"Nothing." Tommy snapped at her without turning from the glass.

"Let's get ourselves ready for bed and we can play Rummy or something." I sounded embarrassingly cheerful, like Mommy on a bad day.

Tommy's voice was like an anchor, all slow and under layers. "I am ready."

"You're going to wear all your clothes to sleep?"

"If I'm sleeping with a bunch of girls, I am."

"Okay." I thought of the T-shirt I had planned to wear with the iron-on of The Fonz. "I'll wear mine too."

"Well, I'm putting on my P.J.'s." Eddy ran out again. "I'll be right back so don't start yet."

"You guys are lucky." Tommy finally turned his long lashes and pink mouth to me and a shock ran through my spine.

"Maybe you guys could stay here too. There's plenty of room. You should ask. At least for the summer."

"Every other weekend and holidays alternate years. They worked it all out in court. We weren't even there."

"We have the same thing." I nodded. "It's okay, I guess. No one asked us either."

"You guys have a radio?"

"Yeah, sure. It's in one of the boxes in my room. It's my great-grandfather's transistor. You want to come look with me?"

"Nah. I just thought you might have one already out. Skip it."

"I could get it. It wouldn't take long."

"No, that's okay."

"Are you sure?" I felt something slipping away from me. "'Cause it really wouldn't take long."

"I'm sure." He shoved his hands in his pockets. "Do you have cards?"

"All the games are on those green shelves. Remember, they used to match the walls in the old house. The shelves, I mean."

"Monopoly's cool but it takes a long time." He said running his finger over the boxes. "Othello's good but only two people can play. Clue, Parcheesi, Life, Scrabble. Forget it, let's just play Monopoly."

"I like that game." I jumped from the bed and did my best casual stride. "I always beat Montgomery."

"Should we invite those guys?"

I erupted inside. "They won't want to play anyway."

"Hurry up, Eddy. We're going to start without you if you don't get your butt in here." He handed me the money box. "Here, Ariel, you be the banker." He smiled and for one moment, everything was perfect.

But Oscar the fish didn't make it through the night, our first casualty.

*   *   *

Ragtag. That's the best way to describe our clan walking to town. Tommy was still in yesterday's blue and white flannel despite the eighty degree temperature. Eddy wore a permanently-stained gingham sundress with bloomers. Neither had combed their hair. Isabelle had hip-huggers and a "Rainbow House" T-shirt.

Merlin looked clean in his khaki shorts and baseball cap but had neglected to shave for three days now. Herbert's collar was the same royal blue as his Bermuda's and he wore black socks with hard shoes. Even at eleven years old, I knew that was wrong. Montgomery's shirt was on backwards and Cory wore his on his head like a wig. I had an airbrushed French-cut T-shirt with seagulls on it that Sandy had given me from the last time she and Dad went to Ocean City. The wooden soles of my Dr. Scholl's clacked against the pavement where the rubber had worn off. Mommy was in a scoop-necked red shirt that clung to her slim body. Her jeans were too big but she said she had to buy them that way to get the length right. We walked down the middle of the road in a clump, moving to the side whenever a car or pickup passed.

The trek was about forty minutes one way but that meant not taking any of the side paths for exploring. Woods lined the road with an occasional clearing for a home or grazing field, then met with the Patapsco river about halfway there. The railroad tracks were on the other side of the river, then just trees. A highway overpass stopped the wilderness. Past that, the road bent around Patapsco Package Goods before crossing the river into Carroll County.

We straggled across the bridge, stopping to look at an old caboose sitting beside the tracks. Main Street started at the S.S. Feed & Grain warehouse and ran past the combination drugstore/soda fountain/hardware store and finally to Harris' Grocery. The screen door jingled when we pushed it open. An old woman with pink-grey hair looked up from the cash register as we filed past the small ice cream freezer and down one of the store's two aisles. The pink-grey head was distorted in the rounded mirror above the glass meat case but I could still tell it was us she was looking at. I chose a peach and went to the cash register.

"Y'all want a bag for that?" She held her hand out for my fruit.

"No thanks." Isabelle dug in a change purse.

Eating our pears, grapes and apples, we passed a craft shop and the two-lane bowling alley. At the fire station, we turned around and walked back toward Howard County.

"Is this a real city, Mommy?" Montgomery turned his face up to hers. He looked like a fleshy question mark.

"Well sure it is. Of course it is. Would they have a bowling alley if it wasn't a real city?" Laughter spilled out of her mouth and down onto his face like a summer rain.

"But there's no post office. Where's the doctor live? They don't have a library or a pool or anything."

Mommy stopped giggling and looked straight at him. "You have your own pool now. And you always hated the library."

"I liked the library." I said it under my breath but hoped she'd hear it.

Mommy tucked the tag inside the back of Isabelle's shirt then ran her hand onto her shoulder. "Your kids are going to love it here, Isabelle. Don't you think?"

No matter how tall I got, Mommy could always talk over my head.

Chapter Two

Mommy had the windows down and my hair snapped at my eyes as we pulled away from my school for the last time. She was talking about Sammi coming and Merlin trying to cook brownies for them from a box mix. I kept seeing faces in my eyelids; Katie, Kim, Danny Tagliani, Skittles, Totsie MacNamara, Bruce, James Moore, Cindy. They were all saying goodbye. Chester had punched me in the arm and Jeannette had cried. Katie said she'd stay in touch but that's not the same as being next door neighbors. Her parents used to fight so loud we could hear it in our house but they were still married.

My teacher, Mrs. Gochenaur, said that everyone was going to a new school next year, junior high, so not to feel so bad. But they were all going to the same new school and I wasn't even in the same county anymore.

They had served grilled cheese with tomato soup at lunch, my absolute favorite. I ate it really fast because I wanted to take a last walk around before recess. I got picked to be on Angie's team for zone dodge so, of course, we won. It had been a good day and a whole summer of no school lay ahead of me but I kept seeing faces on my eyelids.

*   *   *

My finger ran through the clay-stained sand. A and T. A + T. T loves A. A loves T. AW + TH. TH and AW, 2gether 4ever.

I wrote each letter with care then wiped it all out and began again. Gravel cracked at the bottom of the drive and I stood, kicking sand everywhere to erase the letters. Nana's station wagon pulled past the bushes and up to the porch. Her silver hair and Cherokee-influenced profile moved behind the finger-smeared glass. Jumping out of the sand pile, I wiped my hands on my jeans and ran beside the car as it pulled in. Sammi bounded out and her tiny arms reached up and around my slight shoulders and my kiss almost missed her mouth. Brown-sugar hair tickled my nose and ear. Anne got out of the front seat looking up at the house while Nana helped Rayne out of her seat belt. Anne and Rayne shared rope-like hair the color of sun streaming through honey then snow, and their profiles recalled Nana's.

"Well, hello there, Ariel. My, how you have grown and look at that hair. Boy, did it get long." Nana pulled Rayne's dress down. "Is their Mama here? We're all real anxious to see her, aren't we girls?"

Isabelle came running out of the door yelling. "Mama! My babies!" Her brown braid bounced off her back when she jogged down the steps. Sammi let go of me and ran to her.

Anne pulled away from their group hug, and posed next to the car. "Who's hauling all this shit in?"

The laughing and crying stopped and Nana looked to Isabelle then at Anne. "Don't use that tone, darlin'. Come say hi to your mama. She took the day off for you." Nana's eyes urged Anne.

"Big whoop. Maybe she just wanted a day off. We sure make a good excuse."

"Anne, can we not start yet?" Lines hardened around Isabelle's mouth. "Your grandmother's leaving in an hour. Let's make it a nice visit, okay?"

"I already visited with Nana. Nana, wouldn't you say we had plenty of visiting time this last year? I think Nana and I are all visited out, Mom."

"Okay, Anne, you've made your point. But don't ruin it for us. Your room's the only empty one on the ground floor. Go ahead and unpack."

Sammi looked at the toe of her firehouse-red sneakers. She always got red ones, no matter how many new colors they came out with. Her stuffed dog, Bill, was red too. I didn't even have to look, I knew he was in that car somewhere, not in a box, but somewhere she could still see him or touch him. She had even brought him to her first communion. Isabelle loved that stunt.

Nana ended up staying for supper and Merlin's brownies so I didn't get to show Sammi any of the grounds. Sammi thought our room was cool and that we should decorate with four-leaf clovers cut out of construction paper and a rainbow painted on the A-shaped wall at the far end of the room. I wanted to cut pictures out of *Seventeen* and *Vogue* and tape them on the wall. We both agreed we needed pictures of horses.

Sammi popped the catches of her suitcase and stacked clothes in her chest of drawers. I sat on my mattress watching and running my hands over the used-to-be-white fake fur on Bill's ears.

"We finished school yesterday. I left my uniform at Nana's."

"They only had girls there?"

"Yeah, only girls. And we all had to wear the same uniform."

"Did you have bussing?"

"Bussing?"

"Yeah, you know, when they bring kids from other school districts in, black kids. We had it starting last year. It was stupid though 'cause they only brought two buses so each class only had about two black kids, if that. How would you like it if you were the only white kid in your class? I thought the whole thing was stupid. There was one kid, his name is Chester, he used to get in fights all the time. He used to do really mean stuff to me. Once, he made me lick the chalkboard when he was supposed to be cleaning it. I felt really stupid but then he became my friend. Then William and Angie became my friends too. Nobody can beat Angie at zone dodge. Nobody. Do you think they'll have bussing at this school? Maybe it's a black school and they're bussing us. It tasted really gross, the chalk I mean. It was sort of sour."

"Ariel, can we just not talk for a little while?"

It was like a fist was coming up from my stomach into my throat. My eyes were hot. Sammi's hands were smoothing out T-shirts, folding shorts, re-rolling socks.

"Don't be mad." She threw a sock ball at my head. "I didn't mean anything."

"I'm not mad." I threw the socks back.

"Yes, you are. Admit it." She hit my ear with the socks.

"You're full of it." I hit her nose.

"You brat!" She threw the socks and a shirt. "You're never wrong, right?" Another pair of socks and some underwear.

"That's right!" A training bra, a pillow, Bill.

"Wait! Stop! Bill, are you okay?" She petted him twice then dropped him on the floor and lunged at me. I screamed when she grabbed my hair.

"Say uncle!"

"No."

Her hand twisted and yanked. "Say uncle!"

"Fine. Uncle. Whatever. Get off of me."

Sammi pulled her fingers from my hair and flopped back onto her mattress.

"Here." I offered her the training bra. "God knows I don't need it."

"That's true."

"Brat."

*　　*　　*

"Hand me that brush, would ya'?" Merlin pointed to a push broom. "The container said to just pour it straight onto the vinyl and scrub. Gimme that bottle, Ariel."

I leaned over the plastic bottle of electric-blue cleanser and dragged it between my legs to the edge of the pool.

"Kinda heavy, hey kid?"

"Kinda."

He uncapped the bottle and poured. He had an easy manner that made me feel like he might be on my side if I disagreed with a grown-up, like he might shoot them a look that said to take it easy on me.

Mommy handed all the kids small scrub brushes and Herbert connected a long silver handle to the official pool scrub brush that came with the house.

Isabelle pulled the garden hose out of its coil and over the edge of the pool. "Pour the water in now?" Her voice was almost as familiar as my mommy's and had been in my life just as long.

Merlin tightened the handle on the push broom. "Not too much. It just needs to be able to lather a little."

Herbert looked up from the silver pole. "Wait a minute. A lather? Won't it be awfully slick? I think it's going to get slick, Merlin." Herbert always said things like that, logical, smart things.

"Okay, Isabelle, turn on the water." Merlin pushed the liquid soap around the shallow end with the brush. "Come on, Belle. Ready when you are."

The water came rushing from the house and ran past Merlin's bare feet down into the dark emerald-green algae slime in the deep end, lush like moss under a shady tree. "You guys be careful coming down the ladder." He took his first step toward the edge where the hose hung off. The whole thing seemed to happen in slow motion. First his foot flew up, then his butt went down and his hands made a loud SMACK on the vinyl. His first attempt at standing spread his legs apart. His knees came out from under him and he landed on his belly on attempt number three. "Turn off the water!" He went down on his hip.

Isabelle ran to the wall and turned the spigot. The water came gushing out faster, then turned slowly off.

Merlin put his hands out in front of him. "Isabelle, I've had some time to rethink. This appears to be a hands and knees job."

I giggled following Sammi down the ladder. Mommy was stacking towels on an aluminum beach chair with plastic slats.

Isabelle and Herbert kept saying how careful we should be. Rayne got onto her hands and knees right away and sort of skated that way. Sammi and I scooted around on our butts and ran into anyone still standing. The Rolling Stones were on Anne's radio and she had put the speakers facing us in her windows. She and the grown-ups worked on the side walls while we kids scrubbed the bottom. The diving well got more and more full of foam.

"Can we go down the slide?" Montgomery looked like a store window puppy wanting to be adopted.

"Absolutely not. Absolutely. You could really get hurt, honey."

"Let him, Mommy."

"Not funny, Ariel. My children are always trying to kill each other off. Do you get that, Isabelle?"

"Oh sure, Madeleine. It's human nature, like Cain and Abel."

"How would you know, Mom?" Anne interjected this thought from the sidelines like she was throwing a second puck onto the ice.

"Anne, everyone's having fun. Let's not get into this right now."

"Gotcha, Mom. We'll do it later when no one can hear you, right?"

"Right, Anne. You win. Now stop."

Rayne slid by Sammi and me on her hands and knees and screamed as she went flying over the edge into the diving well.

"Rayne." I slid down after her. Sammi came crashing in on top of me and green slime and soapy-foam squished between our bare legs.

"Geronimo!" Montgomery squealed, sliding down the slope onto the three of us.

"Come here, Rayne. Give me your hand." Isabelle lay on her belly and extended her arms.

"No, Mommy. It's fun in here."

"Come on, Rayne. Enough now. It's filthy down there. Give me a hand."

Rayne's slime-covered fingers opened to reach Isabelle's. Isabelle leaned over the edge further. Rayne's fingers wiggled.

Swoosh. Down came Isabelle head first. Foamy green slime dripped off her braid and down her wet T-shirt.

"That's a good look for you, Mom." Anne snickered.

"Thanks Anne. I'm always looking for your support." Her white teeth looked funny set in her green face. "Come here, Anne. I have a secret for you."

"No way, man."

"Oh, come on Anne." Sammi put her hands together like a prayer.

"Yeah, come on. You can trust your mother, can't you? Just a little closer."

"No." She laughed and backed away.

"Get her girls!" Isabelle scooped a handful of slime-foam and slung it at Anne's wavy hair. Montgomery hit her feet and ankles. Sammi got her on the shoulder and I missed and hit Herbert. He looked over his black-plastic-rimmed glasses then looked back down again and continued scrubbing. Anne fell onto her knees running toward the ladder. She gathered handfuls of foam and threw them indiscriminately at our heads peeking out over the diving well. Merlin scooted to her side and took aim at the taller heads, Isabelle's and mine. Our slime was easier to scoop though, and greener. Mommy busily moved the towels closer to the house before getting hit on her second trip. Herbert continued scrubbing. Rayne kept hitting us in the back or on the tops of our heads since she was too short to throw over us. Her white-blonde hair was lima-bean green and she looked like a baby sea monster. Mommy turned on the water and put her thumb over the end of the hose as she came down the ladder making that woo-hoo-hoo laugh sound.

Herbert was still scrubbing but I could see his sides shaking so I knew he was chuckling. Merlin knocked him over and it was like a signal to us. "Attack!" The foam clung to his grey and black beard, dripped over his white undershirt, soaked his black socks. Merlin pushed him and they slid over the edge into the diving well knocking us all over. Herbert's glasses clung to his wide head as he struggled with the rest of us to stand up. Screaming and laughing got all mixed together. Anne pushed Merlin over and down we went again. Then she sat and slid down the edge with Mommy right behind her. The deep end was all arms and legs smacking and slapping until we got our bearings. Everyone was glistening green. We stood looking at each other and laughing.

Then we just looked at each other.

Without a word, Merlin lifted Rayne onto the shallow end and we helped each other out of the well. The ooze slickened the slope so Isabelle and Herbert fell back in twice before finally pulling Merlin out. Over the edge of the pool, behind the split-rail fence that separated us from our next door neighbors, I saw four small children staring at us shining green in the sun.

*   *   *

The pavilion was the size of the skating rink in Laurel. Grey concrete ooze showed through the long logs and the whole building looked like something in a history book. The rustic structure seemed even bigger from inside with a concrete floor interrupted eight times by massive logs supporting beams and roof buttressing. Wagon wheels hung down by chains with electric candles in them like Old West chandeliers. Posters of men in cowboy hats had names printed on them, like Van "The Virginia Reel" Madsen, and were stapled into the wood beams above.

A coffin-length stone fireplace had a sooty hearth and sky-high chimney. On the opposite wall were huge sliding barn doors through which we could see the sloped back field. The grown-ups had put a short-weave carpet down in one corner and lined the walls with bookcases full of my Barbies and their clothes and Montgomery's Match Box cars, Tonka trucks and plastic squirt guns. Sammi and Rayne's toys were in unmarked boxes. There was another carpet in front of the fireplace, still rolled up, an expansive wooden stage, two feet tall, and a large mahogany wardrobe on wheels.

"Cool!" Sammi ran to the wardrobe.

"We're supposed to finish unpacking, remember?" I exhaled like I was irritated.

"Look, it rolls. The latch works."

"So?"

"So, we can hide in it. We can move it around. It'll be like that book with the lion and the witch. Get in."

"You get in." I tried to stare her down but my eyes kept running away.

"No, you do it first." Her eyes could always outrun mine.

I stepped into the closet and Sammi slammed the door shut. I put my hands out to steady myself and my fingers shot through a spider's web. I wanted to wipe my hands but the wardrobe moved out from under me. I was spinning around in a circle and Sammi was cackling and the spider web was clinging to the hair on my arm and I screamed. "Stop!" Sammi kept laughing and I kept spinning. The darkness felt like a blindness and the outer corners of my eyes ached. "Stop, stop!" Then, BAM!, everything stopped and I slammed into one of the walls.

"Oh shit. Ariel, are you okay?" She banged on the walls trying to find the front. "Ariel?" Metal scraped with the opening of the latch. At first, she looked like a black angel with light coming from behind her. "Oh shit. I'm sorry. You ran into the stage, see? Man, I thought you got hurt or something."

"Are you trying to kill me?" I rubbed my hands and arms on my pants.

"It was supposed to be funny."

"Well, it wasn't."

"Well, maybe you just don't know how to have fun!"

"Well, maybe you're just a meany."

Sammi's eyes rolled. "Maybe you're just a nerd."

She turned and ran toward the shelves giggling. "You can't catch me. La la la la la la."

I walked slowly toward her pretending not to care.

Sammi must have bought it because she dropped the subject entirely. "Hey, let's walk to town."

"I thought we had to unpack."

"We'll do it later. Come on." She ran to the path next to the neighbors' split-rail fence. I caught up with her and we passed the pool and the fruit trees and walked out onto the road. It looked warped from the heat rising off the blacktop. I felt like I was playing hooky. Sammi kicked a rock, always keeping it right in front of her. I found a rock too. It made a loud "clack" every time I hit it with the tip of my wooden Dr. Scholl. Mine made me run from side to side to keep up with it. Then I hit it with the tip of my big toe and it rolled up over the buckle on the adjustable red leather strap and flew off sideways.

Sammi spoke first. "Don't you have a bike?"

"Not anymore. It got stolen a week before we moved. They took it off our front porch. Dad said there was a big gang who has a truck and that's all they ever do is steal bikes."

Sammi hit her rock perfectly straight while looking at me for a moment in curiosity.

"He said they come at night and steal bikes then drive them in the big truck to a place where they sand the numbers off and paint them a new color. Then they sell them. I don't see how they'll ever sell mine though because my banana seat was tilted funny and no one else could ride it. A long leg person will have to buy it, I guess."

"I guess." She repeated me absently.

I could still see my bike, its white seat with pink stripes and matching pink paint all over. Once my bell-bottoms had gotten stuck in the chain. I wiped out in front of the Hobart's house, ripping the red-white-and-blue seersucker bell-bottoms and skinning my knee. I couldn't detach the bike and it tripped me when I tried to get up. I carried it beside me and stumbled to the Hobart's front door and as I stood there with the bike in my arms, a hole in my pants, and blood running down my leg, Tommy rode up on a wooden skateboard. There was no way to hide the bicycle and it would not reach the ground while my pants were still in its teeth, so there I stood while Tommy walked by. He said he'd get his mom and I died inside.

"It's too bad your bike didn't make it out to here. Nobody would bother to drive a truck out this far for a stupid bike." Her foot stepped over the rock and she left it behind in boredom. "Maybe you'll get another one for your birthday. You should ask for a ten-speed. Those ones with the banana seats are for kids."

"A ten-speed? Do you have to learn how to ride them?"

"Look! Horses!" She jumped and clapped. "Do you think we'll get to ride them? I wonder whose they are."

"Do you know how to ride?"

She had grown apart from me. I would never find her through all these miles and years. She no longer looked at me. "Sure. I learned at Nana's. I wish they had an Arabian. They're the best."

I may not have known horses, but I knew books. "Did you read that book about the Lipizzaners? They can practically fly. And they're born black but then they turn totally white. Isn't that weird? Have you ever seen one?"

"No. I've never really seen an Arabian yet either. You can tell them by the arch of their neck."

"Do you have your bike?"

"No. You wouldn't believe the stuff we've lost moving. The first time we moved, I thought maybe stuff was just in storage but now I'm thinking that our stuff's just gone. Maybe Mom gave it away."

"She wouldn't do that."

Sammi kept looking at the horses. She stepped lightly on her red Jack Purcel's with her feet turned slightly outward from years of ballet. The white rubber toes flashed in the bits of sunlight that fell through the trees.

"Who do you suppose lives out here?" I looked at her, hoping to reconnect.

Her exaggerated hazel eyes never left the horses in the field. "Out where?"

"In these houses? We must have passed four houses already. But, I haven't seen any people."

"Maybe we're in *The Twilight Zone*. Do do do do." She chuckled.

"What's that?"

"What's what?"

"The 'twilight zone?' What is it?"

"It's a TV show I think. Mom says it. I think it's a place where things are strange, you know? Not the way they're supposed to be, like maybe a monster came and ate all the people and we're the only ones left."

"Maybe no one ever lived here. Maybe it's a ghost town or maybe the people are invisible. Maybe they're all old with no children and no one ever comes outside. Maybe they steal children and hide them like in *Chitty Chitty Bang Bang*."

"Chitty Chitty Bang Bang, we love you." She sang through smiling teeth.

"Wait, wait! Give me your arm." I wrapped her arm around mine. "Weeeeeeere off to see the wizard..."

We sang together skipping to the right twice then the left, right twice, left twice. "The wonderful Wizard of Oz." We flew past two more houses. "We hear he is a wiz of a wiz if ever a wiz there was." My lungs itched with pollen. "If ever oh ever a wiz there was, the Wizard of Oz is one because..." We looked at each other getting louder and louder. "Because, because, because, because, because..." We stopped at once and screamed at each other so that I was breathing her exhales. "Because of the wonderful things he does!" Sammi jumped and twirled and I skipped two right, two left. "We're off to see the wizard, the wonderful Wizard of Oz." I held my side to stop the cramping from all of the skipping and singing and breathing and laughing.

I read aloud. "Redden Acres."

"What?"

"Redden Acres. That's what the sign says." I pointed.

Sammi pushed her bangs from her eyes and looked up the tree trunk to the small wooden sign. "Do they all have names?"

"The one we just passed did. Ours is Crowsfoot Estates but they're changing it to Lemonade Farm."

"Lemonade Farm? What's that?" She swiped at some tall grass.

"Our farm. They're gonna call it Lemonade Farm, you know, for, if life gives you lemons...'"

"That's cool. Lemonade Farm. Okay." She nodded.

"Yeah, it's cool. Lemonade Farm. Where do you live? Oh, I live at Lemonade Farm. Cool! So, who do you like?" We both knew I was talking about boys.

"No one, I guess. I still miss Steve sometimes. My last school was all girls, you know."

"Oh yeah. Which one, Starsky or Hutch?"

"Starsky, definitely."

"Me too." We agreed and I felt everything in me balancing. "Fonzie or Ritchie?"

"No contest. Fonzie."

"Yeah, he's cool. But Ritchie's nice too. David Cassidy or Donny Osmond?"

"David Cassidy, easy."

"Really?" It was like a record needle was skating across the quiet album of my stomach.

"Donny Osmond's a nerd. He's too...something."

"But David Cassidy's hair stands up funny in the front. I don't like him." I stared ahead. How could she like David Cassidy? Something inside me tore. What if she had changed her mind about Tommy too? What if she thought he wasn't cool?

We crossed the Howard/Carroll county line. I followed Sammi into the drugstore past the wood-paneled soda fountain. She walked to the counter and waited. I stood beside her.

An old man with a big nose came over. "May I help you girls?"

Sammi tilted her head back. "Yes, a pack of Salem and a Marlboro hard pack."

I stood there looking at her looking at him.

"Aren't you a little young for cigarettes?" He chuckled. I was just about to run when he reached up and grabbed two packs.

"They're for my mom." Sammi's voice was smooth.

"One dollar ten." He held his hand out expectantly.

Sammi dug into her pocket and pulled out two ones. I stared at the exchange. She put the packs into her pockets and took the change. "Let's go." She grabbed my arm. "Come on."

I followed her to the grocery where she grabbed a pack of gum. I picked up some Wacky Packys. At the county line, I looked at her. "Your mom doesn't smoke."

"No shit, Sherlock."

"So, who are the cigarettes for?"

"For us. Don't you smoke?"

"No. Do you?"

"Sometimes."

We walked quietly to a path where all the plants looked like umbrellas with little white flowers growing beneath. We followed the river to a small clump of rocks and sat. Sammi hit the Salems against her palm then took the plastic off and opened the foil top.

"Want one?" She pushed the pack toward me.

"No, that's okay." I opened my candy. "I've got this. Want one?"

"Nah." She lit the cigarette and pretty grey smoke curlicued out of her lips.

"How did your parents tell you?" My nose tickled with the queer smell of burning tobacco. "I mean, when they were breaking up, what did they say?"

"They didn't really. You should try this, it's cool."

"They just broke up?"

"Yeah, I guess."

"They told us at a family meeting. I think Dad always hated family meetings. Daddy said he loved someone else. He loved two women and he wanted to be with the other one. He cried, you know. I've never seen him do that. I got really scared. Montgomery asked if it was his fault. I knew something was coming because every night for a week, I heard Mommy crying. I asked what was wrong once but they said, 'Nothing.' Mommy cried a lot after he left. I don't think it's fair. I asked who else he loved and he said Sandy, the woman we accidentally bumped into the week before at the mall. She's very pretty and she has long hair. She wears makeup and stuff. Mommy just wears that eyelash stuff and lipstick. I think Dad's going to come back. I think this is like a vacation or something."

Sammi looked away and threw her cigarette into the river. "Come on, Ariel. Just try one." She lit another. "They're mint flavored."

"They are?"

"Yeah, here. Put this in your mouth." She handed me the slender stick. "Okay, now light it off of mine. Just put your tip on my tip and we'll both breath in."

Our cigarettes kissed as I pulled air into my mouth.

"You have to do it a few times." Sammi puffed to show me.

I touched my tip to hers again. Finally, it lit and smoke came billowing out of my mouth. She was right, it was sort of minty.

"You're not inhaling. I can tell."

"I don't want to." I puffed at the cigarette watching grey clouds exit my mouth. It wasn't so bad.

"Anne's going to teach me smoke rings."

"I want to do them, too."

"You have to inhale first."

"Oh." I tried to hold the cigarette like Sammi did, perched very casually between her pointer and index fingers. "Laverne or Shirley?"

"Definitely Laverne."

*　　*　　*

Anne was unpacking when we delivered her Marlboros. We sat on the bed and watched her dumping pale green and baby blue eye shadows into a drawer. She looked at us through her mirror, painted sunshine yellow with "Angel" in curvy letters on top. Painted tears ran down the side of the frame. She unpacked shirts, all lace and macramé and gauze with embroidery. Her jeans filled a whole drawer. She stacked her records on the floor, Buckingham & Nicks, Pink Floyd, David Bowie. Beside me on the bed was a doll with a fragile china head and a chip on its chin. Its teeth looked very real and its eyes were glass. It always gave me the creeps. It wasn't meant to be played with. Next to it was the loved-up worn-out lamb she'd had since birth.

Anne watched herself twisting the wire feet of a plastic bluebird onto the top of her mirror and draping blue silk morning glories down the side. She turned the knob on her radio and found a station. "I love this song." She crossed to a box of *Vogue* magazines.

"Me too." Sammi ran a lavender ribbon through her fingertips.

Perfect faces spilled out of the box when Anne tipped it over. "Why don't you stack these next to the records, Sammi?"

"Why don't you?"

"Why don't you get out!" Anne's voice cut through the air and struck at Sammi.

"Why?"

"I said so."

Sammi got up from the bed and I jumped up to follow.

"You can stay, Ariel. Stay."

Sammi kept walking. I looked back at Anne.

"Do you know the name of this song?" Anne picked up some spilled pencils.

"The one on right now?" I was getting scared. "Yeah, I think it's 'Shining Star,' right?"

"That's right. It's a good song."

"I know. You used to listen to it when you stayed at our house that month."

"Do me a favor and stack those." She nodded toward the *Vogues*.

I looked at each cover before placing the next on top. Sandy-blonde wind-blown hair, kinky curly brown hair, round hazel kohl-lined eyes, almond blue eyes, half-closed brown eyes, freckles, square jaws, pouty mouths, thin lips spread over perfect teeth, dimples, pointy chins - and all in exotic bright clothes.

"Patti Hanson's the best." Anne stated this in such a way that it instantly became law.

"Who's she?"

"The one in your hand." She snickered and I knew it was at my ignorance.

A beautiful, natural face stared at me. She had blue eyes and long blonde hair with just a little wave in it. Freckles topped her nose bridge and her mouth was slightly open, sexy. She looked just like Anne.

"You could be a model." I hated sounding like a fan but I wasn't skilled enough to pull the naked adoration out of my tone.

"Yeah, but you're supposed to be tall. Five-eight, I think. I'm only five-two. Mom says it's not that glamorous anyway. She said nothing's really the way it looks."

For one moment, one precious second, my height was good because Anne had said so.

"Hey, hand me those shoes, will you?"

I hoped I grabbed the right ones and she took them from my hands.

"Thanks. Oh, and those too. Do you know when we're allowed to swim?"

"I think in a day or two. Mommy said there's too many chemicals right now. How do you walk in these?" I held up a pair of platforms.

"You can try them."

I pulled the buckles tight then stood up. It felt like when I used to dance on my daddy's feet. Nothing stayed where it was supposed to.

"My God, look how tall you are in those."

I flopped back down on the bed, gangly and deflated. "I can't walk in them anyway."

Anne balled up bikinis and threw them in a small drawer with socks. She had the stringy kind with darts in the tops. Anne knew she had a beautiful body and was never ashamed for other people to see it.

I pictured myself at Anne's age with her perfect figure. I would walk beautifully in my platform shoes and blow perfect smoke rings. I would wear gauze shirts with no bra. Tommy would tell everyone how much he loved me and other boys would be jealous. Then I would be discovered as a model and have to move to New York to be on the cover of *Vogue* and Tommy would follow me.

"Ariel, hand me those shoes if you're done with them."

I unbuckled. I could have learned to walk in them if I had wanted to. After all, they were a perfect fit.

*   *   *

It had been Mommy's idea that we kids explore the grounds before dinner. Sammi and I walked behind Rayne and Montgomery to make sure they didn't get lost or hurt.

The path was barely visible under the new summer lushness. The grass and vines thinned out beneath the trees. Rayne was humming the *Winnie-the-Pooh* song and looking up weather-scarred trunks. It was darker and cooler under the canopy of leaves. Then, it ended. Suddenly, we were in a field of tall, dry sandy-colored weeds. They tickled our underarms as we ran with our hands held out like airplanes. Sammi found a praying mantis and we all stopped to look at it.

The path sloped gently downward to a small plateau covered with dead vines. Montgomery was the first to step into it and a thousand tiny snaps accompanied his footfall. Rayne jumped in after him, creating crackling little noises like a swarm of centipedes' feet clicking on glass.

"Rice Crispies!" I ran in after them.

We were a symphony of snaps and crackles and pops. Rayne tried rolling in it, putting a network of tiny scratches on her bare arms. This was one of those magic places that parents wouldn't believe. "A whole field of Rice Crispies? Never."

The path went sharply down to a giant pool of water with a fence around it. Next to it was a small brick house with no door to keep us out. Inside, it was so cold the hair on my arms stood straight up. A low concrete ridge divided a small dirt path from a creek with a shiny milk can at the bottom. Sammi reached in to touch it then jerked her hand out. "The water's ice cold."

We all put a finger in to test it.

"I hope the pool is warmer than that." Rayne shivered dramatically.

"I bet there's snakes in there." I made my eyes bigger to scare her.

"You think?" Sammi looked around.

We all looked around for snakes. I was checking the dark rafters just above our heads when Rayne let out a piercing scream. Sammi and I screamed too then we all ran out.

"What was it?" Sammi's voice was more tentative than usual.

"What?" Rayne tilted her head in a question.

"What made you scream?" Impatience pinched at my nerves.

She looked up at us silently, not blinking. "My elbow hurt and it made me hurt."

I looked at Sammi. She shook her head and went sing-song. "Liar, liar, tongue on fire."

The grass was shorter and lush and our feet made squish noises, left indents. Trees lined a huge field of Queen Anne's lace. I

42

stopped to run my hand over a spray of minute white petals. The blooms tickled at my waist and Rayne's snowy head barely stood out above them. Montgomery tried furiously, and in vain, to break one of the thin stalks. Sammi bent down and disappeared. I lay down beside her. Rayne and Montgomery joined us and we looked up at the perfect blue through a web of white lace and green stems. Everything felt quiet and reassuring and I reached over and held Sammi's hand.

Rayne was the first to jump up. She ran toward a tall clump of vines creating a small shelter. We searched for a break in the foliage and finally ripped one. I'd never seen anything like it. Twilight-dark inside, a few dozen tree trunks supported the network of greenery we had seen from outside, but inside all was death. There was not one sprout, not one leaf, just dying, brown emptiness.

"This is Witch's Forest." I was proud to name it.

"It's a fort." Montgomery made gun and bomb noises.

I touched a trunk and decayed bark fell into rusty dust at the pressure of my fingertips. Startled, I jumped back and fell over Montgomery's kneeling figure. We smashed into decayed leaves and musty root rot.

Sammi looked up into the trees. "Maybe we should leave."

"I have to pee." Rayne's little voice wrapped round us like a lasso and pulled us out of our indecision.

We gathered in the darkness before running through the hole back out to the light.

Chapter Three

The day they finished painting the Lemonade Farm sign was the first day we could go swimming. Herbert and Merlin labored with the wooden signboard while Isabelle and Mommy arranged a ladder beneath giant hooks.

I couldn't decide whether to wear my one piece or my bikini. The one piece would be better for swimming but the bikini might make me look older. Besides, the bikini was blue which seemed to be Tommy's favorite color.

"Which should I wear?" Sammi held up a tomato-red one-piece and a bandana-print bikini.

Something like screaming ran through my head and stopped just before my mouth. "What does it matter, you don't care if Tommy likes you!"

She was smiling with one in each hand and her small nude breasts mocking me. "Which one looks better? I think the bikini, I don't know."

"You should wear the one piece. You're going to want to dive and stuff and you don't want to keep checking to see if your top is still on or if your bottoms fell to your ankles. Besides, red's your favorite color. We'll probably go swimming again tomorrow anyway, you can wear the bikini then. Maybe you should wear a T-shirt over top so you don't burn your shoulders. That's what me and Montgomery do at the beach."

"Maybe I'll just bring a T-shirt."

"You could wear it down there and take it off if you change your mind." I held my breath waiting for her to choose, feeling guilty that I had manipulated her over some boy who didn't seem to notice I was a girl.

She threw a long v-neck men's undershirt over the one-piece and hunted for her towel. "I just had it a second ago."

I turned and looked at my two suits.

Sammi was still searching. "How could I have lost it? This room's too small to lose anything. Why does this always happen to me? Is it on your side, Ariel?" She looked to me over her shoulder. "Ariel, do you see my towel?" She was still smiling and the smile cut right through me.

"No, I don't know where you put it." I picked up my one piece. The shiny fabric slid easily over bird legs before clinging to my hips. "Can you tie this?" I indicated the strings at my neck.

"Do you have a T-shirt?"

"I'm not sure. Maybe they're still packed."

"Here, take this one. We'll be twins." She handed me another oversized undershirt. Had she always been this nice?

"Twins." I pulled the shirt over my suit.

Everyone's towels were by the pool but no one was in the water. Rayne was running through the sycamores to the signpost down front.

Sammi pointed. "I guess they're down there."

The bushes lining the front yard concealed most everyone from our view. Only Herbert's ashy-black, wiry hair stuck out above the leaves. I could hear Mommy yelling commands and small voices laughing. We stepped through a break in the bushes. Everyone except Anne was crowded around the base of the signpost. Mommy stood back saying things like; higher! make sure you're holding the ladder tight enough, kids! don't look down, Herbert!

Herbert and Merlin were on the ladder lifting the sign. The first word was in script, lemon yellow with a black outline. "Farm" was in block letters. A glass of lemonade was painted onto the sign and at its base, half a lemon with some slices beside it. The giant metal loops at the top of the wood slid over the hooks. Herbert and Merlin came down and we looked at the sign, swaying slightly to and fro.

"So, I guess it's official." Mommy clapped her hands. "We're really here now."

"Yeah, I guess so." Isabelle itched her cheek with the back of a dirty hand.

"Well, good then." Mommy said it like she'd just decided it was so.

"We should take the ladder down before someone gets hurt." Herbert was a born dad.

Merlin tickled Sammi. "Well, I think I know some Lemons that need to try out their new pool!"

"Yeah!" We squealed and ran back through the bushes and up the hill. My Dr. Scholl's slapped my heels as I ran past sycamores, dotted berry trees and laden fruit trees. Anne glistened with oil on the only lawn chair. Her stereo speakers sat in the windows facing the pool. David Bowie's "Changes" wafted to us on the same breeze that carried the fragrance of maturing grass and clover.

"Nobody jump in." My blood rushed with the sound of my own authority.

Cory spun his arms like propellers to catch his balance at the edge of the pool and Tommy stopped midway across the diving board.

"Everyone come here." All the kids except Anne joined me beside the pool. I kicked off my sandals. "Let's all go in at the same time."

"Okay, I'll count to three." Montgomery held two fingers up.

"No, let's hold hands. That way we'll be sure to go in at the same time." I grabbed Tommy's hand and Sammi took mine. We lined up with the younger kids closer to the shallow end. "On the count of three."

"What if someone doesn't go in?" Edwina looped her finger into Tommy's cutoffs.

"We all have to promise. If you don't want to go in, get off of the line now or someone might get hurt."

"No, I don't want to." Eddy's eyes lowered in shame. "I just thought what would happen if someone didn't jump."

"Everyone promise now." Sammi put her hand to her heart.

"I promise."

"Promise."

"Cross my heart."

"I swear."

"Stick a needle in my eye."

"I promise."

"Okay, on the count of three." I was the leader, totally in control. "One, two, three."

Splash.

I held tight to Tommy's hand but my T-shirt floated up so that I couldn't really see him. He tried to let go and I hung on a moment longer until he shook free of me and swam to the surface. Cold water rushed through the warm spot where Sammi still held my hand and I pushed my shirt down to look at her. She made a funny face at me and we both lost our air laughing and had to rush past the bubbles carrying our "ha ha's" to the surface.

My senses flooded when we left the quiet blue. Montgomery was splashing Cory. Birds called from every tree. Rayne and Eddy's wet feet slapped against the stone mosaic surrounding the pool. My lungs warmed with honeysuckle air. David Bowie sang "Oh! You Pretty Things." Tommy hung from the end of the diving board doing pull-ups and counting, the wet lashes beneath his eyes making him look like Raggedy Andy. Anne lay in her lounge chair soaking in sun. Her perfect figure filled out her string bikini and her hair fell through plastic slats and mingled with pink clover. I started for the ladder on the shallow end and was almost hit by a speeding Eddy, flying from the sliding board.

"Sorry, Eddy." Rayne's voice slid from the top of the ladder.

"You meant to do it!" Eddy choked, rubbing her eyes.

Sammi and I went up the ladder at the back of the sliding board and coaxed Rayne onto it. "We'll hold your feet." She was afraid to go the entire length of the slide so we lowered her down over the first big bump then let go. The waves in the slide made her scream jump like Tarzan. Sammi gave me a big push from the back so I was airborne between each bump and the fear was exhilarating. I swam over to Tommy and put my hand over his on the diving board as if it were an accident.

"Sixty-seven, sixty-eight."

"Tommy, you want to try the slide?"

I pictured him holding my waist while I sat between his legs. We'd go down the slide together with him holding me tight. After landing, I'd turn to face him and we'd kiss, water running down our faces, his arms around me, our eyes closed. When I finally opened my eyes...

"Seventy-five, seventy-six, seventy-seven. In a minute, okay? Seventy-eight, seventy-nine."

Anne called for me to help her when she was ready to turn over. Sammi refilled Anne's glass of water while I rubbed baby oil on her back. Red lines from the plastic slats ran from side to side on her skin.

"Anne, did you know that you should use something with sun block in it?" I tried to make my voice small.

"Ariel, do you want to help me or not?" She threatened to take the bottle back, to fire me from my newly appointed position as the one person allowed to touch her. "You don't tan as fast with those."

"Yeah, but they're better for your skin."

"Mind your own business, Ariel. Did I ask for an opinion?"

"Well no, but..."

"That's enough oil."

I lay the bottle down after snapping the pink plastic lid shut. The grown-ups were watching us from the kitchen window - snickering and pointing. I felt like I was in a zoo.

"Try going down backwards." Sammi turned around to illustrate.

"You go first."

"Chicken?" She flapped her elbows.

"I'll do it!" Cory was always willing to try something stupid and potentially dangerous.

"No, I can do it." Sammi climbed to the top of the ladder and sat backwards. "Here goes." She let go and went flying down the board. Her back smacked against the water and she coughed coming back up. "It's great. Do it." She choked while she spoke.

Cory went next and Tommy finally came to join us. I went up behind him on the ladder so when he turned around, he faced me.

"Sayonara, sister." He pushed off and his face disappeared.

Sister? Did he mean like a real sister that you would never kiss or a sister whose a really good buddy or like a partner or someone you look out for or someone who's so close they're like family or what? I lay down on my stomach and slid down after him.

"Ariel, come here." Sammi smiled mischievously. I swam over to the edge and joined her. "No, come here. Get out of the pool." She motioned with her arm. "Come on."

We walked away toward the pavilion, Pillows trailing behind us. I watched for bees in the clover.

"I have to ask you something." Her face was all anticipation. "Do you like Tommy?"

Heat pushed up through my face. "Why?"

"Just do you?"

"Sort of."

"I knew it, I just knew it."

"How come you knew?" I felt all see-through.

"Do you think he wants to go with you? Does he know you like him? Didn't you used to like him a long time ago?"

"Three years." A sigh escaped. "When I was eight, we were playing football beside their house and he tackled me and, I don't know, ever since then, I just liked him. I don't think he knows it though. I think he sees me as Eddy's friend, you know, like a little sister."

"But she's Rayne's age."

"I know, but I hung out with her a lot. She's really nice. I slept over a couple of times. I kinda liked seeing him brushing his teeth and stuff, you know? He's going to start high school next year."

"Cool."

"Yeah. Do you think he likes me?"

"As a friend?"

"No dummy, you know."

She looked over to the pool. "I don't know. You want me to find out?"

"Oh my God, if you told him, I would die. I'm serious. Maybe you could find out without telling him that I asked you to."

"Okay. You stay here. No, come. He might get suspicious. When we get there, swim away from me so he's not scared to tell me."

"Don't ask him anything because he'll know I asked you to. Just be casual, okay?"

"Okay, okay."

We jumped back in the water and I swam to the deep end. Sammi swam to Tommy and said something to him. He looked over at me and nodded then looked back to Sammi. My heart banged against my ribs. They kept talking and Tommy put his hands on his hips and nodded again. Sammi bobbed up and down in the water then left him and swam over to me.

I blurted before I could stop myself. "What did he say?"

"I didn't ask him."

"What did you tell him?"

"I asked him if he wanted to spend the night in the pavilion with us. I told him we should ask if we could sleep out there, just the older kids.

"Why?"

"He said yes. So we just have to get permission. Which one should we ask first?"

"Your mom will say no. What about Herbert?"

"He'll say to ask my mom. Let's ask your mom."

"Okay. Should we invite Anne?"

"She won't want to go."

Mommy did say yes but suggested that it might be fun for all of the kids to sleep outside. I started to "Aw, Mommy" her but she got that "Don't start with me" look so I gave up.

We ate dinner in a rush so that we could get our provisions into the pavilion before dark. Sammi's sleeping bag was like a fake quilt on the outside and mine was bright bubble-gum pink, Peeps yellow, and white with giant cartoon flower petals on it. Sammi made sure that Tommy unrolled his navy all-weather nylon bag next to mine. We plugged my transistor into a socket on one of the giant wooden roof supports but it wouldn't turn on.

"Dad told me the circuit box is in the workshop." Tommy was suddenly the guy in charge.

"I'll go with you." Sammi sent me a look.

"Yeah, me too." I jumped up feeling obvious, awkward and exposed. I thought only an idiot couldn't tell what we were up to but Tommy said okay and the two of us followed him.

The workroom was like Dad's only bigger. There were saws and electric tools and half unpacked boxes of nails and hooks. Tommy jumped up cricket-like onto the scrap-covered work table and opened the spiderwebbed circuit box. Everything he touched brought light. All the wagon wheel chandeliers, the outdoor lights by the windows and the workshop lights came to life.

"It works." Montgomery yelled to us from the post where the radio was plugged.

"We don't need all these lights, which do I turn off?" Tommy kept flipping switches. "Forget the outdoor ones."

"No." I yelled before I could close my mouth around the word. "Leave them all on for now. We can turn some off later."

"Whatever you say." Tommy smiled and I felt like a giant dork, like a feathered, flashing, swollen, neon dork.

Whatever I say? I say we run off and get married. I say we have a boy and a girl and live in our old neighborhood and watch the kids go sledding. I say we have dinner parties and serve red wine and light candles and stay up till Johnny Carson. I say we kiss for hours. I say we take the kids to Enchanted Forest and Wheaton Regional Park. I say we go to Supplee Lane and watch the fish chase the silver pull-tabs we put on the kids' rods. I say we rake leaves into giant piles and take turns jumping into them. I say we always have cakes for birthdays and never come late with the Tooth Fairy money. I say we stay married forever and live happily ever after.

"Thanks." That's what I said.

After some argument, we decided to listen to WPGC FM 95 because it was my radio. Sammi suggested a game of Truth or Dare but I couldn't think of one truth I'd want to know from Cory, Montgomery, Eddy or Rayne. Rayne suggested a seance but the one we'd had at their old house still had Sammi spooked. All the board games and cards were inside so they wouldn't warp.

"I know what we can do." Sammi took charge now. "You guys have to swear not to tell, no matter what it is."

"What is it though?" Montgomery cloaked himself in paranoia.

"Just swear." Sammi didn't let her authority waver.

"What if it hurts? Tell us first." He was going to cling to this.

"Montgomery, do you want to do this or not?"

"I don't know yet. Tell me first."

She sat there staring at him with unamused round hazel eyes. "It's a grown-up thing."

"What grown-up thing?"

"Montgomery! Leave or swear, one or the other."

It was just the type of ultimatum I would have given him too if I hadn't been getting more and more scared of what Sammi was going to make us do.

"Okay, I promise." The corner of his mouth lifted.

"Check his fingers." I knew him so well.

"They're not crossed, I promise."

"Let us see."

His hands came slowly out from behind his back as he untwisted his fingers.

"Toes too." Sammi was one step ahead now.

"No, don't!" I threw my arms up in front of my face. "He's got stinky feet."

"Okay, then just swear."

"I promise."

"Not promise, swear!"

"I do." He yelled louder than he needed to.

"Okay. Everyone swears, right? Okay. Hold on." She ran to her balled-up pajamas and pulled out the Salem's.

"Those are cigarettes!" Montgomery's face twisted into panic.

"No shit, Sherlock." Even though I'd stolen that from Sammi, it made me feel superior.

"You swore." Sammi reminded him with a crooked smile.

"No I didn't. I said, 'I do,' not 'I swear.'"

"Come on, Montgomery. Just try them." Sammi whispered like we were entering a conspiracy. "I'll light it and you guys can all try it."

"I'll take my own." Pride filled my voice out like air in a balloon.

She handed me one and lit two more, passing one along. I'd never lit one by myself and was worried about catching my hair on fire but it wasn't so hard. I felt really cool, like one of those girls the Fonz would snap at. We tipped the ashes into the giant fireplace. Tommy took one of his own and asked if he could use mine to light it. I felt seventeen. The younger kids were pretty awkward except Rayne who handled the little white wand with more grace than anyone.

"Did you learn smoke rings yet?" I questioned Sammi in an effort to show off.

"Soon."

"Don't forget to teach me." I got the words out between puffs. I had just crushed my cigarette out in the fireplace when Mommy and Isabelle came in.

"Woooooo hoooooo." Mommy greeted us while Sammi and Rayne threw their cigarettes into the ashes and jumped up.

"Hi Mom." They said it in unison.

I kicked the Salem pack toward Tommy and he put his foot on it. I felt like a giant cigarette, like smoke was pouring out of me and everything around me smelled of ash. They kept coming closer so I moved away. Isabelle sat on Sammi's sleeping bag and motioned for them to join her.

"We're going to bed any minute now." Sammi kept that cool authority in her voice.

"Really?" Mommy made her eyes big. "I'd stay awake until I couldn't stay awake any longer. I always wanted to have slumber parties when I was younger."

"You could have one tonight in your room, Mommy." It sounded fun when I said it.

She giggled and looked at Isabelle. "Ariel, honey, adults don't have slumber parties. They're for when you're young."

"Why?" Montgomery tilted his head to the side.

"Well, its just not done, honey." She leaned over and kissed his forehead. No reaction. Maybe she had a stuffy nose. Maybe he didn't smell as strongly as I must. I let her walk over to me. "We just wanted to check in on y'all. Don't forget to turn off all these lights." She kissed my forehead too.

Isabelle got up and started for the door. "You kids get some sleep, okay?"

"We will."

They closed the door behind themselves then waved passing a window on the way back to the house.

"Oh my God, what if they saw us in that window?" My heart pounded so fast it made me dizzy.

"They didn't see anything." Sammi's voice was beginning to amaze me.

I wanted to learn this power to believe the things that come out of my own mouth. "I can't believe they didn't smell anything, I mean, Mommy walked right up to me. She even kissed me."

"Where did the cigs go?" Sammi searched her sleeping bag.

"Tommy's got them." Edwina pointed to his feet. We looked to the green and white pack, half-crushed beneath his toe.

Sammi ran to him and pushed his foot away. "Shit, look what you did." She shook the cigarettes into her palm. The ends were flat and a small tear ran across the middle of each one. "Shit. Well, maybe I can fix them. Anne showed me."

"I don't want to smoke anymore." Eddy's voice was so tiny and she suddenly looked like a little kid and I wondered what Sammi and I thought we were doing. "Can't we play anything else?"

Sammi broke one of the cigarettes at its tear. She rolled the piece without a filter between her fingers dumping a small bit of the tobacco onto the hearth, then she twisted it shut. She rolled the filtered end, emptying the white collar of paper. Then she pushed the twisted part into the collar down to the filter, licked her pointer and her thumb and pressed the spit onto the seam. "There."

"Let's go watch TV." Montgomery pleaded gently.

"You go." I sounded strong like Sammi. "But don't come back. Sleep inside."

"Why don't we bring the TV here?" Cory suggested this with a bucket of hope.

"Guys, quit it." Sammi lit the short cigarette. "We're sleeping outside."

"Yeah." I backed her up. "What's the point of sleeping out here if we bring a TV?"

"Then why did we bring the radio?" Montgomery was always causing problems.

"It's not the same, dummy." I hated it when I called him that. "You can bring a radio into the woods with you if you want."

"Not that one, it's the old fashioned kind." Cory nodded at the radio sitting on the pavement.

"You better shut up!" I screamed because I couldn't do the voice anymore, I felt myself losing. "That was my great-grandfather's radio. He kept it on the porch. He's dead now and this is what I got so you better just shut up." I walked across the concrete floor down to the carpeted area with the toys. I hoped Tommy was following me. I tried wishing him there as if just wanting it would make it happen. I pictured him comforting me, telling me they didn't mean anything by it, asking me to forgive them for being so insensitive.

I snuck a peek over my shoulder when my foot reached the carpet but no one was behind me. Sammi was smoking. Rayne and Eddy were pulling their bags away from the group. Montgomery was fiddling with the tone and volume dials on the radio. Cory was biting his cuticles. And Tommy was... gone. I went running back to Sammi.

"Want a puff?" She acted as if nothing were awry.

"Sammi, this is going all wrong!" I tried to stay cool, keep my voice a whisper. "There's all these kids here and now Tommy's gone. You're not helping me at all."

"He's just peeing, you retard."

It took a minute for me to get it.

"Do you want a puff?"

Tommy came back through one of the side doors. "We really should turn off those outside lights if we're not going to go back to the house." He walked to the workshop.

"This is a complete disaster. I'm going inside." I felt a tight spot on my throat.

Tommy came back in carrying a rubber mallet. "Hey, what do you suppose those guys are doing inside?" He sat next to me and bounced the mallet off the floor.

"Watching TV?" I laughed like it was a joke, though I knew I couldn't have explained why it was supposed to be funny.

"I bet they're sitting around talking about therapy and bullshit like that." Sammi laughed at her not-funny thing too and I felt saved.

"Does your mom talk about that junk too?" Tommy touched my ankle when he said it and I felt all electric.

"My mommy's getting a Masters in it." I played my ace. "So I know she's the worst."

"Oh God, poor you." Tommy laughed too and all was right with the world.

"Let's have a pity party." Sammi had the perfect punch line.

We all made pity noises. I felt like I was part of something for that moment.

*   *   *

One week after we opened the pool, kids started showing up. Our house was the only one with a pool on all of Patapsco Road. Happy and Crane were the first ones to start hanging out just behind the line of bushes. We could see them from the top of the slide. They would stand there talking to each other casually as if they weren't waiting for us to invite them to swim. After the third or fourth day of casual fence line standing, they finally walked right up the lawn and over to the pool.

"Hi."

We looked at each other. Anne gathered her magazines.

"This here's Happy. Some folks say Hap. I'm Crane. We're from down the road a piece."

No one spoke.

Crane shifted his weight. "You guys must be the new neighbors."

"What kind of name is Crane?" I treaded water.

"It's a bird."

"Oh." I bobbed in the water a little.

"What's your name?"

"Ariel."

"Ariel? Isn't that some kind of dog?" His voice held no malice.

"No, that's Airedale."

"Oh." He shifted his weight again. "So, what's Ariel?"

"It's a fairy."

"A fairy? You mean like a fag?"

"No, you retard, like a sprite. A little... never mind."

"No, I know what you mean." He nodded his head.

"Does your friend speak?" Sammi wasn't buying it.

"Oh sure." Crane looked at Happy. "Say something, Hap."

"Hey."

"What's your name?" Crane was definitely the chatty one.

"Sammi."

"Why do you have a boy name?"

"Why do you have a bird name?"

"Be nice, Sammi." I didn't want them to leave yet. They seemed like they might be our age.

"I'm Montgomery."

"That's kind of a strange name too. Are you guys some sort of hippies?"

"No, are you?" Sammi was getting tough on them.

"What?"

"Nothing."

"You guys live around here?" I wanted to save it all.

"No, we came by bus." Crane snapped and I thought those sounded like parting words.

"They have busses here?" Sammi didn't know he was kidding. She suffered selective naiveté. "Oh, I get it. Very funny."

"Yeah, so funny I forgot to laugh."

"Shut up, Montgomery." I just knew he'd scare them away.

"Hey, Airedale, is that your little sister?" Crane asked pointing to Rayne.

"Not really."

"I have a name." Rayne hit the water like a gavel smacking wood.

"Are you guys sisters?" He pointed back and forth between Sammi and me.

"What's it to you?" Sammi challenged him while I shook my head no.

"Are you guys all cousins?"

"No."

"We are." Happy came alive momentarily.

"Really?"

Like Cory, Happy had thick, short bones with tan skin and dirty-blonde thick hair. Crane was long and skinny, even his nose, criss-crossed with a jagged scar, and his skin was starkly white against very dark hair and eyes.

"So, what are you?"

"None of your beeswax." Rayne smiled.

"Aw man. Forget it. Let's go, Hap."

"Do you guys swim?" I wasn't sure what I wanted and handed them the reigns.

"Yeah." Hap answered anxiously.

"Got a pool?" Sammi smiled and looked evil to me for a moment.

"No."

"Well, come visit us sometime. Maybe we can all go swimming." Her arms were crossed between the two pieces of her bandana-print navy bikini and her hair was drying in patches, forming tufts. Her feet were in third position.

"Yeah, okay. That's cool." Crane walked back down the hill with Hap following behind him slapping at tree leaves.

"Bye, guys." I felt all churned inside. "Sammi, what'd you do that for?"

"What do you mean?"

"Why couldn't they swim today?"

"They're nerds. Besides, it's better to have the pool to ourselves."

"Don't you forget it!" Anne snapped the dirt from her towel. "See?"

"Oh."

"Kids, come help me with these groceries." Mommy yelled from the parking lot.

"Jeeze. She always does this. Come on, Montgomery."

"In a minute."

Sammi and I rounded the house and walked onto the chunky gravel on our toughening bare feet.

"Here, honey." Mommy handed me a watermelon. "Careful now." There were two. Sammi carried the other. "Just leave them on the porch and come get these bags."

"Mommy, you got Life again. I hate that cereal."

"Well, then Montgomery must like it. One of you eats it. I got Cheerios too."

"Boring."

"Don't start. Get the door, would you sweetie?"

Who was going to eat all of that watermelon? Dad hated watermelon so we never bought it back in Laurel. He always got mint chocolate chip ice cream from High's. No fruit. We'd eat small fruit like apples and grapes but once Mommy got a melon and he said it took up half of the Goddamn fridge. It was an embarrassing fruit anyway, I never knew what to do with the seeds.

"Put the cereal in there." Mommy pointed absently toward the sink but we were supposed to know she meant the cabinet. "And go ahead and get that last bag."

Thomasina rubbed against one of the melons then followed me inside.

"Wooooo hoooo." Mommy yelled up the stairs. "Isabelle, Herbert. Woooo hoooo."

"Let's go." I nudged Sammi.

"How about cutting the salad, Ariel?"

"Mommy."

"Sammi, Ariel will be there in ten minutes."

I wanted to stomp my feet but I had promised Mommy I wouldn't do that or bite my nails anymore or else I'd lose my fifty-cent-per-week allowance. Her humming and lalalaing made me want to scream. I washed and tore the iceberg lettuce and dropped it into the large mixing bowl. "How much?"

"About half. Where is everyone? Herbert! Merlin! This house can be so big."

I chopped tomatoes, broke broccoli stalks, sliced carrots and sprinkled sprouts. "Can I go swim now?"

"Sweetie, it's almost time for supper. Can you set the table?"

"Mommy." I whined like a three-year-old. Even I wished I'd grow out of that.

"Ariel."

Isabelle's brown Datsun B210 pulled in and she, Herbert and Merlin got out.

"Hey, nice melons, Madeleine."

They chuckled at Merlin's joke while I was still trying to get it.

Mommy gestured her chin toward the pool outside. "Sugar, could you call the kids to the table?"

"Just yell out the window."

"Ariel, I'm asking you."

She was right there. Why couldn't she do it? I always had to do everything. "Dinner!"

Sammi and Rayne wrapped their towels around their waists like sarongs and Montgomery turned upside down and shook his long hair like a dog before settling in to eat.

We got waffle butts from sitting on the bentwood chairs. Isabelle cleared the plates, her thick, auburn hair fell over her eyes when she asked if we had packed.

"Packed?" Montgomery's face fell.

"For your dad's." Rayne knew the routine. "Tomorrow's the Friday they come."

"Oh."

"Okay kids, it's melon time." Merlin clapped his hands together. He and Herbert moved the wooden picnic table from the yard onto the flagstone porch. Mommy came out of the kitchen carrying a big knife and Isabelle had a roll of paper towels. Merlin split the green stripes revealing the freckled red meat. He made each piece huge, too big for one hand.

I sat on the steps and let the cool, sticky juice run down my arm and off my elbow. I looked to Anne to see if she spit the seeds. I was still waiting when the first seed hit my cheek. Merlin guffawed hysterically at his joke. I spit my seeds at his ankles and hoped he'd still like me. The ones that hit Mommy's hair stayed stuck, looking like June bugs. Merlin kept getting them down the front of Isabelle's French-cut T-shirt. Huge chunks of melon shot out of Montgomery's mouth and we kept yelling, "Chew first" at him. One bounced off Herbert's glasses leaving a slime mark. I laughed so hard that I swallowed a whole mouthful of seeds. Anne hit her mom in the back of her head with a rind. Then we all jumped in the pool. Isabelle's T-shirt clung to her and Mommy's jeans made a funny squoosh noise when she walked back to the house. The four perfect brunette kids next door stood like descending stair steps at their fence line and watched us go back inside.

*   *   *

Dad said they had a pool at Sandy's building so be sure to bring a swimsuit. Mommy said they might take us out to eat so be sure to bring a dress and shoes. Montgomery said we might see kids from our old school so I made sure I brought play clothes. There was no way I was going to be able to bring that bag downstairs. Sammi said you get used to it and you can leave stuff at his house so you don't have to carry as much. Anne kept saying, "This is bullshit," and Isabelle kept saying, "Anne, watch for Rayne." Rayne didn't say anything but I found out later that Sammi had forgotten to pack any underwear for her.

I had only seen Sandy once and that was months ago, before Dad moved out. She was pretty like Mommy but she had hair like *I Dream of Jeannie*. She called it "honeydew blonde." She stayed in the Volkswagen Bug while Dad brought our bags out.

Mommy walked us to the door. "Have a great time. Frank, you have our number?"

"I just called you yesterday."

"Have fun, my babies. Call if you need anything." She waved at us pulling down the drive.

Sandy's voluminous ponytail bounced over her shoulder then settled back onto her chest. A gold necklace with her name on it rested on a burgundy blouse that matched her gauchos and knee-high leather boots. I guess it was cold where she worked. "Hi kids. Your dad and I are so glad you could come over this weekend. We have some treats for you at the house."

"I thought you lived in an apartment." Montgomery sounded innocent but I felt my gut tighten.

"You're right, it is." She smiled and I could feel her stomach was tight too.

"It's a nice apartment, Montgomery. Swings, pool, sandbox and kids." Dad explained it all in a way that said we were done questioning it.

Do you like Shakey's pizza?" Sandy's voice was so full of hope that I knew we could only say yes.

"We always ate at Pauly's Pizza." I don't know why I told her but I knew it was aimed at pain. "They have a giant giraffe there with lollipops in its neck and when you stand on the bench, you can see them spin the dough in the air."

"They have wooden paddles to get the pizza out." Montgomery smiled Mommy's smile.

"Well, Monty, we'll have to go there sometime. But tonight we're going to Shakey's."

"He doesn't like the name Monty." My eye caught Dad's disapproval in the rearview mirror. "Well he doesn't, do you?"

"It's not my name."

"See?"

"I'm sorry, Montgomery. It won't happen again. So, you like pizza a lot?"

"It's okay. I like burgers better."

"Except he doesn't like anything on them so it takes an hour for us to eat at McDonald's. They have to make it special for him."

"He'll grow out of it." Dad moved his hand from the gear shift knob to Sandy's knee.

It was really dark inside the pizza parlor. Dad packed his pipe with tobacco while the waitress laid the menus in front of us.

"Mmmm, this sounds good." Sandy sported a hopeful grin. "Pepperoni and mushroom."

"Dad, I'm not eating mushrooms." I considered myself to be relatively easy to please, but everyone who meant anything to me knew I hated mushrooms.

"Can we get plain? Extra cheese?"

"Montgomery, we're not getting plain." Dad stated this with finality. "I say we get pepperoni and mushroom, that sounds good."

"But, Dad, the mushrooms."

"Ariel, you can pick them off. Miss? Yes, we'll have a large pizza, half pepperoni and mushroom, half plain with extra cheese. We'll split a pitcher and the kids will have Cokes."

"Root beer!"

"Root beers. And be sure to bring the salads before the pizza."

"Dad, I hate salad." Montgomery's voice was whiny now.

"Three salads."

"How can you hate salad?" Sandy looked truly mystified.

"He's always hated salad. He hates it really bad. He spits it out every time we make him try it again."

"It's a phase." Dad said it to Sandy and made it sound true. "Ariel loves salad, don't you, Ariel?"

"Not with mushrooms."

Dad lit his pipe with a match. The flame jumped up and down when he puffed.

"I've hated mushrooms longer than Montgomery's hated salad."

"Sandy bought some sleeping bags for you guys so it will be like camping in the living room. Isn't that a nice treat? They stay warm up to thirty degrees below."

I could only hope that feature would never get tested.

"Can I have a quarter for the juke box?" Montgomery bounced as if on springs.

"Sure."

"Sandy, don't give it to him."

"Why not, Ariel?"

"Just don't."

"I don't see why not. Frank, is it okay?"

"Sure."

Montgomery snatched the quarter and dropped it on the floor. He leaned over to pick it up and dropped it again. Surveying the choices, his face was all green and orange in the light.

"He's very sweet." Sandy smiled at Dad.

The salads came and Montgomery sat waiting with his empty plate.

"Mine's very good." Sandy smoothed the paper napkin on her lap. "How's yours, Ariel?"

I scraped some of the orange French dressing onto the side of the bowl. "It's pretty good."

"How's yours, Frank?"

"More beer, Sandy? Hand me your glass."

Then I heard it.

"Oh yes they call it the streak..."

"This is it! Look a dat look a dat Hmmmmm. Lookadat lookadat." Montgomery was laughing and bouncing on the wooden bench. "Lookadat lookadat. Git yer clothes on, Ethel!"

"How many songs do they give you for a quarter here?" I could hear my own exhaustion.

"I don't know. Four? Five?" Sandy shook powdered cheese onto her slice.

"Great." I picked errant mushrooms off the pizza while we listened to "The Streak" play six consecutive times.

*   *   *

I shoved the Barbie I called Carrie under a pile of toys when Sammi walked in.

"Valerie gave us underwear this weekend. It's really silky. Do you want to see?"

"Sure."

Sammi pulled the back of her shorts up to reveal deep maroon silky undies like they wear in the magazines.

"Wow, nice."

"You want to go to town?"

"Sure." I grabbed some change and we headed out into the sun. A girl was playing with those horses we always passed, leading one around with a newish, green nylon rope.

"You think she'll let me ride them?"

"I don't know, Sammi. She doesn't even know you."

"I mean if I was her friend."

"Maybe. I would, but maybe she doesn't like people to touch them. Let's sing the wizard song again."

"I bet she would if we were friends. Wouldn't you?"

"I would."

Crane was far too leggy for the bike he rode and his legs went out to the sides as he peddled toward us, past us, then back around from behind. "Going to town?"

Sammi looked to the horses vanishing behind us.

Crane swept his hair back with dirty fingers. "You guys going into town or you going visiting?"

"Town." I wondered if I was supposed to answer him.

"Oh yeah, town. That's good. What are you getting in town? My uncle owns part of one of the grain places. I could get you some cheap."

"We're not getting grain." Sammi sounded bemused and angry at the same time. "We're just going for a walk. Just us two."

"Oh. I get it. Okay. Well, maybe I can come swimming sometime soon."

"Yeah, maybe." Sammi smirked and I was pretty sure Crane wasn't getting an invite anytime soon.

Crane rode away with his legs making those exaggerated circles. He was kind of cute, the way his hair fell straight into his eyes sometimes and that funny way of talking, the crescent scar across his nose bridge apnd cheek, his eyes, very big with long black eyelashes. And, he was taller than me. Almost no kids were taller than me.

"You know what?" Sammi's face held a secret.

"What?"

"That's what!"

We both giggled. I felt safe. "Do you sleep in a bed at your dad's?"

"Me and Rayne share a pull-out."

"We slept on the floor in sleeping bags. Do you like Valerie?"

"Sure, she's really nice. She's really pretty too. Did you see the underwear she gave me? Oh yeah, that's right. Anyway, she's cool."

"Sandy's hair is fake." I had her attention now. "She calls it a fall. It's a fake ponytail. Her hair's only about that long." I put my hand below my chin.

"Let's try Marlboros this time, okay?"

"Are they minty?"

"No, but you'll like them. Anne smokes them."

"Do you have skates?"

"Roller skates? No." She swatted at a fly near her face.

"I wonder if you could stuff Montgomery's. I was thinking maybe we could go skating in the pavilion tonight. Wouldn't that be fun?"

"Can't. Family meeting tonight."

"You have those too?"

"No, for everyone, all the Lemons."

We bought the cigarettes and sat at what was becoming "our spot" to smoke some. Every few minutes, a car would pass on the road above us and my neck would shrink into itself, hiding turtle-like, making the whole thing more fun and less fun. These didn't taste as good but I still got a little dizzy from them. I imitated Sammi, holding my cigarette straight up and poking smoke rings into the air. I tried to flick my ashes like she did but I succeeded only in creating a spray of waste. She shot her butt into the passing river with her thumb and middle finger and I threw mine at the water using my whole hand.

Sammi stared at the horses the whole time we passed that farm on the way back. She kept talking about Arabians and Bays and Quarter horses. The clacking of my Dr. Scholls was my only contribution.

"You sound like a horse in those shoes."

"I do?"

"Yeah, here." She pulled reeds from the growth beside the road and handed one to me. "It's a crop. Hyah!" She smacked her thigh with the reed then took off skipping rhythmically. I copied her and matched her gait. We were horse and rider at once. We trotted, cantered and galloped the whole way home smacking our thighs as we went.

Everyone was already eating when we got there. We served ourselves the last of the salad and a hamburger casserole.

"Ariel, did you write notes for this family meeting? She's so efficient, she writes notes for the family meetings." Mommy bragged and I wished I had the perfect notes.

"Nobody even told me about it."

"Ariel, I just told you this afternoon."

"Well, it must of been Montgomery because nobody told me."

"Ariel, I most certainly told you."

It was one thing to not have the notes but I wasn't going to take the blame. "Montgomery, did she tell you about it?"

He lifted his chin from the side of his plate. "Yeah."

"See?"

"Well, I knew I told somebody."

And that was that. We left our dishes in the sink and went into the giant living room. The grown-ups settled on three mix-matched couches and we sat on the shag rug with cats snuggled in our laps.

Isabelle sat with her back to the fireplace making her the leader. "Okay, this is the first ever Lemons' family meeting. We're going to do gripes, complaints and rules first then warm fuzzies. Madeleine, do you want to start?"

"No, you go ahead. I've got that chart to do after the gripes."

"Herbert, any gripes or complaints?"

"No, I'm fine thanks."

"Merlin?"

"Oh, just that tool thing. Herbert didn't you want to say something about the tools?"

"Oh yeah. Try not to touch my tools."

Merlin shook his head. "Someone went into the workshop and played with our tools and that's definitely a no."

Mommy pulled at a thread in her hem. "Does everyone understand the rule?"

We nodded almost imperceptibly.

"Does everyone agree to the rule?"

"Mommy, we got it."

"I'm just trying to be fair, Ariel. This is not a dictatorship. You are entitled to your opinions and I was just asking for yours, okay?"

"Okay, okay. Can we just go to the next thing?" I hated when I talked down to her.

Isabelle looked to her index card. "Okay, so the tools are settled. No one touches them. Well, there aren't very many gripes tonight so I guess that's good. Okay, so rules. Now these rules were put together by all of us but if you don't agree to any of them, we can talk about it. Everyone needs to be back at the farm by dark."

"You mean the kids, right?" Anne dared everyone.

"Well, yes, the kids."

"And which am I?"

"Anne, you'll have your own curfew, okay?"

"So, I can basically ignore all of these rules?"

Isabelle sighed. "No. I mean, some are for all of us."

"So, can I leave?"

"Anne, you will stay. Okay, so back by dark. Everyone must clean their own messes in the kitchen and the playroom."

"Yeah, so if you make a mess in the playroom, Merlin, be sure to clean up after yourself." Anne was having fun now.

Isabelle looked back down to the white card. "Don't put any boxes or bottles back into the fridge or pantry when they're empty. No wet towels on the floor. Same with bathing suits. Don't go into anyone's room without permission."

"Now, there's a good rule." Anne agreed but it still sounded like a disagreement.

"How are we supposed to get to our room?" I said it with panic I knew it didn't warrant.

"Well, obviously, you have to be able to do that. But don't worry, we're going to cut that new door soon."

"So? We'll still have to go through Rayne's room."

"Rayne won't mind, will you?" Isabelle ran a hand over Rayne's honey-snow hair.

"This is such bullshit."

"Anne!"

"No, really. Don't you guys get it? They don't care if you go in each other's rooms, only theirs. None of these rules are for them. This is such bullshit. Family meeting. It's more like family... I don't know but something really bullshit."

"Isabelle, I can't have all this cursing going on." Mommy's eyebrows slanted into that disapproving look.

"Anne, can we talk about this later? Let's just get through the meeting, okay?"

Anne sat silently. She vacated her eyes and went to that place teenagers hide from everyone else.

"Okay, enough rules for one meeting. Madeleine, do you want to do the chart?"

Mommy pulled a piece of loose-leaf from behind her. "This is our chores chart. Everyone has a chore and we'll rotate every week." She turned the paper over and pointed. "Here's your names, the dates are along here and the chores are here."

"What kind of chores?" I hated this.

"Are your names on there?" Sammi took up Anne's sword.

"Yes, they are. The chores are vacuuming." Mommy only got one chore out before we jumped on her.

"The whole house?" Rayne's voice leapt up octaves.

"Yes, but lots of the floors here are wood. Sweeping, weeding, dusting, bathrooms, kitchen, watering, and on and on. I'm going to post this on the refrigerator and you have until the last day of the week to finish the chore. If you don't do it or trade it with someone who will do it by then, no allowance."

"Okay, Mad, I think it's time for warm fuzzies." Merlin looked at some words he'd written on his palm in ball point.

"Do you want to start, Merlin?" Mommy sounded hopeful and I was glad he'd rescued her.

"Sure. I want to thank everyone for getting along these first few weeks, especially the siblings. Good job, guys."

"Who are the siblings?" Sammi itched her earlobe.

"You guys. Brothers and sisters."

"Oh, I thought they were the neighbors or something."

Everyone laughed really hard and the tightening in my stomach started to go away.

*   *   *

I liked how the dirt felt in my hands. Warm earth on top gave way to cooler beneath. I worked the squash row with Herbert. It was too late to plant a lot of things but Mommy said we'd still get some berries and lettuce and that our Fall garden would be beautiful.

We had grown stuff in our backyard in Laurel. Mommy would wait until the strawberries were filling the air with their scent, until their vines tangled each other and spilled out over the borders of the garden, then she would ask Montgomery and me to help her pick them. We'd put them all in colanders and rinse them inside. It was hard to wait and sometimes I had to eat a dirty one even though a cat could have peed on it. Dad liked to pick a bowl full of purply-red ragged-edged lettuce and let Montgomery dry it in the salad spinner.

Isabelle said she wanted to have pumpkins, that she and the girls loved fried pumpkin seeds and pumpkin pies. I tried not to be jealous that I wasn't one of "the girls." We all wanted to have corn. Herbert was worried since we'd never grown any of this stuff but Isabelle read directions from seed packs and Mommy, well, Mommy did what she did best, turned a blind eye to the obstacles and faithfully sang while plunking seeds into the ground.

We finished planting before the sun went down and watered with a blue sky turning a promising pumpkin behind us. Isabelle went in to start a dinner of store-bought food with Merlin and Rayne. Montgomery helped Herbert put tools away. I stood at the top of the tilled field watching water pack down loose dirt and trying to imagine that from this patch of nothing, a cornucopia of treats would grow.

*   *   *

Tommy pushed the giant red door on its track and we got our first glimpse of the barn. It was symmetrical with a giant hay bin and a tack room on either side. That's why it seemed strange that the back door was off to the left a little. The tack room on the right was open and we peeked in at the web-filled space.

"A trap door." Montgomery stared down a hole in the floor near one of the bins.

"That must be where they threw the hay down for the horses." Sammi looked down with him, her Jack Purcel's curling over the edge.

"Then, what's that giant door in the back for?"

"That must be how they got the hay in, you know, from the fields. Hey, look, these ladders go all the way up." She started to climb one of the ladders overlooking a hay bin. "Oh my God, guys. Be really careful cause there might be holes in the floor."

"Why?" I climbed behind her. From above, it was easy to see the swiss-cheese flooring the rotting hay had created. "Wow."

"What? Let me see." Montgomery always had a greedy way of asking for things. Plus, he was slow, testing each footfall before applying weight.

"Get out of the way, Montgomery. I'm coming down." The ladder shook with our weight. Tommy put his hand on my waist and sent electricity through me and out the hair standing on my arms. I pictured him carrying me like a honeymooner over to a safer place. He would set me down without letting go of me and stare at me with those brown eyes then slowly lean in for a tender kiss on the lips.

"Ariel, come on." Sammi nudged me. "Look, I bet you could get up on this if you tried."

The roof of the tack room was only seven or eight feet tall. Tommy went first then helped Sammi and me up. Yellowed newspapers were everywhere with pictures of people with hairdos like Mommy's old wedding photos.

"What year is it?" I looked over Tommy's shoulder and felt my breath rebound from his shoulder back up into my nose.

"Look, this one is 1956." Sammi held the paper up.

"This one is 1956 too." I showed her mine.

"Here's a 1954." Tommy flipped the pages of his.

"Wow, this is wild." Sammi pointed at a photo. "Look at their clothes. What an ugly shirt that guy has."

"My dad has a shirt like that." Tommy snickered.

"Yeah but he didn't used to wear his hair like this helmet-hair thing that my mom did."

"No, I mean he has a shirt like that now."

I yelled across the barn to the roof of the opposite tack room. "Be careful, Cory." He was helping Montgomery up while Eddy watched from below with Rayne. Tommy put his hand right through a spider's web, like it wasn't even scary, to grab another newspaper. He scanned the front page then dropped it on top of the others. I ran my hand across the old faces and felt the stiffness of the paper. "I bet some of these people are dead now."

"Probably. Especially the old ones. They're probably goners." Tommy picked another from the stack.

"You guys are gross." Sammi declared it and I wondered if it was true.

"Let's look downstairs." Eddy peered up at us, lonely.

Sammi dropped the pile of papers. "Yeah, this is getting boring." We followed her out the barn, down the rocky slope and into the dark hallway on the lower level.

The scent of old hay was overwhelming - cloying and heavy. The stalls on the right were too dark to see but the ones on the left opened out onto the pasture. The floor was bumpy beneath our feet and the sound of hay shuffling echoed low off the heavy wooden stall doors and stone walls.

Sammi kept walking out onto the concrete porch and summed up the pasture. "Wouldn't it be cool to have a horse here? God, it would be so great. We could get rid of all these weeds and cut them down and we could put hay in the bins and clean one of these stalls out. God, it would be so cool. Don't you think?"

"Sure, I guess." I felt that familiar anger I had for the neighbor's horses, anger that they held more fascination for her than I did.

The weeds had definitely taken over this part of our property. They were taller than Rayne or Eddy and I could practically hear the ticks crawling around. Montgomery walked over to my side and I reached out to him. "Tag, you're it!" I ran back into the stall and down the dark hallway. "Montgomery's it! Run!" I ran up the side of the hill. I ran past the hole in the floor and back to the door overlooking the pasture. I heard small throats squealing as a bewildered Montgomery figured out who to chase.

Sammi and Tommy were the first ones in the barn after me. She ran up onto the roof of the tack room. He stood in the middle of the floor with his chest heaving beneath his brown plaid shirt. The light thunder of the rest of us coming around the corner put panic on Tommy's face. Cory flew in and took a running jump down the trap door. I looked at Tommy then at the hole. Down he went. It was at least seven or eight feet to the ground. Tommy was looking back up from where he'd landed on the rocky floor.

"Open that stall door! Open it!" I was a thinker, not a jumper.

Tommy got up and pulled the stall door over until it was beneath the trap door. I lowered my feet first and stood on the top of the stall door then crawled down it like a ladder. Sammi came down behind me.

"In here." Tommy whispered from a dark stall. I pictured myself curled up in a ball next to him with his arms protecting me from the impending danger. I felt the soft hay beneath us, nestling us. I felt his quickened breath against my salty neck.

Sammi screamed in my ear. "Aaaaaaaaah! Here he comes!" She grabbed my arm. "Oh shit! Here he comes. Come on!" We ran, hand in hand, back up the side of the hill and into the tack room. Sammi closed the door and we stood behind it looking out the dirty windows. "Are they coming?"

"I can't see anything."

Hooks and dowels and saddle stands came out from the other wall.

"Can you see him yet?"

The window was cloudy like someone had spilled coffee and smeared it. "I can't see. You look."

She rubbed the glass with the butt of her hand. "It's on the outside too. Shit. I can't see."

"I told you." I tried to make out shapes through the brown film. "Maybe we should go back on the roof."

"No, let's wait. What if they see us?"

"I don't even hear anybody, do you?"

"Maybe they went back to the house."

I smiled. "Maybe it's that zone your mom always says."

"What zone?" She was still looking.

"That zone. The one where weird things happen. Remember?"

"*The Twilight Zone?*"

"That's the one. Do do do do."

"Yeah, do do do do."

We were tittering softly when the door flew open and hit me on the shoulder. My throat burned with a scream. Sammi grabbed my arm and ran right into Tommy's chest. I ran into her back and we both fell on top of Tommy. For a moment, we were just kids, not boys and girls, just kids. Rayne was holding her crotch, tee-heeing her high-pitched little-girl laugh.

We were dusting ourselves off when Montgomery came in, breathless. He stretched his arm out to Eddy and gasped. "You're it."

"We're done, Sherlock." I looked at him like he was damaged and felt it hurt my heart.

"Oh." He leaned and put his hands on his knees to breathe.

"Who wants to go to town?" Sammi was in a new moment while we were still dusting off the last.

Montgomery was against it but we went anyway. We smacked at giant droopy leaves as we ambled down the now-familiar road. We glanced at the girl riding her horse using only the green nylon rope. We kicked rocks until they disappeared in undergrowth. We waded and fished out smooth pieces of glass from the river bed. We found sitting rocks in the middle of the river and kicked at the water with our shiny white feet. We watched passing cars and laughed at Rayne's terrible knock-knock jokes. We rolled our shorts up higher to get better tans and put our hair behind our ears. Then we got hungry and walked back to our giant, old mansion on top of its grassy hill and left the door unlocked behind us.

Chapter Four

She wore her hair in tight little braids that barely moved on either side of her head as she spiraled through the air flying end over end. She defied all of the laws of gravity and never let her smile so much as droop. She seemed like perfection incarnate and I fell in love with her along with the rest of the world while she racked up perfect 10's and changed the face of gymnastics forever. Her name was Nadia Comaneci and though she spoke very little English, her drive and graceful strength spoke volumes to me. My head in my hands, I lay everyday on the green carpet, my eyes captives of the screen. I liked it so much better than all that jungle Vietnam guerrilla stuff we had to watch for so long. I remembered asking Mommy where the gorillas were - that they kept saying there were gorillas on the news but I'd never see any. She had laughed but then she looked very sad.

I'd watch Nadia then I'd go out to the pavilion by myself and try cartwheels and forward rolls, ending each with a hyper-arched back and arms extended like hers. I pictured the screaming fans and the flashing cameras. I pictured myself walking up to receive a gold medal for America. I pictured them laying the roses across my arms and a tear crawling down my cheek. I was victorious, a hero. I was the world champion. I was the center of attention. I was sitting on my ass on a two by six mat having just fallen for the millionth time. Rayne came in the pavilion and I jumped to my feet.

"Is Sammi in here?"

"No."

"What're you doing?"

"Nothing."

"Mom wants Sammi. Do you know where she is?"

I knew why I was mad but I wasn't sure why I was embarrassed. "Maybe she's riding with Alice again."

"Why didn't you go?"

"I don't know. I guess cause I'm doing this."

"What are you doing?"

No way could I admit to winning a gold medal. "Nothing."

"Do you like that girl, Alice?"

"She's okay, I guess."

"I don't like her. Sammi's always over there."

"I don't really like her either."

Rayne smiled, revealing missing teeth, and we giggled at our secret. We walked barefoot back to the playroom and rearranged the chairs to build a sheet fort. Parts of the sheet sagged on my head but it was mostly well set up. The record player whirled in the middle and our first selection was a sing along. "If you want it, here it is, come and get it." We played it a few times then put on "War" and shouted in deep voices. "Huh! What is it good for!?!" Rayne picked mostly the 45's with the green apple on the label. We spilled our bowl of dry Cheerios twice trying to maneuver around and both times just put them back in the bowl and kept eating.

"Do you know this one?" Rayne looked at me like I was a grown-up.

"Who is it?"

Rayne ran her finger under the words as she read. "'Yoko Ono.' Japanese maybe. Maybe it's one of yours."

"I never heard of them. Put it on. Maybe we'll know it when we hear it."

"What is this word?"

"Kyoko."

"What is that?"

"I don't know. Maybe it's some kind of food or something."

She looked up at me with big, blue eyes. "Then why isn't it supposed to worry?"

I grabbed the 45. "Oh yeah. I don't know. It must be a person. They're telling them not to worry."

"Give it back. I want to play it."

She pushed a yellow plastic disc into the center of the record and dropped it onto the turntable. The speaker crackled with raw needle noise before the high-pitched howling began. "Dooooooooooooooooooooooooooooooooon't." Rayne and I looked at each other. "Don't worry, don't worry, don't worry."

Rayne tittered then I laughed until I coughed and tears ran down my face. Rayne held her stomach then moved her hands down between her legs and rocked. "You're going to make me pee. Stop laughing."

"Turn it off."

"You turn it off. I can't move."

I lifted the needle and brought it back to its cradle then looked at Rayne when I brought it back to the edge of the vinyl and dropped it. "Dooooooooooooooooooooooooooooooon't."

Rayne jumped up overturning the Cheerios and ripping the sheet from under books holding it down on the chairs. I heard her small feet slapping hardwood floor in the hallway then the tile of the bathroom. I took the record off of the turntable. The toilet flushed. I put the Cheerios back in the bowl. Rayne's feet came back. I replaced the books and pulled the sheet tight.

"You're a brat, Ariel."

"Oh come on, that was funny. You got to admit that's a funny song. That's the stupidest song I ever heard in my whole life."

"Yeah, it's the stupidest song in the whole country."

"The whole world."

"The whole world and the moon."

I threw my arms wide. "The whole universe."

"It's the stupidest song in the everest of ever."

"It's the stupidest song ever written."

"In infinity."

"In infinity infinities."

"That's the stupidest song anyone ever sang ever ever."

I smiled. "Let's listen to it again."

"Okay."

*   *   *

"Isn't there some law against this?" Anne was on her knees. "Child labor laws. Don't they say we don't have to do this bullshit? I'm pretty sure this is against the law."

"Anne, just do it." Sammi pulled weeds from the cracks between the concrete tiles surrounding the pool. "It's not going to take that long."

"Is there really a law?" I was never sure what was real anymore.

"Shut up, Ariel." Sammi ripped dirt up with the larger clumps of weeds.

Isabelle fussed. "Samantha, leave the dirt in the ground. I'm not coming over there again. You know how to do this right."

"Mom, I'm not getting dirt anywhere."

"Don't talk back to me when I ask you to do something, Samantha. Anne, where are you going?"

"I'm done." Anne had dropped her spade and was halfway to her lounge chair. She loosened her shirt knot then stripped to her bikini top.

Isabelle wiped her face with the back of her hand and rouged her cheekbone with orange earth. Her T-shirt was dark wet under the arms and between her breasts. She flipped her thick auburn braid onto her back and leaned back. Sammi caught my eye and didn't smile. I yanked another dandelion from the dirt and threw it into the bucket. Herbert mowed near the pavilion and Mommy pulled weeds in the shrubs toward the front of the house.

Sammi pulled the back of her terrycloth shorts down stooping to grab another large clump. "Pass the bucket, Ariel."

Still on my hands and knees, I pushed the grey plastic toward her. "Do you want to go swimming after this?"

She didn't look up. "I'd rather walk to town. I'm dying for a lollipop."

"A lollipop?"

"A lollipop. Remember? Lollipop?"

Then I remembered our new code for cigarettes. "Oh yeah. A lollipop. Really? But don't you want to go for a swim? It's so hot out."

"Let's swim in the river, okay?"

"Okay." Even my legs were slick with sweat. My hair felt like shag carpeting on my back and neck and specks of dirt were stuck all over my arms. Yellow jackets flew around the clover in the grass. Water bugs spun in circles on top of the glassy pool. Everything seemed to enjoy the day more than we were. Rayne pretended to trim the bushes with one half of a pair of clippers while Merlin boxed off the shrub tops with a full pair above her. Herbert hummed in and out of sight pushing the mower in rows. A fly kept at my nose and eyes until I thought I might cry. Blood ran to the surface of the small cuts in my palms and stung like lemon. "How much more?"

"We started somewhere over there, didn't we?" She pointed to the handrails with a freshly yanked weed.

"I thought we started at the sliding board."

"Go look."

"You're closer."

"Jesus, Ariel." She stood up and walked over to the sliding board. "You're right."

"Thank God."

"This is still going to take hours. Don't be so perfect, okay?" She winked. "Let's just finish so we can go walk."

I swatted at the fly and hit myself in the nose with a dirty ragged fingernail. "This stinks. Do you really think there's a law?"

"Ariel, just let's hurry so we can go."

My knees hurt from my weight and the small grainy rocks on the tiles. The fly was at my ear so I shook my hair and long strands stuck to the sweat on my neck and forehead. "How long have we been out here?"

"Ariel, you're just making it worse." She wouldn't look at me. She pulled giant clumps out all at once and threw them in the bucket.

"The Hobarts are coming tonight."

"Good. Let's sleep out."

"Okay." I shook the dirt from some spiky green leafy weed. My shoulders ached from being hunched over for so long. I was too young to ache and old enough to know it.

We pulled all the green from between the concrete tiles until we were back at the sliding board.

"Let's go." Sammi had no victory in her voice.

Isabelle was still grooming the dirt around the shrubs and Mommy pulled weeds from around the new sprouts in the garden. Montgomery watched from inside the dining room because of his allergy to bees. Herbert filled the mower with gas. Rayne and Merlin chuckled over some private joke and Anne lay in her chair glistening. There were always so many people in our days now.

We didn't wash before leaving. Sammi's knees were as red as mine and she had some blood trickling down her left shin.

I tried a smile. "Which one, Lenny or Squiggy?"

"Come on, Ariel, I don't feel like it."

"Fine, be that way."

Her bangs bounced against her restless forehead. The whoosh and babble of the Patapsco rushing by was soothing in the absence of her voice. She pulled at the back of her shorts, staining the white trim with clay.

I pictured us teenagers walking in our platforms with blue jean bell-bottoms and macramé tops with no bras over our b-cup breasts. I pictured our boyfriends, Donny Osmond and David Cassidy with their arms around us. We talked about teenage things like driving and beer and streaking and we kissed and smoked. I pictured us in town, the guys buying us ice creams for the walk home. I pictured them taking us to a concert that night in a big limousine and...

"Ariel, lets go in here." She motioned to the path leading down to the river bank.

"What about cigarettes?"

"You mean lollipops?"

"Yeah, lollipops."

"We'll get some later. Come on."

I followed her down the dirt trail, my Dr. Scholl's smacking against rocks and tree roots. The water was very clear here so it was easy to see that it was at least three feet deep near the rocks I knew we'd try to get to. I left my shoes by the shore. Samantha kept hers on. The flow was pretty warm near the top but as we waded further in, there were pockets of cold running past our ankles. We muddied the water when we walked, dislodging brown silt full of flecks of fool's gold that caught light and danced brightly away in the current. She let her fingers drag creating personal disturbances in the river. My stomach contracted as the shock of cool ran higher on my body. Samantha used dripping fingers to push the hair from her eyes. Her hand jitterbugged, swatting at a fly passing. The tips of my long hair tapped the water's surface but didn't penetrate. Sammi crawled onto the flattest rock and pulled her knees up into her body. Rivulets trickled through the maze of downy hair on her legs. I scrambled up and sat next to her, the heat from the sun-baked rock coming up through my denim shorts.

"What do you think will happen to our dads?" Her eyes were sincere so I knew she wasn't kidding.

"In what way?"

"I don't know. I mean, do you think they'll be okay?"

"You mean without us?" I hadn't thought about it until then and suddenly I was worried. I pictured my dad leaving the Laurel house, his belongings gone, his wife and children in a farmhouse forty minutes away by car. I saw him living with Sammi's dad, Bentley, in their old townhome (though I knew he was mostly at Sandy's now). He had stayed in Bentley's basement, surrounded by cardboard boxes marked "pottery" and "magazines" and slept on a pull-out couch because Mommy had the bed. He said he and Bentley got along better before he moved in and that he had to drive longer to go to work. He said Mommy had taken everything and that he was living like a college boy. He said Isabelle had all of the good kitchen stuff and that he and Bentley had to eat out a lot and he missed cooking. He said that was why he couldn't stay on a diet and lose "that last ten." What was his life like without us? Did he still eat a dish of Breyer's chocolate chip and watch *Sonny and Cher* in bed? Who sampled his food creations for him? Did Sandy go out to movies with him like I used to? Who held his plastic cup of wine in the car when he took fast turns?

A single droplet of sweat ran down Sammi's cheek. "I think my dad misses us. He would never say though. Valerie says he does."

"I think my dad misses us too."

"Does Madeleine date?"

"What do you mean?"

Sammi unlocked her arms and let her legs unfold onto the hot flat rock. "I mean is your mom seeing somebody?"

"Not really. There was this guy but they broke up. It was really short."

"Who was he?"

"A doctor. He was rich and they were going to get married even though they had just met but then we never saw him again and Mommy said he was just in love with being in love so that was it but at least he gave us the PONG game before we left."

"Do you like Merlin?"

"Do you?" I wasn't sure what she was getting at.

"Mostly."

I waited for her to elaborate. She stared off down river. Finally, she picked up a small pebble and threw it into the water. "Sometimes I don't like him and I don't know why. It's nothing he says or does. Just sometimes he annoys me. Is that mean?"

"Maybe. I don't know. I think he's the coolest. He's always so nice to me and even Anne talks to him."

"Yeah."

A little school of minnows sat in the shade beneath our rock for a minute. I watched them dart around exchanging places with one another over and over like musical chairs. Sammi looked down too. "Fishies!"

"Minnows, I think."

"Where's a rock? Do you have one over there?"

"What if you hit one, Sammi?"

She threw a small piece of tree bark down at the water. It stopped on the surface and floated swiftly away. "Shit." Then her fingers found a loose pebble and she threw it down with childish might. The minnows parted too quickly to really watch, then regrouped more slowly when the threat was gone. "Cool."

"Yeah, cool."

*   *   *

We finished supper as quickly as possible and ran out to the pavilion with our sleeping bags. Sammi had a box of Triskets and I carried the radio. We manipulated the sleeping arrangements to get Tommy's bag next to mine then pretended we didn't care who slept where.

Montgomery and Cory wore only cut-offs but most of us had T-shirts over swimsuits because the air was beginning to cool now that the sun had gone down. We left everything set up for our slumber party then ran to the pool dragging formerly-brightly-colored tattered beach towels behind us. I kicked at the water with the tip of my foot to test the temperature but was pushed in before I could decide whether it was too cold or not. Slim little bodies came into the water all around me. Squeals and screams were the major form of communication.

Too much water was flying around hitting me randomly so I dunked down into the semi-serenity of the dark underwater. All of the noise was muffled here, cushioned, once removed. And the water was predictable and all-encompassing.

Sammi's hands wrapped around my sides and pulled me up. "We're playing Marco Polo. Come on. Montgomery's it."

"Marco."

"Polo."

"Marco." Montgomery's little blonde head was highly visible even in this dim light and most of us swam faster than him.

"Polo."

He reached at phantom voices, his arm splashing limply into the water with no one beneath it. "Marco."

"Polo." Sammi and I camped out in the deep end knowing he wouldn't come for us until he had run out of choices in the shallow end.

"Marco." He opened his eyes for a millisecond and Rayne screamed when he lunged for her.

"Cheater!" I hated all this tricky crap he pulled.

"I didn't."

"Yes, you did."

"Whatever, you guys." Tommy hung from the diving board near me. "Just keep going, Montgomery."

"He did cheat." I looked to Tommy to agree.

"Who gives a shit? He didn't catch her. Let's just play."

"Marco."

"Polo."

"Marco." Montgomery was coming straight for the deep end now, having seen what a gold mine it was.

We scattered, screaming, and swam to edges to sneak by him untouched. "Polo."

"Marco."

"Polo." We were all in the shallow end, giggling and splashing at him.

"You guys, let's not play this anymore. It's no fun."

"You jerk." He always did this. He always quit when he couldn't win.

"Come on, Ariel. It's no fun. The pool's too big. I'm never going to catch anyone. Let's play war instead, boys against girls."

"Up your nose with a rubber hose." I latched my hands to the aluminum ladder and kicked my feet like I was riding a bicycle. The dark was beginning to take over and the water looked like tar swirling around my bobbing knee-caps. Tommy swam down to the deep end again and started with the pull-ups on the diving board. Sammi and I followed him.

"Thirty-six, thirty-seven." His ribs bounced in and out of the water. "Thirty-eight, thirty-nine, forty."

Eddy's blue lips quivered while she dog-paddled toward us. "I want to get out, I'm cold."

"Forty-five. It's all in your mind, you sissy."

"I'm going in. It's too cold." She paddled back to the shallow. Rayne followed.

I got that now-familiar feeling of stomach tension. "It is kind of cold, Sammi."

"Come here, Ariel." She swam to the shallow.

Rayne and Eddy wrapped towels around their tiny, dripping bodies and made "brrr" noises while scooting back to the pavilion. Rayne's towel dragged through the grass and clover and dirt, collecting bits as it went.

"Ariel, I think you should kiss Tommy." Her breath tickled the dew on my ear.

I said nothing and felt my middle tighten.

"Come on, you know you want to."

"I can't."

"Come on."

"What if he doesn't like me?"

"He's liked you since you were five. Why would he stop now?"

"But not that way." I thought I might cry.

"I'll ask him."

My raised voice surprised me when I heard my "No" echoing off the back of the house. Tommy stopped his pull-ups for a second then continued. I smiled an ugly, crooked smile at him.

"I know how to ask him. He won't know you wanted to know."

"Yes, he will."

"Fine, forget it."

"Wait. Sammi, he's going to figure it out."

"Never mind." She swam to the side and pulled herself out. "It's freezing. Let's go in."

I looked to Tommy and followed Sammi. Cory and Montgomery were playing with the dirty pool-filter basket and Tommy's counting floated past them over the sheet of black coolness.

*   *   *

I felt my nose freckling in the morning sun. Giant black flies circled my still-damp hair and hummed in my ears. They landed on my arms, my sleeping bag, and my roasting cheek. I swatted at the ones that assaulted my eyelashes and lips only to have them land again on other lashes, my forehead, my chin. I ducked into my bag and found it hot and damp like a Texas day. Defeated, I sat up. Black flies climbed through Rayne's yellow-white hair, over Sammi's deep set eyes, through Tommy's peach fuzz, into Montgomery's delicate ears, between Cory's stubby fingers, and around Eddy's cursed leg hair. Noses twitched and fingers lifted but no one else awoke.

The hum grew in my mind. I couldn't believe they didn't hear it, couldn't believe they slept with those filthy, tickley monsters all over them. I pictured them completely covered with flies, all black and humming. No one moved but nothing stayed still. I pictured them as under a live blanket. I saw the blanket settle then lift in nervous response to a twitch, then settle again. Then it lifted again then settled again only now it was flat, everyone had disappeared.

"Sammi, wake up."

She swatted at my poking finger and rolled over.

"Sammi... Sammi." Her body moved loosely when I shook it.

Rayne's head lifted to face me. "What's wrong?"

"Nothing, I was trying to wake up Sammi."

"Why?" Her pale blue eyes opened and closed slowly, so slowly.

"Montgomery. He's allergic to bees. I don't think he should be out here with all of these bugs."

She reached her hand over to his undershirt and tugged. "You have to go in, Montgomery. There's bugs here."

"Bees?" He jumped upright.

The whole platform came to life with a murmur of "bees" but no actual bee materialized to rescue me from an explanation about flies and blankets moving and people disappearing. "Wow, that was a close one. It's gone now. It flew out that door."

Six heads turned to face the open door. Six heads turned back to look at me. Then we rolled our bags amidst the buzzing of big black flies and went back to the house.

We filled bowls with Cheerios and Life and poured different levels of milk. Anne passed us in her bikini carrying a *Vogue* and a bottle of baby oil. We changed and ignored the half-hour-after-eating rule and jumped in the pool. I caught Eddy in Marco Polo then she caught Rayne and then Rayne got tired so we switched to Sharks and Minnows. Anne's stereo played Hall & Oates. Sammi and I cut small hearts out of construction paper and lay them on our skin to make tan tattoos. I felt myself changing colors.

Sammi rolled over to face me. "Ariel, it's now. You have to kiss him today."

"I can't. I can't just go over there and kiss him." Tommy was laying on the diving board with one hand falling lazily into the water.

"Don't worry. I have a plan. For real." She smiled and I believed her. "Come on."

I followed her to the diving board and watched her lean over Tommy and whisper something to him. He sat up and we all three walked along the fence line past the pavilion, down the hill, almost to the State Park.

Sammi wrapped her towel around her like a sarong and I did the same. "Okay, Ariel, truth or dare?"

What was the plan? "Truth?"

"Truth. Okay, have you ever kissed a boy?"

"Kiss like kiss or like a brother?"

"A real kiss. A guy-girl kiss."

"No, have you?"

"You can't do that. You have to ask 'truth or dare.'"

Tommy jumped up onto the fence and hooked his feet beneath one of the rails.

I still didn't get the plan. "Okay, truth or dare?"

"For me? Why don't you ask Tommy?"

"Tommy, truth or dare?"

"What?"

"Truth or dare?"

"Dare."

I was baffled. I had never dared anyone to do anything. I remembered hearing it at recess, "I dare you... I double dare you," but I had no idea what to say. I pictured him hopping around on one leg or licking a rock or something but these all seemed stupid. Besides, I liked him. I didn't want him to have to lick a rock.

"What's your dare, Ariel?" Sammi rewrapped her towel and itched one ankle with the other.

What to say? I could tell him to yell something or run somewhere.

"Come on, Ariel." She was trying to say something with her hands. Something about Tommy. Something about Tommy and me? Tommy moving? Tommy pointing? Tommy and the woods? Me, Tommy and walking?

I was lost. "I dare you to tell the truth."

"What? You can't do that? Can she do that, Sammi?"

"I don't think so. I never thought about it. Jeeze, Ariel. Couldn't you just dare him to do something?"

"That's my dare."

"That's cheating. Tommy, you don't have to do that. Come on, Ariel, make up a dare."

"Fine. I dare you to run around the whole field."

Tommy jumped down and ran up the hill along the fence.

"Are you crazy?" Sammi was red with anger.

"What? I couldn't think of anything."

"You should have dared him to kiss you. I was signaling you. You should dare him to kiss you in the woods."

"I can't do that. He'll know I like him."

"Then I'll do it. Next time you get a turn, make sure you pick me."

"But what if he says no?"

"He can't. It's a dare."

"I don't want to be a dare. Dares are for bad things."

"They're not just for bad things."

"Yes they are."

"No they're not. Shhh, here he comes."

Tommy was running really fast. He was showing off. Boys could be so silly. He slowed down then flopped over with his hands on his knees. The stripes on his shirt expanded and contracted with his ribs. Sammi retied her towel and winked at me. I was still learning winking. Tommy stood and wiped his face with the bottom of his shirt. Sweat beads clung to his upper lip and formed damp clumps of hair around his face. His breathing slowed and he smiled at me. I turned to Sammi, certain he could see the blood pumping in my temples. Bam, bam, bam... dear God, can they hear it?

"It's your turn, Tommy. You get to pick now." Sammi retied her towel again. Hers hung nice and low on her hips and the slit exposed one thigh. She looked like a fashion picture. Mine was all bulky at the waist and hung down like heavy curtains, all gathered and sagging.

Tommy jumped back up on the fence. "Ariel, truth or dare?"

Sammi flashed me a conspiratorial "oh shit" look.

"Truth."

"Would you ever French kiss a guy?"

"What?"

Sammi smiled. "With your tongues."

"What? No. Really? That's gross."

Tommy nodded. "I think so too."

"You guys are sissies. Your turn, Ariel." Sammi winked.

I looked to Sammi, my heart slamming against my ribs. "Truth or dare?"

"Dare."

Damn her. "I dare you to..." What? Who cares? Why couldn't she just pick truth so it would be her turn to dare Tommy? "Hop on one foot and sing 'Day by Day.'" Stupid, so stupid.

"Day by day. Day by day." Her arms flapped as she hopped and her breathing got more labored. "To see thee   more clear ly, love thee more   dear ly." Her towel fell to the ground and she hopped away from it. "Day   by   day."

"Yeah. Woowoo! Bravo. More. More!" I picked up her towel and brought it to her.

"My turn. Tommy, truth or dare?"

Put me out of my misery. Say it so we can finish. I pictured Sammi daring him to kiss me. I pictured him smiling at me and taking my hand, walking down to the path in the woods. I pictured him taking me into his arms, kissing so softly like in the movies where everything is beautiful and everything notices us and agrees with us. I pictured him pulling back, looking into my eyes and whispering that he loves me. I know then that we will always be together and that we will have babies and love them too. I pictured him holding my hand and us coming out of the woods "going together."

"Truth."

"Truth?"

Truth? Not truth. Fix it, Sammi, God, someone, anyone.

"No, dare. Can I take it back?" His eyes squinted against the sun.

"Sure. Okay. I dare you to kiss Ariel."

"Kiss her?"

"On the mouth."

"What if she doesn't want to?"

"Too bad. That's my dare. Once I've dared, you have to do it no matter what it is."

"Is it okay, Ariel?"

Is it okay? No, it's stupendous. It's five years of day dreams coming true. It's Tommy plus Ariel forever. "Yeah, it's okay."

Neither of us moved. Sammi leaned against the fence to watch. Tommy started silently toward the woods. It was going to be just like my fantasy. I had to walk quickly to keep up with him so my towel loosened and fell to the ground. I pulled it around my slim hips and tied it into a perfect knot with the slit down my right leg.

Tommy stood under a tree far enough down the path to be invisible to Sammi. There was a root pushing out of the ground at his feet and we stood on opposite sides of it. He was looking down, leaving me to wonder where to point my eyes. I shifted my weight so that my right knee came through the slit in the towel. I looked at my knee then at the top of his head. I was just about to refocus on a tree when he looked up and stared right into me. We leaned forward from the hips and I closed my eyes. I felt a slight brush against my lips and opened my eyes to find Tommy running up the path and back to the fence. My first kiss. I felt warm and tense and red and frozen and sweaty and dizzy and breathless. I ran up the path after him.

Chapter Five

I always got to pick the menu for the whole day of my birthday. That was one thing moving to the farm hadn't changed, so I had my favorite annual "sugar cereal," Lucky Charms, for breakfast. Pink hearts, yellow moons, blue diamonds, and green clover. Mommy hated it.

I'd had a few pool parties since my birthday is in July, but this was my first one in my very own pool. Mommy and Isabelle floated balloons on top of the water and bought paper plates with horses on them and matching napkins. Herbert grilled the barbecue spare ribs. Sammi filled a colander with fresh strawberries still dripping with water. Merlin was in charge of the salad and Montgomery brought out iced tea. The men had dragged the picnic table from the pavilion to pool side just for this occasion. It was supposed to be a surprise but the cake, I knew, would be chocolate with chocolate icing - my favorite. Smoke drifted from the grill across the roof of the house carrying the news of my barbecue to houses miles away.

All my life, I had wanted to be twelve. Two, twelve, and twenty-one were my three favorite numbers. Now I only had one left to do.

Twelve. Just the sound of it thrilled me. Who would have thought I'd ever be twelve? Soon, I would drive and date and go to high school and work at McDonald's and wear bras and high heels and makeup.

I pictured myself in a fancy outfit I'd seen in Anne's *Vogue*. A silver halter sat provocatively on my size B breasts. A thin, silver belt ran through the loops of the black satin slacks that hugged my rounded hips like Saran wrap. I stood atop silver platforms with small black butterflies clasping the ankle straps. My hair was curly and wild with a bugle-beaded black beret. My face was painted in reds and blues, all glossy and sparkly. I was Farah Fawcett. I was Patti Hanson. I was Anne. My date was Donny Osmond in a suit with purple socks, our favorite color, and we went to a party then walked holding hands.

"Happy Birthday to you..." Everyone gathered around me. I looked at all of these familiar smiling faces that didn't look like mine and wondered if this was supposed to be my family now. All these neighbors and friends, what was this?

I wished silently for me and Tommy to start going together and I blew out the candles. Everyone cheered. I leaned over and whispered to Sammi, "What's twelve like?" Her birthday was just months before mine so she checked out each year for me.

"Twelve's pretty good." She started to lean away then pulled me to her. "I'm holding out for sixteen." She winked and I smiled. We both knew that was when life really began.

*   *   *

I was still shoving clothes into a plastic JCPenney bag when Dad's Volkswagen pulled up to the porch. I heard the rumble of the tiny engine and the spit of the rocks then silence and a light door slam. Sammi, Anne and Rayne were already gone. Bentley and Valerie had picked them up early to go to a matinee of *Silent*

Movie. Isabelle was setting the table for four when I ran through the dining room. It was such a big table for just four. She had the cloth napkins out and was making them into boat shapes.

Merlin stood at the stove. "Madeleine, do I stir it continuously or stir it then let it sit?"

Dad looked over Mommy's shoulder to Merlin. "What are you cooking, Merlin?"

"Oh, I'm not. Mad's cooking up some gumbo."

"Seafood gumbo?"

Merlin guffawed. "We could barely afford the chicken."

Mommy looked over her shoulder through her curls, "Just stir it when it bubbles then turn it down."

"Merlin, is that the roux? You have to stir that continuously." Dad had that same superiority in his voice that I didn't like in mine. It wasn't enough for us to be right, Mommy had to be wrong.

"Merlin, it's okay to just stir it when it bubbles. I'll be done in one second."

Dad chuckled. "One second is all it takes to go from golden to burned."

Mommy ignored him. "I just want to walk the kids to the car, say goodbye to the birthday girl."

"You can do that here, can't you?" He looked out to the car then back to Mommy. "I'll walk them to the car."

"You left her sitting in the car?"

The looks between them were getting more layered, harder for my juvenile mind to read.

"We're in a hurry."

"Do you have the check?"

"I'll give it to Ariel." He was already halfway out the door. "Don't burn that roux, Merlin."

"Sure won't, Frank. Bye guys, have fun."

"Bye. Bye Mommy."

She leaned down to hug us. "Bye bye, my babies. Have a great time at the Tall Ships. I'll see you on Sunday."

Sandy looked beautiful with her *I Dream of Jeanie* hair-do and her floral-print dress and white heels. Dad loaded up his pipe and off we went to Laurel for the rest of my birthday. I had heard about this whole post divorce two-holiday thing but this was my first time experiencing it. Dad started his pipe lighting ritual, holding the match momentarily on three different spots and pulling in puffs of smoke. The car filled with the sweet smell of burning tobacco until he pushed the small triangular window open.

"So, what did you think of your bike?" He stole a look at me over his shoulder.

"Oh, Dad, it is so great. Did you see it? It's brown and there are a couple of orange and yellow stripes on it. Three speeds. It's so great."

"I helped pick it out. It's from all of us, you know." Sandy tossed her ponytail to the other side of her head. "We thought you'd like the three-speed. Your old one didn't have any speeds. Did you ride it yet?"

Montgomery pushed the door lock down, pulled it back up, pushed it down. "She's scared to."

"No, I'm not."

"Uh huh."

"Nah ah. I just didn't learn the gears yet. I want to read the book first."

"What book?" Sandy's brow crinkled.

"The one that came with it."

"It tells you how to ride it?" She was still crinkled.

"Ariel, just get on it. It's just like your old one only easier to ride."

Dad had spoken. The subject was closed. I would learn to do loop-de-loops by the next time he came.

We ate at The Magic Pan. I had to do the whole cloth-napkin-in-the-lap thing and remember forks. I wiped spinach soufflé from my chin and couldn't decide whether or not to put the soiled napkin back on my clean lap. Montgomery avoided all of it by dropping his napkin on the floor early on and using his sleeve instead. They would never let me do that.

Last year, Dad took me out, just the two of us. We went to the Golden Plow. I wore the pink and white floor-length gingham dress that Mommy sewed. He took me into the bar where a band played on a small stage with red and yellow lights behind them. Peanut shells covered the floor and stuck in the straps of my white sandals. A candle lit Dad's chin while the red and yellow lights changed his complexion over and over. The band played my favorite song, "Wildfire." A hostess led us to our table and gave us menus. Dad's was printed on a two-tone camel-and-coffee ceramic jug. Mine was on a wooden chopping board. He ordered for both of us and drank wine and smoked his pipe. We talked about music and pottery and school and movies and UFO's. I felt like a grown-up on a date. The waiters sang "Happy Birthday" to me and brought me a small cake with a candle on top. It was the perfect birthday.

Sandy asked if I'd like to go to the ladies room with her. I slid out from the table and followed her into the tiled room. We entered separate stalls and talked through the wall. "Your dad and I have another present for you at home. How'd you like your bike?"

"It's great."

"We thought you'd like it. Do you like the color?"

"Yeah, it's okay."

"It won't need washing as much. It's a good color."

I exited the stall and waited by the hand dryer. Sandy came out carrying her white purse. She looked at herself walking toward the mirror and washed her hands with lots of pink liquid soap. "Did you wash your hands?"

"Yes." My hair fell from behind my ears when I looked down.

"Oh, I didn't hear the water."

I moved aside to let her run her hands under the dryer. She pushed the button with a painted nail and made washing motions in the heat. "A color like that won't show dirt as much so you won't have to wash it that much."

"Wash it?" I couldn't remember ever washing my pink bike. Are you supposed to wash bikes? Did Mommy wash it for me and just not tell me?

Sandy put on some rosy frost lipstick and dabbed with a Kleenex then pinched the gold clasp of her purse closed.

My dessert was already on the table when we returned, ice cream wrapped in a crepe with whipped cream, chocolate syrup and shavings on top. No one sang and there wasn't any candle but Dad and everyone wished me a happy birthday.

Sandy turned to Dad. "She loves her new bike. You were right to pick the brown."

"Ariel." Dad smiled and packed his pipe. "We have another gift for you at home."

"Your dad and I picked it out together." She beamed at him.

"Goody." I finished my crepe and placed my napkin on top of my plate. No one else had put theirs on the table yet. Montgomery's was still on the floor. I considered placing it back in my lap but it probably had syrup on it now. Thankfully, Dad pushed his chair back at that moment. Puffs of smoke swirled off his head as he led us out of the restaurant.

Dad and Sandy had pretty much moved in together now. Climbing the stairs of the apartment building, my JCPenney bag banged against my shin. Montgomery carried a pillowcase full of his clothes over his shoulder like Santa. Sandy wiped her feet on the gold carpet swatch in front of the door and slipped the key into the lock. Our sleeping bags were coiled next to the couch. After dropping our bags next to them, I ran to the kitchen looking for some sort of present.

"Ariel, do you want to watch some TV before you guys turn in?" Sandy was pulling the straps from behind her heels to rid herself of her extra three inches.

"I want to see my present."

"You dirt ball." That was Sandy's favorite nickname for us.

Dad threw his coat over a chair and pulled at his tie. "She wants to see her present. Bring it out." We exchanged smiles and he lifted his eyebrows, made his fun face.

Sandy disappeared into the bedroom and shufflings gave away some sort of metal noise. Maybe a zipper tab clicking. "We picked it out together." She peeked her head around the corner. "Close your eyes." More metal noises and some sort of slick sound.

"What is it?" Montgomery burped. "Oh, I know."

"Can I open now?"

"Sandy, did you get film today?"

"Can I open my eyes?"

"I thought you were going to get it. Didn't you say you were going to People's Drugstore today?"

"Can I open now?" I wanted to peek but I didn't.

Dad got impatient with Sandy. "I said for you to get it."

"We'll get it tomorrow. I have to go to People's for pantyhose anyway."

"I'm opening my eyes now."

Dad patted my knee. "Open your eyes, Ariel."

It was a navy blue vinyl overnight bag, wheels on the bottom and zippers on the side pockets. It was like a sack on wheels, opening at the top, with handles to drag it by.

"Now you won't have to carry that plastic bag." Sandy uncrossed her legs and leaned forward to show me the pockets.

"See, it rolls, Ariel." Dad pushed it back and forth.

It rolled and zipped and had pockets and handles. It was weatherproof and had a warranty. The wheels rotated and it even came with a spare tire. A suitcase. A bag. Something to carry my stuff back and forth. A tote. Back and forth. Back and forth.

So twelve is a brown bike that won't show dirt and an overnight to bring my stuff from the farm to the apartment, from the apartment to the farm.

*   *   *

Montgomery double-knotted his shoelaces and pulled his blue and yellow striped tube socks to his knees before climbing onto his bike. I rode around the pavilion practicing shifting my three gears, still not sure why I was supposed to want them. Dad said it would help me to climb hills. Everything would be closed in town but I'd get those loop-de-loops if it killed me.

I pictured myself going over jumps, flying like Evel Knievel over a giant chasm, landing and spinning to a sharp stop with dirt flying from under the back tire. I pictured myself popping wheelies, drawing figure eights and weaving through cones. Swerve right, swerve left, swerve right, swerve left.

"Okay, Ariel, I'm ready." Montgomery climbed onto his bike and rode up to meet me. We had to push down hard on the pedals on the dirt path from the pavilion to the gravel drive. I dismounted and walked my thin wheeled bicycle down the slope. Montgomery bumped up and down over the gullies and ridges on his boy bike with wide wheels and bright green paint. He rambled down and spun to the right when he hit the pavement of Patapsco Road.

"Wait for me." I jogged down holding my handlebars.

"Hurry up."

I came around the hedge row and found him sitting there with one leg as a kick stand. "You made me stop. Now I have to pedal more to get up the hill."

"I can't ride on the gravel. I'll pop a tire or something."

"Sissy."

"It's brand new, Montgomery. You want me to wreck it already? You never take care of your stuff."

"So?"

"Sew buttons on a shirt. Come on."

The slope started almost immediately. We had to press and press to get any sort of speed going. I tried different gears and, sure enough, found one that made it easier to climb, not faster, but definitely easier. We passed the neighbor kids; Jay, Kay, Elle, and Em, standing at their fence line. We passed the Conners' driveway and Happy's house at the top of the hill. Montgomery got to the apex before me and started down.

"Wait up." I came over the crest and saw him pedaling his feet even as his bike sped up on its own. We flew quickly past bushy fence lines and tall, tall trees. Still, he pedaled.

"Slow down, Montgomery, this road is for cars."

He rounded the bend where the road leveled out. I lost sight of him for a moment and saw the car screeching to stop. I remember no movement, no sound, no sights.

Just blackness, just black silence.

When I regained myself, Happy and Crane and Happy's older brother were trying to pick up my bloodied brother and put him in the car. His white "Spirit of '76" T-shirt was ripped at the collar down through the shoulder. It was soaked in red, burbling blood. His fair hair was matted to the left side of his face with more of the sticky liquid. His arms hung limp while Happy's brother pulled him to his chest and carried him to the car. Crane and Happy were pasty-faced and wouldn't look at me. Happy's brother yelled for them to get into the car. They slammed all of the doors and drove off.

My head was filled with gauze. I picked up Montgomery's bike and propped it on a nearby tree. I thought about someone stealing it but couldn't figure a way around it. I started up the steep hill but I couldn't pull enough air into my lungs and my calves burned like someone had poured boiling soup inside of them. The top of the hill seemed to get further away with each pressing of the pedals. I crept past the tall, tall trees and the bushy fence lines. I pushed up to the border of Happy's yard at the top of the hill. I didn't allow myself the usual moment of glory before beginning the downward ride to the farm.

I raced past the Conners' and the four-faced fence line and hit the gravel at the base of our driveway. BAM. The seat jumped down then slammed into the soft cushion between my legs. Pain shot up my spine and through to the front of my forehead. It felt like my nose was bleeding, like my breath was shocked out of me, like my legs were numb with heaviness. I pressed as hard as I could. Right, left, right, left. Every bump rammed the seat up at me again. Right, left, right, left.

Happy's brother's car was in the drive and Mommy was in the passenger seat with Montgomery on her lap. Her face was red and white at the same time. Montgomery's blood dripped from his neck wound down his left arm and onto Mommy's white shorts and bare thigh.

Mommy's voice was trembling. "We're going to the hospital. No one's home so go next door and stay with Bobbie until someone comes home, okay, my angel?"

I nodded. She pulled the door shut and they drove off. I dropped the bike and rubbed my bruised crotch. Tears dropped involuntarily from my eyes making fat water marks on my already stained T-shirt. I heard the sounds of an animal caught in a trap, deep wounded screams, and realized it was my own throat making them.

Bobbie lived in the next farmhouse in the back of her stable. Her farm was smaller than Virginia's next door and she didn't have as many horses or as big a ring for riding. Virginia even had an additional indoor ring.

I approached the entrance to her barn slowly, checking for her Great Dane. He barked when I neared the first stall then I heard the snap of the metal chain holding him tightly to the back fence. "Bobbie?"

A horse whinnied in answer.

"Bobbie?" My voice sounded small, panicky. The dog continued barking. I lifted my hand to the door I'd never entered before, the door to her private world, and knocked.

"Bobbie?"

I rapped with my fist and later with my foot before sitting in front of the door with my knees under my chin. The dog continued. I sang.

"Jesus loves the little children, all the little children of the world. Red and yellow, black and white, they are precious in his sight. Jesus loves the little children of the world. Oh, Susannah, oh don't you cry for me. For I'm going to Louisiana with a banjo on my knee. He's got the whole world in his hands. He's got the whole wide world in his hands. He's got the whole world in his hands, he's got the whole world in his hands. Somewhere over the rainbow, way up high. There's a place la la la la la la la la la. We wish you a merry Christmas, we wish you a merry Christmas, we wish you a merry Christmas and a happy New Year. The itsy bitsy spider went up the water spout. Down came the rain and washed the spider out. Out came the sun and dried up all the rain and the itsy bitsy spider went up the spout again. She ran calling Wildfire, she ran calling Wildfire, she ran calling Wildfire. And they call it puppy love. La la la la la la la. Come on now, there's a song that we're singing. Come on get happy. A whole lot of love is what we'll be bringing, we'll make you happy. I'd like to teach the world to sing in perfect harmony. Grow apple trees and honey bees and snow white turtle doves. Bobbie!"

Bobbie came around the corner carrying a saddle. The sun made a scratchy halo of her blonde hair and her face was all in shadow.

"Ariel, what are you doing here? Where's Sammi?"

"Can I come in your house? My mommy said for me to come here."

She balanced the saddle over a stall door and put her hand on my shoulder. "Is everything okay?" I don't think she'd ever touched me before.

"Montgomery got hit by a car."

"Dear God. Is he okay?"

"They went to the hospital. No one's home. I have to stay here. Is that okay?"

"Well sure, hon." I followed her upstairs. "Here doll, sit down here. You can watch some TV while I finish with my chores. I just have to do a few things around the yard. Will you be okay if I leave you here? I don't want to leave you if, you know, you need anything. I mean, I guess I could stay. Here, here's a *TV Guide*. You can watch anything you want. Oh hon, you must be so upset. You sure you don't want me to stay?"

"I'm fine."

"Did you eat? I could make you a sandwich or something if you're hungry."

"I'm fine, thank you."

"Okay, maybe later. Maybe when I get back you'll want some. Do you want a soda or something? I have Coke. Do you want a Coke?"

I nodded.

"Oh good. Okay, a Coke. With ice?"

"Ice is good."

"Coke with ice. Oh hon, I feel for you, I do."

She disappeared into her kitchenette. I heard the vacuum seal on the refrigerator break, the crack of an aluminum can, then ice popping and shattering as carbonation hit it.

"Here doll. You sure you don't want a sandwich? I have cheese and crackers. Nothing? Okay. I'm right outside if you need me. I'll turn on the TV. Okay? Call if you need me. I'm right downstairs, okay?"

"Thank you."

Sesame Street was on the television. I looked at the TV Guide but I had no idea what time it was. The dial was hard to turn. Soap opera. Soap opera. Cartoon. Soap opera. Marcus Welby. Sesame Street.

I sat on the orange plaid couch and watched "Marcus Welby." I pictured Montgomery in the hospital. Dr. Welby fixed him. Montgomery smiled and sat in his hospital bed with balloons around him. The music swelled and the credits rolled.

Emergency was next.

Bobbie came back smelling of hay. "Hey hon, how you doing? I see you found something to watch. That's good. Can I get you anything? I feel like a sandwich. You?"

The phone rang.

"Hello? Yes, she's right here. Okay. Yeah, she's fine. That's good. Sure. Sure. Okay. No trouble at all. Okay. Bye." She replaced the phone in the cradle more gently than I'd ever seen her do anything. "Someone's at your house so you can go home now."

"Was that my mommy?"

"Yeah. She's still at the hospital but someone's home now so you should be okay."

"She didn't want to talk to me?"

"She'll call you later."

"Is Montgomery okay?"

"He's fine. They'll tell you all about it at your house, okay?"

I put my glass next to her sink and started back to the farm. The air was still thick with humidity though it was nearing suppertime. Isabelle's Datsun was sitting in the drive. My bike was propped against the brick wall of the laundry room, though I didn't remember putting it there. Pillows and Thomasena followed me into the kitchen. "Isabelle?" I walked through the dining room and down past the living room to the front staircase. "Isabelle?" I stood at the bottom of the stairs to Isabelle and Merlin's attic. "Isabelle?" I climbed their stairs and knocked. "Isabelle?" Her door had pictures of fairies and twisty trees and princesses shellacked onto it. I ran my fingers over the ridges at the edges of the cut-outs, tracing a mushroom, a vine, a troll. "Shoot."

The kid's wing was also empty. Montgomery's room was a mess with clothing and stuffed animals all over the floor. I went back down to the dining room and looked out the windows. Someone was near the pool coiling a garden hose. "Isabelle?"

Her back snapped upright and, for a second, I thought it was Mommy when she turned to face the windows. "Ariel? I'm outside." She had the hose looped around her arm and continued to coil it while I approached her. "Did you talk to your mom?"

"No."

"She didn't call you at Bobbie's?"

"Did something happen to Montgomery?"

Isabelle stopped coiling for a moment. "Weren't you with him? You remember what happened, don't you?"

"Yeah. I mean did something else happen?"

"But you do remember he got hit by a car, right?"

"Is he okay?"

"He's fine." Moms have a voice they use, a dulcet hypnotic tone that makes you think everything will always be fine forever.

But I still had to make sure. "He's fine?"

She finished with the hose and walked toward the bushes to hide it. "He's fine. He's just fine. Very lucky."

"Did he stop bleeding? He looked like he was bleeding a lot."

"Ariel, why don't we fix something to eat. Have you eaten? Did Bobbie feed you? Let's make you something."

I followed her back to the kitchen, passing my bike again. "Shouldn't we pick up Montgomery's bike?"

"Pick it up?"

"It's still at the bottom of the hill. I couldn't bring it back."

"We'll let someone get it later."

"But won't someone steal it?"

She opened cabinets. "What do you want to eat?"

"Don't you think we should get it now so nothing happens to it?"

"I think soup would be good. No, it's still too hot. A salad?"

"Can we?"

"Can we what?"

"Get the bike."

"Ariel, forget about the bike. It's probably a wreck anyway."

My face flooded with heat and my eyes turned fire. "It is not!"

I fell twice on the way up the staircases then collapsed on my mattress, my stomach convulsing, my eyes spilling tears.

The woman at the desk peeled the backing off of a sticker and pushed it onto the front of my shirt. "Visitor." Dad and Sandy and I filed into the elevator and floated upward to the second floor. Painted stripes on the floor led us to the children's wing. Montgomery's door was open and through it I could see Mommy sitting on a vinyl chair next to his bed. She had her hand on top of his and was cooing at him. "No, my angel. You have to wait a couple more days." I walked in first with Dad and Sandy as my shadows.

Montgomery turned his face toward me. "Ariel!"

A tube ran from his arm to a sack near the bed. Tubes came out of his nostrils and went to somewhere unseen. A giant bandage covered the side of his neck and part of his tiny shoulder. It was stark white (a white long forgotten at the farm) with browned blood stains. I navigated through the tubes to hug him lightly. He felt so small and delicate in my arms, like a wisp of smoke or a dandelion seed. I sat on the edge of the bed while grown-ups exchanged nervous hello's and Mommy and Dad settled into uncomfortable looking chairs.

"How much do you remember now, Montgomery?"

Mommy smiled and patted the top of his hand. "He's still a bit foggy, Ariel."

"I remember more now, Mommy."

"He says he remembers more but he's heard the story so many times now, we can't really be sure. He remembers June and even a little of July but still no Tall Ships, no birthday, no three-speed bicycle, no trip into town, and definitely no accident."

"Mommy, I think I remember something about the Tall Ships. They were wooden and some were black and they were tall, right?"

Dad laughed a low throaty laugh. "I see what you mean, Madeleine."

I smiled at Montgomery who was straining to see Dad over my shoulder. "That's good, Montgomery. That's exactly right.

106

They were tall, tall, tall. And some were definitely black and wooden. And they had those colonial people for the bicentennial, remember? You don't remember my birthday at all? The barbecue? Swimming?"

"Maybe I remember swimming."

"What do you remember instead? I mean is it just blank or blackness or do you just think it's last June or what?"

"I thought it was June when I first woke up but Mommy explained it to me."

Mommy straightened the blankets around his chest and leaned back into her chair. "It's traumatic arthritis."

I gave her one of those you're-so-stupid looks. "Amnesia. When you lose your memory, it's amnesia."

"What did I say?"

Dad shot her the same look and I immediately hated both of us for it. "You said arthritis, Madeleine."

"Amnesia. Right, like in the soap operas. Well, it means that he knew who he was and how to do math and all of that but he couldn't remember anything connected to the accident."

I tried to picture a black spot in my mind. I tried to think of how it would be to be lost in time, to forget living part of my life. For once, I couldn't make a picture. All that came up was me in a hospital bed with people buzzing around paying attention to me and hanging on every fragment I could recall.

I pressed my hand to his bandage. "Does it hurt?"

"It's not as bad now. Did you see my bear?"

The nurses had propped a six-foot stuffed bear in a corner of the room. It was brown and worn from hugging. Mommy smiled a warm, lip-covering-teeth smile at me. "Those sweetie nurses bring it to the new children. Montgomery's had it for three days now."

"I want to keep it."

"Sugar, everyone wants to keep it, but it's just visiting."

Sandy shifted uncomfortably. She had not spoken since her greetings. Her honeydew-blonde Jeannie ponytail hung down over her left shoulder. She held her white purse with both hands. "Maybe we could get you another bear."

Mommy looked up from stroking Montgomery's hair. Dad turned around to face Sandy's figure in the doorway. Only I spoke.

"He already has a bear at home. He has a million animals at home. Besides, that thing's bigger than his room."

Sandy fiddled with the clasp on her bag. "I'm going to get a soda. Anybody want anything?"

Everyone refused.

*   *   *

Montgomery stayed in the playroom watching TV most of the day. Our daily-tanned bodies made him look sickly in comparison. He couldn't swim or roughhouse or get dirty or sweat or ride a bike or anything. We would wake early, as usual, and play in the barn, run like horses, walk to town, swim and slide, roller skate in the pavilion, hike to the river, explore in the woods, and roll in the fields. Montgomery would watch TV. The adults would go to work, cook, get groceries, swim, sunbathe, go on picnics, talk and laugh. Montgomery would watch TV. We would throw pillows at each other, run in a yard full of bees, draw letters in the sandbox, snuggle the kitties, climb trees, sit on the window ledges, balance on the fence line, and race down the back hillside. Montgomery would watch TV.

Mommy's door was closed but I could hear her soft crying. I knocked before pushing it open.

"What's wrong, Mommy?"

"Nothing, honey. Mommy's just sad today."

"But why?"

She removed the pillow from her lap and wiped her cheek with her fingertips. "I'm okay, my sugar."

"Then why are you sad?"

"It's not your fault." Her head dropped and her top lip tightened holding back more tears.

"Did someone hurt you? Do you want some toilet paper? I can go get you some toilet paper if you want."

Her curls shook. "No, my baby, I just need to be still for a little while. I'll be fine."

I pictured myself rocking her in my lap. I sang her a lullaby like she had sung to me. I pictured myself bigger than her, able to hold her in my old, bentwood rocking chair. I pictured her quieting, looking calm, feeling safe.

"Mommy, do you want me to get Isabelle or something?" I rubbed the top of her hand lying on her lap. I pushed wet hair from her cheek and forced my lips to smile. "Come on, Mommy. It's okay."

Suddenly, her shoulders shook. Tears rolled down the crevice beside her nose, down to the corners of her mouth. She smeared the tears with her hand but they continued to pour. "No one's talking to me. Everyone's avoiding me. I've never felt so alone in my life."

"I'm here."

"Yes honey, I know you are. But everyone else is staying away. Ever since Montgomery was hit, they're all staying away. I feel so stupid. I thought they'd come together for me, be there for me, and now I'm alone."

"Well, maybe they're busy."

Her voice ran up into a new register. "Too busy to talk to me?"

I didn't know how to fix it and felt so small and young and stupid. "I'm sorry, Mommy."

"I know honey. Why don't you go play with the kids? I'll be okay."

"I know what to do, why don't you call Dad? He'll talk to you about Montgomery."

She smiled and wiped some more tears from her chin. "I can't. Don't you worry, okay? I'm fine. You go play."

Maybe all of us felt alone sometimes in this crowded house. "Do you want to play cards? We could play Monopoly or Othello if you want."

Long arms wrapped around and pulled me into the warmth of her breasts. "I love you and I love you."

"I love you too, Mommy."

*   *   *

Strawberries, blueberries, raspberries, strawberries, and more strawberries. I liked the words "tend" and "harvest." We were tending and harvesting our garden. I felt like a pioneer, like there were no grocery stores and we were living off of our land, hard work, and wits. We had made these berries. I snuck a few before handing them to Isabelle. She poured them into a metal colander in the sink and let the water run over them.

"That's enough, Ariel, you can go swimming if you want."

"It's the boys' turn first."

Isabelle smiled Sammi's mischievous smile. "Oh, it's skinny-dipping day, is it?"

"Yep."

I passed a towel-clad Cory, Tommy, and Montgomery on my way up the stairs. Sammi was in our room cutting photos out of a magazine. "Look, isn't this one great?" The sleek, chestnut horse ran with its long, black mane streaming behind it.

"That's cool."

Sammi's hair was the longest I'd ever seen it and she had tucked the front pieces behind her ears. The back pieces curled down around the base of her neck. As if on cue, she scratched at the eczema it created on her hypersensitive skin. She turned pages looking for another perfect and unattainable horse.

"You need a haircut."

Her head popped up and brown eyes smiled at me. "No shit, Sherlock."

"Want me to cut it?'

"Yeah, right." Out came the scissors to free another horse from its pages.

"I can do it. I cut Montgomery's and I cut mine. I'm good at it, I promise."

"You're crazy." This horse was a Palomino, caramel colored with a vanilla swirl of mane and tail.

"I promise I won't mess it up."

"No way, José."

My argument was interrupted by squealing from outside. Sammi and I looked at each other then at the small windows across the room. Laughter rang through our walls while we scrambled to find the source. The field was empty. The pavilion looked hollow. Rayne ran to our doorway tee-heeing too hard to speak in full sentences. "Come. Boys. Look." She disappeared, tittering with Eddy.

Sammi and I found the two of them standing at a window, pointing and giggling. Through the wire screen, the boys splashed and jumped in the water.

Eddy hit my arm. "Wait. Look, wait." Cory pulled himself out of the pool and ran to the ladder of the sliding board. His body was a dark, rich brown with the exception of the strip of pink where his swimsuit would have been. He sat at the top of the board and pushed off. His body shuddered slowly down the board, his small, white behind sticking to the finish. Our eyes were glued curiously to his pre-pubescent penis bouncing up and down while he descended. We laughed at the absurdity of the sight of him jolting downward as much as we laughed at our own nervousness.

The boys barked orders at one another then Montgomery climbed the stairs. He was pale with sunburn marring his shoulders and nose. The bubbling antennae scar crossed from the back of his neck to the front like a sash. Cory passed him a plastic bucket of pool water to pour down the slide. Montgomery pushed off and flew down at what seemed a million miles per hour then slapped the water with his bare bottom before sinking below the surface. We screamed laughter then covered our mouths afraid of being discovered as peeping Toms. Even over their lower, louder voices and Montgomery's warnings of "covering yourself when you hit," they had heard us and their heads turned in the direction of our windows. We ducked but knew we'd been seen. We crawled to the parking lot side of the room before speaking.

Rayne giggled. "Did you see that? He flew straight over the bump into the water."

Sammi's whisper was overly audible. "Slap!"

"Do not pass go, do not collect two hundred dollars." I laughed at my own joke.

Eddy scratched at a cluster of old mosquito bites. "Do pass go, pass everything. Whoosh!"

We heard another slapping splash through the window and giggled with hands over mouths. But loud laughs bounced around the room, and they weren't coming from us. We stopped and looked at one another before creeping along the floor to the staircase. Herbert, Isabelle, Merlin, and Mommy were standing in the dining room windows, crowding each other out for a glimpse of the boys flying down the board and smacking the surface. Mommy's woo-hoo-hoo was the loudest accompaniment to each slap. We stood behind them watching Tommy swoosh down Indian style and Cory backwards and Montgomery all balled up. Herbert turned and saw us at his elbow and tapped Isabelle who looked down at us before she stopped laughing. "What are you doing here?"

Sammi tucked bits of hair behind her ears. "Nothing."

Mommy wiped laugh tears from her face. "Why don't you go upstairs and get undressed. It's your turn next, isn't it?"

We ran upstairs, pulled clothes off and wrapped towels around our slight bodies.

Following Sammi downstairs, I held my towel tightly to my chest. "Don't you think they'll all watch us too?"

Sammi stopped and looked to the window then returned to me. "We'll just tell them they're not allowed."

"What if the boys look?"

"They're definitely not allowed."

We were very clear on our rules about people staring but I could see the shadows on the dining room screens, hear the snickering of small boys upstairs, and after every slap of my bottom on the flat of the water, I swore I could hear, "Woo-hoo-hoo."

Chapter Six

There wasn't much wrong with the first person who came to look at the spare room, but he stared at us as if we were of another planet. We knew we would never see him again. If the lady with the sailor dress hadn't come on the day the baby snakes started coming through the air ducts, she might have stayed. The lady with the two children didn't understand why we couldn't make room for her kids since we already had so many here. When she suggested Anne give up her large, private room for them, Anne lost her manners. "No way! Who the hell do you think you are, lady?" The lady called Anne a discipline problem and suggested Isabelle beat her with a stick then grabbed her kids and left. We all voted no on the very nice man who smelled bad. None of us could understand the man from Korea.

During the second week of interviews, Mommy said she thought she had found the one. She said she sounded very nice over the phone and that she was "a sweet, old lady." Luisella Panarella arrived before lunch while the house was still fairly cool. We hadn't seen any snakes in days and Anne was sleeping late. The timing couldn't have been better. The woman had a small, grey poodle that sat in her handbag panting. Little jingling bells ran along the hemline of her floor-length emerald green skirt and gold piping trimmed her gauzy, pink duster. She was built like Santa Clause with breasts and her grey hair was piled on her head with pins sticking out of it. "Call me Ella."

Sammi and I ran from the living room into the yard, giggling and whispering. "Call me Ella."

Isabelle and Mommy talked to her for a long time. They jingled through the house, up and down stairs. Sammi and I were swapping silly insults about poodles in purses when the three of them came up our staircase. Ella jingled to the top and surveyed our space. "You have bees."

Mommy looked out of the window to the nest on our sill. "We've screened one of the windows but they get in anyway so we haven't gotten around to the second window yet."

"Would you like for me to ask them to leave?"

Isabelle smiled. "Excuse me?"

"I'll talk to them and ask them to leave. I can speak to animals."

We exchanged looks of disbelief. Clearly, this lady was a kook even by our standards. But it had been a long, hot summer in the attic and it would nice to have two windows again - no matter how small.

Luisella shooed us down to the bottom of the stairs. Mommy and Isabelle stayed there and listened in curiosity while Sammi and I ran outside and watched her from the lawn down below. Her gold-trimmed sleeve occasionally waved out of the window in a sweeping motion but mostly she rested on her elbows talking to the nest. Eventually, she disappeared. Moments later, she reemerged with Mommy and Isabelle on the patio. They escorted her to an antique looking car and waved goodbye. We ran to meet the moms.

"She was weird." Sammi crossed her eyes.

Isabelle pulled the door shut behind her. "She was very nice. I like her best so far."

Mommy stopped briefly at the refrigerator. "She was eccentric, not weird."

"Mommy, she was weird."

"Well, she can afford the rent, so I hope she grows on you."

Sammi and I stared at each other, our jaws slack. I spoke first. "That's it? You're letting some wacko with a poodle who talks to insects move in with us?"

Mommy turned around and gave me her "don't argue" face. "We're not letting her, we're choosing her. We only have two more appointments so I suggest you get used to the idea of her."

"This sucks." I stomped my foot for emphasis then ran up to our bedroom, Pillows at my heels. At the top of the stairs, several bees lay dead. There were bees near each window ledge and on each sill. I peeked outside, careful not to touch any of the still venomous stingers. The nest was empty.

Sammi startled me. "What?"

"They're dead."

She took in the small corpses strewn around our floor. "Holy shit."

"Yeah."

She picked up a shoe from her laundry pile and pushed at one of the tiny creatures. "Wow." She leaned out of the small window to inspect the nest. Whack! Whack! The nest fell to the ground below and did not leave its usual hive of nervous bees behind. "Wow."

"Yeah."

We sat stunned for a moment before yelling. "Mom!"

"Mommy"

"Mom."

Mommy and Isabelle thundered up the stairs. Mommy's voice was nervous. "What, my angel?"

We showed them our new collection. Isabelle tip-toed through the carcasses to check outside of the window. "Are you sure they're dead?'

"Look." Sammi flicked one. "I knocked the nest down, but it was empty."

Mommy woo-hoo-hoo'ed. "Far out."

Isabelle pulled herself back into the room. "I thought she was just going to talk to them. Didn't she say she was going to tell them to leave or great harm would come to them?"

Mommy was still tickled. "Maybe they got so scared they had tiny heart attacks."

Isabelle fixed a twisted bra strap with two hands. "We should have had her talk to those damn snakes while she was here."

"Yeah." I joined in the laughing. "Or Montgomery."

"Ariel!" Mommy's eyes cut through me with sharp disapproval. "Why don't you stay up here and clean your room. This place is too small for you to have so much stuff lying around. And get rid of these bees before your brother steps on one and has to go to the hospital again."

My foot involuntarily stomped again.

"And there goes your allowance. Say, 'Yes, Mama.'"

That was always a finalé to any argument. It was her unbeatable tag line.

"Yes, Mama."

*   *   *

But the "bee charmer," as she was known by then, never did move in. Carol had been the last to interview, and by all accounts, the best. None of us kids had met her yet but the grown-ups kept saying how much we would like her, that she was one of us, that she was a true "Lemon."

Sammi and I were late for supper that night because Virginia had more stalls than usual for us to clean. We made one dollar and fifty cents for each one. Mucking stalls entailed pitching all of the old hay and hosing down the food and water bins then wheeling the straw and piss and manure out to the side of the barn and up a wooden ramp to the top of the giant pile of smelly compost. We lined the clean stall with new straw then went up to the feed loft and threw down bundled hay, then filled their water bins and put grain and hay in each trough. We'd each try to earn four dollars and fifty cents usually, but this particular day, we finished, our hands blistered, with six dollars apiece. We ran home to meet the new roommate about fifteen minutes late.

Everyone was seated around the long table eating salad and spaghetti with meat sauce, a low budget specialty. It took a minute to search the faces for the newest one. Carol had thick dark hair cut like a large, fluffy bowl. Her voice was melodic, her smile was charming, her eyes were sparkling and friendly. She looked about Merlin's age, older than Anne but younger than Mommy. Isabelle said she worked doing some sort of sales and that her cat's name was Tigger. She cut her food into very small pieces.

"You must be Sammi and you're Ariel. You two look just like your mothers."

I felt suddenly pretty.

I served myself salad. Rayne passed me the spaghetti and I passed it to Sammi. Rayne smelled the bread then passed it. She smelled the butter then passed it. Then she leaned toward me. "You stink. You smell like caca."

Isabelle looked to Carol, her voice was jagged. "Rayne, that's not polite. Everyone's eating."

"Well, so am I and she stinks like caca. I can't eat."

Sammi leaned forward in her chair. "Shut up, Rayne."

"You stink too. You both smell like peepee and caca."

Isabelle stood up and removed Rayne from her chair. "Come with me." They walked out into the hallway and murmured.

Montgomery sniffed Sammi. "She's right though. Horses."

I dropped my fork loudly on my plate. "Who asked you, Monty?"

"Mom, she called me Monty. She's not supposed to do that."

"Ariel, don't call your brother names." Mommy smiled at Carol. "So, you've never had kids?"

"No. I've never been married."

I leaned into Sammi. "What's wrong with her?"

Sammi covered her mouth to prevent spitting spaghetti when she chuckled.

Anne had to push past Rayne and Isabelle to join us for supper. She sat in her usual chair. "What stinks?"

Montgomery snickered in his annoying way and we heard Rayne join in from the hall. Smack on cloth. Then crying. Small feet running up the stairs. Isabelle came back in quietly and sat down.

It wasn't until Anne needed the parmesan that she noticed Carol. "What the fuck is she doing here?"

All of our heads snapped to Anne. Isabelle was red. "Theresa Anne Busch, go to your room."

"Go to my room? That was my fucking gym teacher. How could you do this to me?"

Now our heads turned to Carol. "I taught gym in Evergreen Hills. I had no idea. Anne, if it's any consolation, I taught hundreds of students. I don't really remember you."

"Well, I remember you." Anne took her plate with her when she left to eat in her room.

Carol shook powdered cheese on her noodles. "Guess I didn't give her a good grade. I feel a bit awkward."

Mommy put on her therapist voice. "Carol, Anne feels this house is already too full. It has nothing to do with you. Did you give her a bad grade?"

"I really have no idea."

"Well, no matter, we all just need to adjust to one more body in this house. Herbert, when will the new bathroom be completed?"

Herbert had been silently chewing. His jaw stopped momentarily. "Merlin thinks we can have it done by next weekend. I say two weeks at the most." His jaw resumed.

Merlin smiled at Carol. "What can I say? I'm an optimist."

Mommy picked up empty plates and stacked them atop her own. "Won't it be nice to have three bathrooms?"

"Way overdue." Herbert smeared the sauce around his plate with a piece of bread. "I still like the idea of a men's room and a women's."

Beyond Herbert's salt-and-pepper wiry hair, I spotted a yellow jacket buzzing in the open window. I held my breath. Mommy spotted it and dropped a fork, CLANK, onto the plates. Sammi held my hand under the table as the bee approached Montgomery. Isabelle gasped audibly. Merlin lifted from his chair but hesitated realizing that Montgomery still hadn't seen the bee and was remaining calm. Carol looked at our faces then at the bee that we focused on. It floated into the open window again and hovered. I thought of trying to shut the window but it had been stuck since we moved in. Herbert had said he'd "take a hammer to it" when it started to get cold at night. I wished the bee would fly away. I wished the bee charmer would come and kill it. I wished Montgomery was in another room safely watching *Happy Days*.

SLAM! The window flew down smashing the yellow jacket. Montgomery's head popped up.

Herbert checked to make sure the bee was dead. "That was remarkable. There's a phenomena called 'collective energy.' Very few studies have been done."

Mommy smiled and clapped her hands. "It must have been the ghost. Montgomery, the ghost saved you from a bee."

"Really?"

She embraced him from behind. "Yes, my baby. Remember I told you about your guardian angel?"

"Hey, Isabelle." I finished my food and stacked my plate at Mommy's place setting. "Who were the last people to live here?"

She picked up the stack and started for the kitchen. "Merlin, was it the Christophers?"

"I think so, Izzy. Hey Ariel, what's up? Why do you want to know who lived here?"

"That's the name of the ghost, Mr. Christopher."

Mommy squeezed Montgomery's slender shoulders. "Sweetheart, they didn't die here. Did they, Merlin?"

"I heard they did. I also heard they were buried somewhere in the walls here and that on nights with a full moon, you can hear them scratching to get out."

Montgomery looked at Mommy, his face pleading and fearful.

"He's kidding, darlin'. He gets nightmares, Merlin."

"I was kidding. They don't scratch, they pound."

Isabelle yelled from the kitchen. "Merlin!"

"I'm kidding. I'm kidding. They're really buried in the basement, Montgomery."

"He's just joking, my baby. Aren't you, Merlin." It was a statement, not a question.

"It's a joke. Just a joke."

Sammi tapped me on the arm and got up from her chair. I followed her up to our room. Rayne was sitting on her bottom bunk. She was combing the hair of her Baby Tender Love. Sammi latched the door behind us. "So, what did you think?"

"She seems okay."

Sammi pulled her shoes off and shook the straw from them into a petite trash can. "What about the Anne thing?"

"What about it?"

She threw her socks into her laundry pile. "What if she's a meany? What if she becomes our gym teacher?"

"She sells machines or something. She's not going to teach us."

"Gym teachers are the worst. They're the ones who do all the extra classes. You know, like, like, driver's ed. or something."

"Oh my gosh, my gym teacher had to teach sex last year. Oh, this is bad. This is really bad. They never ask us what we think."

"Who?"

I shimmied out of my jeans and stuffed them into the pillowcase I kept at the foot of my bed. "The grown-ups."

"Anne's ticked."

I pulled my top over my head and straw shook from my hair onto my bed spread. "Maybe she is mean. Maybe she gave Anne a bad grade."

"I don't like her."

We wrapped towels around us and headed downstairs for the shower. I flicked my fingers under the stream to test it while we waited for the water to heat up. "I guess she's better than the bee charmer, right?"

"No shit, Sherlock."

"It's hot enough. I'm getting in." The water felt good on my itchy skin. The soap was a welcome relief from the clinging scent of urine.

Sammi came in and held her hands up to cover her face, dunking her hair in the shower stream. I passed her the soap and she lathered up as well. "This isn't Alpha Keri. I'm going to break out."

"Can you do my back?"

I turned around and she ran the bar of soap up and down my spine. "Move your hair."

I pulled strawberry blonde strands over my shoulder. The hair stuck to where my breast would be.

"Now you do me."

Her skin was more olive than mine. Mommy said she would age more gracefully than we would. Eczema covered the backs of her knees and her neck, but her back was smooth and unblemished. I lathered her then used my stubby fingernails to scratch her.

"Oh, that's great. My skin gets so itchy from that straw."

"Me too. I hate that."

"Very uncool."

"Okay, you're done."

She covered her face once again before rinsing the suds from her skin. I pushed the plastic curtain aside and grabbed my towel from the top of the toilet.

"Hand me mine."

A small pool formed around my feet as I hastened to dry off. Sammi dried off next to me. Her body was so much more mature than mine. Her breasts were beginning to grow and now she even had a few hairs under her arms and between her legs. We covered ourselves in lotion, a thin gloss from head to toe. I yanked a brush through my hair and Sammi rubbed her towel over her head. She wrapped the towel around her as a sarong.

"Teach me how to do that."

She ruffled her short hair with her fingertips. "Do what?"

"You always do your towel like it's a dress."

"I do?" She was chuckling at me now.

"Never mind." I felt the familiar burning in my stomach.

"You just pull the end over like this." She unwrapped the towel exposing her thin, naked frame and rewrapped it. I tried to follow her and created the same sagging bunched-up mess as usual.

"No, like this." She released the towel from around my ribs and pulled it tightly around me. Her hands worked the top corner into a twist and tucked it near my heart. "There."

It was perfect.

*   *   *

The barn was breezy that day. Lazy wind blew the old straw around the floor where we sat in a circle. Sammi's eyes were devilish. "Who goes first?"

I looked to Tommy, hoping he would volunteer. Brown hair covered his downturned eyes. Eddy and Rayne stared around at the rest of us waiting for some cue. Cory picked at a scab on his elbow and Montgomery drew circles in the dirt on the floor around him. I knew I would never go first, not at something I knew so little about. "You go, Sammi, you've played before."

Sammi placed her right hand on top of the bottle that sat between us all and spun it. It went round and round and round, a slowing glass propeller, before stopping in front of Rayne. We looked at Sammi expectantly. "Well, that one doesn't count."

She spun the bottle again. We followed it with our eyes, rotating again and again, then stopping at me. I chuckled. "This is stupid."

Sammi picked up the bottle. "We have to make teams or something. No brothers and sisters, no girls with girls."

"I'll take Tommy." I spoke a moment too quickly, exposing my intent, and Tommy's head jerked up in response. "Is that okay, Tommy?"

"Yeah, sure. Whatever."

Sammi smiled at me. "I'll take Cory. Montgomery, you can take turns with Rayne and Eddy. Everyone set?"

We giggled nervously at admitting our attractions. Sammi placed the bottle on its side again and spun it around. It turned for what seemed like hours before landing on Tommy. "Now you two have to kiss."

"Right here?"

"Right here."

He pulled himself onto his knees and rested on his hands leaning toward me. I closed my eyes and our lips met. Lightning ran down my spine and through to my crossed legs.

Sammi clapped. "Now, it's Tommy's turn to spin." He gave the bottle a hard spin and it flew around over and over before stopping on me. Sammi laughed. "You guys have to kiss again." I spun and Sammi finally got to kiss Cory. They looked good together, their dark flesh complementing one another. Did Tommy and I look good together?

Sammi spun and Tommy and I had to kiss again. Tommy spun and Eddy had to kiss Montgomery. It felt odd watching my little brother doing something so grown up. He looked so small. His neck and fingers were still scarred from the accident. He was delicate with Eddy, gentle.

Eddy spun and Sammi and Cory kissed again. This kiss was longer, raising the stakes considerably. Sammi spun and Montgomery had to kiss Rayne. Suddenly, I felt very aware of Rayne's seven years. We only pretended she was old enough to do these things. What if we were hurting her somehow? But she kissed my brother with all of the confidence that we had faked.

Sammi was the first to tire of the game. "The problem is it's the same thing over and over. I think we should change it so that we have to do it different each time."

Montgomery tapped on the bottle with a piece of straw. "Different?"

The idea came to me all at once. "I know. We have to kiss each other a different amount of seconds each time."

Sammi's eyebrows went up. "How?"

"We could try to throw rocks out of that big window over there and however many you throw out, that's how many seconds you have to kiss."

I filled the pockets of my shorts with small rocks from the floor then helped Tommy to fill his. We drew a line on the floor that no one was allowed to step over and threw rocks toward the window, a rather large target and very hard to miss, even for Rayne. It was literally the broad side of our barn. We counted up our seconds as each rock made its way through. Tommy and I had to kiss for twenty-three seconds while the others watched and counted. We pressed our lips together and embraced. We twisted our heads back and forth like they did on television. I breathed through my nose and tried to remain cool while the chanting of numbers got louder.

Montgomery had to kiss Eddy for fourteen seconds and Rayne for eleven. Cory and Sammi kissed for twenty-seven seconds. No one wanted to play again so we jumped down to the bottom of the barn and started hide and seek. It wasn't until we heard Mommy's voice that we realized that Montgomery wasn't cheating when he yelled for us to all come out. Isabelle, Mom, Merlin, Herbert, and Carol stood outside.

"Come here, kids."

They were all smiling. Merlin winked at Sammi.

Mommy cleared her throat. "Kids, we have a special surprise for you. My friend Arnold's wife found a pony in the woods and it was all tangled up in barbed wire. She rescued it and brought it home and they have been nursing it back to health." She stopped to take us in, giving me just enough time to hate when she told detailed stories. "They put up all of these lost and found posters and called everyone they could think of but no one claimed the little guy. So, now it's healthy and it's full grown and they need to get rid of it because they just have it chained up on a stake in their yard like a dog and they don't have anywhere to keep it. So, I suggested that maybe you guys might want it."

Sammi screamed. "A pony?"

"Well, I guess so." Mommy grew confused. "Is that a short horse or a young one cause this one's all grown but it's fairly short."

"Oh my God, a pony."

We all went on separate visual dreams of us riding the pony and feeding it and jumping walls with it. Then we ran up the hill and hugged our parents. "A pony."

Sammi and I spent the next week hacking weeds from the field behind the barn. Much of the overgrowth was taller than we were and we had to stop every few hours to burn ticks off of our skin. The field, we decided in exhaustion, was too big for just one pony. So, to avoid clearing all of it, we built a simple fence down one side with old boards we found around the grounds. We drove posts six inches into the ground and hammered nails to rest the slats upon. Then we hacked at the remainder of the field, clearing away at least a decade of unchecked growth. We found smoothed broken glass and old horseshoes. We found an old, rotting storybook and an unopened six-pack of beer. We found broken tools and rusting bits of door hinges.

Then I found the most amazing thing of all, a secret place. Under all of the brambles and stickers and weeds was a small weeping willow. Beneath it sat three moss-covered rocks. I pushed the crackling growth aside and climbed into this secret space. It was quiet and shady and cool. I rested on a moss-covered stone and ran my hands over nature's shag carpeting. The ground in here was moist and brown with small sprinkles of clover. One day I would look for a four-leafed one.

Sammi's voice cut through my peace. "Ariel?" She couldn't see me.

I backed out slowly and chopped weeds. "What?"

"Nothing. I just didn't know where you were."

I smiled knowing I'd finally found something I didn't have to share, and didn't mind the blisters as much as I had before.

*   *   *

I was in the pavilion playing Barbies with Pillows when the first drops of rain battered the tin roof, sporadic at the start then growing in volume and becoming rhythmic. I threw all of my Barbies into their plastic bucket, feet sticking out like plastic french fries, and stared up at the roofing. It sounded like hundreds of machine guns blathering into the metal above me.

Rayne and Eddy ran in through one of the side doors squealing and shaking water from their hands. They didn't see me watching them wring their clothing. Rayne twisted her long hair until water trickled down her elbow. They silly-giggled and slapped each other's wet clothing. Rayne threw her head over and smacked Eddy with sopping tresses. Eddy shook her chopped locks violently back and forth, spraying Rayne with small stinging droplets. They laughed and embraced, pressing their slick bodies against one another. A tickle broke the embrace and they chased each other around the perimeter of the pavilion. They did not break their stride when I joined in.

Soon, Montgomery and Cory pulled in on bicycles. They dropped the bikes near the door and shook themselves like dogs.

Montgomery stretched himself out onto the concrete floor and rolled, leaving a trail of water stained cement in his wake.

"Shit." Anne's voice cut through our laughing. Her cotton top clung to her breasts and her nipples were visible through the shear fabric. She was like one of those women in Playboy. I wondered how the boys could stand to look at her in front of the rest of us. They grabbed their bikes and rode in furious circles, faster and faster.

She stayed in the tool room and tried lighting a damp cigarette. "Shit." Match after match flew from her fingertips until smoke billowed from her lips. I knew better than to ask for a puff. We all did. She would offer if she was in the mood for corruption that day.

Eddy ran to the house with Rayne to use the bathroom and returned with Tommy and a bag of food.

Tommy was mostly dry. He had been watching television inside. "Bring me that paper, Ariel."

Everything in me came alive. He had picked me to help him build a fire. I pictured us living in pioneer days. I was wearing a long skirt and a bonnet. I pictured Tommy building a huge fire for me to cook over. I would stir some sort of garden stew with giant potatoes and corn still on the cob, all from our garden. I would rock our baby in its wooden cradle, crafted by Tommy, and bake homemade bread from grain we had grown.

"See if Anne will give you her matches."

"Her matches?" Yeah, I could do that. I could just wander over there, full of cool, and say, "Hey Anne, can you spare a match?" Or maybe I should say, "Anne, we could really use a light over here." Or, "Baby, won't you light our fire?" No, that was stupid.

Anne watched placidly as I approached her tentatively. "What?"

"Hi Anne."

"What do you want?"

"Tommy wants to know if we can use one of your matches."

"Only one?"

I tittered uneasily. "You know what I mean."

"What are you little pyromaniacs up to now?" She pushed her hand into the back pocket of her jeans and pulled out the match pack.

"We're lighting a fire." I nodded my head toward the other room.

Her hand extended the matches toward me. "Bring them right back."

"You bet, Anne. I'll bring them right back."

Tommy's fire lit right up, crackling and spitting while we gathered around it. I smiled at Tommy, hoping he could see my pride. Anne joined our semi-circle and pulled out two cigarettes. "This one's for you guys to split. You want it?"

My hair stuck to the side of my face when I turned to her. "Cool, Anne. Thanks."

We passed the smoldering stick around trying to imitate Anne's casual grip, the way she gently tipped her ashes. We ate cereal out of the box and wheat crackers with no toppings. The rain pinged against the tin roof but its pace slowed until the sun finally pushed it away.

"Later guys." Anne dusted off the backs of her legs and returned to the house. The party was over.

Sammi met us on Patapsco Road on her way back from riding horses with Alice. She was always riding with Alice lately.

The vines hanging from the barn were still dripping fresh rain. Summer sun had killed all the grass that had dared to try to grow in the naked patch of dirt next to the road near the barn and the rain turned it to fudge. Rayne stepped into the rich mud without hesitation and sunk up to her mid-calf. Her laughter and screams mixed into music and we followed her in, allowing the soup to squish through our toes, over our ankles and up the sides of our legs. Dirt clung to the down on our legs. The further my feet sank, the cooler the mud became until I hit a cold, firm bottom.

Walking was a fight against suction and gravity. Those of us who had worn shoes had them yanked from our feet and had to dig them out of the mud. Rayne was brown from her knees down. Her white-blond, still-damp hair gleamed in contrast. Trying to bring her shoes to the roadside, she splatted onto her belly. "Stop making me laugh." The tips of her hair darkened. "I'm going to pee. Stop laughing." She pulled herself onto her knees and held her crotch. "Stop. Stop." She was gleeful and squealing and we couldn't slow our laughing even a little. "I'm going to pee!" Then she fell silent. The whole world held its breath. Rayne's head lowered. "I told you guys to stop making me laugh." A small trickle rolled down the mud between her legs.

"Okay, don't panic, Rayne. It's okay." Sammi reached out to her little sister and pulled her to her chest. "Nobody go over to that part, okay?"

Montgomery reached for my hand but I did not extend mine and down he went. He picked up a glop of mud and threw it into my hair.

"You shit!" I tried to kick mud at him and fell into the dirt pudding. It felt so smooth and cool on my skin, I sat there and let the goop run through my fingers. Squoosh. It was too hard to resist throwing it, so I didn't.

We were chocolate-molded kids when Isabelle's car drove by, slowing down to take in the sight of seven muddied children. They were halfway up the drive before the car slammed to a stop and a car door opened and closed.

Mommy ran down the gravel toward us. "Are you our children?"

Our laughing bodies dripped in glops.

"Isabelle, you were right. It's them." Mommy covered her mouth with both of her hands. "Oh Lordy. We drove by and I said that I wondered whose children those are. They look like they're having a great time but wait until their parents find out. Dear Lord, look at y'all. Look at all of you." Her head shook back and forth involuntarily and she let out a small giggle. "Make sure you hose off before you come into the house." She ran to catch up with the car.

We threw mud at each other and rolled around and jumped and danced and slid on our bellies for a while then caravanned up the hill staining the gravel beneath our bare feet. The hose was coiled near the side of the house, probably Herbert's handiwork. We pulled a length out straight and hosed each other and turned white again from the top down. Mud was still in our pockets and cuffs when we dove into the pool and small clouds puffed around us when we hit the water.

None of us had towels so we snuck up through the staircase behind the dining room and piled into the bathroom to rinse the chlorine off. This had become a new routine since Anne and Rayne's hair turned green. We kept our clothes on so that we could share the one shower. I stayed near the front to control the heat. I liked control and I hated cold.

We passed a bar of soap around and scrubbed at each other's clothes. The shampoo bottle was simultaneously passed and everyone scrubbed the head of someone near them. I chose Tommy's, though I had to reach around Eddy to get to him. We shifted around to let Cory and Sammi up to the shower head. Air chilled my wet skin and I shivered a little.

We shifted again to let Montgomery and Rayne rinse the bubbles from their hair. Their eyes had been closed against the potential stinging of the soap and they moved like moles feeling their way along the tile wall toward the water. We counterbalanced, moving toward the edge of the tub to let them by.

I'm not sure who fell first and I don't know whose hand reached for me and pulled me down with them. A huge blur. The flash of the shower curtain coming down. The clanging of the shower rod against the tile floor. The inner gonging as my skull thudded on the toilet bowl. The screams of seven small people crescendoed in my mind. We lay stunned for a moment, wet bodies on top of wet bodies, before writhing with our bruised arms and legs and backs and necks.

Rayne wriggled free first. She stood at our feet and looked down at the pile of us. "I say no more group showers."

*   *   *

Herbert's kids were not there the day the pony was due to arrive. Sammi and I stood proudly in our fenced-in field, though weeds stuck up in tufts. A trailer pulled up next to the barn. My heart jumped when I caught a glimpse of the brown rear and black tail of our new pony, Princess. Arnold's family had already named her when they found her in the woods. A denim clad man stepped out of the cab and approached us. "These yours?"

Merlin nodded yes. The hatch opened and out backed Princess. Another pony stood in the stall next to Princess'. He was small, a palomino Shetland, and very stocky. The man led Princess down the hill and into the stall we had prepared for her. We pet her nose and let her smell us. Her brown fur was coarse beneath my hand. Montgomery kept at least arms' length from her teeth while she nibbled and snorted at us then curled her upper lip baring her teeth like Mr. Ed.

Mommy's voice severed the darkness inside the barn. "Kids, come back outside."

Montgomery ran down the stones into the sunshine. Rayne waited for Sammi and I to cue her. We squinted against the light and stared up the hill at the still-assembled adults. Anne was propped on the trailer twirling a reed with her tongue. The denim clad man and Merlin talked about something in hushed voices and pointed at the trailer then at the barn then back at the trailer again.

Sammi hooked her thumbs in her overall straps and walked to Isabelle. "Can I go back inside? I want to play with Princess."

"One minute. Not yet."

Sammi reddened. "Why not? It's our pony, right?"

Mommy smiled fiercely. "Everybody gather 'round. We have another surprise for you."

Sammi and Isabelle stood their ground while the rest of us formed a sloppy circle that didn't include Anne. Merlin returned from the trailer. "What would be better than having your own pony?"

I looked to Sammi but she was still staring down Isabelle. Montgomery was trying to touch the tip of his nose with his tongue. Mommy flashed a warm smile at him. "The only thing better than having your own pony is having two!"

Sammi's bangs snapped across her eyes when she turned. "What?"

"Two ponies." The Shetland belonged to someone who had left the country for business. He had asked our landlord to keep the pony until he came back but that was two years ago and still no word. So, we could keep Taffy until that man wanted him back, which could be never.

He was a stallion, a word I always associated with tall thoroughbreds. He had never been broken so we were told we wouldn't be able to ride him but all of this sounded like wind through our ears as the denim clad man backed Taffy out of the trailer. His back was only as tall as my waist but his muscles rippled like a racehorse's when he clopped past me down the hill. Merlin walked the denim-clad man back to the trailer and we waved at him driving off. Two ponies. Amazing.

Sammi opened Princess' stall door. The pony's hoofs clicked tentatively against the concrete skirting outside the stall before she stepped down into our freshly hacked grass. Princess wandered, grazing on weeds and grasses, moving lazily toward our newly erected fence, and sweeping her nose around the untouched weeds on the other side. Taffy followed, stopping every few steps to feign interest in the grassy tufts that tickled at his knees. Princess pushed her shoulders against the fence slat to better reach the greens on the other side. Taffy continued inching along beside the fence.

Suddenly, Taffy let out a snort and lifted onto his hind legs. Princess' head bolted upward dislodging the wooden slat from its posts and nails and sending it backward onto her rump. She started when it smacked her hind quarters and ran wildly around the furthest ends of the field. Taffy, excited, reared in place over and over, snorting and whinnying. Princess answered him with her own snorts. My insides gathered in terror. The ground shook each time Taffy's hooves came down. I pictured the ponies crashing through the boards that separated us and mowing us down with their enormous weight and deadly hooves.

Then it stopped. Princess got preoccupied with a new clump of grass near the back fence, and Taffy walked leisurely along the fence Sammi and I had constructed. I was already planning how she and I would repair the hole Princess had created when Taffy mocked us by walking under the first slat. He barely had to lower his head to pass beneath it then he rubbed the length of his spine on the board, lifting it from the cradle of nails Sammi and I had created, and knocked it to the ground.

My lungs snapped open with a gasp. Taffy ran his ribs against the post then snaked back under the next slat. Half of it fell to the ground while the other end clung to the next post in his path. Merlin chuckled softly.

As Taffy pushed against the next post, it dislodged from its shallow grave and the weight of the still-clinging end of the slat brought the whole apparatus crashing down into the weeds.

Mommy slapped her hand over her mouth after an "Oh my" escaped on a bed of laughter.

My stomach twisted into knots.

Princess approached Taffy and followed him at a distance while they weaved their way through the remainder of the fence, leaving a wake of boards and posts.

Mommy woo-hoo-hoo'ed. Merlin snorted in his rich, deep laughter. Isabelle allowed chuckles to fall from her mouth and down her shirt. Herbert's shoulders moved up and down and Carol wiped a tear from the outer corner of her eye with one hand and held her stomach with the other. Even Rayne and Montgomery giggled to themselves.

My shoulders ached and acid crept up my esophagus and burned the back of my throat. I looked to Sammi. She was already looking at me.

"Good job guys." Anne snickered and walked up the gravel driveway to the house. My chest ached. But we had two ponies.

*   *   *

The house was relatively, and uncharacteristically, empty. I turned on Mommy's stereo. Her room was spacious and free of furniture. A bed on one wall, a dresser and speakers on the other with nothing but carpet and a wall piano in between.

"And now, for the Americans; Miss Ariel Whilone doing her floor exercise." I pictured the crowd all quiet with anticipation. I heard my music cue and launched with a forward roll. I kept my toes pointed and my hands in balletic readiness during my cartwheel and moved straight into my best move, a front walkover.

Two turns and a leap down into a split. Stretch the right arm above my head and the left out to my side then roll out of the split onto my belly then over to my back. A back bend, push out to a walkover and finish with a pretty pose. Satisfied that I had done well, I snapped my back into the Nadia arch and threw my arms up and out behind my head. I pictured the crowd cheering me on. The Americans were all very proud of me. I was a shoo-in for a medal.

The music on the radio continued and I danced a Broadway show, the one for the Rockettes. Then I was the star of a dance on television. My back-up dancers circled on either side of me and complimented all of my moves. We danced with sharp, staccato moves, then low to the ground moves, then sexy, hip grinding moves. I did the "bump" and the "double bump" then threw in high kicks and dazzling spins and turns.

The radio guy started talking about Carter and making peanut jokes so I turned the dial to find something good on another station. Nothing. It was time for my piano concert. I had taken lessons from Mommy's piano teacher in Laurel for six months before we moved. I even had one recital. I knew two songs.

Rayne entered while I was finishing the second one. "What are you doing?"

"Nothing. Just fooling around."

"It sounds pretty." She rested her chin on the glossy wooden top of the piano. "Do you want to play something?"

"I am."

"I mean like play-lady-dress-up."

"Okay." The concert ended and I closed the lid over the keys, sneaking in a bow before exiting with Rayne. We went to the hollow basket chair in the playroom and lifted the seat. Dresses and accessories were shoved tightly inside.

"Who should we dress up as?"

I studied Rayne deciding if she was Queen Elizabeth or Marilyn Monroe.

"I know. Let's be one person. I'll sit on your shoulders then we'll be taller than even your mom." She grabbed at fabric until her tiny hand settled upon a long, red dress. "This is it."

I put on white tights and Isabelle's scuffed white dress shoes while Rayne pulled the red dress over her head. I zipped her in then put a floppy white straw hat on her head.

"Wait. I need a bun."

I brushed her green-white hair into a ponytail and wrapped it into a swirl, securing the end with a fat bobby pin. "There. Oh, wait!" I ran to Mommy's room to grab a lipstick and rouge. Mommy was spread out on her bed reading a letter with a pencil in her hand.

"Oh, hi Mommy."

"Hi, my precious."

"I just need to borrow something. Can I use your makeup?"

"Where are you going?"

"Nowhere."

"What happened to the play makeup Isabelle and I gave you?"

"It's the wrong color, Mommy. I really need red. Can I borrow yours?"

"What's it for?" She was smiling.

"It's a surprise."

I ran down to her dresser and grabbed a silver lipstick tube from the top drawer. Rayne was smearing blue cream eye shadow on her lids when I returned to the playroom. I held up the red lipstick in triumph. "Give me your face." I followed the ridges of her lips closely, being careful to color in the lines.

She smiled a painted smile at me then hiked the front of her dress up. "Stay on your knees." She climbed onto my shoulders then lowered the dress over my face.

I batted at the fabric. "Rayne, I can't see."

"I'll tell you where to go." She was giggling a lot now, pleased with herself and her costume. "Stand up."

Her weight shifted and her thighs clenched at the sides of my head to avoid toppling over. My ears rang and pulsed. "Rayne, Are you okay? Are you steady?"

"Walk over to the mirror. I want to see us."

I held her calves under my arms and locked her feet behind me. "There's a full-length in my mommy's room."

Her hand came down on the back of my head. "Let's go show her. Go left. Lefter."

I moved gently left.

Her hand thumped against my head. "Lefter than that."

We crossed the threshold into the hallway. "Tell me before the stairs."

"Not yet."

"I know, but tell me before." I slid my feet along the hardwood flooring. "Don't forget to tell me."

"I won't." Her little hips cradled my neck and she rested her hands on top of my head.

I kept my eyes downward to follow the lines of the floorboards. It seemed we had walked a long way, six or seven hallways.

"Now! Now!"

I stopped suddenly and Rayne flew forward a bit. Two steps up. Rayne tottered above me. "Go right in a second. Really right. You're going into Madeleine's room. Now just go straight."

I padded onto the short weave pine carpet and moved into Mommy's room.

Rayne's hand tapped at my head. Her voice got low. "Hello Madame. How do you do?"

I heard Mommy's dulcet Southern accent through the skirting. "Well, hello. I do just fine. How do you do?"

Rayne tried to sound proper, almost English. "What is your name, Madame?"

"My name is Madeleine. What's yours?"

"I'm the lady in red."

"Yes you are. Is that your name?"

"Mr. Christopher."

"Mr. Christopher is your name?"

"Yes, Madame."

"Are you a ghost then?"

Rayne paused for a moment. "No, this is before I died." Sweat dripped from every contact point between Rayne's skin and mine and tickled as it ran down my spine.

"I'm going to look in your mirror now, Madame." She tapped my head. "Turn around and go straight."

I followed my memory and her instructions until we stood in front of the full-length mirror. I wanted to lift the skirt and look but I didn't want to let Mommy see.

"Goodbye, it was a pleasure, Madame." More tapping. "Turn around. Straight ahead and a little right."

We made our way back to the playroom and I lowered Rayne to her feet then ducked out from beneath her. Air rushed cool onto my face.

Rayne pulled her hat off and tugged at the zipper behind her. "She really thought we were Mr. Christopher. We should do that again and bring her tea or something."

"Why Mr. Christopher?"

"What do you mean?" Her head was cocked to the side like an inquisitive puppy's.

"Why were we Mr. Christopher?"

Her small, blonde head tilted up at me. "Because of the long dress. Mr. Christopher always wears a long dress when she comes in. We look like her." She stepped out of the dress and folded it into a ball.

I struggled to follow her logic but we all knew that logic was not Rayne's strong suit, she was forever connecting the seemingly unconnected. We pushed all the clothes down into the basket chair and used toilet paper to wipe the color from her mouth and eyes.

Chapter Seven

"Tah Dah!" Mommy's arms were raised above her as she spun in her red cotton sundress. "How does your lovely mother look?"

She was breathtaking. Her sandy hair framed her face in gentle curls. She wore only the slightest bit of make-up, just enough to pull out her own natural pinks and yellows and browns. The dress skated across the tops of her breasts and cinched around her tiny waist then flowed over her hips and thighs before revealing shapely calves and tiny sandal-clad feet. She was a long ribbon of red swirling through the room.

"Where are you going?"

Her face was soft and smiling. "On a date."

A date. "With a man?"

Her laughter spilled out onto the carpet between us. "Of course with a man."

"You look okay." I knew immediately that is was an awful thing to say, worse because I said it only to share my hurt.

Carol walked past Mommy's bedroom door and stopped to whistle at her. "Hot date?"

"Luke warm."

"Well you look terrif'. Knockout. Who is it?"

"Arnold."

"The horse guy?" Carol's face crinkled. "Isn't he married?"

"Recently split."

My face grew hot. "Why him? I don't like him."

Carol and Mommy turned to me. "He gave you a pony." Mommy wore her "don't do this to me now" face. I wasn't sure which of us would cry first.

"He's a creep." I ran out of the room before the tears came, mine.

My room was empty. Sammi was probably riding with Alice again. I cried alone awhile, sometimes raising my voice hoping Mommy would hear me and come to comfort me, maybe even cancel her date. Pillows answered my call and curled into my belly. My voice went up and down as I alternated between listening for Mommy and calling for her in my childish way. Like a tiring infant, I grew bored with my own noise and picked up my favorite book, The Pushcart War. The pages were fat and wavy from years of dog-ears and humidity. The salt dried on my face as I was transported to the streets of New York and the war between the pushcarts and the trucks.

I heard a car pull into the drive and started crying all over again, loudly, fervently, hoping to stop these spinning wheels. I moved toward the staircase and directed my voice down it. I moved to the window and cried out of it. But the engine started again and I heard the gravel crunch as that man drove my mommy away from me. I threw my book at the wall and felt the anger rise up my throat. Pillows jumped up and ran away when I grabbed my pillow and pictured Mommy's face. I hit her and hit her. I stuck my fingers in her eyes and twisted them. "I hate you!" I smacked her and punched her until I fell, exhausted, on top of her. I pulled her into my belly and sobbed. "Mommy."

*　　*　　*

Everything was a battle lately. Rayne and Anne were battling their green hair. The antiquated copper piping was finishing the job the chlorinated pool had started. Now, the Busch sisters had to shampoo over and over while at Bentley's and almost not at all while at the farm.

Isabelle was battling the flies. Sticky orange fly strips hung in every corner of the kitchen. Dark black carcasses clung to them. Still, every room hummed with the sound of tiny wings.

All of us were battling rabbits, deer, foxes, raccoons and every other creature that was glad we had grown them a garden of vegetables to munch on. They had all but wiped out all our hard work.

Sammi was battling Princess. The first day we took Princess to Virginia's ring, it was raining so we went indoors. Sammi and I had been working for two weeks already at getting Princess used to a saddle. Although she had been mounted before, she had never been saddled and she bucked in protest when we tightened the girth. Sammi whispered threats at her while forcing the saddle on her spirited, ever moving body, then held her jerking head tightly in her hands and screamed for me to finish the buckle. I thought for sure that I was frozen, a vibrating mass of adrenaline, but I felt my body move forward, watched my hands reach out before me, heard my heart as I pulled the leather strap and pushed the metal prong through. My desire for Sammi's approval battled with and won over my fear of death-by-pony.

"Jesus." Sammi had no victory in her face. "What a pain in the ass." Princess bucked with less conviction, aware that she had lost the battle but not the war. Sammi held to the bridle straps. She was going to break this beast if it killed her. She placed her foot into the dangling stirrup and pulled herself over the pony's back. Princess bucked a bit in protest then resigned and moved forward at Sammi's slight kick.

I was terrified and proud. Sammi was so brave. Princess followed the outer walls of the rink, trotting at Sammi's prompting, stopping within a reasonable time after Sammi's "Whoa."

I pictured myself in a riding outfit complete with black, shiny boots and a velvet covered hat. I pictured riding my beautiful horse out in the Queen Anne's field. The birds sang back-up to my laughter and the whinny of my horse. Then my horse stopped abruptly and faced the crest of the field. Silhouetted by a setting-sun sky stood Tommy on his horse looking down at me. "Hyah!" His horse galloped down through the tall lace flowers. Butterflies flew upward as their perches were disturbed. My horse gave chase and we rode through the field and into the next. I pictured riding through the Rice Crispies and the small creek, and even through the Witch's Forest. Then our horses slowed and we leaned into a kiss. I felt his thin lips press against my fuller ones. "I love you" was said.

"God damn you!" Sammi tried to jump the pony and Princess stopped just before the crossed wooden bars throwing Sammi to the ground. "Did you see that?"

"Yes." I hated lying but surely my eyes had registered something of the event.

Sammi patted the dirt from her pants and stood to the side of Princess ready to remount. She took a breath and hesitated, and though she hid her fear behind frustration, even I could see she was beginning to lose her bravado. "Damn."

"Why don't we try walking her over it first without a rider?"

Sammi looked down at the saddle. "Okay." She took the reigns over Princess' ears and ran in a circle to give them both room to make it over the jump. Sammi leapt over it. Princess followed her right up to the jump then skidded to a stop. Sammi flew backward and hit her spine against the crossed logs. Her eyes grew glossy red but she would not let herself cry. She stood and grabbed the reigns once more. "Come on, you stupid cow." We both stared in amazement while Princess gingerly lifted her right hoof and placed it on top of the jump. She stepped over with the left and followed by putting a hind leg on the jump and crossing over.

"What in the world?" I don't know why I had always assumed every horse knew innately how to jump, but I had. No one would believe us if we told them Princess' interpretation of this obstacle. Still, we had both just seen it. We were going to have to teach this horse what jumping meant.

Sammi was dumbfounded. All of her cursing stopped and she stared at Princess pushing her hoof around in the dirt. We looked to each other and laughed. It was an unsure laugh and stopped quickly.

I looked to Princess then rested in Sammi's eyes. "Maybe another day."

"I guess."

"Taffy or Princess."

"David Cassidy."

Then we laughed well.

*   *   *

Summer was ending and we could all feel it. Living in this odd gathering of people in these rural surroundings had somehow made more sense during summertime. Now, school loomed ahead and reality threatened our lifestyle.

A storm swelled the Patapsco and prevented us from even wading on our trips to town. But things had calmed and Mommy and Herbert gave us permission to swim in the river. We ran to our rooms and threw on faded swimsuits and shorts and threadbare tennis shoes and grabbed towels on our way out of the house. We didn't want grown-ups to go but Mommy was insistent and invited herself and Carol along.

The field was overgrown at its edges from a lush, rainy summer, and flattened in its center from horse hooves and games of tag and small bodies rolling downhill. Sammi and I grabbed tall weeds and stripped them into riding crops. We rode our imaginary horses down the path along the fence line and into the state park. Rayne and Eddy followed behind, imitating our every action. Cory and Montgomery were giggling at some private joke I was sure I wouldn't find funny. Tommy walked with Anne just ahead of Carol and Mommy and I wasn't sure if I was jealous of my sweetheart giving her attention or my idol giving him attention.

Vines and laden branches overhung the path. It was as if nothing existed outside of this wall of green, nothing but the baby-blanket blue sky. At the river's edge, spinach green water rushed past us with audible speed. Mommy second-guessed the whole swimming idea but was just as anxious for a last summer dip as we were. The water was still cloudy with the mud of the storm and it had lost some of its languid warmth. I dipped in slowly, letting each section of my body adjust separately to the temperature. Sammi, Tommy, Cory, and Montgomery rushed in past me, splashing unprepared sections of my skin. Anne spread herself out on a rock and smoothed baby oil over her perfect curves. We swam fiercely against the pull of the river and out to a great, flat rock that split the flow.

Mommy moved haltingly into the river. The water broke against her long legs and she let out a woo-hoo-hoo. She reached down and cupped the the water with her hand and ran it down the tops of her thighs before venturing further. I saw my own movements in hers. She slowly sank in and let the water flow over her head before pushing back out into the sun. She was a mermaid, sparkling wet, trickling with reflected diamonds.

Water bugs scampered along the ever-moving surface and floating leaves buoyed wayward ants. We tried a game of Marco Polo but found it too hard. We collected bits of worn glass and particularly colorful rocks from the silt beneath us. I brought Sammi's rocks with me to the shore and placed them in our pile. Anne called me to oil her back.

Her skin was freckled and soft beneath my fingertips. "Anne, don't you worry about wrinkles?"

She cupped her untied top in her hand rolling over to face me. "What?"

"All this sun. You're going to look thirty-five by the time you're eighteen." Her eyes locked on mine and I knew I had betrayed her in some way. I could only hold my breath and hope she'd still like me.

"How do you know I'll live to be eighteen? I look good now, don't I?"

It was inarguable.

I finished and watched water bead up on my own hand.

The battle against the current soon tired us and we grabbed up our rocks and walked back into the woods.

Herbert and Merlin were tarring the roof of the pavilion when we returned. They recruited Mommy and Carol, who climbed the ladder to the roof in their still-damp swimsuits. The recent rains had revealed just how badly the roof needed repairing and another storm was due in the next day or so.

Their height appealed to us so we climbed the fruit trees in the front yard. I chose the chokeberry. It was one of the tallest but much easier to climb than many of the others. The berries stained my fingertips purple and red as I ate from the branches. Sammi was in the pear tree and I envied her those sweet fruit. Tiny feet dangled like ripe human fruit from the foliage of an apple tree, a plum tree. I heard the light thud of cores and pits hitting the ground. They could hear me spitting small seeds. Every rustle and shimmy brought more ripe berries to me and soon my thighs and arms were covered with stains.

A car came cautiously up the drive and pulled into the parking area. I could hear the faint drift of Mommy's voice screaming, "I am Woman" as she stood on the roof with her arms outstretched. She stopped suddenly and looked down to the two men in suits below. Everyone climbed down from the roof and there was lots of hand shaking. I went back to my nibbling and my search for the perfect sitting spot. I climbed up a bit further testing the thinner branches before putting my weight fully on them. I was cautious like that. The leaves were more dense up here and everyone else was almost invisible in their perches except Cory, who was dangling from the apple tree.

I settled into a nook formed by the trunk and two large branches and let my body relax. The first plum didn't hit me but I saw it zing through the leaves just below me. Plums. Who was in the plum tree? Maybe it was Tommy flirting with me. I grabbed a handful of berries and threw them but their weight would not carry them to his perch. I heard the rustle of leaves as apples and pears and plums drifted from tree to tree, then the smack of someone being hit.

"Hey, kids! Cool it!" Merlin's voice carried itself up to my lofty seat. "Sorry about that." Merlin was talking to a suited man who was dusting off his shoulder and smoothing his thinning hair. "Everybody down."

Cory let go and fell to the ground like an overripe fruit, and several of the kids jumped down easily. It took me the longest to come out of my high perch in my tall tree. We gathered around in our faded, ratty swimsuits, our skin smeared with dirt and fruit stains, and smiled at the two men in suits. Most of us kids were used to these guys, we'd seen ones just like them before.

Herbert shifted nervously with a half-smile on his face. "These are my children. This is Tommy and Cory and this is Edwina." He never called her that. "I apologize for their appearance."

"No, not at all. We were kids once, weren't we Burt?"

The other suited man nodded and laughed in a stifled snort.

"What with summer ending and everything..."

"Really, Mr. Hobart, no need to explain. Nice meeting you kids."

Eddy grabbed Tommy's hand before gathering herself. "Who are you?"

The two men looked to each other and smiled. Burt stifled a snort again and the other addressed Eddy. "We're friends of your dad's from work. I'm Cal and this is Burt."

"But this is the weekend."

Herbert moved to Eddy and placed his hand on top of her head. "I'm sorry. She's at that age."

"No, not at all. We have kids too, don't we, Burt."

"Sure do, Cal."

The two men turned and led the grown-ups to the house. I felt skinny and dirty and half-naked. "Eddy, they just want to ask some questions. Your dad's probably getting his security clearance reviewed or something. They always do that. It's no big deal."

"Did they do it to your dad?"

"They do it to all our dads." But I'd never been worried before that the review wouldn't go well.

We all went swimming in the pool. My stains faded but would not let go. I looked bruised.

It would be years before I realized that not all dads worked with my dad. Not all dads had a clearance or needed it reviewed or got polygraphs but it is the nature of childhood to assume that a family is a world, the only world. The men stayed about an hour then drove onto Patapsco Road and back toward civilization to report back to the government on how Herbert was living and whether the world was still safe for democracy.

*   *   *

Mommy's birthday was going to be our last big bash of the summer. She had chosen a movie during the day and a pool party at night. Sammi and I were very excited for the movie. We were going to go to Columbia to see a *Pink Panther* sequel. Columbia was a city of sorts and we couldn't wait to get there. Sammi wore Anne,'s hand-me-downs; a pair of Levi's and a gauze top. I wore a pair of Dittos jeans Mommy had gotten at the JCPenney back-to-school sale. We dressed Rayne in one of Sammi's, formerly Anne's, wrap-around skirts with a plaid shirt tied at the waist.

It took three cars to get us all to the theatre. We each had one dollar for concessions. Sammi and I combined our money and shared our popcorn and Coke. I wanted to sit next to Tommy but he was looking at posters by himself and I knew he'd sit where he wanted.

Mommy looked pretty in the red sundress she always wore with a little red chord tied around the waist. "Ariel, do y'all need to go to the bathroom, honey, because now is a good time."

Isabelle whispered too loud at Sammi. "Remember what I told you in the car."

Sammi exhaled and told Rayne to go to the bathroom. Rayne walked away in her ill-fitting outfit and Isabelle straightened Sammi out. "I could have done that. I asked you to help me watch her. I need your help with all of this, Sammi."

"Okay, okay." Sammi looked down at her red Jack Purcel's and started toward the restroom door when out came Rayne. She was smiling and walking as if she were wearing a tiara. Which one of us would have the heart to tell her that the entire back of her wrap-around was wet with toilet water?

We filed into the theatre and sat in two rows, kids and grown-ups. Tommy sat with the boys. The lights dimmed and I pictured Tommy and me on a date. We were holding hands and watching some romantic movie. He smiled at me when the dialogue matched his thoughts. Then he put his arm around me and at some point... we kissed.

Sammi and I finished our popcorn early in the movie and took turns sipping the Coke. The movie was exciting and funny with lots of gadgets, a cool cartoon and a giant diamond. We punctuated it with Mommy's woo-hoo-hoo's and an "Ooh, punch that guy!" from Rayne. I felt like the Beverly Hillbillies.

Afterward, we got back into our cars and drove to the lush green that is Sykesville. Dinner was burgers and hot dogs on the grill. We put the speakers in the windows facing the pool and played John Denver while cooking and eating. Mommy danced with Merlin and Isabelle. She even got Herbert to do "the bump" with her. The sun was setting when we lit the candles on the strawberry-drenched angel food cake. The air chilled so the water felt warm. Merlin's teenage sister, Adrienne, was there and she and Anne held hands and jumped in the water at the same time. It was the first time I'd ever seen Anne depend on anyone for anything.

We rode the slide in the dark, plunging into the black water from a black sky. I always marveled at the quiet under the water compared with the squeals and music and laughter above the surface. Merlin and Herbert tossed us around like beach balls. Carol and Isabelle and Mommy performed a fairly bad water ballet. Jay, Kay, Elle and Em watched from beyond the fence until two police cars pulled up and asked us to keep the noise down.

The grown-ups went inside and drank some more while we set up in the pavilion. Sammi pulled me to one side after we had laid out our sleeping bags. "Did you see Anne and Adrienne?"

"Yeah." I used the same reverence I sensed in her voice.

"They just trusted that each would go. I mean, they trusted that they would both jump in at the same time."

"It was neat."

"Let's become blood sisters."

"What?"

"You know, blood sisters, when you rub your blood together."

Our mothers had been best friends since before they simultaneously became pregnant with us so I had always considered Anne and Sammi and Rayne to be sisters of a sort. Still, there was something dark and romantic about this idea and I was seduced immediately. "Okay."

Sammi ran to the house and returned out of breath with one of her mother's broaches in her hand. "Come on, let's go out back." We snuck out of the back of the pavilion. "Give me your finger."

"There's no light. How can you see what you're doing?"

"I can see. Just give me your finger."

I stretched my hand out to her and uncurled my right index finger. I'd had a fear of hypodermics all of my life but somehow this was different. Somehow, this crude needle seemed safer. I closed my eyes as she pushed the point under the surface of my skin. It was dull and painful. She pulled the pin out and blood formed a small bulging drop sitting on the surface of my fingertip. She pushed the pin into her own fingertip and pulled it out without wincing. We moved our fingers toward each other. The blood ran to my wrist as we touched our fingertips together and rubbed them around.

"Now we're blood sisters forever and ever."

I nodded. "Forever and ever."

We went back into the pavilion and I felt a new confidence in our friendship, a new sense of sisterhood and I understood why she had done it. We slept around the empty fireplace and Tommy gave me a goodnight kiss. Sometimes you have perfect days and don't know it but this one I could feel and I didn't want it to end.

*   *   *

School was looming ever closer. Dad and Sandy couldn't understand why I wanted to spend Labor Day weekend at the farm. They planned picnics and barbecues and swimming at their apartment complex's pool and said it was just like the farm. But we were all becoming creatures of that place and our green hair and dirty fingernails gave us away even in a small city like Laurel. Sandy bought me some school clothes at the Hecht Company and wondered aloud at my most precious hand-me-downs, the ones from Anne. They didn't get any of Montgomery's private jokes to me.

"You sleep in sleeping bags at the farm, don't you?" Sandy couldn't see how it was different and I didn't have the vocabulary to explain it. "This is a better pool than yours. Look, it even has a high dive." But it had no slide and it was filled with people I didn't know, people who wore shiny new suits that they didn't dare wet.

It seemed silly to cry and, of course, I missed my dad so much it made me mad, but I was beginning to crush under the weight of their perfectly chlorinated pool. I wanted to go home. Not even to the farm, but to my old home, my old school, my old friends, my old neighborhood pool.

Monday came and Sandy and Dad brought us back up the gravel drive. Mommy was waiting on the porch, shucking fresh corn from the garden. Sandy stayed in the car tugging at the cursive pendant spelling her name in gold. It clashed slightly with the silver glitter on her T-shirt declaring "Foxy Lady." Dad gave Mommy a check then started up the Volkswagen and disappeared again. I always missed him most just then, just as his engine's rumble faded.

"So, my angel, how was your weekend?"

"It was okay."

Montgomery went inside with his overnight bag and left the door open behind him.

"Honey, can you get that?"

I dropped my bag and stomped toward the door. "How come I always have to do everything? He never does anything."

"Ariel, don't do this. He's younger."

"So? When I was his age I still had to do everything."

"My heart, he'll always be younger."

"This is so unfair."

"What's not fair?"

"I always have to do everything and he never gets in trouble and I don't want to go to a new school. This is all your fault."

"Come here, precious." I hesitated then moved slowly toward the lap I had wanted to rest my head in all weekend. "I'm sorry you have to go to a new school but you'll make new friends and soon it will all be fine." She ran her hand along my waist-long hair like I was a cat. "Sammi will be there with you."

"But Mommy, this is junior high. They make you go to a bunch of different classes. I might not even see her. And this is a weird place. What if all of the kids are mean or already know each other or something?"

"Ariel, it's going to be fine. Everything will work out."

"It's just not fair. I don't want to be divorced."

Her tone became crisp and I knew the conversation was coming to an end. "Well, life is not fair."

Chapter Eight

Tuesday was trash day. Sammi and I had to drag the glossy black Hefty bags down the front yard to the side of the road. We ran to the barn and fed Princess and Taffy then ran back to the bend in front of our house and waited. Pillows waited alongside us and rubbed his ribs against the hem of my jeans, purring loudly. Sammi and I didn't have watches but it seemed like we waited a long time. The bus was almost empty when we climbed aboard with only the kids from Windriver Estates, the suburban area at the top of Patapsco Road, already seated. The driver introduced herself as Pepper. Jay, Kay, Elle and Em would ride the same bus as Montgomery and Rayne so we drove past their house without stopping and continued up the hill. Hap carried no books and no lunch bag. He walked past us and nodded. "Hey."

"Hey." Our voices were soft and in unison.

He sat in the back and looked out of the window. At the next stop, we picked up Crane and Alice. Alice sat across the aisle from us and Crane brushed past to sit with Hap.

"First day." Alice threw her book bag casually beside her on the green vinyl seat. "I wonder if we'll have any classes together, Sammi. Do you think?"

"Who knows."

Who cares? Didn't she know that it was much more important for Sammi to have classes with her best friend since birth, her almost sister, than with some neighbor?

We stopped again to pick up Crane's younger cousin, Tuffy Redden. She raced up the stairs and sat in the back. Crane muttered something and Tuffy hit him. "Shut your face."

We didn't stop again for at least ten minutes until we had already driven the length of Patapsco Road and turned left and entered foreign territory. There were more girls than boys but the bus never truly filled up and we pulled up in front of the school without me really getting a feel for our new classmates.

The building was one story and rambling, like our elementary school but larger and more complicated. They did the home rooms by the alphabet so Sammi and I were separated almost immediately. She went to the A through C room with Mrs. Hattley and I went to the U through Z room with Miss Addona. I found it with the map they distributed at the door to newcomers, room 24C. The letter was because room 24 was a big open space with four dividers separating four classrooms. Wouldn't we hear each other throughout the room? We would. I missed my name the first time it was called because of the cacophony of names being called from different parts of the alphabet in different sections of the room. "Dade?... here... Setzer?... here... Dewey?... here... Spaulding?... here... Whilone?... Whilone?..."

"Oh, that's me."

"Ariel Whilone?"

"Yes, that's me. I mean, here." And that's how my day started.

I had math first and was placed in the wrong class.

The teacher smiled and looked mad all at one time. "Well, I'm sorry, but your records must have said that you're supposed to be in this class. If you have a problem with that, you need to take it up with the front office, little miss. In the meantime, I suggest you sit down and take some notes so you don't fall behind."

I wasn't likely to fall behind in a class I'd already finished.

Next was science, then geography. Geography was in room 24B so at least I didn't get as lost finding my way. I sat near the back of the room in an empty row. A girl sat next to me. She was thin and fairly tall with long hair like me, but her hair was greasy and stringy and when she turned to face me, she looked like a plate of spaghetti, all red, oily and surrounded by string. "What are you looking at, Green Giant?"

I turned away and tried not to look left for the duration of the class. My teacher, Mr. Williams, was black. It wasn't until then that I realized how few blacks I had seen so far. None in homeroom. Only one in math and none in geography. Maybe they didn't have bussing here.

"Whilone? Is there an Ariel Whilone?"

"Yes, me. Here, I'm here."

"Hiding in the back, I see."

Was I?

Next was reading, another class I'd already finished. My teacher was young and blonde and busty with rounded thighs, Miss Sheridan. "Well, you're in the class for now so stick around and you can have your parents call later to straighten it out." Then she read a poem that I liked about taking the path that's not worn down by millions of feet.

And then came gym class. We were given uniforms and lockers and taken on a tour of the group shower area. Terrifying. At the farm, showering together was silly and fun and tangled familiar flesh. These walls echoed with the ghosts of girls hiding developing breasts, bleeding without wounds and washing off the shame of mothers and fathers afraid of tube tops and pubic hair.

Then lunch. The tables were long and rectangular with orange plastic chairs on both sides. I pushed my tray along metal rails and collected the pieces of a meal; a carton of white milk, bent silverware, a paper napkin, a plate of meat loaf with tomato sauce and skillet potatoes and a bowl of Jell-O with dry-edged whipped cream. I gave the lady in the paper hat fifty cents. Sammi was nowhere to be seen and I recognized no one. I walked to the furthest table on the left, the one under the windows, and sat facing the room. The food was okay and I was hungry, but I was only pretending that it was interesting to look at. I finished it too quickly and dug around in my book bag for things I knew weren't there. I finally pulled out the map and my schedule of classes and read it over and over. My two elective classes were left. One was art, the other would rotate; two days wood shop, two days metal shop, and one day of home economics. Today would be metal shop.

I got lost and ended up at the library twice on the way to metal shop. My classmates were disinterested but I liked my teacher, Mr. Burks, a bulky guy in a flannel shirt with a bandana tied into a cap. His voice was as rough and loud as the metal-working machines.

The last bell rang and we flooded into the halls. I didn't bother going back to my locker and searched for my bus right away. 739. 739. 739. It was near the front of the line. I stepped inside and Pepper smiled. "Long day?"

"Yeah."

"You'll get the hang of it, sweet pea. Just keep on truckin'."

"Thanks." I liked it when grown-ups talked to me. I sat closer to the back and watched for Sammi in the window. She came out of the building with Alice and two other girls and a boy. The boy was beautiful with black hair and blue eyes and he was smiling at Sammi and laughing with the girls. She waved goodbye to them and bounced onto the bus then sat with Alice.

"Hey, Sammi. I'm back here." A lead weight had settled into my stomach.

"Hey, come sit up here, Ariel."

I picked up my bag and moved to the seat across the aisle from them to sit alone. Sammi picked up her bag and sat next to me. I filled with gratitude. "How was it?"

"It was okay. We didn't have any classes together."

"No." Tears worked their way up my ducts.

"Alice's in my sixth period. Right, Al?"

"Miss Addona." Alice waved to someone outside.

"I had Miss Addona too, Sammi, just for homeroom though. Did you have to go to metal shop?"

Alice snickered. "Oh brother, Mr. Burks. He's a nightmare. You'll learn to get sick of him."

154

She was so familiar with Sammi, as if they were friends for years. How could Sammi let her talk to her that way, laugh with her that way, our way?

"Hey, Sammi, you want to get off at my stop? We can go riding if you want."

My fingertips itched. I wanted to bite my nails.

"Nah, maybe another day. My mom will want to hear about my first day."

What would Sammi tell Isabelle? Would she tell her how popular she was going to be? How well she fit in and found her space here? Did she even know it could have been different?

The bus emptied out and finally dropped us in front of our house. Pepper waved. "Bye y'all. See you bright and early."

Sammi walked down toward the barn and I followed her. She grabbed a brush and comb to groom Princess. I went to Taffy's stall and checked on his feed. I could hear the metal scrape of Sammi pulling the coarse hair in Princess' mane and tail.

"Ariel?"

I was so glad she had broken this bewildering silence. "Yeah?"

"What did you think of that school?"

"It'll be okay, I guess."

"Yeah, I guess."

I let myself out of Taffy's stall and joined Sammi. "Some of my classes are wrong."

"What do you mean, wrong?"'

"I already took them. I should be in the next class."

"So? Just stay and get a good grade."

"I got a good grade before."

"Well, excuse me."

I looked down at my hay-covered shoes. "Did you like it?"

"I'm not sure yet. Ask me next week."

We let the ponies out then went up to the house. As had become our custom, I took out two tiny orange juice glasses and filled them with milk. We threw back the shots and refilled the glasses until most of the carton was gone. We walked out to the pavilion with our pack of cigarettes tucked inside of Sammi's waistband. I carried the matches in my front pocket. We sat outside of the back door and lit one to share. Sammi inhaled and blew attempts at rings. "Our moms should be home soon. I thought Madeleine was supposed to be here already."

"I thought so too. It seems like she's never here."

"That's cool."

I blew smoke out into the grass between my legs. "I guess."

"She's dating, huh?"

"Yeah, I guess. Arnold mostly."

"So? My mom dates Merlin. Carol goes out on dates."

"Carol's not a mom."

Sammi pressed the cigarette into the grass and moved it around until all of its embers burned out. She pushed the butt into a crevice between the wall and the ground. "Well, that's life."

"I guess."

*   *   *

It was too hot for baking but Isabelle stayed in the kitchen for two hours molding colored marzipan dough into fruit shapes and heating it to golden-edged in the oven. We drank iced herbal teas out of hand-thrown pottery mugs with my dad's signature carved into the bottom. The marzipan cookies sat on a plate in the center of our group and we grabbed at them intermittently during the meeting.

Isabelle dusted her fingertips on a paper towel and washed her cookie down with a swig of tea. "Gripes anyone?"

No one spoke for a moment. Maybe we'd get out of here early and I'd still be able to see *The Six Million Dollar Man*. Then Herbert cleared his throat. "Who's leaving bottles all around the edge of the tub?"

Mommy looked mortified. "Someone is leaving bottles around the tub?"

"Not glass bottles, shampoo bottles. Near as I can tell, there are a dozen shampoo bottles in there and they all fall in whenever I move in there."

I remembered the rule out loud for the group. "Only one bottle of shampoo and one bottle of conditioner per bathroom."

Mommy smiled at me. "That's right, Ariel, but sometimes grown-up women have to use special products for their hair."

"For God's sake, Madeleine, she's got green hair." Anne smiled at me like a Cheshire cat. "I don't know if anyone has told you guys this, but you have green hair."

"Anne, if you're going to be difficult..." Isabelle was stern in the setting of her brow.

"This is crap. Herbert is complaining about you guys and your hair junk trashing up his bathroom which you guys agreed to share and you're gonna say I'm being difficult?"

"Enough already, Anne. Herbert, we'll get our stuff out tonight. Agreed everyone?"

Carol and Mommy nodded without enthusiasm.

"Any more gripes?" Isabelle sipped from her tea again loudly. She had forgotten it wasn't hot tea. "Okay, let's move on to rules. New curfew for school nights. Madeleine?"

"I think we need one. Until daylight savings, I think seven is fair."

Isabelle shot Mommy a look of betrayal. "I think that's a bit late, Mad, don't you?"

"Well, that's what Frank and I chose."

"Really? What about you, Herbert? When do your kids have to be in?"

Herbert re-crossed his legs in discomfort. "I don't know."

"But when you and Janet decided, what was it?"

"Seven? Maybe eight? Six? I'm not sure, to be honest. She handled the kids."

"It was until the street lights came on, Herbert." I liked knowing answers.

"Well." Isabelle looked down into her empty cup. "We don't have street lights anymore. Six-thirty. Fair enough?"

The adults' heads bobbed and another rule was passed down.

We ended the meeting with Isabelle reading vividly from *Watership Down* and my head resting in my mommy's lap as she stroked my hair. Home is wherever Mommy's lap is.

*   *   *

Sammi and I dragged the Hefty bags over the brittle grass of an early first frost. We fed and brushed the horses until we heard Pepper honk for us from the road then unlatched the stall doors so Princess and Taffy could graze all day.

We sat near the back and waited for Hap and Crane and Tuffy and Alice to join us. I pulled my kneesocks up under my jeans and played with the metal barrette in my hair. It was late September and some of the leaves had already started their change into red and yellow. This was the time of year Marylanders boasted about, "They may have nicer weather, but we've got the seasons." Hap and Crane made fun of Tuffy almost the whole way to school, as was their custom. Though a part of me wanted to stop their tauntings, the bigger part of me was just relieved it was her and not me so I sat in silence occasionally interjecting a "That's not nice," or a "Come on, guys."

We pulled up in front of the bland brick building and waited to file out of the bus. Pepper smiled at Sammi and me passing by. My day centered around Ms. Sheridan and the reading class I didn't need to take. We were supposed to memorize a poem for our next assignment and I was working diligently to find just the right one. Every day, she'd read poems to us and introduce us to new authors we could choose from. I loved the sound of the words strung together, verbal pictures that my mind would wrap around and fill out. Sometimes, a kid would titter and bring me back from my fantasy into that small cinder block room. I hated them for it and called them names in my mind, "idiot," "party pooper," "ignoramus." Class would always end too quickly and I would stay and ask Ms. Sheridan questions for a minute or two before leaving.

I dreaded lunch everyday. I'd fill up my plastic tray with a square meal, pay with the humiliating bright red paper ticket they gave those of us on the government-subsidized hot lunch program then exit into the cafeteria. I'd hesitate for a moment, looking around for some familiar and welcoming face, but, it was always like opening the refrigerator repeatedly in the hopes that new food would magically appear. I walked over to my long table by the window and sat facing the room. Ozepher Wildes sat across from me and three seats up. She had started sitting there a week ago and we'd look up from our food and smile at each other once in a while.

Ozepher was an outcast from the word go. Her skin was so black it was almost blue and it shone with oil. Her hair was always in braids that ran down her head and into small primary-colored plastic barrettes, the ten-for-a-dollar kind. She only had three outfits as far as I could tell and each was a variation on the other, a cotton blend shirt with a jumper over it and knee socks, usually red, with black utility shoes. There was not one thing wrong with her that regular bathing and money couldn't have fixed but she wore her poverty in her gestures at this point. She was tentative, gave herself permission for nothing. Her very presence frightened and fascinated me. I would look at her blemished face and her chipped brass-alike buttons even when I didn't want to.

Something in me knew I was supposed to move to another table the first time she sat with me. Birds of a feather and all of that. I didn't want people to think I liked her or that we were friends or anything. With Sammi making friends in every direction, I still had a chance at becoming popular. But I stayed the first day and by the second day, the second time that Ozepher flashed her frightened smile at me and asked in a too-soft voice if it was okay to sit, it was too late. Today, I found myself even wanting to ask her things about herself. Where did she live? Did she have a million brothers and sisters? Were her parents still together? What did they do? What did she want to be when she grew up?

I was running these questions through my mind, trying to select an inoffensive one, when I heard someone calling to me. "Ariel? Ariel Whilone, is that you?" I looked up and around until my eyes rested on a petite brunette whose face tugged at my memory.

"Tina!"

"Ariel!"

Ozepher silently watched Tina and I embrace. Perhaps she knew that our chance at speaking had passed. Perhaps she hoped to make two new friends instead of one. I couldn't know. All I knew was that I was rescued from having no friends. Tina had gone to school with me until third grade when she moved to who-knew-where. Here. Though she had gotten a few years older, her freckled face looked almost the same.

"Sammi goes to school here too, Sammi Busch. Do you remember her?"

"Yeah, oh yeah, sure I do." She put her tray down next to mine. "You guys all moved out here?"

"We moved to Sykesville."

"Never heard of it but that's okay. I live just down from here. Glenwood. Nice place, I guess. You guys take the same bus?"

"We live in the same house."

"Same house? What do you mean same house?"

It wasn't until that moment that it ever seemed strange to me. The more I tried to make it sound normal, the odder it came out. "Yeah, we moved into a big farm house. It's her family and mine and the Hobarts, remember them?"

"Sort of. Wait. Do you mean your whole neighborhood moved into a house together? Didn't the Hobarts used to live behind you guys?"

"Yeah. I mean, no, not the whole neighborhood. Just the Buschs, us, Herbert Hobart, Sammi's mom's boyfriend and some lady."

Tina became hushed and leaned into me to protect her words from Ozepher. "Sammi's mom and dad broke up?"

A wave of shame rushed over me. "Mine did too."

"Oh." She pushed her food with the tip of the fork. "Sorry." She sat quietly for a moment. Discomfort filled the space between us. "That's a lot of people. Is it a big house? Must be big."

"Pretty big."

"You have a maid?"

Ozepher looked at me. I looked away. "No."

"Wow. Hey, how's Montgomery?"

"He's good. He got hit by a car this summer but he's all better now. Maybe you could come home on our bus once and see everybody."

"Yeah, maybe."

We finished our lunches and went our separate ways.

Tuffy was always inviting Sammi and me to go riding with her at her house and we always said no though I wasn't sure why. But after school, Sammi said yes and we got off of the bus under the Redden Acres sign nailed high in a tree. Tuffy led us up the two dirt grooves that formed their driveway. We followed her into her house, a small two-bedroom with very little light and piles of magazines and newspapers and dishes and clothing on counters, in corners, filling chairs. She asked us to sit at the formica table in the center of the dingy kitchen and offered us orange drink from a pitcher in their antique refrigerator. We sat looking around the room and at each other while Tuffy ran down the hall and disappeared into a room. Our metal-framed, plastic-seated chairs squeaked with every uncomfortable shift of our bodies as we gazed at wooden plaques covered with Jesus and lacquer. Sammi motioned with her head toward the sink filled high with at least three meal's dishes. She leaned into me and whispered. Her breath tickled my ear and rustled my hair. "Her mom must work."

I looked at the only photo in view. Framed in tarnished brass, it sat in the living room on a cluttered dresser. The black-and-white man was big, thick, wearing overalls and a white shirt with a tie. The woman was small and further diminished by her proximity to him. She wore a floral dress and flat shoes and adorned herself with one simple hair ribbon tied high in otherwise mousy hair.

"I don't think the moms out here work, Sammi."

"Yeah, maybe not."

Tuffy entered the room in dirt-stained jeans and a pink sweatshirt with a kitten on the front. She looked at our glasses and then at us. "It's no good?"

I looked at Sammi and she looked at me. "What?"

"The drink, it's no good? You hardly touched it."

"No, it's good." I picked up the nearly-full glass and sipped.

"You don't have to drink it if you don't like it."

Sammi took a sip. "It's very good, Tuffy, really."

We drank in gulps until we had emptied our glasses and brought them to the sink. Tuffy led us out of the back door and across the grassless yard to the fence that held the horses back from us. Four horses watched us approach. Tuffy pushed their noses from the gate and let us in. We followed her to the barn and saddled three. I still felt insecure pulling the bridle onto a horse and was grateful that we had decided on bareback so that I could avoid the ordeal of saddling a horse single-handedly. We rode around Tuffy's yard then out of the gate and onto Patapsco Road. The horses' shoes clicked metallically on the blacktop surface as we plodded past Alice's and Crane's houses. Crane's horses snorted at ours. Sometimes, Sammi would make that clicking noise out of the side of her mouth to speed her horse up a bit. Tuffy pulled out a cigarette hoping to shock us. We passed it between us and let the smoke drift behind as we rode. We turned back at Hap's house and headed to Tuffy's again. Tuffy's voice rose above the rhythmic clicking of the horses' hooves. "You guys like my cousins?"

I squinched my face into a question mark. "Your cousins?"

"Yeah, Hap and Crane."

Sammi laughed. "You guys are all cousins?"

"Well, not really. But Happy and I really are, blood and everything. Crane's family is related by marriage or something like that which I really can't remember. Mostly cousins."

"Yeah, me and Sammi are mostly sisters." I was glad Sammi didn't disagree.

We came around the bend and passed the creepy house with the old woman and hundreds of cats. "Ever been there?" Tuffy caught me staring. "She makes everyone call her Ms. Marchesa Fontaine but her name is Mary Smith or something. She's a kook."

"She's got a lot of cats." I could always offer the obvious.

Sammi kicked my leg. "No duh, Ariel."

Cats littered the lawn, perched on the fence with their tails swinging, posed on the rooftop, lounged on the porch and sat sentry in every window. We had five cats now that Carol brought Tigger with her. I thought that was quite a lot. "Is she a weirdo?"

Tuffy lit another cigarette and passed it. "She's not dangerous or nothin', she's just weird. She doesn't leave that house much. I'll take you there once if you want."

We nodded in fascination.

Tuffy's house was just around the bend so we took one last hit of the cigarette before throwing it onto the street to burn out.

The horses weren't wet so we put them in the barn and helped Tuffy feed them.

The walk home seemed longer without the horses beneath us. It was getting dark earlier and the sky was dimming. We searched the side of the road for long thin reeds and quickly found two with just the right snap to them. Sammi made the clicking noise with the side of her mouth and I copied her, galloping into the sunset, two farm girls on non-existent horses.

*   *   *

Raking the Ultra Shag carpet brought me back to Mayfair Drive and made everything seem normal for a minute. Staring down into the long avocado-colored strands running through the plastic rake, I could almost hear Daddy's Volkswagen pull up out front, his keys jangling while he walked up from the carport, the music in Mommy's voice greeting him after a long day of work.

But Daddy wouldn't be driving up and Mommy was late. She'd even missed supper. A new feeling was growing inside of me, crawling from the back of my head to the front, a feeling of worry over her. What if she got hurt? What if she wasn't okay? What if she never came home? What if she was dead?

I stood on the couch and raked rows into the carpet, picturing my new life without Mommy. They'd let us stay here for awhile I guess. Isabelle and Merlin could raise us. No wait, they'd send us to Dad's and we'd sleep in sleeping bags.

I finished the carpet and went back into the old section of the house to put the rake away. I reminisced about Mommy holding our hands and jumping over the threshold, heard her silly woo-hoo-hoo, smelled the richness of her perfume, White Shoulders, sometimes Joy, "the costliest" for special occasions. I trudged up the stairs and wondered how Montgomery would handle the news. The romance of the attention I'd get faded into the terror of living without Mommy and I realized all at once how much I'd taken her for granted, how many meals she'd served, how many times she'd smiled in the face of despair, how much I'd feigned annoyance at her because she wasn't jaded like me so she must be stupid.

I lay my head down on the playroom daybed and a tear dropped from my chin to my shirt. How foolish I'd been to have wasted all this time with her. Then I felt that comforting hand stroking my hair. Oh, how I loved the feel of her pulling my hair from my face, gently running her palm over me making me feel precious. I looked up to take in her robin's-egg-blue eyes and curly hair but when I looked up, no one was there. I heard a noise across the room and a toy wooden monkey fell from the dresser near the door.

"Mr. Christopher?"

I looked around but I was too afraid to get up.

"Mr. Christopher?"

I sat waiting for what? A response? I touched my hair but everything was normal.

"Is there anyone there?"

"Hello, my baby." My mommy's voice flowed over me like molasses before her smiling eyes found me.

"You're late." I meant to say that I loved her.

"I met some new people and decided to eat with them. How was your night?"

"Terrible. I did my chores and I've been just sitting here waiting for you." The exaggeration stuck in my stomach on its way from my bowels and out of my mouth.

"Well, I'm home now. What do you need?"

"I needed you to be home."

The skin between her eyes creased. I'd gone too far and her sympathy was fast receding. She took a deep breath then reached out and stroked my hair from my face. It was the same as before when she wasn't here except for the warmth. How could I have forgotten the warmth? She stood up. "Time for bed."

I wanted her to follow me to my room and tuck me in but she kissed my face, rubbed the lipstick on my cheek with her thumb and walked out after putting the wooden monkey back on the shelf.

*　　*　　*

Tina was waiting at the lunch table when I put my tray down. Ozepher sat in her usual spot and smiled meekly when I joined them. A girl with long dark-blonde hair sucked on a box of milk next to Tina.

"Hey Ariel, this here's Jillian. Jillian, this is that girl I was saying about. We've been talking about you behind your back. I was trying to explain your house to her. I don't know if I remembered everyone though. Probably not but she gets the gist. She lives not far from you and has two older sisters, right Jillian?"

"Yeah."

Ozepher chewed small forkfuls of cubed vegetables, taking us in.

"Did you guys hear about Boo Walker? Mr. Brant and him got in a big, big fight. I heard it was pretty close to a fist fight."

I looked at Tina blankly. "Who's Boo Walker?"

"Boo Walker. Black guy. You can't miss him. He's sitting right over there. The one in the black satin jacket with red and white stripes. The one getting up right now."

I looked to the table where I knew the blacks sat. It was large and round with only ten or so people around it. A lanky boy, wearing a black satin jacket and tight blue jeans, was getting up from his chair. His hair was a thick afro that stood at least four inches from his head. Mr. Brant, the vice principal, watched him stand and flashed him a disapproving look.

"What?" The voice boomed from the dark mouth.

"Are you done eating, Mr. Walker?"

The hair on my arms stood on end.

"Yeah, I'm done. Is there a problem?" He was standing defiantly now, his chest pushed out and his nose high.

Mr. Brant approached him and pushed his suited chest against the satin of Boo's jacket. No one was stopping them. Mr. Brant whispered something into Boo's ear and Boo's face changed. I felt the rage pushing up inside them both as their chests continued to exert against each other. We couldn't hear what Mr. Brant was taunting Boo with, but it was working. Boo's feet twitched and his hands clenched.

"Do it, boy. Hit me." Mr. Brant voice was still low but all of the cafeteria sounds had died away as we all strained to hear every syllable. "Do it, boy."

I looked at Ozepher who looked away, quietly pushing her food around her plate. It was wrong to call him "boy" that way and parts of the room could feel that. My eyes ran over the bodies frozen into their places. Almost all white faces. Farmer's children. The dark-skinned faces were mostly at that one table and they were covered with fear and rage. I felt rage too.

"Hit me, boy, I dare you. Go on, boy. What are you waiting for? DO IT, BOY!"

The whole room jolted when Mr. Brant pushed Boo into a wall, smacking his head into the pastel-painted cinder blocks. Boo looked as shocked as we felt. He pushed himself from the wall and Mr. Brant's fist came pounding into him. "Come on, boy. Hit me!" White fists flashed again and Boo's body flew back into the wall. Some of his friends at the table were half out of their chairs but no one moved to his side. No one stopped Mr. Brant when he pulled Boo from the wall by his shoulders. No one said a word while he shook him and screamed into his face with spit spraying from his lips. "You tough now, boy? You tough now?" No one followed them when Mr. Brant bent Boo's arm behind his back and forced him out of the cafeteria.

The room was silent for several minutes after they had gone. Then a dull whisper grew into a cacophony of exclamations. "Did you see that shit?" "He should of clocked him." "I'd have taken him out." "Nigger had it coming." "I heard they had a fight earlier." "Brant is a pig." "Boo's a sucker." "That's what he gets for sassing all the time." "Why are people always fighting in this school?" "That's right, he's a boy. I'll tell him to his face." "Them blacks are always starting shit." "Fucking bussing." "It's our school." "Brant is going to get in trouble some day." "This place sucks."

Ozepher quietly placed her paper napkin on top of her tray and carried it to the trash while exiting the cafeteria.

I wasn't hungry anymore. "Tina, are you finished? Let's go."

"And miss all this? This is primo gossip."

"Jillian, do you want to go?"

"Naw, I'll stay."

Tina looked happy. "Come on, Ariel. Stay. This is cool. Everyone's going to ask what we saw. I don't want to be left out."

"Okay, I'll see you guys later." I stepped into the hallway and was relieved when the door closed behind me, shutting off the noises. Boo was in the front office waiting on a vinyl couch. He was looking at his hands. I felt a long overdue tear wander down my face.

Tina was right. The rumor spread quickly and those of us who had borne witness were of immediate interest to those who hadn't. One girl kept complaining that she had gone to the bathroom and had missed the whole thing. People wanted to know who started it, a blow by blow, how it ended. I listened to the variations on the theme. Boo started it by sassing Mr. Brant earlier in the day. Mr. Brant roughed him up a little but Boo had it coming and maybe this would keep "them" all in line.

I replayed it over and over in my head but I couldn't make my replays match their story. Sammi rode home on someone else's bus and Hap and Crane and Alice and Tuffy traded stories of what they had heard.

Mommy was home and I ran and hugged her until tears streamed down and made blotches on my dingy, pink T-shirt.

"What, my angel? What's the matter, baby?"

"I don't want to go to that school anymore, Mommy. Don't make me go there."

"What happened, honey? Did someone make fun of you? Was someone mean to you?"

"Mommy, it's not safe there."

"Ariel, quit being dramatic. Tell me what happened."

"The vice principal beat up a kid for no reason."

"Beat up?"

"Punched him and threw him into a wall and stuff. And Boo didn't do anything back."

Mommy pushed her hair from her forehead. "Well, I don't think things like this happen for no reason and I don't think your principal goes around just hitting people."

"Mommy, I watched the whole thing. He just hit him for no reason. He kept calling him 'boy' and daring him to hit him."

"Boy?"

"Mommy, I don't want to go there again. What if he decides he doesn't like me. No one tried to stop him."

"He's not going to hit you, Ariel."

"Mommy, please. It's an awful school."

"Honey, there isn't another school. Do you know how far away everything is? Now I'm sorry that there was a fight at your school but you need to just stay away from all of that and go to that school."

"But, Mommy."

"Say, 'Yes, Mama.'"

'Fine!" I ran through the playroom, through the closet, through Rayne's room, and up to my room. I threw my fists into my pillow and kicked at the floor until I felt exhausted and ridiculous. Then I turned on my lamp-on-a-clamp and read about Lipizzaners and Arabians prancing around fields.

I pictured myself a horse with a long mane and tail. The wind turned them to streamers as I galloped through a field of Queen Anne's lace. I pictured a rainbow filling the sky and pretty blue birds flying along with me. I pictured a pony, a small foal, running beside me, looking up to me with loving, round eyes, a face full of trust. I slowed and whinnied at my baby and nudged it with my nose. I nibbled at her mane, laced with lovely pink ribbons. We nuzzled each other then she followed me while we ran parallel with the rainbow.

*   *   *

Merlin and Isabelle were great at doing Halloween. They had the house covered in string webs and orange and black construction-paper spiders of orange and black that we kids had cut out. Sammi, Rayne, Montgomery and I picked all of the remaining pumpkins from the now sparse garden, leaving the raccoon bitten ones behind, and brought them all to the flagstone porch. Some were bigger than basketballs and just as orange, but most were smaller, bowling balls that forgot to take their vitamins. There were over a dozen.

Isabelle brought knives out and big cooking spoons. Mommy gathered black Magic Markers. We sat Indian style or on our knees, and drew faces. Merlin went straight to carving, scooping the guts from the sun-colored orb and plopping them in a large metal mixing bowl. Mommy drew a scary face with triangle eyes and plunged a knife into the shell. The insides were cool and wet between my fingers scooping out pulp. There was something vaguely sexual about it that I couldn't wrap my brain around and decided to push aside. Montgomery put his fingers to his tongue and recoiled at the taste.

Anne padded across the flagstone in bare feet. Her jagged-hemmed skirt dragged the ground. She sat close to me and Sammi after selecting a medium pumpkin and a shiny serrated knife. We joked and pointed at each other's handiwork while Anne worked away silently. Isabelle helped Rayne so she wouldn't cut herself. We put the finished pumpkins along the front porch and the sides of the driveway. We put one in the center of the dining table and surrounded it with dry leaves, red and yellow. Anne continued to work silently on hers.

Crane and Hap had explained the routine for the neighborhood; no costumes for us grown-up kids. Trick-or-treating was strictly in Windriver Estates, so Rayne and Montgomery could get a ride up there if they wanted to get candy. We could meet up with the Patapsco-Road kids, if we wanted, for prowling.

Anne finished her pumpkin as the sun was going down. We all marveled at the face, frightening and magical, full of swirls and arches and fiery spikes. She left her knife on the flagstone and carried the head to her room.

"Anne?" Isabelle picked up the knife and followed her. "We could put that in the center of the table so everyone could share it."

"It's mine."

I sputtered in adulation. "It's beautiful, Anne. Wow."

Isabelle hesitated in the archway of Anne's door. "Don't you want to display it where everyone can see it?"

"No."

"Suit yourself."

Anne's door closed and she was lost to us again. Merlin and Mommy were frying pumpkin guts and seeds in pans of butter and salt when Herbert finally got home from work to join the festivities. Mommy wiped her hands on a shabby dish towel. "Oh no, Herbert, we forgot to save you a pumpkin. Ariel, go run to the garden and see if there are any more."

"Mommy, it's dark out there."

"That's okay, I don't need to do a pumpkin." Herbert shifted his coat to his other arm and sneezed. "I'm going to turn in early. Long day. Long day."

He trudged to the staircase and we heard his heavy feet plodding upward, fading into the front of the house. Criss-crossing past it, a quiet knock bounced gently down the long hallway and into the kitchen to mingle with the sizzling and popping of frying seeds. Mommy and I looked to each other for an answer. It was the first time anyone had ever knocked at our front door and we had forgotten the appropriate response.

Finally, Merlin saluted us. "I'll get it."

"I got it. You guys cook." Isabelle trotted down to the door which was already knocking again. She didn't have to unlock it, we never had figured how to get that door to latch. We heard the chirping of children's voices and the booming of an adult. I peeked to see the costumes of little goblins and found Jay, Kay, Elle, and Em dressed as three little witches and a vampire. Their father was in a windbreaker and smiled amiably at Isabelle. It was the first time any of us had seen him. "You won't get many trick-or-treaters around here. Seems like you got enough under your own roof."

"Yeah, we have a few."

"Yup, I'm taking the kids up to Windriver. That's the best place. The houses are closer. They got street lamps too. That's the place to go."

"Thanks for the tip. Maybe we'll do that."

"Yup, I'm loadin' up the car in about a minute. We just thought we'd come by since you guys are right next door. Last year we skipped it. Old couple. No kids. You guys got a lot of kids here. That's for sure. Yup. Seems like there's a lot of people here. You guys all related?"

"You better get a move on if you want to hit all of those houses before it gets too late, right kids?"

Four brunette heads shook up and down and four small voices rang out in unison. "Right."

"Okay, well goodnight. It was good to finally meet you. Have fun trick-or-treating. Goodnight." And with that, she closed the door. Merlin placed a hot pad on the kitchen table and sat a frying pan full of toasted, buttery pumpkin meat on top.

"Anne?" His voice blew down the hall and Isabelle walked through it toward us. "Soups on. Come and get it."

To my surprise, Anne opened her door and emerged to share with us. Silently, she picked up a salt shaker and scattered its contents into the pan then grabbed a fork from the pile on the table and tore pieces off and ate them. Sammi and I sat down next to her. We pulled pieces out of frying pans and blew on them before devouring them. Salty, stringy, buttery pulp warmed my tongue.

Anne put her fork in the sink. "I'm going out."

Isabelle snapped her head up. Her mouth was still full. "Where?"

"Mom, I already told you I was going out with friends tonight. We're just going to drive around."

"I want you home by eleven. Who's the friend?"

"Eleven? Get real. How am I supposed to get them to drop me off then?"

"Figure it out, Anne."

She left the room and Isabelle moved to the sink full of dishes. "Am I crazy? Eleven isn't unreasonable for a fourteen-year-old, is it?"

We kids knew she wasn't asking us. Merlin put his hand on her shoulder and kissed her cheek. "You're not crazy. A little kooky maybe, but not crazy."

"She's just asserting herself." Mommy brought the forks to the sink. "All perfectly normal."

Sammi tugged at my sleeve. "Let's go."

We threw on jackets and yelled goodbye walking out the side door. A voice tried to catch up with us. "In by nine, guys."

We took Rayne and Montgomery with us. Screw Windriver Estates. Alice, Crane, Hap, and Tuffy were coming down the hill as we were climbing up it. We met near the front of the neighbor's house that none of us knew. No kids, no dogs, no horses. No street lamps. The twilight-zone house. Tuffy lit up a cigarette and offered us one.

"We've got soap." Crane pulled a bar from his pocket. "We were thinking, you know, a couple of cars and stuff."

Montgomery shifted in his shoes. "We could get in trouble."

For once, I agreed with him. "What's the point?"

Crane's eyebrows lifted. "It's Halloween. What are we supposed to do?"

Rayne blew smoke out. "Get candy."

Alice smacked Sammi's arm with familiarity. "We don't get candy out here. Too much room between the houses. You have to go to Windriver for that and that's just for little kids."

Sammi stomped out the cigarette and looked up. "Cool, let's go."

What? Why were we doing this? Who were we going to do it to? How bad would it look if I said I had a stomach ache and had to go home?

Tuffy smiled devilishly. "We were planning to start here. These people never come out."

My voice sounded foreign to me, high and tight. "So why bother them?"

"Oh brother." Crane handed Sammi the bar of soap and Hap pulled out a half-roll of toilet paper. Crane stretched his long arm out toward the other side of the street and pointed. "The mailbox first."

Rayne wrapped toilet paper around her hand a few times, tore it from the roll, then draped pieces over the latch of the box and the red flag. Crane wrote illegible expletives on one side of the box and Sammi wrote "trick-or-tr" then ran out of room on her side. We moved as quietly as eight kids can down a gravel road in the dark and left bits of toilet paper on their fence, stopping occasionally to write with soap on a slat. We crept closer and closer to their home, shushing each other every few footfalls and giggling with mischief all the way. Alice neared the front and waved us down, crouching to approach their porch. On all fours, I moved tepidly in the back of the pack.

We missed the first light in the back of the house so we were shocked into statues when the entire house came to life. I sprinted with no regard for the others, trying to outrun my guilt, trying not to think of Montgomery and Rayne behind me. Crane flew past me, rocks flinging up at me as he disappeared into the black ahead of us. A metallic clacking noise mingled with the yelling of an old man. "Git! And stay out!"

We gathered into a circle back on the roadway and flopped over to catch our collective breath and stop the cramping in our middles.

Crane spit then lifted his head without straightening his back. "Damn. Old coot had a shotgun."

"What?" My senses returned all at once.

Tuffy coughed and cackled. "Must of gotten a bonus or something. He didn't have one last year."

What world was this? "A gun?"

"Come on. Let's go down to your next door neighbor's." Crane was off down the hill with us following at varying speeds.

Montgomery reached for my hand and I let him take it. We congregated by the giant mailbox at the foot of our driveway to collect ourselves.

"I bet you could fit her in there." Hap nodded at the mailbox and Rayne.

"I bet you could." Alice seconded the idea.

"Give me a boost." Rayne yanked the latch down and pulled herself into the box while Tuffy lifted her foot with locked hands. Head first was ruled out. A group effort lifted Rayne feet first into the box. She tucked herself into a little ball and was just about in when the headlights hit us. Sammi slammed the box shut and a small "ow' escaped the metal as a pickup truck wound down to a stop. A window rolled down and a teenager with long dirty-blonde hair looked out at us. He chuckled at Hap stamping out a cigarette. "Any of y'all live here?"

"I do." I stepped away from the mailbox and felt Rayne's long tresses sweep against my arm. Startled, I looked back at hair hanging down out of the side of the box. "She does too and so does he."

The boy ignored Montgomery and looked to Sammi. "You two Annie's sisters?"

"Me." Sammi smiled at the boy who lit a cigarette and took a swig from a can of Pabst. "She's up at the house if you want her."

"Cool. Y'all stay out of trouble, ya' hear?"

"Yeah, sure." Sammi flashed another flirtatious smile. "Can we bum a beer off you?"

"You old enough to drink, little girl?"

Rayne pushed the door to the mailbox open and pulled blonde out of the crevice.

"What's that?" The boy pointed with his Pabst can.

Seven heads turned to Rayne then back to the truck where the boy stared slack jawed.

"Can we have a beer or not?" Sammi was determined.

"Sure, take a beer. Catch, little girl."

The truck sped up the driveway as Hap helped Rayne down from the box. The can let out a fizzy, popping sound when Sammi peeled off the pull tab. Tuffy lit a cigarette and we passed both around the circle. The beer was bitter on my tongue and I decided I would only pretend to drink it each time my turn came. Montgomery coughed and said it went down the wrong pipe. Rayne drank it like cola and soon the can was emptied into our various bellies.

Sammi, emboldened, started up the hill back to our neighbor's. "Come on, guys, we still have to get this house."

"I have to pee." Rayne stood her ground. "I have to pee."

The beer must have hit Sammi too because she stopped and came back to Rayne. "We'll go over here, okay?"

"Why don't we go inside?"

I saw my chance to end this madness. "Yeah, let's go inside. It's stupid for all of us to pee out here."

"No, if we go inside, we'll never get out again. Come here, Rayne, we'll go behind these bushes. You guys go away."

The group moved further up the street and we pulled our jeans down. Rayne frowned. "I already went a little. I couldn't hold it that long. It's you guys' fault. You know I can't hold it."

"It's okay, just take your underwear off and put it in your pocket." Sammi was used to this. "Or are they too wet?"

"No, that'll work." She wrestled with shoes and jeans. "You guys wait for me, okay?" She zipped her jeans back on, double-knotted shoes back onto her feet, then stuffed her floral cotton undies into her back pocket and we went back to the road to join the group, having peed, unnoticed, on our own front yard.

We snuck quietly to the bushes around Jay, Kay, Elle, and Em's mailbox. The low-lying shrubs were covered with vines spilling over into their short driveway.

Crane moved as stealthily as his long legs would allow. "Let's get the car. Who's got the other soap?"

"I do." Tuffy moved behind him to the car's rear bumper.

We heard the distant spit of gravel under tires but paid no mind until the headlights reached the road near us. Tuffy and Crane dove under the car and the rest of us fought for foliage in the tangle of vines and bushes. The pickup roared by blasting Lynyrd Skynyrd. We stayed frozen in our places until we were sure that all traffic had stopped. Crane wrote on the driver's window and Tuffy started on the passenger's. Sammi pulled the vines from her legs and threw toilet paper over the mailbox while Montgomery took rocks from the ground and placed them inside.

Sammi nodded. "Yeah, that's good."

Everyone was getting into the act and I felt like a chicken. Part of me wanted to run home before someone came outside and cocked a shotgun at us. Part of me wanted to be the cool one wearing a leather jacket and daring to do something, I don't know, daring. Rayne's undies hung from her back pocket like a kerchief. Something daring and with undies. They waved at me like a taunting flag. Something daring and with undies. I pulled the underwear from her pocket and walked, as frightened as I had ever been, to the front of the car. I crouched down low and came up behind Crane.

"Look out." My whisper didn't carry and I had to nudge him. "Move." I felt urgent. Blood ran through my veins at a hundred miles per hour. I checked the road for traffic, then the house to make sure no one was looking. My knees felt mushy straightening up to reach the top of the antenna. I was hanging the undies on the car antenna when the approaching headlights hit me and turned me to stone. Jay, Kay, Elle, and Em were returning from their candy collecting with their dad at the wheel. The porch light popped on and the wife came to the door.

I pictured myself going to jail for this inexplicable crime. I pictured telling Mommy - worse, making it make sense to Dad. I pictured everyone coming to visit me in my striped outfit and making fun of me for being the only one who got caught. I pictured it being reported on my college applications, my job applications. My life was over. I had vandalized with underwear.

My feet moved without connection to my brain. I blindly followed Sammi over the fence and into our yard, running breathlessly into the back of the pavilion where we collected for a pow wow.

"Holy shit, Ariel. That was so close." Sammi's deep breaths interrupted her staccato speech.

"I thought we were all busted for sure." Tuffy looked stricken. I thought of her huge black-and-white father in his overalls and animated his photo into a screaming red-faced man.

Hap stared down at his shoes and kicked dirt with one toe onto the top of the other. Crane tapped Hap's arm and motioned with his head. He cleared his throat until Tuffy looked at him. "Time to go, Tuff."

"What?"

Hap looked up. "Time to go. We gotta walk back. Didn't you hear him?"

Tuffy looked mad. "All right, already."

Alice moved from Sammi's side to join the exiting group. "'Night guys. It was fun, huh?"

Sammi shot her a thumbs up. "Cool."

Maybe I had missed something. Had we just had fun and I didn't know it? Maybe that was cool people's fun and I was just too big of a nerd to get it. Maybe I was a sissy, a fraidy-cat.

A breeze, cool and humid on my face, pulled my hair over my shoulder. "We should probably go in."

Sammi looked to the small blonde heads of Rayne and Montgomery. "You want to sleep in the pavilion tonight?"

Rayne waited to see what the majority vote would be. Montgomery saw his chance to stop the fast wheel we'd been spinning on. "It's too cold and we don't have any firewood this week. You have to wait until they cut some more."

I hesitated, waiting for Sammi to show her mood. She looked toward the dark pavilion. "Oh, they didn't do that yet?"

I pounced. "No, Herbert's been working late and it takes two people."

"Yeah, it is pretty cold out here. I guess we should just go back inside." Sammi led us back to the old farmhouse with its glowing pumpkins all around. "Hey, we could tell ghost stories if you guys want to."

Rayne showed her age, rubbing her eyes with balled fists. "Maybe tomorrow."

We walked to the unlocked front door and knocked heartily. No one came. We knocked again and waited. Merlin was laughing, red-faced, when he opened the door a crack to see who was there.

"Trick or treat."

"It's okay." He yelled up the front staircase to someone invisible. "It's our kids." He smiled at us and his eyes seemed funny, distant. He let us in and handed us candies from the bowl by the door then took the bowl with him and ran upstairs. He yelled to the ceiling. "Hey guys, wait 'til you see what I've got."

We passed Anne's empty room heading for ours. Montgomery asked if any of us wanted to watch TV and watched it alone when we all said no. Sammi helped Rayne into her pajamas and tucked her into bed then joined me in our loft. "Anne said she was going to see 'The Exorcist.'"

"That devil movie?"

"Yeah."

I thought of Anne's room far below all of ours. "Won't she be scared to sleep all by herself?"

"She said she wouldn't."

"I would."

We fell into sleep talking in broken, sluggish sentences. I dreamed of being in a car. Mommy and Daddy were fighting and Daddy kept going faster and faster to scare her. Montgomery and I sat in the back, checking our safety belts and staring at the road flying up at us. The creaking of the stairs blended into the road noises in my dream so I awoke with the shock of Anne's voice.

"Are you guys awake?" Sammi did not stir. Anne sat on the edge of her mattress. "You awake?"

My eyes focused on her shadow-body in the dark. "I am."

"What'd you guys do tonight?"

I was too sleepy and too thrilled about having a private late-night conversation with Anne to find the question odd. "We went out and soaped houses and stuff. We shared a beer. What did you do?" My brain slowly came back to real life.

"I saw a movie, 'The Exorcist.' Do you know the story?"

Sammi sat upright with a jerk. "What?"

"Anne went to that movie. Do you want to hear the story?"

Sammi's face was soft, drowsy. "Uh huh."

Anne rambled through a story whose high points were vomiting green stuff, a flying bed, and a spinning head. She imitated the devil's voice and described the girl's deteriorating physical appearance.

My head filled with pictures. "Aren't you scared you'll have nightmares?"

"Nah. I've seen scary movies before." She started down the stairs. "The steps in the movie were narrow like these. Goodnight guys, sweet dreams."

Sammi and I found each other's silhouettes through the blackness. The gory pictures danced in my head like a mobile. "Are you scared?"

Her head betrayed a confessional bit of a nod. "No, but I'm glad we didn't go see it, aren't you?"

"Definitely."

We snuggled back down under our covers and drifted into an uneasy sleep when the creak of the stairs brought us back to consciousness again. I didn't breath, waiting to see the face of our enemy. The moon lit Anne's hair glowy-blue around her. "You guys mind if I sleep up here?"

Sammi didn't speak. She lifted the corner of her bedding inviting Anne to share her single mattress. I closed my eyes and the nightmares dancing across the inside of my eyelids were replaced with the comfort of having Anne in the room and of knowing that she, too, was scared.

Chapter Nine

The trees looked like naked scarecrows, stark and craggy. Leaves covered the browning lawn in a quilt of burgundy and gold. Tommy, Cory and Eddy worked alongside the rest of us raking the immense yard. One thing I was learning about communal living was that everyone had different traditions that they clung to especially hard in this new environment. We were all astonished whenever we found people didn't do things "the right way."

I remembered Dad helping me make the pile in our old back yard. He'd shape it funny or make it really tall so that it was more fun to jump into. Montgomery would run haltingly then jump low into the pile. Mommy would fall backwards like the Nestea plunge commercial. Sometimes she would pretend to make a snow angel with the leaves. Dad and I would rake the pile in tighter again then he would jump in and roll around. I would run and fly into the dry bed face first. The smell of soft mildew and dry death encircled me. Tiny pops and crackles filled my ears and the sun came through a filter of sharp angles and minute cracks. I would lie still a moment and just enjoy the natural blanket then start to borough through, letting the edges scratch at me until I fell out onto the brittle, browning grass. Then Dad and I would gather up the leaves into two metal trash cans, pushing them down hard to pack them in, and set the cans on the side deck next to the pottery kiln. The next day, Mommy and Daddy would have a racu party and invite a dozen grown-ups from the classes Dad gave in the basement and they would dip and paint their pottery. They'd fire some in the regular kiln but the main attraction was the small racu kiln Dad built into the hillside. They baked the pottery then pulled it from the kiln with long, metal tongs. A tipsy friend would hold the lid of the trash can while the piece was thrown inside and the leaves burst into flames from the heat. Then aluminum would crash against itself as the lid was slammed down to extinguish the flames. The tongs would search out the lip of the pot or bowl or vase, now scarred with the veins and blades of leaves. A bucket of water sat next to the trash can and the tongs placed the still-searing piece down into it. Steam rose from the popping and bubbling of hot meeting cool and the piece was further scarred with blisters and their remains. Everyone drank wine from clear plastic cups and the odd and beautiful pots and vases lined up along the deck for everyone to admire.

Herbert said jumping in leaves was stupid and "counter-productive." We all giggled until we realized he was serious. There had been a protracted discussion of the merits of completing the job quickly and efficiently versus the merits of just goofing off and eventually finishing. Herbert decided that we should divide the yard and Tommy raked in rows and scooped every leaf into the dark plastic bags until their patch was pristine. We squealed and laughed at moppy hair full of debris and funny body positions assumed in the launch toward our large pile. Herbert pretended not to look and dutifully removed the leaves that drifted on breezes from our antics to his clarity. Isabelle was crowned "Queen of the Fall" when her hair held a nest of leaves. Merlin was named the king to honor his creative jumps. The sun set and the air chilled and we finished up and returned to the house for a family dinner with three extra chairs pulled to the table for the Hobart kids. Mommy served spaghetti made with chicken and a salad on the side and we fell asleep early with full bellies.

The morning was sunny and I missed the pool. Sammi was curled into a ball facing the wall. Her ribs moved only slightly with her gentle breathing.

"Sammi." She didn't twitch. "Sammi, are you awake?" I waited to see if she had heard me then raised my voice a bit. "Hey Sammi, are you awake?" Her ribs continued expanding and contracting rhythmically. "Shoot." I pulled on some socks and walked quietly through Rayne's room, where Eddy slept in Rayne's spare bunk, and into the playroom. Cory was in Montgomery's room. Tommy was still asleep on the trundle bed when I padded in. I stood quietly near his head and tried to memorize his face, tracing the bend of his nose in my mind, the arch of his eyes, the hills and valleys of his lips. He was the most beautiful boy I'd ever seen. I was too mesmerized to move when he first came to life, too fascinated by his motion. He jumped at the sight of me and my heart crashed onto my feet.

"Is it morning?" His eyes shielded themselves from the morning sun by blinking and forming little slits.

"Hi."

"Ariel?"

"Good morning."

He pulled himself up and we smiled at each other. I wanted to marry him. I wanted to curl up next to him and feel safe.

Sammi appeared in the closet door that led from Rayne's room. "Hi guys. What's up?"

"The sky." It was our normal exchange. Sometimes I'd say, "Prices," or "My height," then we'd smile somewhat secretly.

"You guys want to walk to town?"

We threw on sneakers and jeans and traded our sleep shirts for sweaters and jackets. We didn't ask the others to come and hurried our exit to avoid turning them away. The grass was still crunchy from the last of the night frost and I could feel the air putting pink on my cheeks. Walking in the shade, we dug our hands down into our pockets, pushed through the thinning bushes and stepped down onto Patapsco Road. It was early still but one neighbor was in the yard working on some pipes and another was tuning up a truck. Only the dogs were out at Hap's and Alice was nowhere in sight. Tuffy was in her front yard winding some rope when we passed her house. We waved.

"Hey, wait a minute." She dropped the rope and skipped down to the road. "Where are you going? You going to town?"

I nodded.

"I don't think anything's open yet."

Sammi kicked a fence post. "I didn't even think about that. Shoot."

I looked up the hill and saw Tuffy's father checking us out from the side of the house. He made me nervous and I turned away as the hair rose on my arms. "When does it all open?"

"Nine, I think. You want to go riding, you guys? We could ride for half an hour if you want."

Tommy wasn't much of a rider, even more unsure than I was, so he looked hesitant. Sammi, on the other hand, jumped at the chance to ride a full-sized horse and without taking turns. Tuffy's Dad was running wire through a hole in their fence when we passed him. "You finish that rope, girl?"

Tuffy did not look at him over her shoulder. "It's done. I'll finish the rest of the stuff later."

"Don't you screw around too long. This house don't run itself, you know."

"I know. We're just going for a little ride. Don't sweat it, Pa." She looked to Tommy and rolled her eyes for him. "Men."

We headed into the field and collected some of the horses. I chose the same one I had last time and threw a bridle over his head. I led him to a rock and used it to climb up to his back. Sammi gave Tommy a leg up then she and Tuffy mounted their horses expertly. The animals knew the path along the river without guidance and we meandered along against the flow.

Tuffy pulled a cigarette from her training bra and lit it. "I hate weekends."

I walked my horse up closer to hers. "What?"

"Weekends. Too much work."

Tommy chuckled. "We had to do leaves yesterday."

"Exactly. Plus I have to spend the whole time at home. Gets me sick of my dad."

The horse heated my thighs and I placed my hands on his neck to warm them. "What about your mom?"

"Dead."

My eyes went wide.

Sammi grabbed at an overhead branch. "What's your mom do?"

"She's dead, I said she's dead."

"What do you mean? I mean, why?"

"She got sick and died when I was little."

I rewound the mental images of her home with its dirty dishes and piles of magazines. "Wow."

Tuffy remained cool. "It's shallow here. You want to cross?"

We so rarely crossed the river. The railroad tracks there were active and nothing else but trees could be seen. No incentive.

Tommy shifted on his horse's back. "Nah. We shouldn't go too far. Your dad seemed like he was going to want you back soon."

"Yeah, you know how men are." Her voice seemed flirtatious and a twinge of jealousy crept up inside me.

Sammi looked puzzled. "How are men?"

"Oh, you know. Don't they, Tommy?"

I looked to Tommy. Bless him, he looked as bewildered as the rest of us.

"You know, always wanting to know where you are, where you're going, telling you what to wear and stuff. Crane likes me to wear no underwear."

My blood raced. "What?"

"You know, as a turn on or whatever. What do you like, Tommy?"

My face went red and my heart moved so quickly, I thought it would take flight. "Why does Crane care if you have on undies?"

"Oh, come on, Ariel. Sammi, tell her."

"Tell her?"

"God, you guys are either faking or you're really behind. Doing it. I did it with Crane."

I felt my head shaking, betraying my disapproval and dismay. "Isn't he your cousin?"

"Hap too."

Sammi stopped her horse. "You mean Hap is your cousin too or you did it with Hap too?"

"Both."

Tommy laughed nervously. "You're making this all up."

"No, I'm not. Have you ever done it, Tommy?"

"Me?"

We sat silently atop horses waiting for him to speak. "I'm not saying."

I flashed him as close as I could come to a reassuring smile. Tuffy turned her horse back up the path. "Oh brother."

We followed her back to the field behind her house with an awkward awe. She was younger than any of us. Tommy and I still lived by the "no tongues" rule and were quite happy with that.

The horses weren't sweating so we stripped off their bridles and thanked Tuffy with as few words as possible. Tuffy's dad eyed us receding down the drive and heading quietly to town.

*   *   *

Sammi was brushing Rayne's hair for school and hit my leg with the brush when I passed. "Can you pick another outfit? She doesn't like the one I picked."

Rayne's head yanked back then reset. "It's for a little kid. Pick another one, Ariel."

Sammi dragged the brush straight down the top of Rayne's head to find the part. I pulled a sweater from a low shelf and searched for a matching skirt. Rayne peeked at me through her hair. "I want to wear jeans like you guys."

"Where are they?"

Sammi removed a barrette from her mouth to speak. "They're all dirty. They're in the hamper, Rayne. Come on, I'm going to miss the bus. Just put that on."

"Up your nose with a rubber hose."

"Forget it." Sammi slammed the brush down on the mattress and walked out. "Come on, Ariel. She can dress herself."

"No, Sammi. Come back."

I was torn but Sammi was right, we would miss the bus. We grabbed the Hefty bags by the door and dragged them down the hill to the street then ran down to the barn to brush and feed Princess and Taffy. Pepper honked the horn and we ran to meet her at the bus stop. Pillows ran after us and sang a meow as we climbed into the open yellow door. Sammi plopped down hard on the vinyl seat and stared into the metal back of the chair in front of her. "I'm sick of this."

"School?"

"No. I mean, yeah, but no. I'm sick of having to do all the work."

"Yeah."

"The chores are bad enough and the ponies and our rooms, but now I have to do our laundry and dress Rayne and we have to clean that new bathroom. Do you have to do laundry?"

"Mommy does it." I was immediately sorry I had spoken.

"See? That's what I mean. It seems like I'm doing all my mom's work."

"Well, maybe it's because she has to work now."

"Your mom's starting to work."

"But not every day."

"She just wants me to do everything. It's not fair."

"Maybe you should talk to her. Maybe Anne can help with stuff." I wished I had a solution. I needed her to be okay.

"Never mind."

"I can help with the laundry." Feeling her shut me out, my heart throbbed. "And I can help with Rayne more."

"Forget it, just forget it."

"Sammi, I..."

"You don't understand."

I had lost her. We sat in silence. My chest ached and my stomach churned with acid. She sat away from me now, her head looking out the window and her back forming a wall at me. She breathed onto the window and formed a circle of fog on the pane. Her finger traced the name of the most beautiful boy in school, Matt. She breathed again and wrote her name below his. She stared for a time longer then faced me with courage and sorrow in her eyes. "Matt's mom said he shouldn't talk to me anymore."

"What? Why?"

"She says he shouldn't hang out with a girl whose parents are divorced." Her huge, round brown eyes welled.

"Really?" It finally came home to me why we instinctively whispered about our parents.

"She says that I'd be a bad influence."

"Bad influence?"

"Something like that. Broken homes. I don't know."

"What are you talking about? You didn't do anything bad, did you?"

Sammi got very quiet and shook her head no. I looked down into my hands and then over to Sammi's. Her skin was dry and irritated by eczema. She lifted the back of her hand to her nose and wiped. "I just asked if he wanted to come over some time and ride Princess or something. He said he had to ask his mom." She looked away again. I wanted to stop the bus and give us a day off. I wanted to hold her hand and pat it like Mommy would. She spoke into the glass creating a new ring of fog that brought their names back to life. "I never get to... Why can't we be like normal people?"

"They're really gone, aren't they?" My jaw quivered involuntarily.

"What?"

"Not what, who."

"Oh brother, then who?"

"Our dads."

"I guess so."

My jaw shook and shook. "Is your dad going to marry her?"

"I don't know."

"Is your mom going to marry Merlin?"

"I don't know." She cracked her knuckles. "What about your dad?"

"I don't know. But, sometimes I think maybe so."

"Yeah."

We turned our heads to the front of the bus and stared as the first snow flew into the windshield and bounced off either side.

186

* * *

Mommy had her clock radio on while she readied herself for some seminar. The morning was grey and snow had been falling for hours now, off and on. "I just don't know, even with snow tires. It doesn't look like driving weather to me. Maybe I'll slap two boards on and ski there."

"That bus isn't very safe, Mommy, maybe I should stay home today."

"If I have to go, you have to go."

"So, don't go."

"Oh darlin'." She flashed me a movie-star smile and splashed White Shoulders onto her wrists then dabbed them behind her ears. Even in the grey of winter, she radiated like the sun from her southern home.

"Shouldn't we call the school or something to make sure?"

"Honey, they'll announce it if you don't have school. Why don't you brush your hair and finish getting ready so you don't miss the bus when it comes."

Isabelle's voice came alone down the hallway and jerked Mommy's head up into the air. "Madeleine? Are you sending them to school?"

"Aren't you?"

Their voices crossed each other in the hall. "Mad? What do you think?"

"I'm waiting for the radio. It still says one hour late for P.G. County so I'm getting them ready but I have to go soon."

"Madeleine? We live in Howard County now."

"I told you, Mommy."

"Shoot."

Isabelle came into the room with a robe gathered around her, auburn, tangled waves obscuring doe-like eyes. "So, what does it say for Howard?"

"We'll have to wait again."

Isabelle left with her voice trailing behind her. "Tell me when you find out."

"If we don't have to go, can we go sledding or something?"

"Why don't you go for a winter hike? If you get out of school, I mean." She clasped a bracelet on her wrist and slid two clip-ons over her earlobes. She reached instinctively to where her Aqua Net always sat and sprayed a cloud of acrylic around her hair.

The snow was falling in big, fat, floppy flakes now. We knew that meant it wouldn't last as long but it usually scared even the most fearless drivers off of the road.

The man started the announcements again. It didn't matter what county we moved to, it always seemed to be the last one announced. "Prince George's County, two hours late..."

Oh, please don't do that to us. Please not the one hour late then the two hours late then the day off. Either the day off or forget about it.

"Carol County, closed. Howard County, closed."

"Yeah!" I clapped my hands before I even knew I had done it. Mommy smiled then looked out the windows at the pristine white front lawn.

"Now can I go play?"

"Have fun, honey."

"Are you going to go? You shouldn't drive in this weather."

"Well, we'll see honey."

"Call them and tell them the road is closed. It practically is, Mommy. Stay home."

"Lordy, it's been a long time since you asked me to stay home with you."

"Not with me, I'm going outside to play, remember?" Her face dropped a little and I felt a wave of guilt run up through me. "I don't want you to drive, Mommy. Stay home and play with us. Call them." I turned and ran out of the room.

Sammi was brushing Rayne's hair into a ponytail. Montgomery was watching *Mr. Magoo* on TV. They jumped at my voice punching through the air. "Guess what, guys? No school!"

We became a quickly moving machine, stripping our clothing and dressing again, layering tights and long johns and socks and turtlenecks and sweaters and jeans and mittens and scarves and boots and knit hats. Sammi and I helped Rayne with hers and I even volunteered to help Montgomery get the zipper going on his jacket. We ran out of the house and toward the pavilion to find sleds. Sweat collected inside my layers as we dug through piles of family collectibles. Ours appeared first and further disheveling brought the Busch's to light. Only two sleds, stacked and dusty, for the four of us. I tried pulling ours by its licorice-like red rope but the powdery blanket gave way too quickly and the sled kept sinking into slight drifts. We sent Rayne inside for a bar of soap. I pulled a mitten off and rubbed Zest along the runners, coating them slick. Montgomery ran his mitten along the other removing dust and rust. We rubbed until the bar was in shreds then dropped the sleds on the snow to be dragged by their red ropes but nothing helped. The sleds would not move.

Back in Laurel, we would close Mayfair Drive at the top and bottom and sled down the well-packed snow, lightning quick. Here, the road was full of blind spots, as Montgomery well knew, and the snow had not been packed by the passing of fathers making their way to their government posts. Mommy came out in slacks and a sweater and called to us. "I'm making a bowl of snow ice cream. Who wants to help?"

Excitement shook vibrato into Rayne's voice. "I will."

We all would, it was the only time Mommy would offer ice cream for breakfast. We scooped the snow into large metal mixing bowls. Mommy helped us measure out milk, sugar, vanilla extract and coloring. Montgomery made his brown and I couldn't stifle a "gross." Rayne used almond extract and colored hers pink. We ate from each other's bowls and added spoons of improvements. For a minute, everything felt exactly as it had always been. Everything felt traditional and familiar.

Sammi and I went down to check on Princess and Taffy. Princess was miserable in her stall. Her hair had grown thick over the last few months making her look fatter. She was itching to run in the virgin snow. I threw the door open and she jumped off of the concrete landing into the white velvet. She buried her nose in it then threw her head back creating a spray in the air. Sammi and I followed her lead. We had finally found a playful use for this dry, powdery, fluffy snow that would not stick or pack. We made a storm with hand scoops of it thrown up high. Princess snorted foggy breath out and reared onto her hind legs, kicking more snow into our personal blizzard. Sammi continued, unfazed. I always envied her ease around Princess, around all horses. I felt my legs carry me involuntarily away from Princess and her flailing hooves. I flinched at her every move. The moment was gone for me, I would be too busy staying safe to romp with a playful pony in a self-made snow storm. "Let's go for a walk."

Sammi was throwing snow into Princess' face and laughing at her large tongue swiping at errant flakes. "Now?"

"Yeah, we'll get too cold if we wait."

She looked doubtful but neither of us liked the cold much so I let Taffy out and Sammi smacked her mittens together as we headed for the road. Princess continued to root through the snow and blow it into the air. I finally got it, she was looking for grass, not playing. I didn't tell Sammi.

"Let's go this way." I pointed left, away from town. "We've never walked this way, really." So, we went the direction of Windriver Estates on the road of unblemished snow and knee-high drifts. A field of corn stalks jutted up through the white like blonde beard stubble and a fence post stood empty with just the hooks left where a sign would have hung. "Do you see a 'No Trespass?'"

Sammi scanned the ground and the nearby trees. "No, do you?"

"No."

Sammi smiled all sly-like. "Let's go."

"It must belong to someone though, don't you think?"

"So what? It's just a corn field, it's not someone's yard or anything."

I took one last look for a red and white sign telling us to keep out but there was nothing, nothing but a field that looked like it needed a shave. "Okay."

We walked up the slight ridge and stumbled through unseen obstacles. Most of the stalks had been broken off below the surface of the snow. Rocks and other debris moved under our feet. Sammi tripped first and dragged me down with her. We pulled ourselves up again and made our way along tentatively.

I pictured myself as a pioneer, as Laura Ingalls. I pictured walking through a huge snowstorm. I had to lean into the wind that pushed against me and forced me back. I was carrying food to my family, bread and dried fruits. I was alone against this storm and they were counting on me to make it through and save them. I walked with my eyes down and watched the stalks passing beneath me like mile markers. I secretly enjoyed the stumbling, the hardship, that would make my victory all the more valuable. I pictured my scarf blowing out behind me like a flag, my long prairie skirt pressed against my legs.

"I'm starting ballet again." Sammi's voice reached into my daydream and pulled me out. She was swatting at pieces of dead plants that stuck up in dark scratchy-looking tufts. "Mom found a place in Columbia."

"Is it the same place you used to go to?"

"No, it's closer to here. The lady was trained in Russia. Pretty cool, huh?"

I fought back envy. "Great." I fought back loneliness, knowing it would mean even more time apart for us. "When do you start?"

"Next week. I'm so excited."

I fell into silence listening only to our breathing and the muffled sound of snow packing beneath the weight of our feet. The field stopped at a split-rail fence and we turned without a word and headed back home. Our footprints and those of an occasional animal were the only markings in the surface. It made me feel important and alone like the guys who walked on the moon.

Merlin and Isabelle were trying to have a snowball fight with Carol and Montgomery. The snow still wouldn't pack and their snow blobs traveled only inches before disintegrating into bits.

We stripped in the laundry house and ran into the kitchen in our long johns. Mommy was boiling water and lining up mugs with strings hanging from some of them. "Well, two snow bunnies. Hot chocolate or chamomile tea?"

"Chocolate." I almost yelled.

"Tea." Sammi was allergic to chocolate. It was the only reason I wouldn't truly want to be her.

"Okay, bunnies, hop on upstairs and get changed and it'll be ready lickety-split."

The house was freezing. It was bad enough during cold days but windy days made it almost unbearable. The grown-ups' half of the house, the newer half, had inadequate heat - but our half was downright freezing. We put on sweaters and jeans and I felt dressed until Sammi pulled dancer's knit leg warmers over her ankles and up her shins. She always knew how to make an outfit uniquely her own.

Herbert was sipping tea in the kitchen when we entered, warming his hands on the mug and breathing in steam through his trimmed beard. Rayne was stirring things for Mommy.

"One tea for you and a hot chocolate for my favorite daughter."

"I'm your only daughter, Mommy."

"Details." She kissed the top of my head and returned to the stove. "Rayne, how about you go sit with your sisters and I'll bring that to you."

Rayne took the last vacant seat and crossed her ankles. Mommy brought her hot chocolate with extra milk to the table and sat it on a hot pad I had made from cloth loops in arts-and-crafts class one summer.

Herbert blew on his tea. "Has anyone heard tomorrow's weather forecast?"

Mommy looked to the ceiling as if searching it for the answer. "Now, I did hear something. Shoot, what was it?" She stirred chocolate into simmering milk. "I think they said snow. Something about a front coming in. Now, wait. Maybe that was last night." She held a pensive look for a moment longer then dropped it abruptly for a smile. "Well they either said snow coming or not. I don't remember which."

Herbert threw out his tea bag and walked away from the noise of snowbound children. I looked at Sammi and we both laughed. Rayne laughed with us and Sammi stopped. "You don't even know what you're laughing at."

"Yes, I do."

"What?"

"You guys, so there."

Mommy went to the kitchen door and pushed it open only a crack to hold back the wind and cold. "Ollie ollie in come free! Get it while it's hot." She closed the door and shuddered against the weather.

Snow days always ended up being longer than they needed to be and we all felt tired rather early. The icy rain was just beginning to fall when we left the grown-ups' warm rooms and put on more clothing to sleep in.

*   *   *

A layer of ice made a Vaseline gloss over everything. I punched my foot through and felt the snow pack tightly beneath my weight - great for snowballs. "Figures."

This time we only got two hours off. Herbert, Isabelle, and Merlin had gone to work and Mommy would be leaving soon. We dragged the garbage bags down to the street then trekked to the barn to feed and brush the ponies. We opened Princess' stall door and watched her move slowly across the icy concrete. Pepper honked for us to come back to the bus stop just as Princess put her first hoof through the sheet of ice. I pictured Princess walking through the field and slicing her ankles to shreds on the sharp edges of broken ice. I grabbed her halter and pulled her backward onto the concrete before she could walk out any further.

"What are you doing?" Sammi's mittened hand reached for Taffy's stall.

Princess yanked at my grip while I pulled her to the stall and yelled for Sammi to shut the door. Pepper honked again and Princess reared in confusion. I jumped back, finally remembering that I was terrified by Princess and her spontaneity. She bucked and kicked and even Sammi screamed in fear. I pulled myself up the slatted wall, climbing it like a ladder. Sammi jumped out and yelled for me to come to her. Princess wheeled around, kicking and rearing. Her hooves pounded the wall next to my legs and Sammi and I both screamed and closed ours eyes for a moment. I reached out for Sammi's hand and crept across the wall toward her then jumped at the stall door before I was truly in range and it was only Sammi's adrenalin-filled tug that wrenched me over the barrier. We sat on the frozen cobblestone flooring until Pepper's last honk brought us to our feet. She was just pulling from the side of the road when we ran into the street screaming after her. She slowed and the flashing red lights alternated on the back of the bus as we sprinted to catch up.

"Didn't think you were going to make it today, kiddos."

We flopped down, our breath struggling to catch up with our recent expenditure. Sammi panted until it became a laugh. It grew and grew until the bus rang with the music of her relief. My shock fell away and my voice became her harmony. We laughed all the way to the end of Patapsco Road, never explaining it to the few kids that boarded the bus.

School was empty, with those who made it to class bundled in layers of mismatched knitwear. We moved through the shortened day with one eye on the windows hoping for an early out. Ms. Sheridan read us poems about winter and snow. The lunch room was quiet and all of the usual cliques were in disarray. Ozepher Wildes and I had the entire table to ourselves. We smiled at each other and enjoyed the lack of judgment in the air. There were no lines for the equipment in metal shop class so I was able to work on my tool box until it was almost finished. No one called me "beanpole" or "Q-tip" or "Green Giant" or "flat as a board" or "skinny" or "daddy long legs" or "nerd" or "brainiac" or "x-ray" or "skeleton" or "bones" or "skyscraper" or "flagpole" or "stick figure" or "carrot top" or "Ariel airhead" or "Ariel venereal" or "deri-Ariel" or "welfare baby" or anything. The day passed quickly and soon I was with Sammi on our way back to our snow covered farm. I tapped her knee and smiled. "You can brush Princess today if you want."

Rayne and Montgomery joined us in the pavilion and we listened to the radio, built an inefficient fire, and roller skated and rode bikes round and round the concrete expanse. Sometimes, I forgot about Dad leaving, forgot about switching schools and leaving the old neighborhood and just roller skated during a snow storm and knew it would be all right.

*　　*　　*

Herbert wasn't there for our family meeting. Montgomery promised to fill him in on the chapters he missed from *James and the Giant Peach*, a favorite book I'd already read twice. After the meeting, I followed Mommy up to her room and watched her undress in front of her bare windows wondering secretly whether my body would ever be as curvy as hers. She was what I thought of when I thought of the word "woman." Mommy pulled her nightgown over her nude torso then stopped to look out the window. She walked closer to the wavy panes and stared. "Honey, go get Merlin, would you?" I walked over to look and Mommy's arm pushed me away. "Go on, honey."

From her door, I screamed into the vastness of the adult wing. "Merlin, Mommy wants you." I waited a minute then screamed again.

"Stop all that yelling and go get him." Mommy stayed at the window.

Merlin's feet padded above us coming down from the attic.

"Merlin, do you see that light down there?"

We all saw it, someone was in the spring house. They moved in and out of the building, their flashlight illuminating the snow around them and patches of the brick walls of the spring house. Merlin picked up the phone and dialed.

"I'd like to report a burglar... 961 Patapsco Road... Well, they're not at the house yet but I can see a car of some sort parked down there and someone's walking around." He rubbed his forehead between his thumb and pointer finger. "They're sending a car but they said the weather will slow them down a bit."

Isabelle joined us. The flashlight continued to dance around as Sammi came into the room along with Carol. Sammi had put Rayne to bed and Montgomery was also sleeping. Anne stayed in her room in ignorance while we waited, in varying degrees of fear, watching someone move around on our property with unknown motives. Finally, a police car pulled up. Its headlights shone on the other car but the distance and fallen snow prevented us from distinguishing its color or type. Two policemen with flashlights approached the stranger. We heard the muffled barking of commands while they stripped the burglar of his flashlight. They pushed the man into their car and pulled up our drive. Merlin ran to the side door. "Stay up here, I'll talk to them."

We all ran to Carol's room overlooking the parking lot. Mommy and Isabelle tried to get Sammi and me to go to the kid's wing but we weren't about to miss this excitement. The cops got out of their car and approached Merlin who danced in the snow in his sock feet. They exchanged a few words then went to the car and pulled the stranger out of the back. A dark man bundled in scarves and a fur-lined hat climbed out of the back looking like a Russian from a scary spy movie. My hand clenched. Who was this intruder, this freakish fur-hatted man?

Herbert.

We laughed for days about Herbert's near-arrest for trespassing and breaking-and-entering. We called him a robber and a burglar and Merlin called him, "A threat to society as we know it."

We laughed until the day Herbert came home early. Mommy said those men who came the day we were in the trees asked why there was a police report with his name on it. She said they didn't think it was funny at all, even when Herbert explained about trying to keep the pipes from freezing and having to get Merlin to identify him. Mommy said they weren't much for humor. It was creeping upward, even the grown-ups were beginning to wear our farm life on their sleeves. Somehow, Anne still escaped.

Anne was falling in love. His name was Kevin and he came over one day and poked his head into the playroom.

"Hey."

We were mesmerized. He was blonde and beautiful and short, just taller than Anne. We called him "King of the Hobbits." Sammi and I couldn't have been more jealous. I pictured him and Anne on their dates. I pictured him putting his arm around her and calling her "Babe." I pictured them walking into a party together, two gorgeous blondes with blue eyes and perfect bodies and faded jeans. He would lean into her and whisper that he loved her and she would let down her walls for him and love him right back. They would kiss heatedly and her shirt would come down on one shoulder. He would kiss her neck and her white flesh would redden. I pictured them getting married and having perfect children and living in an apartment full of Anne's drawings and Kevin's hand-crafted furniture.

Then I pictured Tommy. I pictured us sleeping in the pavilion with our sleeping bags next to each other and his breath rustling my hair. I remembered our first kiss and every kiss since then, his arms encircling me as we toasted marshmallows over the fire in the pavilion, his head resting in my lap when we watched TV. I pictured us, I pictured us, I pictured us.

*   *   *

I started making gifts in November but, this year, I had to make so many more, I was running out of good ideas. Sammi and I both finished our steel tool boxes but neither one of us could give them up after the monumental work we had put into them - cutting, folding, bending, riveting, and sanding metal. They sat side by side on a shelf in the barn. One was filled with brushes, waxy with dandruff, and the hooked pick we used on Princess' hooves. The other was filled with a grain scoop Sammi made in shop and old canvas gloves. For everyone else, we made metal boxes with names imprinted on them and pendants for necklaces. I made hand-drawn cards with poems on the inside and some tree ornaments from acorns, Elmer's glue, glitter and ribbon.

I wanted to buy my mommy something wonderful and expensive like a fur coat or a long sparkly dress with diamond earrings but I had saved so little money. I wished Tommy would give me an I.D. bracelet with his name on it or a ring I could wear on a chain around my neck. I wished we were back at the old house with Dad making us wait at the top of the steps until he got his camera ready. He'd keep saying, "Hold on. One minute," and it would feel like a hundred hours while we held ourselves from rushing down to see what Santa had put beneath the tree. Mommy would tell him to hurry and he would say that he was and then he'd finally yell, "Come on kids, what's taking you so long?" and we'd run down the steps and squeal with delight as the flash from Daddy's camera put blue lights in our eyes. Some things would say they were from Santa and others would say they were from, "Love, Mommy and Daddy." Montgomery would rip his paper and I would carefully open mine at the Scotch tape loops trying to make the moment last forever. It always seemed like he got more than me or better stuff than me but we'd sit and eat miniature Hershey bars from fuzzy red stockings and feel blissfully unaware of how lucky we were.

This year would be a free-for-all with cars coming and going and scattered pieces of families pretending this was better because we got to open presents twice in one day. Dad had us for Thanksgiving so Mommy would get us Christmas Eve and morning and Dad would come later to take us to Sandy's.

I pictured my own little place with my own tree and Tommy and I would hang ornaments and drink warm cider by the fire and give candy to the carolers who sang on our snowy front stoop. We would kiss under the mistletoe and tell each other, "You were the best present this year." He would give me a gold necklace with a heart pendant and I would give him a watch or some other grown-up present.

I closed the Elmer's, walked into the bathroom, sat down and enjoyed the small relief. Then the shower, of its own accord, rained water then stopped. I looked up at the dripping shower head and wondered if it was some trick of old plumbing. Water sprayed again and I stared in fascination as it stopped again.

"Hello?" I'm not sure what possessed me to speak to a dripping showerhead while sitting on a toilet with my jeans at my knees, still dripping myself - but I said it. The shower remained dormant. "Mr. Christopher, is that you?"

Nothing. I scrunched my face. "Mr. Christopher, if that's you, make the shower go on again." I thought I'd have to wait but the shower came on immediately then turned off again. My blood rushed but I was not scared, it was more like a thrill running through me. Did I dare to ask again? No, that's taunting. I asked for a sign and I got it, that's enough. "Thanks." The drips sped up and I wasn't sure if water would come rushing out again but that was it. I stood up and stepped to the tub then tested the handles. Nothing unusual, just a shower doing what showers do.

We got off the bus at the stop near Tuffy's house and walked
in the brisk air over damp gravel covered in rotting, frozen leaves
to Mrs. Marchesa Fontaine's. Mrs. Fontaine was paying Tuffy two
dollars a day to feed her at-least-fifty cats while she went out of
town to visit her sister somewhere out west. We followed Tuffy up
the hill to the white, wooden one-story house with blue shutters
and a small front porch. Cats on fence posts watched Tuffy look
for the key. Cats in windows mewed or stared in feline
indifference. Inside, the smell was overwhelming, a dank mixture
of urine and fake fish and fur licked with spit. Cats came running
from everywhere and rubbed against our legs and tripped us
walking to the kitchen where the feed bowls lined the walls. Tuffy
handed me a bag of hard food and told me to fill all the plastic
bowls. Sammi put water in all of the glass and metal bowls and
Tuffy filled bowls out back in the yard. The cats swarmed almost
the instant that the first kibble hit Tupperware. I love cats but this
was such obvious overkill. At what point did Ms. Fontaine lose her
idea of a normal home and give over to this?

Tuffy slammed the door. "Shit, it's cold out. You done?"

I shook food out of the bag. "Just about."

"Hurry up. You guys have to see this place."

I knew it was wrong to look around this woman's house
without her knowing but I knew equally that Tuffy wouldn't be
talked out of it. And, I was curious.

Tuffy handled Ms. Fontaine's curios roughly and I felt a
nervous constricting of my breath as I worried about getting found
out for the bad girls we were being. The furniture was feminine
and sort of old fashioned, like a doll house. The hallway was dark
and lined with nicely-framed bad paintings of vases of flowers,
mostly roses. My throat tightened when we entered her bedroom.
We had crossed the line and were officially trespassing on a
stranger's property. Tuffy headed straight for the dresser and
Sammi looked under the bed. I stared at the photos on her shelves.
She was younger than I thought or the photos were old, I wasn't

sure which. Her clothing didn't fit any era so lent no clues and a
giant straw sun hat obscured the view of her smiling face in almost
every shot.

Sammi joined Tuffy at the dresser and we looked through her
top drawer filled with receipts and plastic key tags from places like
Niagara Falls until Tuffy hit the jackpot, the thing we would giggle
about for the next few weeks at least.

"Here it is, guys. Look."

Sammi and I thought it was just a lipstick so we weren't sure
why Tuffy was so anxious to show off this trophy. She unsheathed
the tube and twisted the bottom. A cherry-red lipstick slowly
emerged in the shape of a penis. My eyes got round. What could
this be? Why would Ms. Fontaine have it? Would she, could she,
dare touch that to her lips? Holy cow.

Sammi stared silently with her hand over her mouth. "Gross.
That's disgusting!"

"Nerds. Here, put some on."

Sammi backed away. "No way, Jose."

I beat her to the door and we started down the hall together,
avoiding cats and hoping Tuffy would leave the lipstick where she
found it. We walked out to the front porch and bundled our collars
beneath our chins. I sat on the steps of the front porch and Sammi
sat beside me. Tuffy came out lighting a cigarette between bright
red lips. She passed it to Sammi who passed it to me. The tip was
covered in that red, sticky penis-shaped lipstick and I wasn't sure if
I'd gag. "Shouldn't we lock up?"

Tuffy grabbed the cigarette from me. "Nah, Bobby is coming
up."

Sammi exhaled. "Bobby?"

"From down the road. Don't you guys know anyone?"

Did we?

She stamped the cigarette out and stood defiantly in front of
us, her red lips poorly drawn and garish. "We're going riding
without the horses."

What?

"You know, riding?" Her hips moved awkwardly beneath her
pink, polyester-filled quilted jacket.

Sammi's arm hit mine. I looked to her but she betrayed nothing.

Tuffy waited.

I leaned into Sammi. "Let's go."

Tuffy kept gyrating in her black rubber booties while we headed for the gravel drive.

We couldn't just say nothing, could we? She hadn't done anything wrong. We weren't angry at her. I searched my history for some response but I had no history with penis lipsticks and horseless riding. "Thanks for inviting us. The cats were cool."

Sammi looked at me like the geek I knew I was. "Yeah, Tuffy, it was cool."

The gravel squished and crunched under our quickened steps until we reached the road and finally allowed ourselves to speak. I had so many questions that I didn't know where to start, so Sammi did. "Do you think she meant what I think she meant about the riding thing?"

"I don't know. What do you think?"

"First the lipstick, then the riding. I think she meant, you know."

"I think so too. Do you think she really does it or is she just making all that up? Maybe she just talks about it to make us think she's older. I mean, we've never seen anything really. It's just her saying that."

Sammi looked ahead. "Would you do it?"

"It? I don't know. I don't think so."

"Not even with Tommy?"

I felt the panic rise within me. Is that what he wanted? "I don't... No." I pulled at a thread-pill on my mitten. "Would you?"

"With Tommy? No way."

I laughed. We laughed. But inside, I wondered if she meant Tommy was not good enough for her, that she didn't really think he was cool enough.

Sammi didn't look at me. "Do you think Anne has?"

"Do you?"

She faced me. "Yeah. I think she did it with Kevin."

"Gross."

"Yeah."

"So, would you?"

"Maybe."

The very idea sent my head spinning. Naked bodies rubbing on each other. Kissing with tongues. Hands touching me where only I touch myself. Me having to touch him on all those foreign and unpredictable places. I was repelled by every thought but could feel a wetness in my panties as the pictures danced in my brain.

Chapter Ten

Isabelle made marzipan, as usual. Sammi and I stained our fingers kneading in food coloring and shaping small balls into fruits. Some we garnished with cloves as stems. Rayne got the mugs out for the spiced apple cider and put a stick of cinnamon in each as a straw. I liked <u>Velveteen Rabbit</u> but I was glad we were doing something new for this family meeting. Herbert and Merlin were poking at a growing fire when we entered with the trays of snacks.

Mommy sat on a throw pillow toying with what looked like a board game on her lap. "Ooh, let's get through all of the gripes fast so we can do this."

Isabelle passed out mugs. "Anne, we've started!"

Herbert looked immediately tired. "Let's go ahead and start and let her join in."

"Maybe she didn't hear you. I'll go get her." Sammi tapped at Anne's door. "Come on, everyone's waiting."

Isabelle looked to Mommy and had a whole conversation that we would never hear. As a matter of fact, when I looked to the grown-ups, they seemed to be speaking a mile a minute to one another without ever opening their mouths. I wondered if we ever looked that way to them, if there was a secret kid code and a secret grown-up code and you could only know one at a time.

Sammi came back in and sat next to her mother instead of me. She looked at me and her eyes were filled with I'm sorry's and I'm tired's and help me's and I was sure the parents couldn't hear it. Anne came in and sat next to me and I was immeasurably thrilled, I would be the cool one for the night. I smiled at her and she looked at me with a completely indecipherable face. Was that a grown-up code look or did she have a category all her own?

"I have a gripe." Carol stroked Tigger's back. "I'm sick of waiting for everyone to show up before we start. If this was a class, we wouldn't wait to begin because one pupil hadn't arrived."

Anne got red. "Are you talking about me? I'm a lousy five minutes late. What's the big deal? And this isn't a class and you aren't the teacher here, Teach."

"Carol."

"What?"

"My name. Don't call me 'Teach.'" Carol was a bit red now too.

Mommy smiled impossibly. "Okay, so the rule is that we all arrive to family circle on time. Any objections? Okay."

"I wasn't even late." Anne twisted her split ends, inspecting them. She was gone from us now. "This is such bullshit."

"That's it. Anne Marie Busch, go to your room!" Isabelle raised her voice to a level that had become more and more familiar lately.

Anne was stunned for only a second, then she gathered herself and left so quickly that the air spun. Her door slammed across the hall and we all looked from the empty doorway to each other. Montgomery stared into the fireplace and ate a cookie. His voice was a whisper that drifted on the hot breeze from the flames. "No more gripes."

Merlin forced a laugh and looked to the board on Mommy's lap. "Chess, anyone?"

"Yes, let's do the test." Mommy laid the board down and handed us pencils. We answered questions about our favorite things and what we didn't like. She asked questions about what we'd do if something happened and the parents answered with seriousness or knowing glances while we kids used our imaginations. What would I do if my friend canceled an expensive lunch date at the last minute? "A: eat alone at the restaurant? B: go out of my way to let the waiter know that I'd be back soon but that I needed to leave now? C: order the food to go? D: sneak out?" I pictured myself waiting for Sammi at The Magic Pan. I'd already had a glass of water and she rushed in and told me she had to go to an important meeting thing. I pictured the waiter staring at me expectantly, the customers wondering why I was eating alone. I watched Sammi cross out "D" and write "A." Really? What about "E: burst into tears and yell 'That's not fair!'"

Mommy told us numbers that went with the letters we picked and we added them up. We each got a color card and a number then Mommy looked up things in her book and we found out who we were. It said I was a thinker and that I was too worried about getting things right and that I was creative but not intuitive. I wasn't sure what that meant but Mommy and Isabelle nodded in agreement and moved on to the next person. What we learned was that none of us had the same things. Everything came down to these color cards and none of us had the same one. Mommy was bright orange and Merlin was vibrant green. I guessed that Anne would have been a whole rainbow and it made me sad that we didn't get to hear what she would do if the dress she ordered didn't fit quite right. Sammi was red and I knew without asking that she was so happy for that. Herbert was blue and Carol was yellow. Montgomery was pink and we all teased him a little. Isabelle was navy and I was, of all things, grey. I thought I'd be purple or some other marvelous, enviable color but I was grey, just grey. The grown-ups kept talking about the game and swapping answers while we put mugs in the kitchen sink and went upstairs.

I decided not to brush my teeth. Grey people don't brush their teeth before bed. Sammi and I put on mittens and socks over socks to get into bed. I turned off my clamp lamp and looked at the darkness. "Do you think it's bad that I'm grey?"

"No. Your mom would have lied and said you were another color if it was bad."

I thought about that for a minute as my eyes adjusted to the dark and picked out familiar objects. "What if she told the truth about the color but lied about what it meant?"

"Oh Ariel, it's a stupid color. Just forget about it."

"Yeah, right. Cause you got red but if you had gotten grey, you'd be worried, right?"

Sammi breathed low and long. "No. That's why you got grey and I got red."

The tear was down my face and in my ear before I even knew I had shed it.

*   *   *

Mrs. Sheridan called on me to recite my memorized poem first. My teeth chattered with excess energy as I walked to the front of the room and turned to face the class. Everyone stared at me expectantly, or worse, ignored me in boredom, while I chanted from memory. "'Twas brillig, and the slithy toves did gyre and gimble in the wabe; all mimsy were the borogoves, and the mome raths outgrabe."

Mrs. Sheridan beamed and I pushed forward with more confidence. Steven, a smallish boy up front, looked at me with wonder as I spun the story with words that made no sense. I hoped it was wonder, he may just have been confused. But no matter, I felt free for the first time in that school. I didn't think I was learning anything but I felt good.

I pictured myself slaying the dragon and dragging its head back. I pictured myself standing on top of a hill telling the story to the villagers, acting out the parts when I battled the dragon with my vorpal blade. The villagers stared in rapt attention and applauded when I finished with a regal bow. The king put a wreath of flowers on my head with ribbons flowing down over my armor.

"Thank you, Ariel. Well done." Mrs. Sheridan gave me a wink.

I was sure my skin was actually glowing with pride. I carried it with me through the rest of class and on into lunch when I sat with Tina and Jillian. Ozepher lifted her eyes but not her head and smiled gently at me. I forgot myself in the excitement and blurted before I knew I had. "Hi!"

Her head jumped and she opened her mouth to speak.

Tina beat her to it. "What's the big smile for?"

There was no way to explain that I was still glowing from the one fruitful moment I'd had in all these months of school. Tina hated school. Everyone hated school. Even I was learning to at least dread it. "Nothing."

I poked my straw through the experimental plastic milk bag the government had forced onto our district and propped the blob on the side of my plate so the milk wouldn't all squirt out. It sagged, a reminder of the IV bag that hung over Montgomery's bed in the hospital.

"Get up, boy!" Mr. Brant's voice boomed through the cafeteria and all our heads snapped to see him. "Get your black ass outa that chair before I drag it out!"

Boo sat defiantly in his chair. He had shaken his head at first but he was silent steel now. Ozepher tucked her head to her chin in some vain effort to cover her ears or disappear. I wondered if she told her mom about these fights and if her mom believed her.

Mr. Brant leaned down to Boo's ear and screamed into it. "Get your ass out of that chair, boy!"

Boo's hands wrapped around the plastic seat. The room was silent. Mr. Brant tried to pull Boo up by the arm and when he couldn't he became quiet and scarier. "Mr. Walker, move or it will become my job to move you." Nothing happened for a moment then everything happened at once. Mr. Brant grabbed Boo's shirt and tried to yank him out of the chair. Boo stayed stuck to the seat when the chair fell over and Mr. Brant dragged him, chair and all, out of the cafeteria. The collar of Boo's shirt cut into his throat and a button popped. We knew that Boo would leave school bruised and bloody that day. His shirt, one of only four or five he wore, would be torn. I wondered what he told his mother and whether she thought he made it all up.

We animated again and the room filled with young voices. I looked to Tina and Jillian. "How come Boo's mom doesn't get mad at Mr. Brant? Isn't that against the rules that he does that?"

"She probably doesn't have a clue." Tina started eating again as if all were right with the world. "Probably too busy with her own problems."

"Do you think? I would get really mad if he was my son, wouldn't you?"

Tina's eyes were impatient. "She doesn't know, Arielhead. She thinks he's fighting with kids at school. That's what Brant tells them if they call. Golly, you're slow."

"So, when he goes home, she's going to think he got in a fight?"

"Duh. No shit, Sherlock."

I looked at Ozepher but she would not look at me.

"Then what? Then he gets punished by his mom? This is terrible. Why doesn't Mr. Brant get fired?"

Jillian snickered and Ozepher left the table like a shadow retreating at noontime. Tina looked at me like I was still speaking in Jabberwocky. "He's the Vice Principle, dummy. He's the one in charge."

I did feel dumb. I felt like I didn't understand one thing in the universe anymore. I looked to my sagging plastic bag of milk and my plate of fried meat and corn and wasn't hungry anymore.

*   *   *

Mommy left an invisible halo of White Shoulders cologne when she walked out the door to Arnold's waiting car. Anne sat alone in her room with the door cracked. Isabelle walked to the crack while Merlin waited for her on the side porch. Please, no more yelling today. "Anne, we're going now. Make sure everyone's in bed by eight."

The voice drifted through the crack. "Eight. Bye."

Isabelle put her hand up to push the door open then rethought it and walked away. Merlin's headlights filled the window and Anne came into the hallway to watch them drive away. Sammi finished with the dishes and watched the red lights go behind the hedge and down to the road.

Anne summed us up - acolytes. "Wanna come in my room?" She walked away without our answer, knowing Sammi and I would be right behind her. She arranged the pillows on her single bed and leaned her back onto them. A wreath with ribbons dripping from it adorned her wall next to a collage of photos of Kevin. She was as close as I'd ever come to being near a fairy princess and I knew it.

"Heard about Boo Walker today. That really bites."

She did? "You did?"

"It's everywhere. Mr. Brant better hope nobody ever figures out where he lives or his ass is grass."

Sammi ventured. "He deserves it."

I wanted in. "No shit."

Rayne peeked into the crack where the door hinged to the frame and Anne giggled gently. "Step into my parlour, darling." Rayne said nothing but couldn't stop her seven-year-old body from fidgeting behind the door. "Rayne, come in. She thinks we can't see her. We see you. Come in."

Rayne tried to stay still and silent but started a giggle fit. Explosive breaths accompanied her now shuddering body. We waited. Running to the bathroom, Rayne's tiny voice escaped. "Oh shoot."

Anne chuckled. "I can't wait for her to grow out of this laughing and peeing phase."

Sammi's laugh was just like Anne's, I'd have to start copying it right away. She slapped Anne's leg. "Tell me about it. I do her laundry." I wished so hard I was one of the sisters at that moment. Not an almost sister, but a real sister.

Two bodies collided in the hall and the thud resounded.

"Rayne, what are you doing?" Anne looked like she might get up and see for herself.

"Nothing." Then Rayne lowered her voice. "Get up. They'll see you." Montgomery's long hair was clear in the doorway. Rayne pulled at him. "Shhh. Hide from them. They don't know it's us."

"They're obviously working on the 'if we can't see them, they can't see us' theory." I wasn't sure what Anne meant, but I laughed with Sammi anyway, trying to imitate their jolly harmony. Montgomery and Rayne tried poorly to stay invisible behind the door and Anne crossed her room quietly on her toes. Rayne and Montgomery screamed when Anne threw the door open and Sammi and I screamed because they did. We all laughed together for the first time I could remember.

Anne let Rayne sit on her bed next to me while Montgomery cozied into her chair and Sammi propped herself on the bedding box. Anne pulled her tape recorder from a drawer and turned it on. "Testing, testing. One, two, three." She played it back and we sat watching her like she was a magician doing a card trick. "Hi, you're listening to WWLF. Welcome to the show. Tonight, we have lots of music spinning for you and some special guests so stay tuned for the show. But first, this song from Kenny Rogers. Hit it, Kenny." She motioned to us and we followed her lead. "You picked a fine time to leave me, Lucille..." We sang loud and bad until we got to the part where no one knew the words anymore. "Thanks, Kenny. We'll be interviewing him later in the show." She looked us over, selected. "And now for the news with Miss Ariel Whilone, our favorite rolling stone. Back to you, Ariel." She pointed the recorder at my mouth.

I knew it was supposed to be cool to be a rolling stone and prayed to the god of cool that I would live up to the introduction. "Hi, today in the news... Today..." They were all looking at me. I wanted to be funny, I wanted to be clever and quick. My mind went completely empty. "Well, nothing much happened in the world today. More news later." Everyone laughed. More importantly, Anne laughed.

"And now, another song." She put the recorder in front of Montgomery's mouth and he pulled his lips in. Sammi shook her head and waved her off. Rayne smiled and sang loudly. "You picked a fine time to leave me, Lucille..."

I was about to explain to her that Anne meant for her to sing a new song when Anne giggled and joined in. We hummed when we didn't know words then abandoned the song again. "Thank you, Kenny, for that lovely song. And now the weather with Rayne. Get it?"

Rayne giggled so much she almost couldn't speak. "I'm Rayne. The weather is sunny. Get it?"

"Thank you, Rayne. And now a song. You picked a fine time to leave me, Lucille..." We laughed so hard, we spit when we sang. "Four hungry children and the crops in the field..."

"And now, the sports with Montgomery Whilone."

Montgomery's guffaw was deep into the snorting stage now. "I don't know sports. Um, everyone won today except the people who didn't. Now you talk, Anne."

"And that was the sports. And now for a brand new song. You picked a fine time..." My stomach was cramping on the sides from all the laughing. It was one of my favorite feelings. "I've had some sad times, been through some bad times, but this time the hurtin's for real..." Our accents got more and more twangy with each repetition of the song. "And now, that interview with a famous person. Hi, my name is Angel the D.J. and you must be..." She held the recorder to Sammi and we waited for Sammi to decide.

"Kenny Rogers!"

I was sure the tape would just sound like five kids laughing.

"Of course. Mr. Rogers, hey wait, any relation to the neighborhood?"

Sammi deepened her voice. "No, miss."

"Tell us about yourself."

"Well, I had a wife but she left me right when the crops were in the field so now I mostly try to feed my four children."

"That's wonderful, Mr. Rogers. Would you like to lead us in a song?"

"Sure, Angel. You picked a fine time..."

We sang until after ten. My stomach ached like I'd been punched. My eyes were itchy from chuckle tears. I'm pretty sure I had never had that much fun in my entire twelve years on the planet.

*   *   *

The alarm sounded, its metal hammer banging and clanging on its metal casing. Sammi lay unmoved. I watched the kelly-green clock vibrate on top of her dresser and wondered whether I was ready to get out from under the covers and face the icy cold of our room. "Sammi."

Not so much as a roll-over.

"Sammi."

I was just about to exit the warm cocoon of my quilts and trapped body heat when Isabelle came up the steps. I didn't hear her footfalls but her head appeared and grew with each step upward. She was wearing her bright yellow Rainbow House T-shirt from the health food store where she was working. Her long chestnut hair hung in a thick rope of braid. She didn't hunch under the low ceiling, like she usually did, as she reached out and tapped the top of the alarm which fell blessedly silent. Sammi did not stir as Isabelle lay down next to her then melted into her.

Wait, melted into her? I stared at Sammi's bed where she slept alone and replayed it all in my head. Isabelle had come in, turned off the alarm, and melted into Sammi in the bed where she lay.

"Sammi, wake up."

She rolled over, squinted with sleepy eyes. "Morning."

"Where's your mom?"

She smacked her lips and pulled the covers up tight around her neck. "I don't know."

"Isn't she in the bed with you?" Sammi didn't answer right away and I grew impatient with her sleepy drifting. "Is she?"

"What? No."

I could see now that she wasn't. "Sammi, wake up. Where did your mom go?"

"When?"

"Now, after she turned off the alarm, she got in bed with you."

"I thought you turned it off." She was coming-to now.

I got out of bed, undressed then dressed quickly in cold long johns, jeans and a sweater. I ran down to the kitchen where I found Isabelle making buckwheat pancakes. A sweater was pulled over her turtleneck and none of it was even yellow.

"Isabelle, did you come in our room?"

"Don't worry, we all know the rules. No trespassing. Why, is something missing? Sammi did laundry the other day, you know."

"Did you turn off our alarm?"

Sammi came in and sat at the kitchen table. "You made breakfast. Cool."

Isabelle served a pancake to Sammi and put another on the table for me. "Go ahead and sit, Ariel. You don't want it to get cold."

"Did you?"

Isabelle looked puzzled. Sometimes I wondered if grown-ups took anything we said seriously.

"Did you turn off our alarm?"

"Of course not. I've been down here cooking." She poured a bit of syrup on my plate for dipping then went back to the stove.

I knew what I had seen. I for-sure knew I didn't turn off that alarm. I saw Isabelle snap it off as clearly as I saw her flipping pancakes on the stove in front of me. But I was just as sure she wouldn't melt away in front of me now. Why did so little of the world make sense to me?

Chapter Eleven

    I wanted so desperately to love school but Mr. Brant continued to swagger through the halls looking for us to make mistakes and inventing them for Boo if he went too long without sassing him. My classes bored me, I had taken most of them before and just couldn't prove it without the lost records. Stringy-haired, oily-faced kids looked at me with disdain and occasionally shot things at me, small bits of paper or eraser. Construction paper snowflakes hung curling from the walls. Small pools of water condensed inside the windows and the electric clock on the wall moved too slowly.

    I pictured myself far away in a place with pretty, well-scrubbed people in pretty, store-bought clothes. The rooms were clean and light flooded everything making it all bright. I pictured a young, pretty teacher who asked me lots of questions and smiled generously when I got each one right. My classmates gave me little Christmas cards with candy canes taped to them and they all knew my name and liked me. I pictured a school dance with Tommy and me twirling on the floor. My dress touched the ground and was as light as tissue so that it lifted with every movement. I was voted most popular and Sammi was the second most popular and everyone knew that we would become famous models and astronauts and gymnasts.

The bell rang and I almost ran down the hall after closing my locker. Vacation.

Sammi was sitting with Alice when I got on the bus. They were chatting and I was too tired to even let it hurt my feelings - tired of grey days and cold wind and sleeping in my clothes, tired of living in the country with no friends and no Daddy, tired of stomach aches and grown-ups dating, tired, tired, tired. I rode home in silence barely waving goodbye while kids exited one by one wishing good vacations to all remaining on board.

I trudged up the hill and the stairs to the bathroom and turned on the water, lots of hot and a half turn of cold, then peeled off layers of knit. I had one of those chills I inherited from Mommy, the kind that gets inside the marrow and won't let go. The tub continued to fill and I stared at my face in the mirror. I looked pulled down around my eyes and mouth, the same face but my image had somehow shifted.

The water wasn't as hot as usual when I slid into the less-than-half-full tub. I ran my fingers under the stream coming from the faucet. Too cool so I turned the cold down and waited for the temperature to remix itself. Still too cool and now the water already in the tub was getting colder. In a bold move, I turned the cold off completely and swished my butt around to mix the warm with tepid. The water level was still so low and the air was so cold, goose bumps appeared. Why wasn't it heating up? I felt myself cracking. I held out a tentative finger and hoped not to burn as I tested the temperature of the stream. No. I double-checked the cold knob. Off. No. No. NO!

Why? Why couldn't I even have this, not even this small moment of calm and warmth? I pulled my knees into my shivering chest and cried until I was heaving.

*   *   *

We took two cars to the tree farm and parked in a muddy field marked with orange flags. I was the first out of the backseat and stepped right into a good three inches of mud. "Oh, great."

Wooden boards covered the worst part of the walkway but the mud was inescapable. A man gave Herbert and Merlin directions and a piece of paper with some heights and prices printed on it. The farm was hilly and pretty, like small mountains, and trees grew along every walkway. Some had already been cut.

I thought all Christmas trees looked pretty much alike but it turns out there are many different kinds. I also assumed we would find the same ones pretty but everyone had a different kind of favorite. Herbert liked firs and said his family always got those for as long as he could remember and even further back than that. I liked the ones with the long needles that felt soft to the touch but Mommy said they couldn't hold the larger ornaments. She liked the ones we'd always had with the short needles and almost no bare spots. Isabelle said that her kind was the best, it just needed more trimming than the kind Mommy liked.

I walked away with Sammi and Rayne down a parallel path. Anne disappeared. There were many strong, bushy trees here, the kind Mommy liked, but all shorter than her. She liked them taller and this year they wanted an even taller one to "fill the space better." Rayne stopped to pull at the needles of a Norman Rockwell-esque tree while I came around the corner and found it - the perfect tree. It was small, much smaller than I was, a baby still reaching for the sky. Sparse. Four branches sprouted from the trunk which was no thicker than my thumb. And it was crooked, its spindly branches drooped forlornly toward the ground on one side. It was the loneliest tree I'd ever seen in my life and I wanted it. It reminded me of the one in the Charlie Brown special we had watched the other night. "Sammi, look."

"Jeeze, now that's pitiful."

"Don't you like it? Look, it's so sad. It wants us to take it home."

Rayne came around the corner and took Sammi's hand. "Is that a bush?"

"No, it's a tree. Isn't it sweet?"

Rayne looked at the tree with her head cocked then looked up from under a too-big, striped woolen ski cap. "Yeah, maybe it is."

I was determined. "Go get my mommy."

Rayne dropped Sammi's hand and followed the muddy trail back to the rest of the group, her feet making sucking sounds when she walked. The longer I stared at the tree, the more I knew it was mine. It seemed to be telling me that we were its only hope for a home, that everyone else would be too shallow to see the depth of this tree. Sammi ran her hand along one of the underdeveloped branches and down to the tiny puff of long stringy needles at the end. "It is kind of cute."

I smiled inside and out.

Mommy came down the path with Montgomery and stopped near us. "Where is this wonderful tree?"

I looked down at it with pride. "This one."

Mommy followed the length of my finger to the stubby growth in front of it then giggled. "This is the one you like?"

I nodded my head.

Her face got straight. "Why do you like this one, sugar?"

"Mommy, if we don't take this one home, it will think no one loves it and I love it."

Her voice was a gentle lullaby. "Oh baby, that one's not done growing. It doesn't want to be cut down yet."

"But what if it is? What if that's really what it looks like?"

Montgomery moved his feet side to side in the mud, watching his feet manipulate the earth. Mommy took his hand and reached for mine. "Come on precious, We'll check on that tree next year."

"If it looks the same, can we get it next year?"

"Sure, now come on."

I gave her my hand and walked with her, turning to check over my shoulder and catch a last glimpse of the perfect tree. Rayne took Sammi's hand again and we joined the group next to a giant, bushy tree that looked like the kind you find in a department store. It was gorgeous but anyone could see its beauty.

Herbert brought the man with the saw over and they sent us back to the car to wait. The wooden planks were covered in mud now from so many foot steppings. Sammi and I broke off twigs and brought them back for everyone to scrape their shoes. We packed into the back of the car and waited while Herbert and Merlin positioned the tree on the roof and tied it down with twine. Merlin got into his car and Herbert climbed into ours and they started the engines. Mommy played with the radio as Herbert put his arm around the headrest and turned his body to see out of the back window. The car rocked into motion then stopped abruptly. Herbert muttered something that didn't make it out of his beard. He moved the stick thing that came out of the steering wheel and we moved forward the tiniest bit. Then he moved it again, a small jerk then the sound of wheels spinning with no intention of propelling the car. Merlin was already gone along with Isabelle, Sammi and Rayne. Herbert looked around hopelessly. "Madeleine, you steer. Ariel, come help me push."

"Oh, she can't..."

I ignored Mommy and got out of the car. Herbert assessed and I was certain he had some smart way to get us out of this. "Go get some of those boards."

I checked his face to make sure he was serious. They were lodged in the ground and covered with icy mud. His eyes were free of Merlin-like mischief so I walked carefully through the swampy muck and yanked at the boards with bare hands. The first one came up easily but the second, I had to use my body weight as leverage so that when it finally gave, I fell like a clown going for the cheap laugh. I dragged the boards over to Herbert who shoved them beneath the tires. "See if you can get two more."

"Won't I get in trouble for taking all these?"

He was back to assessing.

I found two more and pulled them from the suction of the brown goop. "Here."

He built a ramp with sticks and leaves and boards directly behind the tires. "Follow me."

We walked around to the front of the car and Mommy stared at us with a smiling but expectant face. Herbert motioned for her to roll her window down. "Put it in reverse and only give it a little bit of gas."

She moved the gear thing then Herbert and I pushed as the engine sped up and the car rolled forward the tiniest bit.

"No, stop! Hit the brakes." Herbert pushed back from the hood and walked to her window. "Reverse."

"I thought neutral. That's how Frank always did it."

"Sometimes it's neutral but this time we need reverse." We put our hands back on the hood and got ready to push - mine wet and mud-covered and freezing, his gloved in black leather. "Now, Madeleine. Put it in reverse and give it just a little gas."

Mommy moved the stick again and the car lurched. We pushed. I put all my scant weight into it, wanting to be the strong girl who was able to move the big car. I pushed and pushed even as my hands burned, even as my feet slipped behind me. Herbert made animal grunts and pressed his shoulder to the car. Then it moved so quickly. Mommy squealed happily as Herbert and I lost our grip and our footing and fell, comically, into the mud the car had finally escaped. Mommy stopped the car and popped her head out the window. Her voice was full of music and her hand covered her mouth. "Oh no. Well, you got the car out."

We rose from the mud. I giggled, before I could stop myself, at the mud on Herbert's slacks and in his beard. He stood stunned then chuckled at my mud-dipped hair and chin. "Let's go home." He reached around my shoulder and rested his muddy arm on me.

I elbowed him gently, teasing. "Hey, watch it, you're getting me dirty." It was almost like being with Dad.

*   *   *

Christmas Eve morning was a time of packing overnight bags. Sammi put Bill on top of her bag before going down to Rayne's room to pack hers. I zipped mine and dragged the wheeled base down the flight of stairs, through Rayne's room, across the playroom, and down the last flight of stairs.

We had decorated the tree during the family meeting and it stood in the living room with a few presents from grown-ups to other grown-ups beneath it and cats occasionally batting at lower dangling ornaments. Montgomery was eating iced sugar cookies shaped like trees and Santas, his bag already packed by Mommy and sitting by the door.

"Mommy's going to kill you if she sees you eating those for breakfast."

"No, she's not."

"I'm going to tell."

He licked the powdered sugar, butter, and food-coloring icing and smiled at me. "Tell. I don't care."

Anne wandered in wearing a floor-length black velvet cape over jeans and leg warmers. She opened her arms with a flourish and red satin flashed at us when she reached for a cookie. "Mmmm, who was foolish enough to leave these out? They'll be gone by lunch."

Rayne and Sammi entered and grabbed cookies. Rayne put her hand out to Anne's cape and ran it down along the shiny red lining. "Wowee Anne, where did you get this? It's so pretty."

I was afraid to betray my amazement with her clothes but Anne beamed at Rayne's open admiration.

"I got it from a princess at an open air barter in the hills. I traded your pony for this and a magic wand."

Rayne's eyes widened. "You did not. Really?" She switched to her I-don't-believe-you little girl voice. "Then where's the magic wand?"

Anne, with a mouth full of cookie, held a finger in the air for us to wait one minute, then left the room, her black cape filling with air and billowing at the back. I slapped Montgomery's hand reaching for another tree cookie. Anne came back holding a silver-painted wooden dowel with a silver wooden star at the top.

Rayne gasped so quickly that she inhaled the crushed cookie already in her mouth and coughed over and over while we pounded her back. Her face was red and tear-streaked when she flipped her head back and let her hair fall around her baby-fat-rounded cheeks. "I just wanted to hold it. Can I?" She coughed and smiled between spasms.

Anne held the wand out to her. "Be careful where you point it, it's magic."

Carol came in and made herself a cup of herbal tea. Rayne gave the wand back to Anne who waved it above her head and tapped her on the nose. Carol lit the burner and sat with us at the small table. "That's a nice wand, Anne. Did you make it in wood shop?"

Anne's face froze into that hardened look that the parents had grown so accustomed to. She billowed out of the room and I felt angry at Carol for taking her away from us. Rayne grabbed another cookie and put her most authoritative face on, her I-told-you-so face. "She got it from a princess in the field and now we don't have a pony anymore and she barnered it." She smiled triumphantly and I had no desire to be right or explain it or be a good kid. Carol was still bewildered when Mommy and Herbert entered.

I hiccuped the words. "Montgomery ate cookies for breakfast."

"Did he now? Well, good for him. Everyone should eat cookies for breakfast on Christmas Eve." Mommy was still in her purple robe with orange paisley, the one that made her look like a movie star from the movies that only came in black and white. She rumpled Montgomery's hair and took a cookie for herself. I had wanted a cookie, had wanted to let that icing melt on my tongue. Now I wanted only to deny myself that pleasure that they so readily indulged. Herbert reached over me to grab a cookie and the sight of the crumbs falling into his beard repulsed me. Damn cookies.

Dad pulled up outside. Mommy stuck Montgomery's arms through his coat sleeves while Dad left Sandy in the VW Bug and walked up the icy flagstone steps. He knocked though he could see us all standing there. Herbert opened the door. "Hey Frank, good to see you."

Dad had moved ahead of Herbert and Sammi's dad, Bentley, at work. He wore it with the tinniest bit of pride showing. "Herbert, good to see you."

"Come in, come in." Herbert backed away from the door letting the cold air rush in but Dad stayed in the frame and waited. I grabbed my bag and rolled it to the door as Montgomery shoved a cookie in his pocket.

Mommy walked over to Dad and pulled her crisscrossed robe tight against the cold air I knew she couldn't stand. She opened her arms and hugged Dad who stiffened. "Merry Christmas, Frank." Her wide smile fell as she pulled back from him. She stared at him then shivered. "Well, come on dear hearts, all the warm air is getting out."

"What warm air?" Merlin walked in, a woolly bear, while we hugged and kissed Mommy goodbye. "Hey Frank, how's it going?"

"Pretty good, Merlin, pretty good." He had that tone where you were supposed to ask him more about himself but Merlin must not have heard it because he just lifted a cookie and a mug of Herbert's coffee and sat down. Dad grabbed Montgomery's bag and we waved goodbye when Mommy shut the door, framing her face in the small window.

I missed her the moment the car door closed. This was my first Christmas away from her and it already felt wrong. I knew that Bentley would be there soon to take Sammi, Rayne, and Anne away but I couldn't help thinking that we must be missing something with all those people wearing outside clothes indoors and a plate of cookies sitting on the breakfast table and hot beverages being brewed.

Sandy's *I Dream of Jeannie* ponytail swished when she turned. "Your dad and I have a very good dinner planned for you. And guess what? We put up the tree last week and we got the prettiest new star for the top and new lights too."

Dad banged his pipe against the ashtray. "I'm making a turkey with chestnut dressing and green beans and sweet potatoes with bourbon and pecans. Sandy baked a chocolate cake. I know you like that, Ariel."

I knew I was supposed to say yes but I didn't feel like saying anything. And I was allergic to bourbon.

"Don't you, Ariel?"

His voice was still cheerful but I knew I had better respond. "Yeah."

"Sandy made it for you. I told her how much you like chocolate cake and she baked it for you last night after work."

I didn't want to thank her and I didn't want to respond to Dad. I wanted to turn around and go back home. It hit me rather suddenly that Lemonade Farm was now home. I wondered if Montgomery felt it too. Maybe he still thought of Mayfair Drive as home. As he breathed onto the window and drew swirls in the mist, I wondered if maybe he didn't think about it at all.

Christmas cards hung through the slats of the swinging doors that separated Sandy's kitchen from the dining area. The chocolate cake sat on a glass plate on the counter, covered so I couldn't run my finger in the icing. She served us Triskets with Cracker Barrel cheddar and Dad pulled out our Master Mind game and put it on her kidney-shaped glass coffee table. He disappeared into the kitchen and Sandy went into the bedroom awhile. Montgomery turned on the TV and passed all the soaps before settling on *Captain Chesapeake*, a local show with cartoons.

"No double colors." His mouth was full of crackers.

I had set up my board with a blue, white, blue, yellow combination so I switched a blue out for a black and smiled confidently. "Ready."

Montgomery made his first attempt to match my hidden combination while Ultraman fought evil on TV in a rerun we paid little attention to. Montgomery usually took longer than needed to make it seem he had really thought things through. I crossed my legs in different ways in boredom. Indian style, right leg on top, left leg on top, and that way Mommy, Isabelle, and Carol did for yoga.

He got it in six attempts and it was my turn to guess. He took a long time setting up and changed it several times. Ultraman hit a giant lizard thing in the nose and down it went. Didn't Ultraman ever worry about crushing the people below? "Don't forget, no doubles. You said it."

"Duh."

Right over left. Left over right.

He settled back onto his palms and looked at me. I picked a yellow, black, white, red combination, then moved them around a little. "Okay."

Montgomery looked at my pieces then at his hidden ones. "Did you peek?"

"No, you saw me. I was watching TV."

"You peeked!"

"Did not! Come on, just play."

"I don't want to play anymore." He tossed the board at me and went into the bathroom. The pieces had shaken loose but I could see I had picked all the right colors and almost all the right positions. Sometimes it felt good to be older and at the advantage. This was not one of those times. I wanted to fix things. I wanted him to feel like he could have won. I'd gotten lucky. I wanted to hold him and say I was sorry for all the times I called him dummy. I wanted him to come back and ask me to teach him how to win.

I felt the sides of my mouth fall, felt my teeth press together. More and more, I had the feeling I could do very little right.

Dad motioned with the wine glass in his hand for me to come into the kitchen. "Hey pumpkin, come taste this." He stirred a pot of green beans and onions with a wooden spoon and offered some up to me. He blew on it. I blew on it. Then I opened my mouth and he guided the spoon in. They were wonderful. I had eaten beans at school and at dinners in other people's homes but his were like a whole different vegetable, at once sweet and salty. All of his food was better than other people's. Not even restaurants compared. He must have known this and still he looked at me expectantly.

"Pretty good, Dad."

"Do they need anything?"

I loved when he asked me but I never had any idea what went into food to make it taste this way or that. "No, I think they're just right."

"Try the dressing. I made it with currants and chestnuts." He held a spoonful out to me.

"There's a mushroom, Dad."

He ate the spoonful and got me another. "What do you think?"

Dad had a funny habit of asking what I thought of the food before I had tasted it. Once, I dared to wonder if he would have noticed if I had answered him.

The stuffing was warm and moist with chestnuts that broke on contact and little raisins Dad called currants. It was like a warm fire or a hot bath. There was that much comfort in that spoonful of breading.

Sandy walked in with her lipstick reapplied and a cowl neck sweater atop a shiny purple skirt. "Oh, I feel so much better. I hate those boots. And I had a run in my hose from pulling those socks off and on. Ariel, do you have pantyhose? I always see you in corduroys or knee socks."

"No."

I was wearing corduroys. I had grown out of so many of my clothes and none of my cousins were ever as tall as I already was so the hand-me-downs weren't fitting anymore. The Levi's were worn at the knees and Mommy had patched them with a bit of cloth shaped like an apple and stitched all the way around in red thread. I felt suddenly shabby. I had always been embarrassed at school when the kids stared at the patches but I secretly liked them and knew how much it took for Mommy to sew them. She hated sewing. It was one of the few things that put her in the mood to yell. I hoped against hope that I would get new jeans for Christmas.

"Well, you should try them with a skirt. Do you have any skirts?"

"Yes." I was all at once uncomfortable, as if my whole body were leaned back on my heels. "I have plenty."

"I never see you in them. Do you have dresses?"

"Yes, Sandy, I do." This was bordering on accusation, I felt, but I wasn't sure what the charge was. "I have lots of dresses and skirts. I just don't like wearing them that much." I pushed the card-laden door out and walked back to the living area. Montgomery was sitting on the floor watching Captain Chesapeake read mail from kids who sent him drawings and questions for his sidekick puppet, a sea monster named Chessie.

"Do you want to play a game?"

He didn't look at me. "Cards?"

"Go Fish."

I let him shuffle and deal the deck. He counted out loud. I won three games but he won two and that was enough.

Sandy came out of the kitchen wiping her hands on a crisp holiday dishtowel. "Okay dirt balls, wash your hands for supper.

Ariel, come help your dad take the food to the table." She usually asked me to set the table but it had been made ready before we got there today. She lifted the giant-glass-grapes centerpiece and lay a hot pad in its place. "Your dad has been working on this dinner since yesterday morning. He got up before work to get that dressing started."

I put platters of food down and Sandy moved them around like she enjoyed the extra work. "Did you wash your hands?"

"You told me to help you."

"Go wash your hands." Dad's voice ran through the kitchen and out around the dining area.

"I was going to." My voice was higher, the pitch I used when I was angry. Was I angry? Montgomery wiped his hands on his pants, gross, and sat at his regular spot.

Dad entered with the turkey and hesitated before lowering it. "Sandy, move the cranberries over." His voice was impatient and Sandy was still trying to light a candle. "Would you move the cranberries? This plate is hot." Sandy smiled and blew out the match and searched for a place to put it. Didn't she know he hated to repeat himself? I watched his face harden in frustration. It seemed like she was taking forever though it couldn't have been more than three Mississippi's. "Damn it, Sandy." He exhaled. Her hand was on the bowl of cranberries now and he forced a smile. "This is hot and heavy." He winked at Sandy as he put the platter down then waited ceremoniously.

Sandy was right on cue. "This looks great, Frank. Doesn't it smell good, kids?"

We nodded. Dad extended his hands and we bowed our heads. "Bless this food to the nourishment of our bodies and us to Thy service."

"Amen."

My belly pressed into my jeans toward the end of the meal. Dad pushed away from the table and sipped on his wine. Sandy showered compliments and Montgomery left the table without being excused. It was an extraordinary meal. Even with my little bit of experience with being alive, I knew I would eat few meals as good. But we didn't eat it in the Mayfair Drive house and we didn't eat it with Mommy. I had no room of my own to retreat to here, no place to escape from Sandy's hideous crime of not being Mommy. She kept talking, kept drawing attention to the fact of her existence, kept being cheerful and friendly. "Ariel, why don't you help me with these dishes?"

I knew that was coming. And I knew Dad had littered the kitchen with saucy pots, serving dishes and spoons and drips from many tastings. I hoped she would let me dry this time. Actually, I hoped she would let Dad and Montgomery do the dishes so I could go watch the beginning of *Fantasy Island* but I knew better than to hope for that with any sort of conviction. "Your dad sure does know how to cook up a mess. But that was a great dinner, wasn't it? He worked on it for two days. He got up early yesterday and started that dressing. Wasn't that great dressing?"

"Yeah."

"We're going to have desert later. I baked a chocolate cake. Your dad said that's your favorite."

"Yeah."

I didn't know which one of us to feel sorrier for so I picked me because she could leave and I couldn't. She washed, I dried. She wiped down counters, I dried those. She washed the inside of the sink, I dried that. Then I took the towel to the dirty-laundry pile in the utility room and placed it on top of Dad's work shirts and Sandy's underwear.

We watched TV later than usual and even talked Dad into changing the channel during the local news. The cake was good, the kind from a box mix, and we ate it with ice cream on the side. Dad and Sandy tucked us into our sleeping bags and jostled us and tickled us and I shook free of my moodiness for a time and drifted into sleep.

I dreamt of our car on I-95. Mommy, Dad, Montgomery and I rode inside. I saw the whole thing from far above. The highway was dark with only streetlights and the beams from our headlights making everything clear. We were driving pretty fast but then came the giant dodo bird stomping down behind us, his feet and ringed legs thundering the earth with each step. It was as if I were looking out of the bird's eyes while it threatened to crush us alone in that little car on that empty highway. My breath quickened, my body curled on itself. I wanted to make the car go faster, to get away somehow. The three-toed foot rose again and again barely missing the car as I shook awake.

It was morning, Christmas morning, but there would be no staircase to run down, no Mommy telling Dad to hurry up with the camera. This was a new Christmas, divorce Christmas, and I guessed the old ones would never come again. Montgomery was still asleep so I shook him. "Hey, wake up. It's Christmas."

His slightly-slanted eyelids bobbed up and down over muddy-blue eyes, adjusting to the morning light. "What?"

"Get up, dummy."

Sandy crept into the living room and was halfway to the kitchen before she realized we were awake. "Frank." She leaned over us and did that snuggle thing she liked to do. "Hey dirt ball, what are you doing awake? Do you think you're getting some presents or something?"

Dad came out tying his robe around his naked morning body and Montgomery giggled while Sandy jiggled us. "Go brush your teeth and wash up and we'll turn the tree on."

Montgomery looked confused. "We don't wash first."

"Come on dirt balls. Ariel, go to the bathroom and you two get scrubbed up. I didn't start the coffee yet, Frank."

"I'll get it."

Coffee? Cleaning? Lights? What were all these delays? We're sitting five feet from the tree, for goodness sake. It's time to open presents.

Sandy stood up and looked just as confused and flustered as we were. "Frank?"

"Sandy, just let 'em stay like that. They can wash later."

Still my hero.

*   *   *

I was hanging the new floor-length dress Dad and Sandy got me when Sammi passed me carrying a bag of new clothes and a box of new, red Jack Purcel's.

"That's pretty."

"Yeah."

She unzipped her bag. "Where are you going to wear it?"

"I have no idea."

"Wear it now."

The thought had never occurred to me. I had been smoothing down the quilted skirt, lamenting that I would never wear it before I grew out of it, and besides, I really needed school clothes and all I asked for was jeans, and it was a pretty dress but it seemed I could get lots of other stuff for the same amount of money, but they were so happy when they gave it to me because I had pointed it out once at Hecht's and Sandy had remembered and was pleased to have gotten it knowing that I loved it when really I had liked it a lot but she had loved the idea of seeing it on me more. And the bottom line was... I wasn't sure I deserved it. I was a farm girl now, a twelve-year-old who worked at the stables next door shoveling horse crap. I was getting accustomed to using government-issued tickets to buy lunch at school and didn't even like sugar in my tea or cereal anymore after so many times going without it because we ran out again. I never threw food away anymore, saved a few squares of toilet paper in my drawer in case we ran out, and tried to find new uses for broken toys' parts and games with pieces missing.

"If I wear it, will you dress up too?"

I pulled the dress from its hanger and Sammi selected a long skirt that had once belonged to Anne. We were dressing Rayne when the grown-ups called us and we answered with giggling just-a-minute's. They called three times and wondered aloud what we were "up to" when we finally walked elegantly down the staircase like three models working a runway. Isabelle, Carol, and Mommy woo-hoo-hoo'ed with delight at our hair piled and pinned atop our heads and our long skirts tripping our socked feet.

Isabelle had her hand over her open-mouthed smile. "Well, well. I feel underdressed."

I had been smiling and laughing for so long now that, as I stood there proudly, my face actually hurt. Mommy patted the throw pillow beside her on the floor. "Come sit on your throne, my princess." Sammi and Rayne and I couldn't stop smiling at each other.

The room exploded into activity as we grabbed presents from beneath the tree and passed them around. Montgomery had wrapped all of his in tin foil this year and Rayne had knotted ribbons and shoelaces around hers. We colored the cardboard rolls from inside the gift wrapping with magic markers and called them "doop-de-doo's" then marched around the room with the tubes to our lips like huge kazoos. We ate the cookies we had iced and played with each others' presents. Mommy brushed my hair with a new plastic tortoise-shell-alike handled brush from Carol then I did Sammi's and she did Rayne's. Montgomery and Herbert built something industrial looking with his Erector Set and Merlin kept sticking funny things on it like bows and candy canes.

Carol and Anne read our personality types from a book on sun signs and another on numbers. We fed logs to the fire and cupped our hands around pottery mugs full of hot chocolate with peppermint sticks and teas with cinnamon straws. Even after we were yawning, the grown-ups let us stay up and play with freshly-opened Matchbox cars and puzzles while popping miniature Krackle and Special Dark bars and listening to new Eagles and Captain and Tenille records. I looked around at Mommy and Isabelle and Sammi and Montgomery and Anne and Rayne and Herbert and Carol and Merlin and I couldn't tell where my family ended and the other ones started.

*   *   *

The Hobart kids got there just as the snow really began to come down. We wanted to spend New Year's Eve night in the pavilion but it was far too cold. Instead, we went for a walk on the road, promising to return before dark.

There's a muffled noise that snow makes when it falls at that rate. It's not as loud as the sound of it packing beneath your boots when you plod through it, but it's louder than people think of snow being.

Sammi and Eddy loved it when the flakes would get on their eyelashes so they kept their heads up while they walked. I kept my eyes to the ground for so long that I forgot everyone else.

I pictured my long pioneer skirt with the ruffle on the bottom kicking out in front of me with each step of my handmade cowhide boots. I pictured log cabins in the distance, so far away that I didn't bother to look up to spot them, I was in the middle of nowhere. I plodded through the thick snow carrying supplies to my family to get us through this terrible blizzard, exhausted, but knowing how much they were counting on me to cross this treacherous terrain and bring home some scraps for us to eat. I was Laura Ingalls, the hero of the prairie, coming home to save my family from certain death. I pulled at my shawl and pressed forward. I was strong and resourceful and important.

"What are you looking at?" Sammi knocked me gently.

"Nothing, just the snow."

Tommy smiled and I felt immediately pitiful. Had I had my head down too long? Did they all see? Did I really pull at a shawl I wasn't even wearing? I smiled back.

The snow was really coming down now. We'd walked a good distance toward Windriver Estates and all around were fields and patches of trees covered in white fluff. Our silence was odd. Cory and Montgomery walked behind us, occasionally smacking a signpost for deer crossing or a tree limb that reached too far for the road. Eddy and Rayne struggled to lift their too-big boots they were meant to "grow into" above the growing depth of snow. Sammi and Tommy and I walked side by side, though not together. Only the snow kept talking, its growing muffled silence falling on us and turning our cheeks red. There was no sun and the sky was becoming a darker grey. When we hit the part of the road that looked like a covered bridge for all the trees that line either side, we wordlessly turned around and trudged back to the farm.

Sammi and Tommy and I stopped at the barn while the younger ones started up the gravel drive, Cory and Montgomery pausing briefly to smack the Lemonade Farm sign and shudder the white from it. Princess and Taffy looked fat and woolly in their winter coats and stomped anxiously at not being let out to graze. We brushed them and fed them sticky, sugary-sweet-smelling grain and quickly mucked the corners of their stalls before heading back to the house in the low glow of light that bounced off the millions of reflective bits falling from the sky.

Inside, the comfort of the silence outside was replaced by the comfort of people disrobing damp children and preparing a meal and talking, always talking, about something that mattered less than the sounds of their voices.

Isabelle and Mommy prepared a special supper for New Year's Eve. Friends were supposed to come celebrate but already the phone was ringing with apologies for bad weather. Anne's friends were coming in a van to take her to a local party. She and Isabelle wouldn't look at each other so I guessed that they'd already had the fight about how unsafe the idea was.

Mommy came back to the table after hanging up the phone again. "Well, the Ellises can't make it either." She smiled and her voice sounded tight when she spoke again. "Well, won't we have ourselves a party with all this extra food and drink." It wasn't a question so nobody answered.

Car lights flashed from outside and Anne jumped up. "Later." She ran to her room and then past us again putting a coat on.

The knock at the kitchen door was startling, I had expected a horn honk. Anne was reaching for the knob when the door opened and someone too old for her pushed his head in. "Hey hey, I made it." Anne walked past us again and slammed the door to her room as the stranger stomped his feet before entering the kitchen. "Am I the first one here?"

Merlin motioned for him to join us in the dining room. "Hey, Simon, you know everyone, don't you?"

He didn't mean us kids, I'd never seen this guy and I'd have remembered the cowboy hat. Herbert stood up and reached across the table. "Herbert Hobart."

"Hi, Simon. And who's this lovely creature?"

"Hi, Simon, I'm Carol." She became girlish and extended her hand which he kissed.

"Carol, my Carol." It was like watching one of those shows that comes on after eight p.m., only on those he would propose to her in a day or two and I knew Carol would still be here with her cat, Tigger, in two days. She dated more than Mommy but people didn't slip into darkened rooms with strangers in this house.

The grown-ups put plates away while we kids went upstairs to the playroom. The snow was slowing down outside and the flakes were small, so small now.

"Monopoly?" Eddy held the box up.

"Takes too long." Tommy clicked the TV on and rotated the dial through the UHF stations. "Othello's better."

"It's only for two people." Sammi flopped down on the trundle bed and stuck her feet out in front of her. "The Ouija board."

Rayne's voice came out too quickly. "No, it's too scary. Last time was too scary."

"Ouija it is, then." Sammi bounced up and pulled the box from the stack on the shelves that Dad had painted green in our basement in the Mayfair Drive house. "Get a candle."

We gathered into a circle around the board and Cory turned the lights out after Sammi lit a stubby votive. "Okay, everyone concentrate. No laughing this time. This is serious. We're going to try to find out about Christopher."

Rayne's arms shot out straight at her sides. "The ghost?"

Montgomery sat on his hands and looked to me so that I almost wanted to put my arm around him and tell him it was all in fun, that nobody would hurt him. The candlelight danced across our young faces and mismatched warm clothing as Sammi placed the plastic thing with the see-through window down on the board. Seven little hands found their way toward it and rested fingertips on top.

"Nobody push it." Sammi put her head down. "Who is Christopher?"

Nothing happened.

I looked from Tommy to Sammi and back to the board. Suddenly, the plastic thing moved. Rayne screamed and Montgomery pulled his hand away and tucked it beneath him again. Rayne giggled when the thing moved to the first letter. W. My hand was pushed and pulled rapidly. "Who's pushing it? Are you doing that, Cory?" He shook his wavy hair and stared at the board while we moved to the next letter. O. It moved with such determination that I just knew someone had to be manipulating it. M. "Sammi, quit pushing it."

"I'm not, I swear." A. "What does it spell? Who's writing it down?" N. The plastic gadget stopped. "Holy shit, guys. What's it spell?"

I recounted the letters in my head. "Woman."

"Christopher is a woman!" Sammi looked part devil, part angel in this flickering orange light. "Somebody write down anything it says."

I got up and found a crayon and construction paper and wrote "WOMAN" on it. Rayne started to reach her fingers forward when the piece moved again and she recoiled. Sammi looked up at me with disbelief in her eyes. Y. I wrote down the first letter and watched carefully to see if anyone was pushing it. E. The slow scraping sound made my heart race. S. "Yes, it said Yes! Yes what?"

Rayne moved up beside me and looked at my paper. "Why did she say 'Yes?'"

"I don't know. Were you thinking of a question, Sammi?"

"I don't think so."

Tommy removed his hand. "Maybe she meant, yes, she's a woman." He seemed a little bored and I got scared I might be too young.

Sammi jumped when the piece moved again then looked at Eddy and Cory accusingly. "Did you do that?" Suddenly, the candle blew out and tiny high-pitched screams filled the dark room. I felt Rayne's arms wrap around me and I reached for Tommy but he was no longer there. More tiny screams. I think one was mine. Then the lights came on and Tommy stood near the switch snickering at us. The board sat still and innocent with the snuffed candle still smoking close by. Montgomery turned the TV back on and stared blankly into it. The snow outside had stopped. I waited for Sammi to move or smile. She looked from the board to my paper then up to me. "Let's go scare the grown-ups."

We were back in our element. We gathered into a single-file clump and moved, as quietly as seven kids can, down the flight of stairs. We waited to hear voices but none came. Sammi motioned with one then two then three fingers and we ran down the remaining stairs and into the empty room. Tommy shushed our "where are they's" and led us into the kitchen. Nothing. We bumped into each other turning around and headed past Anne's empty room toward the living room. We waited outside then jumped at Sammi's signal. A collective "Boo!" haunted the empty room.

Cory pointed upstairs to the adult wing of the house and we crept noisily to the landing outside Mommy's room. Tommy shushed us again and pointed to the loft where Isabelle and Merlin slept. "I hear something." We tiptoed down the hall and pulled open the creaky door to their staircase. Tommy and Sammi went in first and we followed tightly behind them. A large laughter tumbled down on top of us in a cloud of funny-smelling smoke that wafted past us and out the door behind us. None of us spoke. Tommy and I caught each other's eyes and turned to leave more quietly than we had arrived. I remembered that smell from an outdoor concert. Tommy must have known it too. Mommy called it funny cigarettes.

Eddy crawled into her father's bed while we walked wordlessly back to the playroom. Dick Clark was standing in a snowy Times Square on the TV welcoming 1977 with music and lots of loud teenagers blowing on noisemakers. Cory followed Montgomery into his room with the Battleship game tucked under his arm and Tommy made the trundle bed up without even kissing me goodnight.

Sammi and I put Rayne to bed then climbed up to our room. We took off our daytime layers and threw on nighttime layers while shivering loudly. Sammi finished first and jumped under her covers. "Happy New Year, Ariel."

"Yeah, you too." I snapped my lamp off and pulled the covers over my mouth to trap my body heat. "Are we supposed to promise not to do something anymore?"

"What do you mean?"

"The revolutions. Aren't you supposed to say a revolution? It's something like I won't get fat or something."

"Do you have one?"

I stared at my slanted ceiling. "No, I don't think so. Do you?"

"Can you say you want to start doing something or do you have to quit something?"

"I don't know. Why? What were you going to say?"

"Nothing, I guess. I just wondered." She pulled Bill in tighter to her. "Hey Ariel, did you get more Christmas presents this year than before?"

"I guess."

"That's what everyone said, that I'd get more presents."

"Yeah."

"Yeah."

*　　*　　*

We woke up earlier than the grown-ups and fixed ourselves bowls of cold cereal. It was still snowy out and we wanted to see if there was anywhere to sled. We got out of our morning bundles and into our outdoor bundles and headed to the pavilion workshop with a fragrant bar of Zest.

The hill behind the house, so good for running and playing, wasn't sloped enough for really good sledding so we trekked into the woods, sleds in tow, and started down the path to the river. None of us were sure we'd find a good trail but we kept the faith and took turns yanking the sleds over brambled spots and tree roots.

The woods were still magical in that way where icicles hang from branches and everything looks like it's from a movie about a princess. An occasional cardinal would break the color scheme, splashing its red wings over icy brown branches and white drifts. Maybe we were awed by the white noise of winter at its finest, maybe we were afraid to discuss walking all this way with sleds in tow and no good hills in sight. We didn't talk much.

We were almost the whole way to the river when we stopped to stare at the hill we couldn't believe we had forgotten, the last yards leading to the river's edge. It was steep, truly steep, and curved sharply right near its foot before crossing a small creek that we couldn't see but knew was there behind white foliage. Tommy dropped his rope. "Who wants to go first?"

Sammi dropped her rope. "You can if you want."

I looked at the giant tree at the bottom where the path made its right angle. "Maybe we should walk down first."

"I'll do it." Rayne smiled innocently.

Tommy kneeled and pressed his padded belly to the wooden planks. He slid the sled forward to the edge, teetered for that cartoon moment that lasts too long and ends in a sneeze or some other silliness, then pushed off with his booted feet. He and the sled jerked staccato down the hill. He curved easily with the trail and came to a halt just out of our view.

He came back up the hill, panting. "Too easy. Maybe it'll get better when we pack it."

"Me next." Sammi sat on top of the sled with her feet on the steering board and slid more quickly down the slope. She came closer to the tree than Tommy had and went a little further toward the iced-over creek.

Cory started down before Sammi was back up. "Cowabunga!"

I decided at that moment that I had to be next. I guess Montgomery did too. "I called it first!"

"No you didn't." Sometimes I argued with him even when I knew he was right just because I could. Sometimes I even won.

"Yes I did. Everyone heard me. You heard me Rayne, didn't you."

"I wasn't listening." She giggled and tried to wink at me. It came off as a facial tick.

"Oh, come on! Did you, Tommy?" He looked for a backer. "What?"

"Forget it." He stomped his foot and I felt that dread I would later learn to call guilt but now only knew as a grey that came over my heart and quieted the good in it. He slammed himself down on the first sled that reached the top and flew down much too quickly. My blood sped up and my throat swelled when he approached the turn at the tree. Inside my eyes, I saw him hitting the tree and felt my remorse as if it had already happened.

Everyone yelled. "Yeesh." "Holy shit!" "Watch out!"

I simply screamed.

But he missed the tree and flew down toward the creek. Prideful and smiling, he came back around the corner. "Did you see that? I went all the way across the creek."

I doubted him immediately, as if he had never been in jeopardy, as if I had never cared. "Bullshit."

Because the world is more fair than I am, everyone else clothed him in accolades and asked him the questions he was dying to answer. I shot him an I'm-not-impressed look and knew when our eyes met that I loved him, that I always loved him, that I would die for him.

I grabbed a sled and waited for Rayne to go before I put my weight down onto it. The trail was definitely getting slicker, faster. My heart banged against the wood beneath me when I pushed off. Like the moment before my first kiss, I was aware of everything as if it had all been slowed down and yet it was all so, so fast. Each bump registered. I saw every errant tree limb. My skin changed temperature when wind rushed against me. The tree loomed ominously as the sled jumped against newly built moguls then it was suddenly there before me. I cut right and leaned hard and heard the scrape of one of the blades against a root as I flew, now truly out of control, down further to the creek and then across it before I knew it was even beneath me. I slowed. It was over. The exhilaration started somewhere around my knees and rushed upward. I wanted to do it again. I wanted to recount every detail out loud then live it again. But I knew the rules, knew that I'd have to hand the sled over to Eddy or Tommy.

Mommy's was the first head I saw topping the hill. The grown-ups had followed our tracks down to the woods. They listened to tall tales of near death experiences and I tried to get to them before the subject was changed but was met at the top with that old feeling of my chest sinking as I realized that my story would never get told, that Montgomery was the star of the moment.

Merlin took my sled and Carol waited behind him with the other. We had been patient in waiting turns before they arrived, but now it was a matter of showing off in front of the grown-ups. For the grown-ups, I guess they had waited all the distance of the hike and didn't think they should have to wait at all. It was fun watching Merlin try to go without hands and Carol just plain steered off of the trail halfway down, but they had broken the magic of our alone time, of seven kids challenging each other in tests of speed and endurance, of furtive looks and unspoken language that needed no translator. Now we were just having fun.

*   *   *

Vacation was closing in around us now, only two more days until the Hobart kids left and school started and all fell back into that same old pattern. So, though we had sledded all morning, we went to the pavilion instead of the house with the grown-ups. Sammi and I traded boots for roller skates and were tying them when four bikes and a scooter zoomed past. They ran along the outer perimeter of the building, each trying to outdistance the other, Rayne and Eddy bringing up the rear.

I tuned the radio to WPGC and Sammi and I skated rhythmically, slower than the bikes and faster than the scooter that Rayne finally abandoned for a pair of skates she was told she'd grow into. She caught up to us and reached for our extended hands which she missed, instead catching my mitten and Sammi's scarf. Sammi went down first and I'm not sure which errant skate knocked me flat, but down we all went into a pile of metal wheels and wet, woolen clothing. The fall had pushed the air from my lungs so I was still dazed and frightened when Rayne's tee-hee cut through my fuzzy head. She was laughing and holding her hands to her crotch, Sammi was lost to us now in some far away place that the sound of her own laughter kept us out of. I laughed too because it seemed the thing to do and because they looked funny and because I was more scared of not laughing and risking being held forever from that place Sammi had escaped into. She tried to get up and flew out from under herself and back to the ground again. Hot tears rolled down our cold, contorted cheeks as she tried and failed again. Rayne wanted to be like Sammi in all things so she did a very bad acting job of attempting to get up and falling down but the absurdity of her trying to fake it was even funnier than the genuine article and we were thrown further into our noises and struggles at breathing. Then Sammi's face changed, abruptly and finally. "Come inside with me."

She was still holding my hand when we reached the side of the house. "Let's go around front, I don't want anyone to see us come in."

I followed her upstairs and tried to walk as stealthily as she did. We didn't go into our bathroom because she said it might not have enough towels. Okay. So we closed the white, wooden door behind us and kept our voices to a whisper as she revealed her secret; in her fit of laughter, she had lost control of her bladder and soaked through her panties, tights, long johns, and jeans.

A load of laundry would be suspicious but so would wet clothes hung to dry. Sammi was going through the same mental gymnastics, trying on all the options and discarding them like ill-fitting clothes. Maybe we could just throw everything in the laundry pile and no one would know. I hadn't said it out loud but Sammi answered. "But they would smell, wouldn't they?" She stripped them into a pile and we stared.

The steps creaked and we pushed the pile into the linen closet then stood on top of it with the door opened just a crack to spy. Rayne would have to be looking for us by now so we planned, without saying it, to wait until she was sitting on the toilet and then jump out at her. The door to the bathroom closed. Sammi and I looked at each other and tried not to even whisper-laugh. We waited to hear the rustling of clothing then the sound of a tinkling stream hitting toilet water. We looked at each other, our eyes asking, "Ready?" then looked out the crack in the door. Where I expected to see Rayne's little blonde head was Merlin's blue-jeaned bottom as he faced the bowl. I could only have seen him for a second and yet I catalogued every detail of this foreign sight. His hands were down in front of him and a yellow-tinted stream ran from the pink, no red, no mauve, bulb in his hand. We were dumb struck. He shook the bulb and tucked it back into his pants then flushed and rinsed his hands. It felt like it took two hours for him to leave.

Sammi gathered her clothes and we walked silently to our wing to collect enough laundry to justify a load.

*   *   *

It took almost a week for us to look Merlin in the face. He would tease us like always but we had trouble even giggling without feeling self-conscious and embarrassed. His generous brown eyes smiled when his mouth did but I feared we would never get past this. We had betrayed him somehow but couldn't apologize without telling him what we'd done.

Sammi and I sat in the green room with *Get Smart* on the TV. The front half of the house was still the warmer half and we did what we could to stay there. I was reading *Misty* for the third or fourth time. The library tab in the back alternated between my name and Sammi's. She was reading the one about the Lipizzaners. Merlin passed us on his way up the front stairs and smiled lovingly at the sight of us resting on each other, reading on the couch. "Just remember, you can pick your friends and you can pick your nose..."

"But you can't pick your friend's nose. We know, we know." And we did. He found at least one opportunity a month to lay that one on us. We didn't care, as gross as it was, we liked that one of the grown-ups talked about nose picking and other silly things. Merlin knew how to keep our attention.

I wanted to mention the bathroom incident to Sammi, wanted to say how hard it had been to ignore his laughing eyes and silly jokes for a week. Instead, I stared out the floor to ceiling window ringed with frost and onto the snow laden tree branches dipping heavy down toward the drifts on the ground and comforted myself with the ephemeral beauty of winter as seen from a warm room.

Tommy came in and I felt that spark in my heart that occasionally accompanied his entering a room. His face was getting more of that downy fuzz that would one day warrant shaving but not yet. He sat beside me and let his hand graze mine and a shock traveled up my arm and into my heart causing it to race slightly. That's how I knew we were in love.

I pictured us already married and this as our house. Sammi would live in the back half of the house with her husband, Cory, and we would live in the front half. We would have had a double wedding, as brothers who marry almost-sisters should. I pictured Tommy's sweet face staring into mine and I love you's tumbling from his mouth.

He took my hand and whispered. "Come on."

Sammi winked at me. I followed Tommy up and up and into my room leaving pieces of my trust behind me like bread crumbs to find my way back to myself. There was something more grown up about his stride, more decisive than usual.

"What are we doing?"

"You'll see."

Two more frightening words had not passed through my ears. What was I going to see? I wanted to flee but we were going together and a certain amount of compliance was expected. I sat down on my mattress and he sat beside me. His eyes struck me as wild and determined. I prepared a "No" in my head and lay back as he leaned into me. We kissed and I tried to talk myself into relaxing into his formerly-safe arms.

Then it happened. His tongue forced its way past my lips, through my slightly parted teeth and toward my own tongue. What the hell? I pushed him away and his whole body became rigid and powerful. "Come on!"

Come on and what? I was so confused. And so twelve. "You said. You said no tongues."

"Jeeze, Ariel. I was just a kid then. I'm already fourteen now." His eyes changed. The determination was still there but a layer of pleading glossed over them and I actually, for just a minute, considered allowing him to invade my body with his tongue. Then the very thought of it overtook my pity and I became as steel. No. The answer would definitely have to be No and stay No for as long as I was alive.

The determination fell away and the pleading in his eyes accompanied a resignation that let me know that in that very instant, he had outgrown me. My heart felt shot through with bullets. He pulled away and smiled my favorite lovely, gentle smile. "It's okay." And a new realization struck me as violently as the last had. There was another girl who would let him try this experiment, maybe even had asked him to. I wondered what she looked like, how old she was, was her hair soft, brown like his? Less than a second passed but the whole world had cataclysmicly changed just like the instant in which Dad said he was leaving.

Life was far too instantaneous for me sometimes.

Tommy stood up, as much as he could under the slope of the roof, and spoke so softly that I almost didn't hear it. "I love you." Then he was gone. Only the curse of our commune was that he wasn't really gone, he was just downstairs and we would see each other as soon as supper was ready, whether we were or not.

It wasn't until then that I allowed myself to realize that he had grabbed at the breasts I didn't have, that he had rubbed himself against my pelvis, that he had attempted to sexualize me and us in a way that my anatomy would have betrayed even if my mind had been willing. I knew we would never speak of it, knew that I didn't have the vocabulary even if I had wanted to.

I lay still and closed my eyes. I pictured Donny Osmond handing me a purple flower and asking me to dance. He sang "Puppy Love" to me and got down on his knee and looked up at me with innocent radiance. I pictured dancing with him in our matching purple outfits, mine a flowing dress with a shredded skirt and spaghetti straps, his a suit with rhinestones. We twirled around and around under a mirror ball and he sang and sang to me and never once tried to put his tongue in me.

Chapter Twelve

Pillows had been missing for at least three days this time. He usually came back fat and triumphant-looking after our many days of panic and calling from the edge of the patio. "Heeeere kittykittykittykitty." These short disappearances we referred to as "hunting trips" and tried to keep our worry down to a minimum knowing that he would return again with a solid belly and sit near a heating vent staring at us with his face all what's-the-fuss-about?

I hadn't put shoes on so I hopped from foot to foot in the slushy leftover snow, calling out with all the power my chilled lungs could find. "Heeeere kittykittykittykitty." I had learned the call from my mommy, or rather had not learned it at all but had absorbed it merely from being her daughter as she had from being her mother's daughter.

The Datsun's lights shot two overlapping triangles up the driveway and finally across me. What should have been Isabelle, Anne and Sammi was just Isabelle and Anne. They walked past me with a speed and focus that said they had not even noticed my hopping body and rolling-tongued cat call. Anne slammed the door behind her and Isabelle threw it open then slammed it again. I was afraid to touch the knob after that, afraid to interrupt the vibration of a door slammed that hard. Instead, I walked through the frozen grass to the face of the house and snuck up the front stairs. Icy blades crunched under my numbing toes as I passed the outside of the living room and came to the flagstone steps leading to the door whose lock we'd still not bothered to fix.

"Ariel." Sammi's voice was low but urgent and I turned with all the shock of a young deer hearing the click of a trigger. "Come here." She was hiding behind the shrubbery lining our driveway. My feet were lost to me now as I obediently made my way to her shaking body. What I thought were sniffles from cold was a runny, swollen red nose that only crying can create. "Come with me." Her mittened hand clasped my bare one and she pulled me toward the side doors. We stopped and remained instinctively quiet watching the silent movie of Anne and Isabelle fighting. Their silhouette's were combative and Anne's hair moved with every violent gesture, every I-dare-you stance.

Then Isabelle's hand came up so quickly that I wasn't even sure I had actually seen it cross Anne's face. It was a moment I instantly replayed to make sure I understood what I had seen. Anne's door slammed so loudly that we reentered the sound era. Isabelle's head fell forward and she covered her face with her hands and shook for a moment. Then, remarkably, she became erect and smoothed her braid with the palm of her hand before walking slowly out of the doorframe. My eyes remained frozen on that spot as if some form of encore might occur or perhaps I froze out of reverence for all that had already gone on. It was Sammi's sobbing that drew me away and made it all real again.

"What happened?"

"Come on." She tried to lead me to the pavilion.

"Wait, I don't have any shoes on."

She looked down at my feet then into the space just past my face. "Figures."

I wasn't sure what figured but I was certain that I had somehow let her down in this, her biggest time of need. The familiar nagging of how odd we'd all gotten tugged at the edges of my feeling like a bad friend. "I'm sorry."

"No biggy."

She looked suddenly old, very old and worn down, as I followed her through all the rooms that led to ours. She peeled her wet layers off and added dry layers over her pink and black ballerina tights. "She hates me now."

"Who?"

"Anne. She hates me."

The gravity of that possibility was too much to even consider and my mouth immediately spun alternatives. "Maybe she was just in a bad mood. Or maybe she's only mad at your mom. She looked pretty mad at your mom."

"No." She pulled her knit cap off and shook her short, static-filled ringlets. "No. She thinks I'm the enemy."

"What happened?"

"It's all my fault but I didn't mean it and now she's going to hate me forever and I can't even tell her what really happened 'cause she's so mad at me. She'll probably never speak to me again."

"That's not true." It couldn't be true.

"It wasn't really my fault, I mean, I didn't mean for it to come out the way it did but Mom was so whatever, so mad or something, that it was too late."

"What happened?" I might finally have asked at the right time.

"You know how Mom always takes me to ballet? And it's all the way in Columbia? And you know how I'm always late?"

I nodded.

"Well, we were running late again and I didn't know that Anne had missed the bus and was waiting for us to pick her up. So, when we got to the part where you have to decide to go to Columbia or Glenelg, Mom turned right and I said, 'Are we going to pick up Anne?' and Mom said, 'You're right, she missed her bus again. I'm not going to pick her up. She can wait. She can wait until we get back.' So she just left her there, left her sitting outside in the cold while I went to class but that wasn't what I meant at all. I just wondered it out loud, if Mom had forgotten or something. So then we picked her up and Anne was so mad and she just started screaming at Mom and Mom was screaming back and I just sat there in the backseat scared and, shit, I didn't know what to say and the whole thing was my fault but I didn't mean any of that at all. So then, they dropped me off at the barn and I fed Princess and then I came up here."

"Wow." Even I was underwhelmed at what a paltry addition I was making to the conversation.

"She hates me."

"No she doesn't. You're her sister."

"You should have seen her face. It was like, it was like she was trying to look-me to death."

I wanted to hold her shuddering body, wanted to tell her it would all be okay and that I loved her no matter what happened. But I knew it would be cold comfort in the face of losing Anne's love. So I sat watching her fall into herself while I rocked myself wishing I could cross the chasm between us. Then, up through the chasm, a scream, no, a yell, cut through the house. "Anne!"

Sammi came back into the space behind her eyes and looked at me then the staircase. We ran like the house was on fire and arrived just as the grown-ups were gathering around Isabelle. Herbert looked tired from another day of whatever they made him do in that secret world of his and his mouth barely moved behind his beard. "Go back to bed, kids. Everything's fine."

I had to see Mommy's face before I would leave this much turmoil, had to see that all was in fact fine. She had Isabelle's head hidden in one of her hands and was whispering something to her so that they were all hair and hands. Merlin came out of Anne's room and motioned sideways with his head to Herbert. "Come on." Herbert followed him and they put on coats and boots. I still hadn't seen Mommy's face but I knew mine was beginning to crinkle in that spot just between my eyebrows. Carol brought two flashlights from the kitchen and tried not to look at us. I didn't care, it wasn't her assurance I needed. Mommy was still nestled into Isabelle when they walked into Anne's room and closed the door.

Rayne asked the question I hadn't dared. "Where's Anne?" Only now, no one was left to answer it.

Sammi swatted Rayne's behind. "Get upstairs and go to bed."   "Tuck me in." Rayne giggled then ran up the stairs.

Montgomery looked at me with that face that said there were too many women here, too many sisters conspiring, too many things he was left out of. I smiled more sweetly than normal because he was right and because he seemed to need it. Then, even more strange, I followed him to his room. "Do you want me to tuck you in?"

He pushed aside his mountains of stuffed apes and rhinos and pulled his dirty blankets up to his chin. "That's okay."

My heart fell like we'd gone over a hill too fast in the car. Had I already waited so long to be kind that I'd lost my right to it? I turned to leave.

"I mean, it's okay if you want to."

He really did have the most delicate face in the world, far prettier than mine really, like a porcelain doll, all perfect angles and peach-colored. He seemed so small and not-terrible at all with his face peeking out from the furry ones around him. I couldn't remember why he annoyed me so much and made a silent vow to be nicer to him. Then I made my hands into shovels and playfully pushed the covers under his little limbs. He giggled and pulled his shoulders up around his ears. My face became a generous smile and without meaning to I kissed his cheek. "I love you."

"I love you too."

I reached for the light switch, then remembered and left it on without calling him a sissy. "Sleep tight. Don't let the bed bugs bite."

Sammi was reading to Rayne and I sat on the covers with her as we finished up our ritual of putting her to bed. We snuck out into the hall and looked out the window in the bathroom. Our breath fogged the glass and it was too dark outside. I turned off the light so we could see out better but everything was all snow and trees and night sky. We went to our bathroom and looked out toward the parking lot, which was better lit but held no answers.

"Downstairs." We spoke in unison so frequently now that it seemed a waste to talk at all sometimes. From the green room, we could see the patches of skittering light Herbert and Merlin created with their unsteady flashlights. Sammi pointed at the ground outside of Anne's room. Her light was off now. Dare we walk into the sanctuary of Anne's room without her permission? I guess Sammi had decided that she was already so exiled that violating this rule couldn't further damage her relationship because she didn't even hesitate when we moved to Anne's door and pushed it open. It was bright enough without the light on, all blue and moony colored, and we passed the pile of clothes on the floor, stepped over her magazines and kneeled on her bed. My forehead felt hot against the icy window as we pressed ourselves to it and looked down to the footprints in the snow that tracked off toward the road. My stomach went achy and mean. Anne was gone. Splotches of water appeared and spread on the bedspread beneath our hands. Sammi might never stop blaming herself for this one. For a second, as I was wiping a tear from the tip of my nose, even I blamed her.

*   *   *

My secret place in the field under the willow tree wasn't as good in the winter, the leafy covering replaced by a labyrinth of spindly branches covered with snow and dangling icicles. I stared out across the hills and pretended nothing hurt.

I pictured myself a princess living in a magic kingdom. Roses and wild flowers bloomed everywhere. I pictured warm lush greenery and vines with gentle tendrils curling down. My subjects loved me and looked forward to doing anything I asked of them. Mommy and Daddy were the king and queen and they smiled at me from their throne and never wanted to be apart. Fairies flitted around and landed on colorful toadstools and put ribbons in my hair.

But the picture wouldn't hold. All I could see was cold, empty white, the white that had enveloped Anne days ago and left us behind speaking in impatient bursts. Only Rayne was cheerful but it struck me as a sort of mania like that time that she accidentally scalded me in the shower and tittered hysterically because she was so scared.

We had all made some sort of silent agreement to unspeak her name. It would be like she never existed except that all the not-saying her name made her the loudest presence in the house.

My bottom got numb against the cold rock so I pounded at the padded tingling when I stood. Herbert's car rumbled past as I walked back to the house. He smiled and waved through the foggy glass.

Mommy smelled of Joy when she pulled my coat off to dry near a fire. She still had her bathrobe on but her face was made up that way she does with only mascara and bright lipstick. I was getting ever taller so my eyes almost met with hers. "Are you going out?"

She smiled conspiratorially. "We're going to a singles dance."

Her smiling open face made me feel bad for being angry with her. "A singles dance?"

"We're going to the church in Columbia. Doesn't that sound fun? I don't even remember the last time I danced. Jean is going to be there and Ruth and Tony, you remember him don't you? From the time we went to see the kites?"

"Is Isabelle going with you?"

She turned away, opened her robe and pulled a purple dress from the wooden wardrobe. She never knew what to do when I disapproved and I disapproved so often now.

"We're all going. You and Sammi will be in charge and we'll be back by eleven or midnight. I told you about this a day or two ago."

"No you didn't." My stomach tightened.

"Well, it must have been Montgomery then." She refreshed her lipstick and slipped low heels over nylons. It didn't seem to bother her a bit that two twelve-year-olds were going to be in charge or that neither of them had been told. She was clipping on earrings, fluffing curls, blotting her lips on toilet paper. I left as loudly and dramatically as I could and was immediately flooded with guilt, overwhelmed. She just wanted to be a princess too and go to her palace ball and meet a prince and have the slipper fit. I hated her for it. I didn't need a princess.

The grown-ups crammed into Herbert's car and waved and blew kisses when they drove off. Sammi smiled at me and I knew we had a secret brewing. "Come here." I followed her to the dining room and Montgomery and Rayne followed from a distance. She was sneaking around like there might still be grown-ups there to catch us. "Remember that party they were going to have? And remember only that one guy came? Well, look." She pulled the cabinet door open revealing bottles and bottles - tall, short, brown, green - of liquor. "Tah dah!"

Rayne's gasp was audible.

Sammi pulled some of the bottles out and placed them on the table. "Rayne, go get us some glasses."

Rayne could barely take her eyes off of the bottles long enough to go into the kitchen. I had seen her sipping the bottoms of wine glasses at parties and knew she had the taste for this that my allergies prevented. Sammi pulled out packets with pretty pictures of tall curvy glasses full of colorful drinks topped with umbrellas and fruit. They said things like "daiquiri mix" and "pina colada mix." She opened one and poured it into a glass then opened a bottle of rum and stirred it in. Even Montgomery's face was anticipatory. I could only feel worry and fear. "Don't you think they'll notice?"

Sammi smiled. "Bottoms up." She put the muddy substance to her lips and gulped then winced. "It's not too bad." Her face betrayed her. "Here." She made a glass for Rayne, one for Montgomery, one for me. We clinked them, like we'd seen the grown-ups do, and drank. It was sharp and burning and too sweet and I felt myself becoming an actor again, pretending I was older, cooler, and hoping Sammi would buy it. I was going to have to find ways to empty the glass that didn't involve actually pouring any of this concoction down my throat. I was going to have to laugh and clink glasses and sip and cozy up to plants and sinks and wait for no one to be looking. I felt the whole night becoming a big burden, a dance where I would constantly have to learn more steps. Inside, I always knew I was slower to bloom than Sammi but I wouldn't risk telling her, showing her. Sammi's head tipped back and the last of her drink slid down the walls of her glass and through her open lips. Her right eye winked involuntarily before she found her devilish face and started mixing more poison. Rayne was halfway through her glass and Montgomery was working pretty steadily on his. I stared at my full glass.

"I'm going to the bathroom. I'll be right back." I closed the door behind me and turned the faucet on to wash the drink down the drain, keeping a bit in the bottom of the glass for credibility. My face in the mirror looked more tired than I remembered.

The radio came on as I returned to the dining room. Montgomery bounced his knees to the beat. Rayne twirled around and around watching her flannel nightgown fill out with air. Sammi had no time for their foolishness, she was mixing another drink. Only this time it was all liquors and almost no mix stuff. Rayne fell into a puff of fabric when her dizziness got the best of her. Montgomery chortled through his nose.

Sammi tinkled a spoon inside of her glass. "Here Ariel, do you want some of this?"

Suddenly, a brainstorm. "No, that's okay, I'll make one."

"No, here, take some of this. It tastes good."

She was smiling and offering her tipped glass. I walked over like I was walking the plank. "Okay, thanks." She poured half in and we clinked our glasses. My gulp was too big and it shocked my body from tongue to tummy. I painted my smile on and wished I felt connected to something, anything.

Rayne's head lolled a little and I grabbed another opportunity. "Hey, Sammi, I'm going to go put Rayne to bed. I'll be right back." Rayne put her hand in mine and I led her up the stairs. She stumbled a bit and I had to admit it was a little funny to watch her tip this way and that. I sat my drink in the bathroom on the way to her room and she tripped on the front of her gown. I picked her up and carried her into her room and pretended I was her mommy while I tucked her in and kissed her on the forehead. Her eyes were already closed and she looked like a snow angel, like all we had left of Anne.

Sammi was behind me by the time I turned around. "I got this for you." She offered my discarded glass. "She must have been really tired."

I took the damn glass. "I think she drank too much."

"She only had one."

"Well, maybe it's because she's so little. How many have you had?"

"Three, no, four. Wait, three and a half because I split that one with you."

"Is that a lot?"

"I feel okay so far."

I had to admit my fears seemed to have been in vain, she looked just fine. "Well, maybe we shouldn't have too much more. Maybe I should pour this out."

Sammi had been kneeling and when she stood to protest, she fell to one side and hit a wall. "Whoa." We sat quietly, waiting to figure out if it was something to laugh about or get ice for. Then Sammi put her head into her hands and shuddered. I wasn't sure if she was crying so I waited a moment more to see her face which came up covered with tears coming from the outside corners of her eyes where her laughing was squeezing them. She tried again to stand up and grabbed for my arm to steady herself. She was laughing so hard that no sound came out and she had to hold her stomach, so hard that I knew she couldn't see me through all of the tears and the air rushing around her head. She tugged on me and we left Rayne in an alcohol-enhanced sleep.

"Let's go dance." Sammi was all enthusiasm and no coordination. Montgomery was still bouncing alone to the beat. Sammi tried to square dance with me but it felt too silly. She danced around and around me, laughing and tripping then laughing at the tripping. I wanted to feel like they felt, they looked so oblivious to our aloneness, to Anne's disappearance, to school and chores and weekends at Dad's. There was so little pain in their faces and I wanted my face to look like that. But I was too scared to drink anymore of that liquor and was already grabbing at the parts of my brain I had felt slip free.

Then, Sammi pulled at her sweater, taking it over her head and revealing a thin undershirt with hard nipples beneath. I was suddenly aware of her nascent sexuality and Montgomery, though bouncing in his own world, was a boy. I grabbed her hand and led her up the stairs to Mommy's room before she tore off her top and danced her pants off. Her underwear hit my arm and she banged out a very poor version of Hall & Oates', "You're a Rich Girl" on the piano. I couldn't help but stare at her slightly rounded hips leaning over the instrument. She sat on the cold, varnished wood stool and I grabbed the blanket from Mommy's bed and threw it over her shoulders just as Montgomery walked in. He was startled into stillness.

"Go back downstairs." I pulled the blanket closed in front of her while she sang and banged on the keys with the blanket weighing on her wrists.

"You're a bitch girl, and you're goin' too far 'cause you know it doesn't matter anyway." Her voice was all volume, as if decibels were a measure of worth.

Montgomery pretended not to look but his curiosity was natural and obvious. "Can't I stay up here?"

I had to scream to be heard over Sammi's singing. "Go to your room or somewhere. I'll come get you in a minute."

"Oooooh, you're a rich girl." She threw her shoulders back and sent the blanket flying. Her legs were crossed over the thickening bit of sandy brown hair growing beneath her belly. I wanted her to stop being silly, wanted her to control herself, and yet, I wanted her to continue so I could watch how far we were capable of going.

"We need more of those drinks!"

"No, no. Put these clothes back on, okay?"

"They're too tight. I don't want to. You're a bitch girl and you're going to far."

"I'm going to go get you something to wear, something loose, okay? Don't move, okay? I'll be right back. Don't move. You're not going to move, right?"

She swayed back and forth on the bench and tossed a smile over her shoulder at me while banging the keys. "Born to be wild."

I ran through the playroom where Montgomery was staring at the television while running his hand over Thomasina. He looked up at me flying past. "Soft." Then he went back to petting the cat. I missed Pillows. Rayne was lightly snoring. I sprinted up the staircase and pulled a drawer open, running my hands over shorts and turtle necks and overalls until I settled on a pair of long johns and a wide, fluffy sweater. I held them to my stomach and raced back to the room, scared of what I might find. The music had stopped. Sammi was gone. I ran through the house peeking in every room. I found her downstairs rolling around on the Ultra Shag carpet.

"Come here, try this." She patted the spot next to her nude body. "Come on, the rug feels really good on your skin."

I'd like to say that I did, that I pulled off my clothes despite the cold and let my body roll unselfconsciously around on the fake lawn of the carpet. I'd love to say that I felt the tickle of the fibers against my cheek, my thighs, my belly. But, I stared at her, paralyzed by fear and responsibility, my head rushing with what-if-they-come-home's. I wrangled her into clothing and only felt the carpet brush against the back of my hand as I pulled the pant legs over her knees. She didn't fight much then got up and started for the dining room where expensive glasses still sat on the table holding forbidden drinks.

"Montgomery! Come help me clean this up."

Sammi went straight for a bottle and I grabbed it from her. "Hey, why don't we go on a walk around the house." I don't know what I thought the walking would do but I'd lost any thoughts beyond, "Do something."

We passed Montgomery on the staircase and I smiled pleadingly at him. He'd never been much for cleaning up and I could only pray that he understood that there could be no traces of our night. Sammi pulled away from me at the top of the stairs and went into the bathroom. "I have to pee."

I wanted to follow her in but decided she was fine, that she had to be fine because the grown-ups were coming home soon. Then I heard a thud. Sammi was yanking at her long johns when I burst in.

"I fell." Her smile was less vigorous. She looked a little sleepy-faced. I pulled her up and threw her arm over my shoulder then helped her into the one-man shower stall in our bathroom. I hated turning the water on her knowing how cold it would be coming out of the ground but I hadn't thought ahead enough to warm it up before. Montgomery came up the steps ploddingly.

"Hey, Montgomery, do you know how to make coffee? They always give them coffee on TV. Can you try to make some coffee?"

"It's just with water, right?"

Who knew? Everything just appeared on television. Happy faced Midwestern moms came in carrying the finished product to their newspaper-holding husbands, or harried best friends ran it to their drunken pals while a laugh track accompanied their footfalls.

Sammi screamed when the water hit her and I feared we might wake Rayne. It got hot slowly but I wasn't watching enough and Sammi screamed again when the water scalded her through her clothing. She slid down the side of the stall and sat in a ball near the drain. Montgomery came in with a mug of black brew and I handed it to Sammi who looked at it with confusion.

"It's coffee. Drink it."

She held it to her lips then stared at the mug while water from the shower head diluted the liquid. "It tastes like shit. Are you making me drink shit?"

"It's coffee. Drink it."

She took one more swig then giggled when it spilled down the front of her shirt and swirled around the drain. "Look, someone shit in my house. Did you shit in my house? Look, look, it's gross. Someone shit in my house! Ariel, get me out of here."

I'd lost touch with her so completely that I couldn't tell if she was kidding or delusional. I helped her to her feet and she looked straight at me for a moment. It was the saddest I'd ever seen her eyes. They looked like they weighed a hundred pounds apiece and in the center of each, reflected in the pupils, I could see a footprint in the snow.

I took her wet clothes off and wrapped her in a towel then carried her to bed and bundled her up. Montgomery was staring at the TV when I took his hand and led him to his bed. "Thanks for helping me." I handed him a stuffed animal and turned out the light. "Sweet dreams."

The dining room was, as I suspected, still a mess - the obvious wreckage of kids not behaving. The coffee hadn't been made without significant damage either. I pulled my sleeves up to my elbows, filled the sink with bubbling water, and dropped the sponge in.

I was tired but awake when I finished cleaning. I appointed myself the only adult and decided to treat myself to some late night TV before bed. I clicked the set on and sat down on the trundle bed in the playroom. It was the middle of some movie that I couldn't follow but I liked being up late so I lay on my side and watched awhile and dared myself to start calling Mommy "Mom."

At first, when I heard the whimpering, it took me a minute to figure out if it was coming from Montgomery's room or Rayne's but her small voice rose into a cry and I pictured Rayne thrashing in her sheets. I resisted getting up, didn't want to be the grown-up anymore. I asked God to make her stop crying. I pretended I couldn't hear her over the TV. Then I resigned myself to get up. I had just lifted my head from the pillow when I heard the rustling of a skirt and saw a blur of purple taffeta go by. Rayne stopped crying and I went back to trying to follow the movie. When the commercials came, I wondered if Isabelle had fallen asleep in there. She still hadn't come out. Then I wondered why Isabelle would be home if no one else was. Then I wondered if everyone was home and whether I'd get in trouble for staying up late and whether I'd really cleaned everything after tonight's adventures. I got up and walked into Rayne's room. She was quiet and alone. "Where's your mom?"

Her voice was sleepy. "I don't know."

"Then why'd you stop crying?"

"Mr. Christopher said it was okay. Can I have some water?"

I stared at her face, too groggy to make up a lie. "Go to sleep."

*   *   *

I hated Valentine's Day. It seemed like a holiday designed to remind me that none of the boys in school liked me and never would.

I did enjoy making cards for Mommy and all of the Lemons. That was what we called ourselves now. I even made a Valentine for Anne, but I tucked it away in the back of my sketch pad.

I decided to rebel against my own anger with the day and wear a defiant and celebratory red turtleneck sweater to school. Sammi jumped when I walked into the bathroom to adjust the collar. We were both used to me walking in while she was on the toilet so I laughed when she screamed. "Close the door!" She spread her legs exposing her panties between her knees. There was blood on the fabric.

"Oh my God, are you okay? Do you want me to get your mom?"

"No, it's my period, stupid."

I was baffled. I knew about periods, knew that older women got them, but was shocked that Sammi, at twelve, could have one - and on Valentine's Day no less. And, once again, she was leaps ahead of me on the woman scale. "What do we do?"

"I don't know. Maybe, I can stop it somehow, maybe if I roll toilet paper or something."

"I think we should get your mom."

She looked down at her panties again. "Shit."

There were so few moments in real life that I felt prepared for. I had seen my mommy put thick diaper-like pads in her underwear but that didn't seem like the solution for someone half her size. I knew Sammi's mind was already where mine was going, why wasn't Anne here?

"I guess get my mom."

I left the bathroom and walked slowly down to the kitchen trying to figure out what to say. "Isabelle?"

"Well, don't you look festive today. You guys are running late. If you're not careful, you'll miss the bus."

Seven thousand possibilities passed unchosen before the words snuck out of my mouth. "Sammi needs you in the bathroom upstairs."

Maybe it was the timbre of my voice or something in my face. Maybe she was edgy from Anne being missing. Maybe she'd been expecting this. She dropped the dish she was washing back into the suds and ran past me with the type of urgency that I knew would embarrass Sammi but that I had hoped for. The blood had scared me. My shirt seemed too red now. I got a little dizzy and ran into the downstairs bathroom to pull down my pants. No, I was still a little girl. I wanted to be relieved but my red sweater reminded me all day that one day, I too would bleed from a place I scarcely knew.

*　　*　　*

Sammi and I got off the bus with Crane, Happy and Tuffy. Some people were going to film their cousin, Timi, because she was in a wheelchair but she drew pictures with her mouth. They told us we could come and watch. I was scared to meet Timi, scared I would look at her in a way that let her know I wasn't used to people being in wheelchairs, and that I'd make her feel weird, or worse, scared that she would actually look weird and scary so that I wouldn't be able to help staring, or worse, scared I would run, or worse, or worse. There was a ramp leading up to the door but the house was otherwise pretty normal. There was a guy wrapping a cord from his wrist to his elbow over and over and another one talking to their aunt. It was evident that we had missed the big deal, we weren't going to be on TV. I looked at Sammi hoping she'd want to leave as much as I did, leave before we'd have to face Timi and her chair and her arms and legs that wouldn't work ever since she got hurt in a car accident and broke her neck because she wasn't wearing a belt. They said she was lucky because she hadn't died. I had my doubts.

The chair didn't make noise rolling up behind me. My scream stopped everyone in the room. I was only startled but my stomach turned knowing that they would all think I was reacting to her handicap. She, a very young and pretty she, smiled gently. "Didn't mean to sneak up on you like that."

My heart was pounding so loudly that I just knew everyone could hear it when I opened my mouth to speak, could hear it echoing in the cavern inside my teeth. "No, no. You didn't scare me, I just, I just, you just, I didn't know you were there."

Her hands rested her on lap and her too-skinny legs sat unmoving in the footrests of the chair. "Hi, I'm Timi."

Sammi looked so cheerful. Was she really that comfortable with this? "Sammi. This is Ariel."

"Are you two sisters?"

We spoke together. "Sort of."

My belly warmed with the realization that we had become sisters of a sort. I'd never had a sister and suddenly, in a moment of trying to simplify things, I had three. Maybe Eddy made four. The rules were getting awfully muddy.

Timi rolled over to her easel and put a pencil in her mouth. Soon a horse emerged on the paper, a beautiful horse by any standards, not just "for one drawn by a mouth." She signed it "Timi GIG" and started another one. I was amazed at her speed, her accuracy, her talent. I tried not to imagine how good she would have been if she hadn't gotten hurt. Crane gave the first drawing to Sammi and I understood that the next would be mine. It was a foal, all knock-kneed and new. She signed it again and Crane brought it to me. I was shivering with wonder. Would I really get to keep this work of art? All for me? "Thank you, Timi, it's beautiful." We say that a lot. I meant it. "Is GIG an abbreviation for your last name or something?"

"It's 'God is good.'"

All the way home, I thought about that, chanted it in my head, "GIG, God is good." I was walking home on my two legs, watching my feet leave imprints in what was left of the snow. I was carrying my new drawing with my hands. Timi couldn't do any of that but she signed her work as a witness to God's goodness. Sometimes life pulled a sneak attack. Sometimes lessons came with diagrams and notes, sometimes they rolled up behind you and drew a picture of a foal with their mouth.

The house looked the same as we walked up but it felt different. Sammi and I were anxious to show everyone what Timi had drawn us. I wanted to tell Mommy about the chair and God and the lesson. Mommy, Isabelle, and Carol were sitting in the kitchen and they got quiet when we walked in.

I took a deep breath before daring to grow up all in one minute by calling Mommy "Mom." "Look what I got, Mom."

She smiled and I could tell she hadn't seen it at all, hadn't heard my bold move. "That's nice, honey."

What would normally be a sinking disappointed feeling was instead an angry ball in my belly. Sometimes I got exhausted by being a kid, by having everything I cared about be cute and something we could talk about later. Sammi was already onto the next thing, having ignored the parent pow-wow, and I followed her to the foot of the stairs where she stopped. Anne's door was closed like it had been for two weeks. Sammi walked over and tapped quietly.

"What?"

I jumped at the sound of Anne's voice.

Sammi wiped at a tear that escaped down her cheek. "Can I come in?"

"Not now."

"Please?"

She stood by the door for a minute, watched the knob.

It seemed like a long time before she finally came back to the stairs with her head down, her eyes unable to connect with mine. A knife poked at my heart as I followed her, still clutching my drawing that promised God is good.

*　　*　　*

Kevin told Anne he was only helping his brother when he confessed to robbing the store. He said that his brother actually did the robbing but asked Kevin to confess because Kevin didn't have a wife and kid to look out for. They gave Kevin six months because it was his first offense. I thought that Anne would be ashamed. I should have known better. She rose to the occasion. She wrote him letters almost everyday telling him, I imagined, that she loved him and missed him and was waiting for him.

She took me out to the field when we had a warm day and I took two rolls of film of her posing like in magazines. I had to carry the camera and the makeup bag and her clothing changes and her brushes and the full-length mirror she used to check all of the poses before I clicked. But I felt honored that she picked me. I would have carried an elephant on my back if it would have made her spend more time alone with me.

Easter was coming and Anne spent weeks working on a basket for Kevin. She'd arranged for a ride to the jailhouse and wanted everything to be perfect. Everyday, she tried on different outfits to wear for her visit. She collected early spring flowers and hung them upside down to dry. She bought foil-covered chocolate eggs and pretty pale ribbons with her allowance and decorated a large wicker basket. She took down her blue silk morning glories and her prized toy bluebird and wound its wire feet around the handle of the basket while singing, "I'm a bluebird, I'm a bluebird, I'm a bluebird, yeah, yeah" over and over.

It was the most beautiful basket I'd ever seen. The wicker was festooned with the cornflower and pastel yellow flowers and ribbons. It was filled with photos, hand-painted eggs, candies and flowers and love. Then, one day, Anne left in a pickup wearing a cornflower-blue and white floral dress and carrying the basket. Hours later, she returned empty-handed and full-hearted.

I filled in the blank with pictures of Kevin in a jumper, tearfully taking the basket and holding her hands while they whispered about staying in love forever. She never told us what really happened.

Easter morning was sunny and warm and we were all grateful. It was the best egg hunt ever. The whole back yard was in-bounds and eggs could be found behind bushes, under trees, in windowsills, beneath the diving board and within the windings of the garden hose. We had dipped them in dye at the last family meeting and drawn on them with crayons. Mine had the crayon first so that the dye had a halo effect. All of Montgomery's had a big "M" on them. I knew it didn't matter how many I found, Mom would make me give Montgomery my extra to make it even. It just didn't pay to be an over-achiever. I found green ones, striped ones, red ones, ones with rainbows and even one of Anne's coveted blue ones with birds on them. She only made three so I wasn't about to give that one away.

We gathered on the side porch and took the only photo I remember of all of us at once. Princess stood in the middle, flanked by Mom and Isabelle in silly straw Easter bonnets covered with bows and fake flowers and the rest of us clumped haphazardly on either side. I wouldn't even have to see the photo to know that Mom and I were the tallest, teetering on our long legs as we did. But I had become enough of a Lemon to forget that we were dressed ridiculously, spanning the array from logo-ed T-shirts to Sears suits, from a haphazardly draped blanket to overly frilly Sunday-go-to-meeting dresses.

Lunch was hard boiled eggs with salt.

*   *   *

Anne's birthday fell on a grey day. She was turning fifteen. I
was in the playroom when she entered and winked at me with a
nod of her head. I followed the snap of her neck and felt glad to be
picked again. I had forgotten to wonder anymore whether Sammi's
feelings would be hurt.

She took me down to her mother's Datsun and we climbed
in, Anne in the driver's seat. "I'm getting my learner's this year. I
need to practice."

Driving into the pavilion, my usual fear of being caught fell
behind me. She drove a figure eight and some loops. I was
impressed by her expertise and suspected it wasn't her first theft of
this auto.

"Now we do parallel parking."

She pulled up next to one of the wooden poles that held the
roof up and threw the shift into reverse. I was awed. She put her
arm behind my neck and looked behind her before backing up and
twisting the wheel. The back bumper tapped the post but I was
used to that with Mom and thought it customary. Mom said that's
what bumpers were for. Anne pulled forward and lodged the car
between two posts. I was so impressed that I didn't notice her
panic. Her hand reached down and snapped off the radio. She
looked at me and then at the posts. She pulled forward and back
without turning and her breathing became erratic. "Shit."

She went forward again and tapped the post then pulled back
and twisted. It seemed that poles and walls had sprouted up around
us. There was only one way out and the wheels would need to go
sideways like Herbie the Lovebug to achieve it. "Shit!" She
maneuvered the car back and forth some more but every inch
seemed only to dig us further into the hole. "Get out of the car.
Motion me."

I didn't know what that meant, only that she was counting on me to do it well. I popped the door open and stood in front of the car.

"No, get behind me. Make sure I don't hit anything."

She pulled forward all herky-jerky until she hit the post then wheeled around to look at me for direction. I was all arms and panic, no help at all. Finally she screamed for me to get back into the car. The weight of my failure pushed down on me, the acid in my stomach rose. Suddenly, she burst out laughing. Relief washed over me and I joined in. We laughed together until my eyes were watering, until my sides hurt. Then she pushed the stick into first gear and inched the car toward an escape. It took seven million eternities but she managed to ease the auto out of its trap and back into its spot in the gravel drive before Isabelle came out to check on the garden.

That night, the driveway was like a concert as teenagers, from Anne's school and those neighboring, pulled up to enjoy her "kegger." Their cars formed rows in the field behind the pavilion. The music from the garage band that had volunteered to play pumped through the air. Even the rain had respect for her birthday and held out. Sammi and I crept to the windows and watched as macramé-clad girls and tie-dyed boys danced to covers of Lynyrd Skynyrd and Jimmy Hendrix. Some songs were slow and pressed the tight-skinned kids against each other. Others were fast and created fit-like gyrations. We covered our mouths when we giggled, as if it were possible for someone to hear us above the talking and the music. We danced to "Stairway to Heaven" like we were a couple, our bare feet trampling a small circle in the newborn grass outside the window. I knew Sammi wanted to taste the beer from the keg. I was happy that it wouldn't be possible. Occasionally, a couple would escape through the side door near us and make out without noticing us snickering uncomfortably in the dark.

And in the middle of it all was Anne, the birthday girl, the belle of the ball, orchestrating who would have fun and how much. I wondered at her control, her stature, until I saw her look off into the ceiling during one slow song and realized with a crashing jolt that she was lonely, pining for her jailbird on this, her night of nights.

Sammi and I snuck back into the house before the police were called to assist removing dozens of cars from our lower acreage. We watched out of the loft windows as kids hugged Anne, tossed kisses at her, and drove off. We watched Isabelle wrap a quiet arm around Anne's shoulder and walk her into the house. And we slept, dreaming of being as grown-up and cool like Anne, loved by hundreds, renegade and solitary. She was all the women we'd ever admired and none of the women we'd known. She was our rock star, our model, our actress, our legend. I pushed the falseness of her smile when she blew out her candles to the back of my head and held onto the picture of her toasting the crowd from the band's stage.

*   *   *

Walking to town, Tommy's hand brushed against mine as our gangly arms swung by our sides. Electricity shot through my vein like I'd hit my funny bone. The hairs on his chin were thicker now and I thought of them tickling some other girl's chin, someone with boobs and pubic hair. The mere thought of tongues touching was still enough to make me nauseous, I didn't even want to picture touching a boy's penis. Even the word was a bit much for me, conjuring up images of scary, fleshy monster-like aggressions. It seemed that there should be a different word for that funny little pouch of hairless dimples that little boys have and the scary, hairy, soggy-looking stuff hanging off of grown-up men.

"Can we stop for a minute?"

I was surprised that Sammi needed to rest. "Do you have a stitch?"

"I'm just really tired today for some reason."

It was rare that any of us admitted to weaknesses so we all waited for some sign as to what we should do.

She started walking again. "Screw it. Let's just get there."

266

We exchanged looks and I felt her for a moment, felt her trying to be cooler than she really was, felt her hoping something would get her off of the hook. I thought of saying that I was tired but settled on nervous chatter instead. "When are those people supposed to come?"

Rayne pulled petals off of a flower and tied the stem in knots. "What people?"

"The pavilion people. Remember they said at the family meeting? The people are going to come and stay in the pavilion for money?"

"I think it's soon." Sammi kicked a stone then abandoned it, exhausted. "In like a week or something."

Cory ran to catch up with us. "Hey, maybe we should sleep there tonight."

Tommy looked at me and I felt a shiver wanting not to want to sleep next to him. We came around the corner past the liquor store and crossed the bridge into Carroll County. I had always longed to kiss Tommy on that spot. It seemed like there was something special about kissing in two counties at once, about being in neither place and both places at the same time.

We bought our candy and cigarettes and started home. Sammi kept falling behind and I found myself slowing down so no one would notice her. Then, she stopped.

"Are you okay?"

"We have to go back to town."

Rayne took her hand. "Come on, let's go home."

"Did you forget something?" Tommy's voice held genuine concern.

"I want to go back and call for a ride. My feet hurt."

Knowing it was a lie, I quickly organized. "Tommy, why don't you walk everyone home and we'll meet you guys there."

"Are you sure?"

Sammi played with the heel of her shoe. "Yeah, you guys go ahead and we'll see you later."

We waved them goodbye and walked slowly toward the pay phone at the liquor store. I didn't ask and she didn't talk. We got to the phone and she held her hand out for my change. "Merlin? Can I talk to Mom?... Mom? I can't walk home. Can you come pick me and Ariel up?... She's with Tommy and everyone... No, they're on their way... Just because... Because!... Because I got my period and I'm too tired to walk."

I was both relieved and shattered. This was what I had to look forward to? This is what it meant to be a woman? Then, skip it. I was almost glad for my embarrassingly bald skin now, my flat chest.

"She's sending Carol. I'm so humiliated. Now, everyone knows. Shit."

"Just the girls."

She kicked the dirt. "And she'll tell Merlin."

"Maybe not."

We sat on a parking lot concrete stump and waited. Sammi lit a cigarette.

I looked around. "What if someone sees you?"

"Who cares?"

She blew a smoke ring. I wanted to make her feel better. I wanted her to smile. I wanted us to be like little girls again, playing with dolls and arguing only over who would get which outfit. I wanted us to be small and safe and found in a lost world. But it was all gone now and I felt it as surely as I felt the sun on my arms. "Genie or Bewitched?"

She looked at me for a moment and stubbed out her cigarette. "Genie."

"Roy or John Gage?"

"Who?" She squished her face.

"From *Emergency*."

"Oh, whichever one has the dark hair."

"Yeah, me too. Gilligan or the Professor?"

We smiled and spoke in unison and I was glad we could still play little girl games. "The Professor."

*   *   *

I helped Isabelle arrange the warm brownies into a pyramid piled on top of a big, ceramic serving platter. Other than the scent

268

of my mother in a cloud of Joy or White Shoulders, the smell of baking chocolate was the most beautiful, most comforting thing in the world to me. I stuck a thin, blue candle in the center of each brownie, admiring the precision of my work as I went. Isabelle washed out the baking tins and put them in the rack to dry.

Sammi's dry hands wrapped around my cheeks as she played, "guess who." I turned around and light and energy were coming from her eyes. "Come upstairs. I want to show you something."

I stuck the big number candles on the top brownie. 2 and 9. Perfect.

The pounding of our feet resonated through the old wooden floors as we bounded up to our room. We arrived breathless and giggly. She plopped down on her mattress and told me to close my eyes. "Wait, first I have to tell you. You know how Merlin is always saying that thing about may the bird of paradise fly up your nose? Okay, now close your eyes."

I did and heard her rustling a paper bag.

"Okay, open them."

She held a small statue of a blue, cartoonish bird flying over someone who had a white splotch on his head. On the base were some words but before I could read them, Rayne yelled for us to come down "before all the hot things got cold and the cold things got hot." Her mom always said that. Sammi pushed the statue into a Spencer's Gifts bag. "I'll meet you down there." She pulled some ribbon and paper off the floor and smiled at the statue.

"It looks really pretty, Sammi."

"You think?"

"Yeah, he'll like it."

Merlin was sitting at the head of the table with a paper crown on his head. He had picked spaghetti and salad. I was glad, even though it didn't sound all that special for a birthday dinner. Sammi came in and put her newly-wrapped gift in the small pile on the pull-out bar. She could barely contain herself during dinner and I found myself getting impatient and excited along with her.

Dinner finally ended and Isabelle brought out the tower of brownies. It was beautiful all lit up like a chocolate Christmas tree. Merlin clapped his hands and I stopped myself from taking credit like I usually would. This felt like Sammi's moment and I didn't want to slow it down.

We sang badly and Merlin blew out the candles with Rayne's help. People were always finding little things for Rayne to do and applauding her minuscule efforts. I couldn't remember ever being praised so much and so often for doing so little but it was Sammi's moment so I let it go.

Isabelle gave him a new tackle box for fishing and made some joke about later that night that I didn't really get. I laughed anyway, though, because I thought it sounded grown-up. He got some more fishing stuff from Herbert and some other boring gifts from the grown-ups and then it was time for the badly-wrapped scraps we kids gave him. I had carved a bar of Irish Spring from Dad's into a turtle. Sammi sat up in her chair as he pulled the paper from the statue. He smiled as he read it out loud. "May the bird of Paradise crap all over you." His face fell and Sammi held her breath. She looked to him to love her gift. Her eyes reached out to him and begged him to see how special it was, how hard she had looked for just the right thing, how many stalls she had shoveled to buy it. He just looked hurt and confused. Sammi jumped up from her seat and ran upstairs. I thought of staying for the brownies and for my gift getting opened but I got up and followed her.

Sammi's face was smashed into her knees and tears wet her jeans.

"Are you okay?"

She just cried. So, I sat there for awhile and when I felt her body invite me, I put my hand on her back and rubbed it.

I heard Merlin's feet on the landing before I saw him. Sammi looked up for a minute then reinvested in her knees. I got up so he could sit next to her and offer the brownie he brought. I wanted to stay but the room seemed suddenly full of a silent conversation that didn't include me. I took my time walking down the steps and heard her explaining about the bird going up your nose and heard him tell her that it was a great gift, that it took him a minute to get the funny joke. I could guess the rest. They would hug and say love stuff and feel safe again. I was glad everyone was okay again but, silently, I wished for Dad.

The clouds had moved in late in the day and the rain was coming down pretty hard by the time we got all of the sleeping bags out to the pavilion. I loved the banging drums and shivering cymbals of the different weights of drops hitting the tin roof. This was a thunder storm so we had the added effect of crackling electrical skies and sudden flashes of blue-white light through the side windows. The giant, impossibly heavy door at the end of the pavilion was open. We'd had trouble rolling it closed after Anne's party.

The radio kept sizzling with the storm's bursts and I was wondered if it was safe to have it on at all, but we were skating and biking in circles and it felt like a disco and I didn't want to lose that. Tommy flew past me on a bike and I wished the corners of my mouth would quit betraying me. Sammi seemed to be doing a lot better, as if today's events belonged to another girl entirely.

Eventually, we settled down and built one of the last fires of the spring. Montgomery handed out the marshmallows after holding his nose to the freshly-opened bag. I browned mine carefully as everyone else furiously blew flames off of theirs and popped charcoal-covered, still-hard-in-the-middle balls of sugar. Of course they were stale, even brand new. Things had a way of getting that way around this house.

We were playing Go Fish when I yelled for everyone to shut up. Montgomery made cartoon noises in response and everyone joined in.

"Shut up! I just heard something on the radio."

"What?" Tommy almost seemed concerned.

"Shhh. I think I heard something about Patapsco State Park."

The radio fuzzed out with every lightning blast but the message was fairly clear. "The bear escaped from the Baltimore Zoo today and was last seen in the park near the Howard County, Carroll County line. Zoo employees want to remind us not to feed the bear and to 'bear' in mind that this is a very large wild animal capable of great violence."

The rain seemed louder. We looked at each other and laughed at once as if we had previously agreed on it. We continued playing cards but the big, open door at the other end seemed to grow larger, get closer. I was fairly certain we could outrun the bear from that distance and jump over into the tool room, but what if Rayne and Eddy needed help and slowed us down? What if someone tripped? What if the bear could jump over the divider too? What if it scratched at the flimsy door until it broke through?

No one dared close their eyes. We just kept pretending we didn't notice how huge and close that door was, how black the night was beyond it. I wondered if anyone else wanted to go inside as much as I did but knew better than to cry uncle and suggest it. Then a loud THUMP outside. Then the whole field outside the door lit up in a flash and we became convinced that we'd seen something black moving through it. It wasn't that any of us said it out loud, we just began too-quickly gathering blankets, pouring water on the fire, turning off the radio and packing up food and dirty dishes like a small army retreating into safety. Tommy and I made sure there were no bears between the pavilion and the house then we all grabbed the hand of someone smaller than us and ran through the rain.

I pictured running for miles with the bear bounding down on us from behind. I pictured Rayne and Montgomery as my kids and Tommy as my husband. Eddy was Sammi and Cory's kid. We ran through fields and forests and past rivers overflowing with rainwater. We ran and ran, carrying everything we owned, until we finally reached the shelter of home. But Tommy wasn't going to be my husband and the picture fell apart.

The grown-ups were in the living room doing we-couldn't-figure-out-what and didn't seem too happy that we were back but we didn't ask what they were doing and they didn't ask why we'd come home to interrupt it. Besides, since the Mr. Christopher stories hadn't gone over too well, I figured a bear story would elicit the same patronizing eyes. We scuttled up the stairs and split into the rooms in our wing to sleep surrounded by rain and lightning and loud thunder and, thank goodness, walls.

* * *

We welcomed any excuse to get out of school so we didn't ask enough questions about Isabelle's request that we help her with the presentation of the four food groups at an elementary school. We pulled up in front of a school and piled out behind her to meet with a guy in a pickup unloading giant papier-mâché foods from the back of his truck. The guy smiled when we walked up. "Who's which?"

Isabelle's voice was filled with the music of excitement. "I don't know. I guess height will have a lot to do with it."

The man unloaded a person-sized milk carton. This wasn't going to be as glamourous as I had originally envisioned. I thought we'd be the center of attention, teachers to the youth, people that they asked questions of. Isabelle was looking at the foods and at us, calculating. "Sammi, why don't you try the milk carton."

We weren't going to be educators, we were going to be giant papier-mâché foods with screened eyes. Montgomery was the T-bone steak, Rayne, the box of cereal, and Isabelle lowered the carrot onto me. With my orange-ish hair and long, skinny frame, I'd been compared to a carrot enough times to make this feel like a double injustice.

Rayne looked so funny moving her feet like a cartoon Japanese person inside the almost-flat but very wide box. We knocked into each other and the frame of the door when we entered the school to wait in the hallway until Isabelle cued us. She told the kids about nutrients, vitamins, and protein. She told them about four, four, three, two and then called for Rayne. I don't know if it was because she couldn't hear inside of the box that covered her down to her little ankles or if she was chickening out - but she didn't move forward. I turned to see if she'd heard and as I searched for her behind screened eye holes, too low and obviously made for bigger people, the wide bell-bottom of my carrot contacted with her cereal box.

Rayne probably tried to stop the inevitable, but had no leverage what with her knees unbendable inside that box. Her descent seemed slow at first, like the box was still deciding whether or not to topple. Then, BAM, the box fell flat and two little feet kicked up and down, back and forth, out of the bottom. It was too funny to resist laughing. We tried to bend and reach for her but each of our foods prevented us. We must have been a sight - a giant carrot, steak, and milk trying and failing to bend to pick up a prone box of cereal. But this was actually pretty normal for us now, just barely a story worth retelling. We might as well have been wearing giant lemons.

Chapter Thirteen

The pavilion people were arriving in a caravan of rust-splotched vans and Volkswagen busses as Dad and Sandy pulled out of the gravel drive. I wasn't sure what a retreat was. All I knew was that we were leaving just in time for more Lemonade stories that we wouldn't know.

Dad took us to the pizza place again. He smoked his cherry-smelling pipe. Sandy tried to get Montgomery to order salad. They told us about new furniture they had at their new bigger apartment and how much we'd like it. I didn't know about Montgomery but I wasn't old enough to care much about furniture.

I wondered what Sammi, Anne, and Rayne were doing with their Dad. A movie? Pizza, like us? It always took me a day or two to shake free of Lemonade Farm when we left. And we'd usually only go to Dad's for two days.

I was tired when we got to the apartment but awake enough to accept Sandy's invitation to ice cream with frozen strawberries on top. We ate in front of the TV, enjoying *The Loveboat* and *Fantasy Island*. They tucked us into our sleeping bags and leaned over us to kiss and wish "goodnight."

I dropped into sleep quickly but awoke in the dark with an excruciating cramp in my stomach. I stared at the cathedral ceiling of the loft until I felt that familiar watering in my mouth that let me know I might not have time to make it to the bathroom. I ran down the open staircase holding my hand over my mouth when the heaving started.

Dad tapped on the door while I held my long hair back and spit into the toilet.

"Are you all right?"

My retching was his only answer. I heard him walk away and return with Sandy. "Can we come in?"

I was embarrassed but I so needed help that I didn't care. I retched again, spilling more strawberries into the bowl. Sandy stood at the door and Dad wet a hand towel and tried to hold it to my head. They said things to each other that I didn't pay attention to until they mentioned leaving to go to the doctor's.

"No!"

More vomiting. More strawberries. More gut-tearing pain crisscrossing my abdomen. I heard a moan and realized it was mine. Sandy flushed the toilet and held the towel to my head when Dad left.

The vomiting slowed down by the time Dad returned, dressed to go out. I hoped he was going for medicine. No such luck. "Get her a jacket or something."

The car trip seemed endless. I had no idea what time it was but it felt very late for someone my age to be up. We pulled into the medical center about twenty minutes later. Dad's sweet pipe smoke sickened me but I didn't say anything, just kept my mouth near the open window and breathed slowly.

The waiting room was too bright. All I wanted was to sleep but my stomach felt like someone was standing on it. Dad talked with the woman at the window. I heard things like, "stomach flu," "appendicitis" and "food poisoning."

The doctor seemed like a nice man and asked that Dad come with us after I undressed. "There's no nurse right now and we're not to examine females without someone in the room." I took off my clothes and hurried into a cotton gown. The doctor came back with Dad, pushed on my right side and asked if it hurt. I answered him with a scream. He moved to my left and I cried. I was sure that it was appendicitis, that only a major operation would cure what was ailing me. The doctor asked me to turn over and Dad backed into a corner with a look of rapt horror as the doctor inserted a gloved finger into my butt. I cried and cried. I cried in pain, in humiliation. I cried for knowing that Dad and I would never look at each other again without this picture buried somewhere deep in our memories. I cried in violation. I cried as the doctor snapped the glove off and tossed it away routinely.

Then it was over and the doctor went to leave the room. Dad lingered a moment then left abruptly with a pressing health question that needed immediate answering. Something in me broke as I realized he was more uncomfortable staying with me than with the man who had done this to us.

*   *   *

Gastritis. Nerves. Tension. Dad parroted the doctor to Sandy. No need to get another upper G.I. since I'd just had one about a year ago and this appeared to be just an upset.

Sandy shook her head and spoke as if I weren't still in the room. "What could she possibly have to be this upset about at this age?"

I remembered a family night when we read an article about stress. It said that the biggest stress builders were divorce, a death in the family, moving, and changing jobs or schools. I knew the article was for grown-ups but other than a death, we'd all gone through each of those in just a year's time. I had moved past asking why my stomach was always in turmoil and into wondering why no one else's was.

I fell asleep to Sandy's guesses about puberty and boys and woke to the smell of sausage wafting up from the small, super-clean kitchen downstairs. My stomach was sore like I'd been punched, but Dad insisted that the biscuits and sausage gravy would be good for me, get my strength back. I avoided the meat and ate as little as I thought I could get away with.

Apparently, the cure for nerves is shopping so that's what we did. We looked at furniture they'd like when they got a bigger place then looked at bigger places for them to put the furniture in. Montgomery was as bored as I was so I didn't tell on him when I caught him fooling around with one of those lounge chairs with the footrest that pops out.

Dinner was at a fun place with fountains and peacocks and drink glasses shaped liked women's curves and plates that were refilled the second we could see the bottom. My favorite was the fried corn fritters dipped in powdered sugar and I talked myself into eating more than my stomach was ready for so that I ached a bit during the entire drive back to their apartment.

The next morning, Dad was showing Montgomery his new personal computer and I tried to imagine if there was anything I was less interested in. It seemed like a machine designed to exclude me from their conversations.

I looked at Sandy's *People* magazines and read about Farrah Faucet and Lee Majors, about Linda Purl, whom I'd always loved, and Elizabeth Taylor. I played solitaire with a deck of airline cards and won more than I lost. I watched reruns on TV. I read a Phyllis A. Whitney mystery that Sandy had just finished. I'd always been able to amuse myself.

Dad and Montgomery worked and played on the computer. It was called a "Pet." I would have preferred a cat.

Dinner was good. I cleaned the kitchen the way Sandy liked, where you wipe the sink down with a dry towel after everything is put away so that it looks like no one's even been in there. I'd gotten the frozen strawberries attached to the throwing up in my mind so I wouldn't allow them on my ice cream. They now belonged to that stack of things I didn't do anymore.

It was Sunday night and though the pavilion people had one day left, Dad and Sandy decided to bring us back to the farm in the morning so that they could get some things done that we wouldn't find very interesting. I resisted the urge to point out that the lighting fixture stores and stereo equipment shops we'd gone to weren't the top of my list of fun things to do. Sometimes, even I could tell when I was being a restless, opinionated preteen.

*   *   *

A dog was barking in the pavilion when we pulled up. The vans were still parked in the back field.

Merlin jumped, startled. "Hey hey. I thought you guys were coming back tomorrow."

Sandy stayed in the car, as usual, while Montgomery and I pulled our overnight bags up the flagstone stairs. I thought I saw someone walking near the pool wearing footy pajamas but I no longer questioned visual information around here.

Mom came out the kitchen door and ran past us, without a hug, to the car. "I thought you were bringing them back tomorrow."

Dad hit his pipe against the bottom of his shoe to shake the tobacco loose. "I told Ariel to tell you on Friday."

"Did you remember the check? Ariel said you promised to bring it this week."

I let the door shut them out behind me.

Montgomery and I wordlessly pulled our bags up to our empty rooms. I stooped to peer out the tiny windows at the end of the bedroom. The dog was still barking. A group of people leaned against the side of the building facing the neighbors' field and looked like they were hiccuping until I noticed stuff coming from their mouths. They were throwing up. Leaning over, in a group, and throwing up together. Little miss footie pajamas walked toward the workshop door with part of her bare hiney exposed and I understood the tension over our early arrival. Bizarre things were happening here, more bizarre than usual.

I heard the thrum of Dad's Volkswagen pulling away and wondered what else I might see if I sat here long enough. The vomiting group walked away from the side of the building and formed a circle while holding hands. They sat down with their legs crossed and looked like a wreath of pretzels. While they lifted their heads to the sky and made nasal humming noises, someone came out and hosed away their prior mess. Jay, Kay, Elle and Em watched from the fence line, fascinated.

The dog finally stopped barking. Three people walked out of the workshop and I ran down to Rayne's room to watch them pass the pool and head out onto Patapsco Road. One was wearing a frilly pink dress with matching hair ribbons and carrying a doll. Another wore overall shorts over bare, swinging breasts and sucked on a baby bottle. The last was a man with a pacifier in his mouth wearing nothing but a towel pinned up like a diaper. I didn't even have time to wonder what was going on with these people before another thought crowded my brain. What would our parents not allow to go on here? These people had obviously lost all touch with their minds but our parents were in charge of our lives. They were supposed to have some sort of grip on reality, weren't they? And had this been going on all weekend? Was this what went on every time they sent us away? And if it was okay for grown-ups to be oversized babies, where did we kids fit in? Who was in charge here?

Someone screamed in the pavilion and I ran down the stairs instinctually. Carol was cutting vegetables in the kitchen with my mother and they turned when I ran in slightly out of breath. Carol put her arm out to stop me. "Where are you going?"

"Some lady's screaming in the pavilion. Don't you hear it?"

Carol looked to Mom with that face that mixes "help me" with "isn't that cute?" and Mom sat at the breakfast table then patted a chair next to her. I was just about to sit down and give her my best suspicious look when Mr. Prickle, the landlord, pulled up in the gravel drive. Mom looked out. "Lordy, Lordy."

Carol put her knife down. "Shit."

They ran out. Mom wore her very best Southern Belle smile. I walked out behind them just as Merlin and Isabelle came up from the garden. Herbert was on TDY, which was government-talk for out of town. Mom, with her extra long legs, was first to get to the landlord. "Mr. Prickle, how wonderful of you to stop by. What brings you by today?... Without calling ahead."

The woman in the pavilion screamed again and my head snapped toward the building even before Mr. Prickle's did. His voice betrayed his usual curiosity about us with an extra dose of fear this time. "What's going on in there?"

Four voices competed. "Therapy!"

Mr. Prickle kept his eyes toward the pavilion as he stated his business. "I came about Taffy. It seems that the owner has returned and he'd like his pony back so we need to coordinate a time for us to come by and..."

More screaming.

"What kind of therapy?"

Everyone looked to my mother, who appeared to be elected. "I believe that they lie over a stool and scream up at the ceiling."

More screaming.

Mr. Prickle took a step toward the building. "Shouldn't we investigate?"

Mom smiled her special southern smile, the one that was so sweet but settled that it made you wonder if you were being rude. "Therapy is a private thing."

More screaming.

Mr. Prickle walked toward the pavilion as if pulled from his center. He walked slowly, afraid, I think, of what he might find at the other end of this stroll. He peered into a window at the side and saw whatever he saw then walked back toward us. Merlin exchanged a look with Isabelle that said we'd be looking for a new place to live soon. Mr. Prickle shook his head back and forth then looked at my mother with as stern a face as he could muster. "Tell them to be more private."

He got back into his long, maroon car and drove off while the grown-ups laughed in relief. Carol stopped and spoke with some seriousness. "Thank goodness the dog wasn't barking."

Isabelle looked befuddled.

Carol smiled and winked. "You know, the dog that barks every time that man and woman... you know."

I didn't know and I guessed that no one else cared that Mr. Prickle was going to take our pony.

*   *   *

I tried to tell Sammi about the pavilion people but all she wanted to know was when we were going to lose Taffy. The barn was oppressively hot that day and I wondered how we'd ever shoveled all this horse shit last summer. But a dollar fifty was a dollar fifty and that's what we got paid per stall. Vaughn was restless as I led him out to another stall so I could muck his and lay fresh straw that I knew would stick to my sweat.

The smell of the horse shit never bothered me. It was almost warm and comforting. But the burning, acidic stench of the piss packed down into the bottom layers of straw that clung to the dirt floor always got to me, made me heady with nausea. I didn't mind laying the itchy new straw or even pushing the full wheelbarrow up the ramp to the top of the mountain of manure and refuse outside. Or even filling the water bucket with cold water from the hose, though I knew it would just lead to more piss. There was even one part I actually liked, scooping out the sweet oats and dumping them in the feed bin. The dust that rushed up my nose as the oats fell from the metal scoop felt like candy and there was still very little I liked more than candy.

"I can't believe he can just come and take Taffy like that. We're the ones that broke him. You couldn't even ride him before. It's no fair."

She was right and I knew we'd never even get a thank you for turning that beast into a domesticated pony but I also knew that kids had very little say in the way things went and that Taffy would be gone before we'd even had a chance to wave goodbye.

I led Vaughn back into his stall. He snorted at the back of my neck and his hot breath tickled the baby hairs beneath my ponytail. I patted his burnt haunches and twisted the heavy bolt behind me as I left. Sammi finished her stall and we stacked the pitchforks next to the tack room. They'd wait there patiently for us to return tomorrow and finish the last four stalls.

I hosed Sammi's hands and calves down and she got mine. We used to squirt each other playfully until it got too cold to be funny, and though the temperature was right again, something had settled into us. This was a job. We were workers. Too young for the IRS to care about, too unprofitable to make a ripple in the economy, but workers none the less. We walked out to Patapsco Road and down to our barn. No one was paying us to muck our own ponies' stalls so they often stayed dirty a day or two too long.

I alternated between feeling sorry for Taffy and Princess and the way we'd come to maintain them instead of adore them, and feeling angry that they even existed since only Sammi and I took care of them.

Sammi led Princess into her stall while I brought Taffy in. Her hair fell over her eyes as she latched the stall. "Do you want to ride?"

I searched her face to see how my "no" would be received. Would she be disappointed? Would she hate me? She looked as tired as I felt.

"No."

She was quiet. Too quiet.

"Is that okay? Are you mad at me?"

"Nah, I'm tired anyway."

We walked up the gravel drive and I wanted to take her hand like we used to when we were younger. Rayne's tiny squeal cut the air like a silly siren. Isabelle had the hose and turned it from Rayne to my mom who let out one of her woo-hoo-hoo's and turned her back. They were washing cars. Merlin was working alongside Herbert whose black socks were covered in white foam. There were two buckets filled with soapy water. Sponges dipped into them then drizzled on their way to various cars. Mom's woo-hoo-hoo's drowned out Rayne's little siren, then Isabelle turned the hose on Merlin and they wrestled lovingly until he got the hose inside the front of her shirt. She broke from him and ran away laughing. He held the hose like a cowboy's gun and dared anyone to take it from him then turned to us. "Hey kids! Come on, join the fun!"

My feet were tired and my knees were sore. My upper back ached and my arms were weak. And washing cars was just more work, wasn't it? But Sammi walked over to the bucket with something that looked like resignation and wordlessly dug around for a sponge. She located one and didn't squeeze it out when she lifted it from the grey, soapy water. She seemed so automatic that I almost looked away and only caught her out of the corner of my eye when she slapped Merlin in the back of the head with the sopping sponge. Smack! He turned his hose on her then on me, guilt by association, and we laughed with abandon, laughed as the water washed away dust and urine and sweat, laughed as the water cleansed us of work and aches and money-making, laughed until the water turned us back into two children playing with a hose while we washed cars with our family.

*   *   *

We were worried about the kittens being born in the old slaves' quarters. Herbert told us that brothers and sisters could have handicapped babies before Mom and Isabelle had a chance to shush him. We visited Mehetabel in the shack everyday before going down to feed the horses, then checked in on her again every afternoon when we got home from school. Sometimes, we checked on her again in our nighties before we went to sleep. Montgomery would beg to go with us and put his hand in mine while we crossed the gravel lot in our bare feet.

Mehetabel had the litter while we were at school on a Tuesday, four little babies. Anne said that there had been a fifth who died but she could be so negative, I never knew if she was telling the truth or just doing her best to prepare us for the cruel world she kept swearing we were living in.

We named them Toby, Tabby, Timmy, and Tammy. I'd always wanted to do that, to name things similarly, but I thought it was cruel to do it to actual children, robbed them of their oneness.

I loved it when their glassy eyes opened, when they shook as they tried to crawl around their mother's belly. They were so small; two black and white, one grey and white, and one tabby. We watched them quickly change from quaking, weak infants to playful kittens chasing each other's tails, batting at each other's faces.

They were the first thing we showed Sammi's friends when they arrived for her birthday slumber party. Eight small pairs of hands reached in to pet and pick up the fuzzy babies.

"They're so cute!"

"Look at this one's eyes."

"Oh my gosh, he's sucking my finger."

I felt important. After all, they were sort of mine and most of these girls had never liked much about me. I allowed myself to hope that this party might be a chance for me to move from my lunch table to Sammi's. School would be out soon but maybe they would come over to swim this summer and maybe, by eighth grade, we could all be friends.

I pictured Beth waving me over while I carried my tray across the cafeteria. I pictured Chris and John smiling as I sat down between them. I pictured myself fitting right into the middle of their conversation and the whole table laughing with me, instead of at me, as I casually tossed my perfect Marsha Brady hair behind my shoulder. I pictured Sammi sitting across from me, passing knowing looks and rolling eyes between us, our secret language. I pictured Ozepher and Tina and Jillian sitting across the room. They looked at me and I knew they wished they were sitting at my new table and I felt suddenly sad. I looked at Boo's table and my heart sank even further, he hadn't been back to school in weeks. I looked at Sammi and she looked at me and I pictured myself in her eyes, pictured myself across the room with Ozepher and knew very suddenly that I would never really feel comfortable with Beth and Chris and John and the rest as long as there was a table with a Tina, a Jillian and an Ozepher.

The kittens mewed sharply when we replaced them until they found their mommy's tummy and suckled again. We went out to the pavilion and Sammi gossiped with the girls about people I didn't know. Someone had kissed someone else even though they had to have known they he was going with someone else and now they all agreed she was a slut. And they didn't like her hair. And her shoes were nerdy. And she smelled bad.

How would I ever survive this kind of scrutiny? How did they? I guess when you're the scrutinizer, you don't get scrutinized.

They never stopped talking as they moved around easily in this unfamiliar space. They unrolled sleeping bags, arranged them, stacked presents near the fireplace, pulled out combs and mirrors to "freshen up," and formed a seated circle without once breaking the steady stream of evaluations of people's jeans, the "way" they said some insignificant thing, how stupid this girl was, how fat that one was, this girl needed deodorant, and that guy's hair was always dirty. I thought of Ozepher's shiny black skin, of her limited selection of dingy dresses, of her oily braids finished with mismatched plastic barrettes. I remembered the time she let it slip that her house didn't really have running water all the time. Maybe it didn't have it at all. What if they brought her up? My chest tightened. I wouldn't be able to stay quiet, would I? Ozepher and I still didn't talk much but I did know that she was as harmless a person as I'd ever met. I couldn't stand the thought of people attacking her and I knew they must everyday.

Isabelle arrived with plastic bowls of pretzels and stove-popped popcorn. Merlin carried pitchers of Hi-C and iced tea. Carol had paper cups, plates and napkins with rainbows on them. The lights went out and we screamed until Mom came out with Herbert behind her. She carried a home-baked coconut layer cake with thirteen candles flickering on top.

Mom's voice was loudest when we sang to Sammi, whose face glowed in the tiny flames. Sammi closed her eyes and made a wish then sent us into darkness again. Mom's voice cut through our adolescent screams. "Oh shoot. Herbert, can you find your way back?"

I felt suddenly conscious of our habit of not planning ahead. It was okay to do things on the fly when no one was around but I felt myself shrinking as I stood still in the dark waiting for the lights to come back on and expose us all for the weirdoes I knew we were. Mom clapped when the room lit up and Isabelle gathered us around the gifts. Sammi unwrapped a comb and brush set, two record albums, and other gifts that made me hope mine were still special. We would be having a family party tomorrow. I was aware of every word our parents said, every gesture, every oddity. The tightness in my chest moved into my stomach as I counted the seconds until the grown-ups would leave and narrow the quantity of things the girls could later pick on. They looked like they were having such fun. Didn't they know how ruthless these girls would be? Couldn't they see the sideways glances as the girls recorded things with each other to be reviewed later?

Mom kissed me too much before she left. I loved it somewhere so far inside of me that it was little more than an echo. And I hated it as I sat there surrounded by the girls' gathering eyes.

We ate until our tummies ached then sat around telling stories before settling into a few rounds of "light as a feather, stiff as a board." I kept wanting to be the one they lifted but everyone grew bored with the game after two unsuccessful attempts to lift Dolores and one time of lifting Sammi up to our shoulders.

Sammi was always the first to fall asleep, I was always the last. I got nervous without her to cushion the distance between me and the girls but some small part of me thrilled when they included me in Sammi's absence. We smoked cigarettes and I tried to blow smoke rings without looking like a fool. Dolores opened her make-up case to replace her toothpaste when Beth got a "great idea."

"I mean, it's practically a rule. If someone falls asleep, you have to put their hand in warm water so they pee and put toothpaste in their hair and lipstick on their face."

I was dumbfounded. I had been troubled by the lack of connection between our worlds but now I felt we were from entirely different planets. And I wasn't sure I liked theirs. I looked around the lumpy sleeping bags and confirmed my fear, Sammi was the only person sleeping.

Dolores caught my eye and for something less than a second, some part of time so small that I wasn't sure it had even passed, I thought her eyes pleaded with mine. Beth handed the lipstick to Dolores whose eyes had resumed their distant critical quality.

"Draw like a clown face or something. Debbie, go fill that popcorn bowl with warm water. Ariel, take her back to the sink."

I was bolted to my spot. I wasn't sure I'd ever move again. Beth brushed her rich brunette hair off of her round face and her black eyes challenged me. "What are you waiting for?"

She uncapped the Crest tube and turned to Sammi's sleeping bag, pulling the top corner down to better get at her hair. I don't remember getting brave. I don't remember coming up with a plan. I don't remember how I got from my paralyzed spot on the floor to the other side of the room but, somehow along the way, I had kicked the popcorn bowl out from Debbie's reaching hands and into Sammi's head causing her to roll away as Beth stooped over her. Sammi grunted unintelligibly while I waited for her to shake the sleep from her head. She smiled at me then retracted like a turtle back to its shell. I didn't want to look at Beth's face but it was as irresistible as an eclipse.

"Dumbass. You ruined it."

Sammi was just as asleep as she had been before. Maybe Beth didn't know how hard it was to wake her in any permanent sense. Or maybe she felt just as rescued from the evil as I did. I looked at her for evidence that I had saved her but found none.

Dolores took the opportunity to cement her position with Beth and crouched over Sammi with the lipstick. She held the bright wand above her face like a saber and seemed to thumb through options mentally before finally lowering the cosmetic to Sammi's lightly-freckled cheek. Beth looked at me with eyes that dared me to rebel, dared me to bring on the barrage of insults she'd been saving up for the nerdy girl she was forced to deal with at her cool friend's party. I felt my body closing in on itself, becoming the spare tire I was beginning to feel like. Dolores' hand moved slowly over Sammi's skin, up to her ear, over her forehead, around her nose. Beth smiled at me and I iced over inside. She seemed to be doing math in her head, calculating a great theorem of some sort.

"Your turn." She thrust the toothpaste into my hand.

Time moved from slow into some sort of fragmentary slide show. April cackled. Beth stared. Dolores smiled as if she were encouraging me to dive off the high board. Beth stared. Debbie nodded and covered her braces when she giggled. Beth stared. I watched my hand uncap the tube and the pool-colored paste flowing slowly out into her hair. I thought of nothing. I just watched it all like a movie. Raindrops fell onto her sleeping bag and I wondered why it was raining indoors. I watched my hand make a design with the paste so that it looked like a wig with a bow on top. I wondered again about the rain. Pubescent braying bounced around the room and through my head like rubber Superballs ricocheting and feeding off their own energy. I watched my hand calmly recap the tube and place it in Beth's outstretched hand. I raised my chin to face her and registered some second of humanity in her that would have disappeared before I could have caught it if not for my time-slicing. I felt a tickle on the peachy imperceptible hair of my cheek and wiped at it with my palm. It was my indoor rain.

Everyone got into their bags and started talking about boys. I knew my job and stayed quiet though I was dying to ask about tongues and grabbing breasts and all the new curiosities in my life.

One by one, they dropped off until only Dolores and Beth and I were left. I imagined that Beth's mistrust kept her awake. How could she ever sleep knowing that people like her were out there waiting for her to be vulnerable? But her body betrayed her and her eyes drooped as Dolores and I started in on stale snacks. Our fingers hit when we reached into the plastic bowl and I thrilled at the idea that she might actually like me. I was almost convinced that we were having fun.

"It must be pretty cool living here. My parents are always breathing down me and my sisters' backs. My dad is the worst. Is yours?"

"Yeah, me too."

The lie hung between us and I panicked realizing I might be blowing my only chance to really connect with her. "Actually, our dads don't live here."

"Who were those guys that came out here?"

"Herbert used to be our neighbor and Merlin lived in the Stone House with Isabelle and they're sort of going together."

"The Stone House?"

"Yeah, it was another commune."

I felt as if a turd had just dropped from my mouth into the space between us. I was better off lying. Somehow I'd always secretly known that. And tomorrow, I'd have to look Sammi in the eye and say I didn't know who put that stuff in her hair. No, tomorrow, I'd have to look her in the eye and hope she understood.

*   *   *

The family party was a trip to Friendly's ice cream parlour. Sammi and I split a Jim Dandy, as usual, the one time a year she'd eat chocolate and just deal with the rash. One scoop chocolate, one scoop strawberry, one scoop chocolate almond chip, chocolate syrup, strawberry sauce, bananas, whipped cream, nuts, and a cherry. I loved the part when our long handled spoons clinked against each other as we fought over the last bites dripping syrup.

We sang loud from the three booths we filled and everyone in the restaurant applauded when we finished. Lucky number thirteen. Now she was a teenager. Not quite a grown-up but no longer a child, like standing on the line between Carroll and Howard counties. Like Anne.

At home, we opened presents and Mom started everyone singing again. Carol put a hat made of newspaper on the birthday girl's head. I was so excited to hand Sammi her gifts. She took the paper off the 45 first. It was that new song, "Thank You for Being a Friend." I loved that song. Then she unwrapped the T-shirt that I got at McCrory's last time I was at The Mall in Columbia. I picked the red because that was her favorite color, the color of Bill the dog and her Jack Purcel's. I saved until I could afford all the letters and had them shape the words in a rainbow, her favorite shape, "Best friends last forever." She smiled that approving smile that let me know I had done well and I thanked God.

Afterward, we went out to the pavilion, just the kids, and roller skated and rode bikes. I had the radio playing and I blame myself because of that. That was the thing that started it all. "Shining Star" came on and Anne stopped skating long enough to say it. "I love this song."

Sammi skated past her. "Me too."

Montgomery pedaled faster to impress us. "Me too."

Anne sat defiantly on the edge of the stage. "I don't really like it, I just wanted to see if you'd mimic me."

Sammi skidded to a stop and stared Anne down. "I still like it."

Montgomery kept pedaling. "I don't really like it."

Sammi and Anne stared at each other. I watched them while my skates vibrated on the pavement. I tried to slow down imperceptibly so that I could keep hearing over the roar of metal wheels on cement.

Sammi was just about to roll away when Anne stopped her with audible venom. "You don't even have a personality, you just have a combination of other people's personalities."

There was so little in the world that was more perfect than Anne but Sammi's face fell and I felt my heart crushed as in a fist and wondered at the cruelty of her words. Anne pulled her skates off in one swift gesture and walked out in sock feet.

Is there a smile that lifts from those depths? I searched for it and found nothing, only lame apologetic grins that I knew couldn't begin to fill the void that Anne's attack had left. Without Anne's love, we were bereft, lost in that bridge between child and adult without a guide.

As if cued by our aloneness, Anne came back in and padded up to Sammi. "Why didn't you defend yourself? Are you going to let people talk to you like that? Why do you take that shit?" And she was gone more quickly than she had reentered.

Sammi skated two more quick circles around the pavilion then squatted to pull off her skates. I sat beside her and yanked desperately at my own.

We walked out together and as soon as the door shut behind us, she opened herself to the tears she'd been drinking back. "Do you think she's right?"

I wasn't sure what the question referred to but I was sure the answer was supposed to be no, so that's what I gave her.

She wiped brusquely at the tears she didn't want me seeing. "I really do like that song, you know."

"Me too."

"I've liked it for a long time, even before I knew she liked it."

We both knew it was a lie but I nodded anyway. "Me too."

"Do you think that? Do you think I'm just a bunch of other people's opinions?"

It had always seemed natural for us to agree for Anne's benefit, to like what she liked. There was no greater, more exclusive club than hers and we all wanted to be a part. But I could see that Sammi didn't want to hear that. She wanted the one about her being her own person and liking the song months ahead of Anne and I just couldn't seem to pull that one from my lips. It wasn't even that I didn't believe it, it was that Anne's approval was just as important to me as fixing this.

I followed Sammi down the hill to the barn and helped her saddle Princess. The man who would never come back to claim Taffy had taken Taffy so we let the hay in his stall rot and concentrated on our remaining pony. We walked out to the field across the street and I watched Sammi and Princess run. The real estate people had already started sectioning the land to sell off as lots for suburban-type homes. Princess jumped the first few rope partitions just fine but the third must have appeared insurmountable to her because she stopped dead in her tracks and Sammi flew over her neck and onto the ground. I ran furiously across the dried-out remnants of a once prosperous corn field and knelt beside her shuddering body. She shook with a ferocity I'd yet to see in our short lives. I rolled her over and readied myself for the warming embrace designed to reassure her. It took a minute for my brain to wrap itself around the twists of her face, she was contorted in unabashed... laughter.

Sammi laughed to herself the whole way back to the barn. The sun was setting somewhere behind Happy's house and played the red notes in Princess' coat. Stalks crunched and pressed pale dust out on either side of our feet.

I pictured us crossing a desert, the sun beating down as we walked slowly whispering, "Water... water..." I pictured dark robes dragging the brittle ground. There was no oasis, no hope of rescue, only walking, more walking.

Sammi was quiet while she brushed the sweat from Princess' stocky muscles, but occasional bursts of laughter pushed through her lips and danced maniacally across the air between us.

I reached for her hand as we walked back to the house with the sky turning that murky blue before the star-speckled black takes over. She seemed not to be there somehow, hiding somewhere beneath herself, and her hand felt dead in mine.

The lights in some of the windows were on and we used them to guide us up the darkened drive. The bushes looked like scary hair with the light shining through from behind. I sent another smile to Sammi but it landed on her downturned cheek and fell off.

The totem tree appeared at the top of the hill and it hit me how bleak it looked at night with its amputated limbs. It swirled on itself, something we might not have been able to see had it been covered with lush springtime leaves. It twisted upward as if it had been caught in a tornado but held tight to its place.

Sammi lifted her eyes and we had a whole conversation about the limbless tree without ever opening our mouths.

Grown-ups were in the kitchen laughing about a joke we had missed. Carol kept trying to add to the story but her own laughter stopped her. Mom woo-hoo-hoo'ed and Merlin wiped juice from his chin. Must have been a good one.

Anne's door was closed. Upstairs, Montgomery's light was out and Rayne had fallen asleep with her overhead lamp on. Sammi pushed the switch down and I followed her up the stairs into our room. I hated the divider wall we had erected after a fight, but I could feel her thanking God for it as she disappeared into what little privacy it offered. Her table lamp went out almost immediately. Feeling lonely in a room with someone else is a special brand of loneliness. I looked at the pictures of horses and leggy models I'd mounted on bright construction paper and tacked into the divider wall. I tried reading *Through The Looking Glass*. I pulled out a small, latched diary I hadn't touched since Tommy and I stopped kissing and pushed the tiny button down popping the strap open.

· "Dear diary, why do I call you that? I'm just writing to me. But dear Ariel seems strange. How did the dear diary thing ever start? Anyway, Sammi and Anne got in a fight and now Sammi's sleeping in her room and I wish she'd stay up and tell me about it or something but she falls asleep so fast. Wait. I hear something."

It was a soft whimpering at first, a hollow sound that gathered on itself and became a bellow. "No! No! Help!"

I jumped up and ran into Sammi's half of the room and we smashed into each other when she came around the corner to see if it was me. We ran down the stairs and into Rayne's room and Sammi shook her too abruptly. Rayne's hysteria rose as Sammi tried holding her screaming mouth into her chest. Little arms grabbed at nothing and Rayne's screaming got even louder.

"Help me carry her upstairs. She's going to wake Montgomery up."

I took as much of her weight as I could from my awkward position and we carried her up the narrow stairway. Rayne's hands banged against the walls. "You're taking me to hell! You're taking me to hell!"

Her eyes were open and frantic. I felt guilty and frightened. I felt like that scared little girl in *Gone with the Wind* who didn't know how to birth the baby. Sammi rocked Rayne on her lap and I ran my hand over her slightly-sweaty hair until her breathing sounded more like ours.

She looked up at Sammi with tired eyes. "What's happening?"

"You had a bad dream."

I chuckled nervously. "Really bad."

"Really? Am I okay now?"

Sammi slowed her rocking. I kept petting her hair and watching this thing called "sisters" that I was only tenuously a part of.

*   *   *

It was the first time we were allowed to play hooky. Just me and Sammi alone all day at the horse show. I couldn't wait. Sammi was taking forever to get dressed and I wondered if I had underestimated the importance of what I chose to wear. I opened a drawer and pushed the shirts around aimlessly, hoping that some magical shirt I had forgotten about, some new, sexy, cool shirt would be hiding at the bottom somewhere.

Sammi spoke over her shoulder on her way down the steps. "Come on, Mom's going to make us late." She turned to me and I gasped. Her breasts were suddenly huge.

"What did you do?"

"I stuffed my bra. Come on."

"You can't go like that."

"Why not?"

I never knew the answer to that question and the Busch women asked it so frequently. "You just can't."

"No one will know us there. We can be anybody we want to be. We can be in high school with cool boyfriends who live in New York and own a business selling... hats."

I could have gone a lifetime never seeing my limitations if I'd been raised without moments like these. It was one of those times when I knew that I was too scared to be like her but I wasn't going to have as much fun if I didn't try. I knew I'd feel stupid all day. I knew I'd want to run to a public bathroom and kill myself from embarrassment but she spoke to some small echo of an individual in me. She spoke to the tiny sliver of me that wanted to be like Anne more than I wanted to be safe, that wanted to live out loud and damn what people thought of me.

I pulled two socks from my drawer. "Can I borrow a bra?"

The first pair, athletic tube socks with blue stripes, made me look like a three-headed monster. I moved to anklets but the pom-poms at the heel looked funny. Sammi finally hustled me down to the bathroom and stuffed balls of toilet paper inside the small pockets where my own breasts should have been. Ever the worrier, I felt immediately guilty for wasting so much toilet paper, a precious commodity in this house, and made a silent vow to use it later.

We wore sweatshirts but needn't have botherhed because Isabelle seemed not to notice any change as she drove us to the Capitol Centre and dropped us at the curb. "Meet you back here at five sharp."

We walked in like two teenagers and sauntered up to the ticket counter then to the arena. It was like a giant bowl with seats all around. The center was full of dirt and wooden jumps and a white horse was flying over one, then the next, with a properly-dressed English rider on its back. The small crowd clapped politely after each jump and more enthusiastically as the horse pulled to a halt and finished its routine.

We found our seats, too high up and not another soul around. Sammi pulled her sweatshirt off and tied it around her waist before sitting. "These seats suck."

"At least no one's in front of us."

"Take your shirt off."

"That's okay. I'm cold."

"Chicken."

True. No rebuttal.

Clapping for the brown mare, I sat down. Sammi squirmed into Indian style in her seat. "We should move down there."

"We can't."

"Why not?" Again, that question.

"Because we have tickets for these seats."

Sammi laughed. "No shit, Sherlock."

"What if they check the tickets?"

"They're not going to check the tickets."

"But what if they do?"

"Then we'll lie and say we didn't know." She was already in the aisle and working her way down the very steep staircase.

I followed with pictures of guards pulling us from our seats dancing in my head. She moved to the fourth row and came to rest next to an older couple. I sat too but my body was anything but at rest.

The next horse was beautiful. I knew Sammi would love it because it was an Arabian, her favorite. I was holding out for the Lipizzaners, the ballerinas of horses. She hit my arm every time the Arabian jumped. Her face was a lamp with illumination escaping through her wide, brown eyes and her gasping mouth. I grew glad we had come, glad we had asked to play hooky, less worried about missed assignments and guards looking for tickets. I settled into my seat some more. Sammi grabbed her sweatshirt and jumped out of hers. "Come on. These seats suck."

"What?"

"It's too close. I can't see anything. We should go up higher where you can see the rink better."

My stomach went into its familiar knot while I followed her up and up and up to the very highest row in the building. There was a haze of risen dust between us and the floor. We were higher than the center screens where they flashed basketball scores. The horses were like the plastic ones we collected and carried around in our pockets. It was actually a little thrilling, like being in a plane.

Sammi threw her shirt into a neighboring seat. "Why don't you take that off?"

"It's too embarrassing."

"There's nobody for miles. No one's going to see. Besides, you're the only one who knows they're falsies."

I looked around at the rows and rows of bare seats all the way around and down and down below us. "Okay." I looked at what I hoped would be my future and tried to get used to the idea of having real breasts. My upper arms kept knocking into them. Unwieldy.

"Look." She ran her fingers over the carvings in the wall. The black paint had given way to the white plaster beneath, spelling things like Huey loves Julianne. "Do you have a knife?"

"Are you high?" I loved using that one ever since Anne had said it to her mom.

"Well, what do you have?"

"Nothing."

"Come on. We have to write something."

"I have a quarter."

"Good, give me that."

I dug into my back pocket and pulled out some change. Sammi rubbed at the wall, and if intentionality had meaning, she would have dug a hole to China. As it was, she made a blurry mess of scratches amounting to nothing.

"Come on." She crawled over some chairs to find a new spot on the wall. She lit two cigarettes and handed one to me.

"I don't think you can smoke in here, can you?"

"Who's going to see?"

I hated these inarguable bits of logic. "Hey, what about my comb?" It worked like a pocket knife where one half was a comb and the other a brush and they folded into each other, kelly green plastic with black bristles.

Now she was cooking. She carved an S and gave up on the idea of spelling out her name. She followed it with a B for Busch then a plus sign. Who would she put? Cory? David Cassidy? I waited as she cut at the paint. J? Who was J? And then another J.

"Who is JJ? Is it that Jeff guy from science?"

"Duh, Jimmy Jarvis."

There were moments where our thirteen years of history siphoned away and left nothing but the realization that Sammi would always be other. I wanted so badly to know who Jimmy was, to give that to her, to give her at least that. And I was certain that Beth knew, Dolores knew. "From reading?"

"You know him, he sits at my table at lunch. Come on, you know. He's so cute."

I ran through everyone at the table in my mind. "The one with the blonde hair?"

"Ariel, come on, Jimmy Jarvis. Jimmy?"

I so wanted - SO wanted - to know.

"Just forget it."

"Wait, is he the one who always wears the corduroys? The one with the glasses?"

"Just forget it."

"No, I know who he is. Does he wear glasses?"

She pushed her cigarette out and I thought she had given up. "No, but he sits next to that guy sometimes."

"Oh yeah, yeah, I know that guy." I didn't and I hated lying but she had made that last effort and I felt I owed it to her. I made a note to myself to look for him next lunch and laughed in all the right places while she told me how cute he was and the thing he had said to her about being as pretty as the *Flying Nun* lady.

She made the A and the W for my name than looked to me. "Who should we put you with?"

"Tommy?"

"No, it should be your biggest crush. When we carve these, it's like making a wish."

"Okay, put D.O."

"Who? D.O.? Who's that? Darrin? Danny?"

"No, you don't know him."

"I'm not putting Donny Osmond."

"You said it could be anybody. You said it should be my biggest wish."

"It has to be somebody real though, someone at school or something."

"I don't like anyone there."

"Then someone we know. Come on, you gotta like someone."

I thought hard and a kaleidoscope of boys passed inside my eyelids. Tommy, Crane, Donny Osmond, Happy, Fonzie, Cory, Merlin, Carmine Ragusa. None of them was my special carve-his-name-into-the-Capitol-Centre-wall guy. "I can't think of anyone."

"How about Jason?"

My face twisted into confusion bordering on panic. "Jason who?"

"The kid in wood shop. He smiles at you all the time."

"The one with the glasses?"

"What is it with glasses? Not every guy wears glasses."

I could hear in her voice that the game was becoming less fun for her so I gave in.

She scratched at the paint. "That's who I'm putting."

Sometimes my life felt like it all fit into boxes of "it figures" and this was definitely one of those times. I'd dreamed of this moment, the moment when I'd finally get my initials carved into somewhere permanent but it figured that Sammi wasn't my boyfriend and it figured that she just picked some guy out of exhaustion with my immaturity and lack of popularity and now my name would be forever linked with J.C., whoever that was.

Sammi ran her hand over the scratches to clean off the paint chips and leaned back to take in the rewards of her efforts. "Come on."

I followed her back down the stairs and we went out into the hall that ringed the indoor stadium. I adjusted the toilet paper boobs while I was in the dental-office-green bathroom stall. I was beginning to like my paper breasts and wished I could wear them to school. My mind followed that train and pictured the chests of girls in my classes. Were any of them wearing socks? Maybe I wasn't the only one left without boobs. Maybe I wasn't a late bloomer like Sandy said. Maybe everyone was just as scared as I was and they all faked it to throw everyone off the trail.

We bought warm pretzels at the concession stand and Sammi filled a tiny Dixie cup with yellow mustard. We walked down the hall until we were on the other side of the stadium then entered another portal. We sat high enough to see the whole rink, low enough to avoid dizziness - and totally alone. She dipped her pretzel into the mustard while I stripped the salt off of mine. She made it look so good together, though it seemed an absurd combination, that I finally had to try it. The vinegar bit at the back sides of my tongue, alternately warm and yeasty then cool and tangy. Maybe she was onto something.

We watched the beautiful horses and I pictured myself in an English riding habit sitting atop a Lipizzaner waiting in the wings for our turn to come out of the chute. I pictured his flowy, white mane between my fingers as I encouraged and comforted him before our big show. I pictured his feet lifting restlessly and heard the breathy snorting from his nostrils. I pictured us entering the ring to a round of applause. I pictured us circling the ring once then flying effortlessly over the wooden jumps to applause that enveloped me like an anonymous hug. I pictured us winning the blue ribbon and the packed arena in a standing ovation throwing red and white roses at our feet.

As soon as the food was gone, we were up and walking again. I was beginning to feel cool. I was beginning to feel like we were cooler than all those people sitting idly and watching the show like it was on TV. We were really here, we were enjoying the here-ness of the show. And we were on a giggle jag. We went down to the lower level and found some seats in the front row. We couldn't trace the horse's swirling movements but we could feel the pressure of the hoofs against the trucked-in dirt. Dust rose up and flirted with our eyelashes, our nose hairs. I sneezed twice. The horses passed so closely that it seemed we could have touched them had we reached out. Sweat sprayed out in a fine mist when the black horse's muscles twitched and the hair shuddered. My own body twitched in fascination, in feeling close to something that alive.

We sat there for four horses then were back on the move again. I realized, too suddenly, that we were looking for boys. Part of me hoped we'd find some but most of me was relieved that no boy's parents would allow their child to skip school to watch horses running circles. The day was longer than I had thought it would be and I wondered if grown-ups had long days or short ones.

Isabelle was late. We dared fate by smoking even after it was already ten after five. Isabelle still seemed preoccupied when she pulled up in the brown Datsun B210, but like I loved about mommies, she pushed through whatever was gripping her fingers too tightly around the steering wheel and asked us to tell her all about our day. It was Sammi's mom so I let her tell most of the stories knowing that I'd get to talk my mom into that sleepy place where her eyelids lower and she protests while acting startled. "I'm still awake." After she fell asleep, I'd be able to tell Carol too and then brag to Montgomery while Sammi told Merlin and Rayne about our big adventure.

When we got home, I started for the door but Sammi held my hand and pulled me to the garden. She pulled a stalk that hadn't grown corn yet and snapped it into two. I followed her while she dragged the leafy stalk down the drive. "Let's go feed Princess."

We held out the stalk and watched Princess chomp on the sugary center. She wasn't a Lipizzaner or an Arabian, she wasn't tall or talented or well behaved, but she was ours. All over America, kids were playing with toy horses, reading horse books and watching horse shows on TV. Sometimes, in picturing all the things I wanted, I forgot to love what I had.

We brushed Princess and talked mindlessly but my heart was full, full of Sammi and the farm and a day of running around as free as wild horses.

*   *   *

We were going to play grown-ups against kids but the grown-ups thought that wouldn't be fair. My team was Isabelle, Carol, Herbert, and Rayne. Sammi played with Mom, Merlin, Montgomery, and Anne - who wandered by just as we chose up teams. Our team was up to bat first. I was horrible at hitting. There was just too much room for error between the hands on the bat and the bat contacting the ball. I always envisioned getting a good chunk of the ball and sending it over the fence but I had to settle for grabbing any piece of it and getting it anywhere on our make-shift diamond.

Mom always cheered for me no matter what I did and despite her being on the opposing team. Sometimes, when I was very quiet inside, I felt my mother's efforts and I knew that not only would I always love this woman above any other, but that I was looking into my own face at thirty-six. It was my obligation to roll my eyes at her oddities but inside, I marveled at her ability to find rainbows in oily parking-lot puddles.

I got to first base because Merlin pretended not to see that it was a foul ball. He smiled at me but didn't do the wink so I didn't feel like we were sharing a lie. He always knew exactly how to skate thin lines. Sometimes, he was my favorite grown-up. He didn't have his own kids but he seemed to understand us more intuitively than the others.

Carol, a former gym teacher, knocked the ball pretty far and I ran down the hill toward second base. The grass was too high and Anne was the only way I knew where the base was. Her hair was braided and she looked like a blonde squaw. We didn't talk, me pretending to be intensely interested in Herbert's ability to hit the ball and her pretending not to notice that she was playing a family softball game. But I could tell she liked me today without any words and I glowed inside.

Carol hopped back and forth and threw me glances that said she was looking to steal a base. I hated that. Why couldn't we just hit the ball and run the bases? Why was there this added pressure to be on the lookout while the next person batted? It was funny how much Carol was a part of us now. More like a long lost relative that we had found again than a renter we had met through an ad in the paper.

Herbert hit the ball hard but into the ground so it didn't get very far before Merlin caught it and threw it to Montgomery behind the plate. Herbert ran to first base in his white sneakers and now familiar black socks. It was strange to me that he saw my dad more than I did. They probably waved to each other in hallways, each holding their own tongue about the other. I loved him being a Lemon because it was like bringing our old backyard with us to the farm. Everyone needs to keep something the same when everything changes. Herbert's black socks and salty beard were an anchor for all the drifting.

Bases were loaded and Rayne was next up. She stood masterfully and I actually dared to hope she might hit it, then she moved into a fit of laughter and I knew this would be our first out. Merlin tried to hit her bat with the ball but she moved it in a spastic jolt of frenetic giggling and the ball sailed past untouched. Rayne was growing so quickly and it was becoming apparent that what she was growing into was Anne. Her ropey, white hair flowed with the same arrogance, her cheeks and nose had been carved with the same chisel. The sprinkle of freckles fell in the same pattern. I realized with a start that Sammi and I would always be adoring Anne or catering to Rayne, that there were women on this earth whose job it was to stand apart from the rest of us and allow us to revolve around them. Rayne would be one of those women.

Isabelle was up next and I made ready to run to home. Sammi stepped on my foot and held it there and we pushed at each other playfully until neither of us was watching the game anymore. I wrapped my arms around her defiantly. "If you go, I go."

She threw her arms around me. "Then you have to drag me home with you."

We smiled and took turns squeezing each other harder and harder. The ball rolled past us and I ran for home. Sammi dragged along with me for a second then went after the ball. I made it home but Carol was tagged out at third base.

I was still huffing when I took up the bat and tapped it on the cereal box we were using for home. I'd seen the tapping done on TV and it gave me confidence, though I had no idea what it was for. Isabelle smiled expectantly from first base. Jay, Kay, Elle and Em watched from the fence. Pressure started to crawl up my spine and squeeze the pleasure from me. Isabelle had always been like another mother to me but never more so than here at the farm. I looked from her to Anne and Sammi and Rayne and marveled at the cohesiveness of their genes, wondered if Montgomery and Mom and I looked so of-a-whole. Everyone was staring at me and I was supposed to be "keeping my eye on the ball" but I kept running the bases with my eyes and pulling in all these pictures of families and of the family that we had become.

Isabelle shook her butt back and forth until Merlin could resist no more and ran over to smack her behind. She ran and he chased her then tagged her with the ball. "You're out!"

"What?" The wheels of logic in Herbert's head spun and he walked over to Merlin. "She was responding to the chase, not the game."

Merlin smiled and tapped Herbert with the ball. "You're out!"

Sammi and I laughed. Montgomery stood up behind me and laughed too. I just started running. Running and running. I grabbed Isabelle's hand and she ran with me. Merlin chased us with the ball as we rounded the bases. Anne sat down and strung a necklace of clovers. We ran in crazy circles and Mom ran with us and Sammi ran too. We squealed and split and ran until we forgot who was on which team and fell in a laughing, puffing heap. Montgomery snorted a laugh. He had weeds in his dirty hair and a grass stain on his knee when I pushed him over. He put fistfuls of dirt and weeds in my hair and I pushed him over again and saw Jay, Kay, Elle, and Em staring at us from the fence line. Everyone was laying down and Sammi pulled me next to her and we stared into the blue abyss and sometimes into each other.

Chapter Fourteen

It was the last week of school. I couldn't wait for it to end. I would miss Tina and Jillian and even Ozepher's silent acknowledgments, but I could see them once or twice during the summer, maybe for a slumber party on my thirteenth birthday. And I wouldn't miss them more than I hated all the fighting and teasing in this place. I could wear my clothes without feeling ugly and poor. I could be around people who mostly liked having me around. And I could eat at the same table as Sammi every day.

Crane and Hap and Tuffy were already positioning themselves to get invited to our pool during the bus rides home. We fed Princess and thought about going for a ride but decided to walk to town instead so she was still out in the field that night, a forgotten chore.

We watched TV. Sammi brushed Rayne's hair and Montgomery lay with his head in my lap. Anne was out with friends. Carol was filling out forms. Mom was playing the piano. Merlin and Isabelle were upstairs in their loft. Herbert was out on a date that we had teased him mercilessly about, a woman from work he'd been hiding from us for about a month.

Mom didn't hear the glass breaking over the sound of "Fleur de Lis." We didn't hear the cackle of teenage boys over the laugh track of "Happy Days." Carol didn't hear the car speeding off over the sounds of her own humming. It was the glow that was finally loud enough to be noticed, the orange glow that illuminated what Merlin and Isabelle thought should have been a darkened room.

None of us heard them jump out of bed. We were still oblivious as they pulled on robes. It wasn't until they came thundering down the stairs - screaming - that all of the sounds fell into their proper perspective. It wasn't until the noises of "just life" were shattered that we realized how good, how sweet, how fragile "just life" was.

"FIRE!"

We were all out of the front door within seconds. Merlin was yelling something into the phone in the green room. We stood on the porch looking at the distant glow of the barn on fire.

"They said someone already called. They should be here soon." Merlin gripped Isabelle and pulled his robe tighter.

I looked at Sammi to figure out what to feel. Everything was all scrambled inside me. Tears dropped from her chin onto her T-shirt. Then, as if shaken from a sleep, she grabbed me. "Princess!"

"Oh my God!"

Mom pulled us back. "Shhh. They'll be here soon." I was about to pull from her grasp but the look on her face, the fear and sorrow, stopped me.

"You know what, Sammi? We didn't put her away today. She's in the field."

"Oh, thank God. But what if she wandered into the barn?"

Isabelle stood on her toes, hoping to find a fire engine coming up the road in the distance. "Horses are afraid of fire. She'll run from it."

Merlin stepped off of the porch and we followed out of curiosity, fear, and the deep desire to control that which cannot be controlled. As the barn came into full view, I started picturing things again but it was all wrong. Instead of fantasies of love and heroism, I pictured everything we were losing; the old newspapers with photos from the olden days, the hatch we'd jumped down during hide and seek. I pictured throwing rocks out of the hay window for kisses. I pictured the personalized boxes we made in metal shop. And I pictured the weeping willow, my secret place, my hiding spot when things hurt too much to talk about.

The siren arrived before the whirling lights did. Two trucks stopped in front of the barn and unloaded. Virginia stood at the end of her drive. Jay, Kay, Elle, and Em stood at their fence line with their mother and father. More trucks arrived and Herbert's green Gremlin navigated through the trucks and stopped to meet us where we stood below the Lemonade Farm sign. "How did this happen?"

It was a question none of us had thought to ask. But he caught on and soon, he was standing silently with us. Nine glowing faces watching sparks fly up and dance dangerously among the leaves, watching strangers pull hoses from trucks and spray water into the blaze, watching flames fold in on themselves under the eaves then curl upward and onto the roof, watching something die.

*　　*　　*

Rain pinged and steamed as it hit the black chunks of wood. Princess was tied to a tree near the back of the field. Virginia offered to stable her until we figured things out but we hadn't gotten around to bringing her up there. We weren't allowed to touch anything inside the ring of charred grass. We walked aimlessly around the back field, taking the remains in from different angles. I crept to the secret spot. It was still intact. Black flakes covered the roof-like greenery but inside, it was as lush and silent as always.

Except that Sammi was already inside sitting on one of the low flat rocks. I sat down on the other. Sammi stared ahead into the weeping tangle of branches and leaves. "It's still here."

"You knew about this place?"

"This is my secret place."

I laughed at my arrogance in thinking I would have been the only one to have enjoyed the magic of this living tent. The branches parted and Montgomery crawled in. "What are you doing here?"

Sammi winked at me. "Your secret place?"

"Did you guys follow me?"

I couldn't resist a jab. "We were here first. How could we have followed you?"

He kneeled down near the trunk and I watched the tiny bits of sunlight play on his blonde hair, dirty with soot. The branches parted again and Rayne came in. "Hey! Why are you guys in here?"

We laughed and spoke in unison. "Your secret place?"

"No fair." She sat on her behind and faced us. There was no more room left but there were no more kids so it worked out.

But the branches parted again. Anne held them to the side like a curtain. "Out!"

I was tired. Loss is tiring. None of us moved. Entering, Anne dropped the strands of leaves. "Move over." She sat on half of Sammi's stone and we waited for her to let us know if this was a talking moment or a quiet moment. With the right incentive, kids know just how to be quiet.

The soot fell through in places and dusted our faces, our hair, our clothes. We looked sillier and sillier but no one made a sound until Anne let a giggle escape. I laughed until my sides hurt. Sammi and Anne laughed on their shared rock. Montgomery laughed through his nose. Rayne wet her pants and we laughed some more.

*   *   *

It was June third. Four more days of school. Sammi had stayed home with a stomach ache but I suspected it was woman stuff.

We were doing gross national products in social studies class when I heard my name on the P.A. system. I'd never been called to the office for anything. Mr. Dupont looked at me and I felt suddenly heavy.

"Why don't you take your books with you."

I closed my social studies textbook and stacked it on top of my ring binder then put my math book on top before walking out of the oddly reverent room. The halls were empty and my Dr. Scholls clacked against the tile flooring. Click. Clack. Click. Clack. The hall was eternal. Click. Clack. Click. Clack. I could see Merlin through the chicken-wired glass of the office. Click. Clack. His face didn't look right. It was puffy, tired, elsewhere. Click. Clack. I pulled the door open. The secretary looked grave, old. That's when I was able to sum up Merlin's face. Old, he looked old. He said nothing for seconds, the kind of seconds that feel like minutes, hours even. "Your mother is in the car."

I didn't question him. For the first time I could remember, I wasn't curious, or rather, my curiosity weighed less than my fear of knowing. I followed him to his Camaro and went around to the passenger side. Mom's long legs were extended out of the car and her head was bowed. When she saw my beaten sandals beneath her, she lifted her face to me and she was a hundred years older than she had been when she kissed my forehead this morning. She was red and seemed swollen, bruised. But it was just the havoc of tears that had come too quickly, had pushed their way out of her and left her beaten in their wake. Her voice was wispy and mottled. "Anne's dead."

"What?" I heard the laughter come up from my gut. Felt my face rebel in a smile, a force field against bad news. "What?"

"Get in the car. We're going home."

The nerves above my lip twitched and my cheeks were instantly wet. Merlin choked. Mom sat forward and pulled the seat behind her so I could get in. I started shaking and my math book fell and splayed on the pavement. "How?"

"Get in the car, my heart."

I was numb as Merlin drove us home. Mom shuddered with tears. "There was a man, a food delivery man at the school. He apparently asked her if she needed a ride."

Merlin gripped the wheel and drove only well enough to keep us on the road. Mom twisted her skirt with her fingers. "I guess she felt like she could trust him since he came to the school once a week."

"Did they get in a wreck?"

"No baby, he killed her."

"Why?" I couldn't have known how unanswerable that question was, couldn't have guessed how many years I had ahead of me with that question unsatisfied.

"Sammi is going to need you to be strong so try to get yourself together for her." Mom wiped at her eyes with a paper napkin from Burger King and handed another to me. I caught Merlin's eye in the rearview. Old, so old. I wondered if I was aging as quickly as everyone else in the car. How old would Sammi be?

We pulled up the drive and nothing was as it had been. Everything was the same but waving branches looked ominous. A single flower looked lonely, frightened. The hedges were foreboding. And the black hole where the barn had been seemed a crater into which we were beginning to slip.

Herbert was in the kitchen arranging casserole dishes on the shelves of the refrigerator. Isabelle was in the living room with Carol's arm around her. Virginia was just leaving and asking us to call if there was anything she could do. Isabelle's sister thanked her for the casserole. Rayne was running around the room doing cartwheels and tumbling, trying to entertain. Mom nodded toward Anne's closed door and I understood that she meant Sammi would be there.

I pulled the insides of my ribs up. I had stopped crying when we pulled onto Patapsco Road so I wouldn't look weepy. Be strong. Be strong. Be strong. My wooden shoes banged against the wooden floors. Be strong. Breathe. I saw my hand reach out for the doorknob. Be strong. Breathe. The mechanics inside the door tumbled audibly as I turned the knob. Breathe. Don't cry.

Sammi was sitting on the floor. Drawers were open and their contents surrounded her. Diaries, photos, hair bobs. The pieces of a person. It was strange to be in Anne's room without her permission. I just knew she'd come in any second and yell at us. Sammi looked up and all the composure I thought I had gathered shattered into shards that fell to the ground as I ran to her. We held onto each other and I couldn't be sure who was comforting who.

Then time lost its place in my mind and I couldn't know how long we rocked and cried. Maybe it was only seconds. Maybe it was days.

Sammi pulled away and avoided looking at me. She put her hands on the papers around her. "I was reading her diary."

I couldn't believe the freedom she must have felt to have done something so bold. I would have never felt that entitled.

"Sometimes I think I didn't really know her."

But how can you know a beam of light? How intimate can you be with a cloud? We couldn't have known Anne. She wouldn't have allowed it and it was more exciting to think of her as "other," to see her as our own personal rock star, our Stevie Nicks, an angel who had alighted on earth without ever really touching the ground.

Sammi flipped through some photos. There was one of Anne in the pool with her perfect young body that would never grow old. One of her in a thick, blue turtleneck pulling some branches aside like she had at the secret place. One I had taken of her on top of Princess wearing Isabelle's antique wedding gown with the high collar and all the lace. And one of her holding her kitty, Mehetabel, in front of the fire in the same dress with her hair piled up loosely like in Victorian photos. I flipped it over. "Here I am waiting by the fire wondering when my prince will ever come..." I put it down atop the others and watched Sammi finger the magic wand Anne made in wood shop and spray-painted silver. Her small shoulders shook again and I almost couldn't understand her words. "It should have been me."

Not knowing what to say didn't stop me from babbling. Anything to surpass the sound of crying. Anything to feel useful. Anything to stop the feelings and thinking. Talking did that. "Don't say that. That's crazy. How can you say that?"

"But it should."

"Quit saying that. Don't say that. And don't say that to your mom. She's already upset. Besides, I need you. I love you. I don't want it to be you."

We looked at each other through tears, two friends who wished at being sisters, and I knew I wasn't lying. Anne was magic but Sammi was real. I held her head on my shoulder and felt the weight of her, felt the texture of her wavy hair, the dryness of her eczema-afflicted skin, the wetness of her tears soaking through my T-shirt. I looked down at Anne's pictures and noticed that they were all just the slightest bit out of focus. Maybe she had always been only mostly here.

*   *   *

Sammi and Rayne didn't have to go back to school. Everyone seemed unusually quiet when they passed me in the hallways. But I was more the center than I had ever been. Tina put her tray down next to mine at lunch. "They said it on the loud speaker, you know."

I punched the plastic milk bag with the pointy end of the straw and sucked.

"They did. Then they did a moment of silence. I think we were supposed to pray or something."

I was grateful for the grilled cheese and tomato soup combination. Comfort food. And the cheese was still runny, just the way I liked it.

"When's the funeral?"

It exhausted me to think of talking but I needn't have worried, she was still on a roll.

"I guess they won't have an open casket. They said she didn't look human. I heard about it on the news. They talked about it on channel four. Pretty wild, huh. And my sister saw it on channel seven. But they caught the guy so that's good."

Ozepher looked at me and her eyes were audible. They were wet and available and cut through the hum in my head. They said that she knew. They said that she'd lost someone and I realized that I'd just joined a club I never knew existed. My stomach felt too full and the cheese in my mouth tasted old and dry. I looked down at my plate as I pushed it away. I'd only taken two bites. The corner of Ozepher's mouth curled up in recognition.

Tina seemed not to see me at all. "Are you going to eat that? Grilled cheese is my favorite. So, that guy's in jail, right? My dad said he'd go to jail for a long time, for his whole life probably. Was she really on a date with him? Why would she be on a date with some old, ugly guy?"

"What?"

"And I heard he has kids and everything. That's gross. Wait, if he's married, why was he out with her?"

My mouth was hot as the words flew out. "She didn't go on any stupid date with him. He gave her a ride. She would never go on a date with him, ever. If you knew her, you'd know how stupid that is. Why would you believe anything he said anyway, he's a murderer. What is wrong with you?"

"Okay, okay. I didn't mean anything by it. Everyone's been talking about it is all and I just was trying to ask you 'cause I figured you'd know."

"I don't really want to talk about it."

"Okay."

I sucked on the milk bag again.

"I mean, it's not like I can ask Sammi 'cause that would be mean and I just want to know, you know? I mean, I never knew anyone who got murdered before."

Black crept up behind my eyes and I felt my consciousness leaving me. Ozepher leapt up from her chair and caught my head before it fell to the ground. I could smell the warm funk of her body oils. My head rested on the grooved corduroy of her jumper.

I pictured a white utility truck moving past me. I pictured it making a u-turn and pulling up next to me. A man smiled and waved. I was in the truck and he was driving. Then I felt anxious. I pictured him turning. My hand scratched his face. He reached below his seat. I pictured a silver flash coming straight at my head.

I came back to myself in the nurse's office. My head was pounding. My heart was pounding. I could hear Carol's voice through the curtain. "It's been hard on all of us, but with kids... I don't know, but thanks for your sympathy." She pulled the tacky floral curtain aside and smiled at me. "You're back. You feel okay? You look like you've seen a ghost."

I felt woozy, like my head was pushing its way through cotton. "Are we going home?"

"Come on."

She led me out to her red Pinto. My skin was cold and tingly on the outside and hot and dizzy inside. I felt like a volcano being tickled by snowfall. My eyelids were thick and lazy. "Is my mom home?"

She leaned over and opened my door from inside. "She'll be home soon." She waited while I put my safety belt on then pushed the stick into gear. "Did you eat?"

"Yeah."

"Really?"

I looked at her moving her eyes from the road to the rearview. Sometimes grown-ups are so smart. Tears welled up in me from nowhere in particular. "I had a little food then I didn't want it anymore."

She moved the stick from second to third. That's the most complicated shift except reverse. That's what Anne said that day in the pavilion. Anne. I felt embarrassed over my crying but it wouldn't stop.

"You're pretty sad, huh?" The engine revved high again. "Do you want to put that in fourth?"

If she meant to distract me, it worked. I was so fascinated by driving, by the freedom to go where you want when you want. I wrapped my hand around the bulb and pulled the stick from third into fourth. The engine dropped down in pitch then hummed evenly. Carol smiled and I smiled back. I wiped at my face with my shirt and she handed me her purse. "There's Kleenex in there."

"That's okay."

"I know what you need."

Sometimes grown-ups did that, left sentences in such a way that you're supposed to respond with some obvious thing. "What?" would have been the right answer here. I liked to ignore grown-ups then and let them finish it when they realized I was too old to play those stupid games of fetch. I started to feel bad when she waited too long to keep going.

"Let's go to the drugstore and get an ice cream cone. What do you think?"

"Okay."

It dawned on me that a bad kid could use this obvious new power we had over the grown-ups. They were finally looking to see how we were doing.

I got a single scoop of mint chocolate chip on a sugar cone and licked the sides, round and round. Carol sat beside me on the curb and ate her strawberry scoop. "You're going to be thirteen soon, huh?"

"In a couple of months."

"A teenager. That's pretty exciting."

"I guess."

"I remember I couldn't wait to be a teenager. I wanted to be like my older sister and go on dates and drive a car and wear cool clothes and get a job."

"I have a job."

"Oh right, at the barn. Yeah, I forgot about that. It's funny now, because I look back and being a teenager was pretty tough. I'd say being a kid is easier."

"Like Rayne, you mean?"

"Sure."

I thought about Rayne screaming that we were taking her to hell, thought about her turning cartwheels in the living room to outrun the reality of death, thought of how much she looked like Anne, how she'd be less able to escape her than any of us. "Aren't you supposed to be working right now?"

"I got off early."

"How come?"

"To pick you up."

"Why?"

Carol took her eyes off her cone and put them on me. "What do you mean, why? Ariel, you're hurting and none of us want you to hurt."

"I've hurt lots of times."

"Honey, we've got to stick together now. This is a terrible thing that happened but it happened to all of us. Your mother put diapers on Anne. Merlin would have done anything for her. Rayne doesn't even know what hit her. You probably know more about Sammi than I do but Isabelle just lost her firstborn child. There's probably not a bigger hurt than that. We gotta stick together now and get each other through this."

"Carol?" This was how I always introduced that I was going to ask something scary and important, I always started with the name as a question. "Do you think of me as Anne's sister?" It was a sucker punch. I knew she couldn't give an answer that would satisfy me, there was none.

She must have sensed the trap because she waited before she spoke. "Your mother showed me a picture of your first birthday party. You were in a highchair at the head of the table and it must have been before you learned the word 'chocolate' because the cake on your tray was yellow. Sammi's sitting on one side of the table and she's got the fattest cheeks you've ever seen and she's got her fists just full of this cake. Then, on the other side of the table is Anne and she's standing on her chair, leaning across the table and she's maybe three or four and she's reaching out across the table. I don't know if she wanted Sammi's cake or what, but she's reaching for something. You have this little hat on and so does your mom." She looked at her cone and licked it some more. "That belongs to you."

*   *   *

Sandy waited in the car again. Dad came up to the door but wouldn't come inside. Montgomery sat quietly while we drove to their place. There was no competition for attention. It was open mic night in the car with no takers. They'd bought a new house, a huge house with only the two of them to rattle around inside. Everything was new and funny smelling.

Dad made an amazing dinner. It rose above my lack of appetite and I even ate seconds. We settled in for the evening news but Dad changed the channel when they started talking about Anne. I wanted to know what they were saying but not more than I wanted to pretend it hadn't happened. We watched a rerun of *Hogan's Heroes* instead.

I tried to picture myself as a pioneer to get the comfort it gave me. I tried to picture myself marrying and having pretty children. But Anne kept dancing through the pictures so I pictured myself just growing up.

Mom had picked out a funeral outfit for me so I wouldn't have to think tomorrow. It didn't help, it gave me a whole new litany of things to review before my mind exhausted itself and fell into sleep. I wondered if Anne was dead right away or whether she died slowly, knowing it was coming to get her. I wondered if she was happy in heaven. I wondered about Sammi and whether I could ever make this okay. And I wondered why. Why Anne? Why so young? Was it a punishment? Would it happen to me? Why is there violence? Are there people who are evil? Would I ever see Anne again? Did she know I loved her, we loved her? Did she love me? Would she remember the day out in the field when I took her picture? Did she think of me as her sister? But mostly why? Why dead? Why taken? Why young? Why, God? Why?

I played an old game where I named the shadows on the wall I blamed for keeping me awake. That one was an airplane. The one on the ceiling was a cloud shaped like a state I couldn't remember. The one across from me was a mushroom with a butterfly on top. I heard Anne's favorite songs in my head, "Sara, Smile," "Shining Star," "Bluebird." I thought of the things I never said. I talked to the canopy above me. "I love you. Do you have any idea how much we looked up to you? You are the most beautiful girl I've ever seen besides my mother. I will never, ever forget you."

The sound of Montgomery crying through the wall lulled me to sleep.

Then it was morning. Sandy's puppy woke me up before she came in. "Okay dirt ball, time to get up."

I dressed without being in my body. I brushed teeth that could have been missing, combed hair that could have turned brown. Nothing registered. Nothing felt real. Today, we would bury Anne.

Sandy made biscuits, eggs and sausage and the puppy ate what I couldn't. Montgomery sat next to me in the car as we drove to Ellicott City, a town famous for its floods. The parking lot was full. So many people from her high school. Kids in black. I followed Dad and Sandy into a pew in the back and looked down the aisles to Mom sitting in the front with Isabelle and Nana and Sammi and Rayne. I suppose Dad had done plenty of things that made me angry but I'd never felt rage boiling up inside me before. Sitting near the exit door like a stranger and looking at my family sitting up front where I belonged, I felt something in me harden against him. He'd diapered Anne too. How could he pretend that he was a tourist?

I looked at the baby faces of the people from our schools, took in the bewilderment of a room that would never again believe in their invincibility. I would never have that now. I would never be an immortal teen recklessly trying on life for size.

Anne's casket was covered with blue flowers and fake bluebirds like the one she put on Kevin's Easter basket. The coffin was closed but I knew that, inside, she was wearing her favorite floral scarf-hemmed dress with her tuxedo tails over it. That scary doll with the teeth was in there too, the one she'd had her whole life, and the lamb with all the fur worn off. I liked that she had all those things with her, all those things she loved.

The priest talked, then Isabelle's sister got up and read a poem from Anne's diary. "Nearer still, I come to the end. I take death's hand and call him 'Friend.'"

Maybe God whispers in the ears of the ones He doesn't give much time to. Maybe He lets them know that they have to do all their living right away instead of working their way up to it. I thought of that day when I rubbed oil on Anne and she asked me how I knew she'd live to see eighteen.

Mom wept. I watched her body, rigid with dignity, shaking to hold in the tears, and still they fell. No one was holding Sammi's hand. I was in the wrong pew. Sammi's hand was empty and mine was the one meant to fill it. Montgomery looked out the window over the tenth station of the cross and Sandy read the program over and over. Dad looked like a piece of granite with an epitaph sketched across it. Inside his stony face was the man who had held Anne when she was an infant. If I hadn't been so angry, I might have felt bad for the man who wouldn't allow himself to mourn this precious child.

We emptied into the parking lot after the service. I wanted to be with Herbert and Carol and Sammi and the rest of the Lemons, but Dad kept his hand on my shoulder and guided us to his car. I didn't realize until we pulled away from the lit-headlight chain of cars that we weren't going to the burial. "Where are we going?"

"Home."

"Why? Everyone's going to the cemetery. Turn around! Where are you going?"

"We're all very tired."

I had been going along pretty well with all this divorce nonsense but, in one sharp instant, my patience turned to anger. I felt betrayed by everyone in the car. Except Montgomery. So, I took his hand and held it in mine as we stared out of our windows and didn't fight over who was hogging the seat.

*   *   *

We hadn't had a family meeting since the barn burned. I sat on a throw pillow with Mom's hand combing through my hair. Merlin started us off. "We have a lot of stuff to talk about, kids."

My heart hurt. I didn't want them to talk about Anne, didn't want them to bring up the barn or fires or murderers or death. I didn't want to think about trials or newspapers. I was tired of having feelings, tired of being heavy and sad and angry.

He nodded some secret nod at Herbert. "Herbert has something he wants to share with us."

Herbert didn't know whether to stand or sit. He shifted but stayed in his place on the couch. "This is harder than I thought."

I got really scared. Mom's hand stopped.

"Good news, folks! I'm, uh, I'm getting married."

I was so relieved that I didn't care when Mom's knee hit me in the back of the head as she jumped up to hug Herbert. Embracing, we were a big bundle of arms and exhales. We settled down again, everyone beaming with romance and much-needed good news. Mom's face was shiny with happy. "When will she and the girls move in?"

Herbert shifted and looked at his hands. "We're getting a house."

No one spoke. This was a goodbye. This was another ending after too many endings.

The celebration caved in and Merlin steered our awkward quiet back toward normalcy. He told us to stay away from the burned remains of the barn. Mom announced the pool would be ready for swimming this weekend. Carol assigned chores and we talked about planting the garden.

Isabelle read from *Willy Wonka* while we sipped lemonade. But inside, I felt everything falling away.

*   *   *

The whole room smelled of new synthetic carpet. A map on the wall showed two streets running almost side by side, Darkest Evening Way and Downy Flake Path. In the middle of the room sat a Lucite-boxed model of the housing development. Darkest Evening Way and Downy Flake Path ran down to the man-made lake. "Little Horse Lake" was scripted on top of the clear blue plastic of the model lake. Little fuzzy trees lined the streets and rimmed the lake. White Monopoly houses ran in sections down each street. A brass plaque read, "Little Horse Landing."

I held Sammi's hand as a chipper, blonde woman led us through "floor plan number two." It was a nice house, a 'townhouse,' she called it. But it smelled so new and clean, so lifeless. Our clothes seemed dingy against the white walls, antiquated compared with the flashy modern furniture.

There were shiny bathrooms, a sparkling kitchen, an optional wooden balcony, a fireplace in the living room, an indoor laundry room, lots of nice things but it didn't feel like anything. It had no mood, no face.

We followed the lady back down to the room with the Lucite-enclosed neighborhood. Mom smiled at Montgomery who sat in the plush, leather chair and looked through slick, colorful foldouts of floor plans. She put her arm around Isabelle's shoulder and squeezed. Mom's enthusiasm was so unflagging that I often found it suspect. But as I watched her reassuring Isabelle, it hit me that even if her enthusiasm over these townhouses was for Isabelle's benefit, her enthusiasm for Isabelle was the genuine article.

Sometimes I loved Mom out of habit, sometimes out of obligation. But moments like these, moments when I saw her for all the things I hoped I'd become, I fell in love with her just for the sake of it.

It had taken two cars to get us all there even though Herbert didn't come and Anne, well, Anne didn't come either. I wanted to go home in Merlin's car and sit beside Sammi but I just waved to her when they pulled in front of us and led the way out of civilized Columbia and back into the farmlands and woods of Sykesville. My chest released when we pulled back onto Patapsco Road and past all the weathered, suburban homes in Windriver Estates, around the familiar bends in the road, through the tunnel of trees, past the barns and horses and then past the ruins of our barn and the sign naming our home. Merlin stopped the car suddenly before we got to the parking lot. Everyone got out of their car so we did the same. Merlin pointed at the dead tree trunk. "Look."

Eight heads turned upward because, near the top, impossibly, tiny green buds were peeking out.

*   *   *

We walked to town in the river, just me and Sammi. The water was pretty high in some places and we'd laugh when the bottom dropped too quickly and swallowed us. We stopped just outside the county line and sat on a favorite rock. The water rushed by on either side but a small spot behind the rock remained calm and I watched tiny fish glimmering like aluminum pull tabs moving on string.

I peeled pieces of moss off the rock and threw them into the water. Sammi tickled the current with a stick.

I put my hand over my eyes to shield the sun and tried to hold everything into them. I wanted to remember the smell of

Pataspsco's river water, the shapes of the trees, the line of the railroad tracks dividing river from woods. I wanted to carry the sound of the leaves in all their different greens being rustled by wind, the feeling of that same breeze stimulating the white hairs on my arms. I wanted to record these particular bird noises, this exact shade of blue sky.

Sammi's eyes were gathering things too.

We sat quiet on that rock for awhile, each on our own mission to never lose this place. Then, she threw her stick into the current and watched it get sucked under and away. "Do you think Anne liked me?"

I almost laughed. "Of course she did, she loved you."

"No, I know she loved me, but do you think she liked me? Like as a person, like a friend."

I wasn't sure who Anne liked and didn't like. Her moods were mercurial, her tastes fickle and her cards were always clutched tightly to her chest. She loved Kevin but she might have outgrown that, had she been allowed to grow. I think we knew more now, having read her poetry and her diaries, than we had known from all the years of trying to understand the mysteries of her heart. But I knew what Sammi needed to hear and she needed to hear it said with certainty. "Of course she liked you. Don't even wonder about that. You're her sister, silly."

"You really think so?"

I did. But what mattered more was that it didn't matter. Anne was tough and angry and sharp but she wasn't cruel. She wouldn't want Sammi wondering these things for the rest of her life. "What's not to like? Think about all those times she did stuff just with you. That was because she liked you, like a friend. She liked being around you."

Sammi picked up a pebble and lobbed it gently into the eddy where the fish swam. "I guess so."

"It's a lot to remember."

"Yeah."

"That's what we've gotta do, we've gotta remember her."

"Remember that time we sang in her room?" Sammi was smiling now and it looked like music to me.

"You picked a fine time to leave me, Lucille." We sang together and swayed back and forth on the rock. If people can be around after they die, I believe Anne was there with us on that rock, laughing and swaying and remembering.

"Hey Ariel, don't laugh but do you believe in ghosts?"

I wasn't sure how to answer. Maybe she wanted to know Anne could visit. Maybe she was scared of being haunted. "I saw some weird things in the house. I don't know what to think, I guess."

She swatted at her leg. "Do you think Mr. Christopher is real?"

"I don't know. Maybe it doesn't matter. Sometimes it was just nice thinking there was someone there watching us, you know?"

"Yeah. Yeah, and she wasn't scary at all." Sammi almost smiled.

"Nope, just another Lemon."

We looked up the river together. It kept flowing at us, threatening to wash us away, but we sat there in the sun like we were on solid ground.

"Hey Sammi, Major Healy or Major Nelson?"

"Nelson, definitely. Which Angel?"

"The smart one, Samantha."

We walked into town. Everything was for the last time. We wandered the two aisles of the grocery and picked through the candy and ice creams looking for a favorite just like we always had. We walked halfway back, stopping to climb over to the waterfall and smoke a cigarette. We kicked rocks passing Crane's and Tuffy's and Alice's and Happy's. We ignored the burned-out hole where the barn used to be and fed Princess at Virginia's. She came out and asked us if we wanted to muck some stalls next week and we said yes because it was true that we wanted to.

"Vaughn hasn't been ridden in a while. You two would really be doing me a favor if you took him out for a ride."

I liked it when you could tell a grown-up was lying so that they wouldn't seem too nice. Then you could say yes without guilt.

Virginia led Vaughn out and we didn't bother to bridle or saddle him. I gave Sammi a boost up and she pulled me on behind her. She held onto the mane, I held onto her waist and we crossed the street into the field that was being divided for housing lots. We walked around the edges of the field then crossed the grassy middle and made funny patterns.

I don't know if it was a snake or just some fantasy that scared the horse, but Vaughn jumped unexpectedly and took off running. I squeezed my legs around the horse tightly and gripped at Sammi. She tangled her fingers into his mane and leaned her body forward. We held on while Vaughn galloped across the field, bucking and trying to shirk us. We held on when he turned sharply and ran up a small hill. We held on when he leapt over a tree stump and again over a fallen branch. Then he calmed down and slowed to a trot. His body bounced lightly beneath us.

And down we went.

The fall pushed most of the air from my gut and Sammi fell on top of me pushing out the rest. I lay stunned while Vaughn came to a stop nearby and bowed his head to chomp on some grass. Sammi rolled off of me and we looked at each other then exploded into laughter. We were getting so good at hanging on for dear life that we were forgetting how to just trot along.

*　　*　　*

Herbert had a separate truck for his stuff. Our truck was big and yellow and very full. Every box was labeled. Kitchen B for Isabelle's stuff and kitchen W for ours. We were dividing along the lines of Busch and Whilone. Even Merlin and Carol were divided among us.

Mom was vacuuming carpets while we loaded up. I caught her crying but she put on a big smile for me and told me how exciting this all was.

Carol and Herbert moved Anne's stuff out. Her room was like that accident in the road that you don't want to see but can't help but look at. I walked by with regularity and looked out the side of my eye to see Anne's stuff in boxes, her life packed away, her privacy shattered. She must really have died because she would have never put up with any of this. Carol marked each of her boxes with an A before sealing them with packing tape in a way that seemed more permanent than I was comfortable with.

Montgomery was sitting in the bathtub. He'd been there for over an hour and Mom said to leave him be, so I did. But, I thought it was strange, a little boy sitting in a porcelain tub with his jeans, sneakers and no water. He was humming.

Rayne retrieved things from secret hiding spots, a Parcheesi piece she put under a corner of carpet, a Barbie shoe she'd kept on a window ledge.

Sammi and I finished up our boxes and lugged them down the winding staircase. I sat looking out the window for a minute. Merlin was carrying tools from the pavilion. The garden was in disarray, having been abandoned when we found out we were moving. The trees that lined the field were growing lush and full with oncoming summer. I saw the ghosts of us playing softball in the back field, heard us laughing and yelling and running and winning and losing. I wanted some sort of moment with Sammi but we'd had too many moments for moments lately so she took the last box and went down the stairs without a look back.

I stood in Rayne's room and looked out at the pool so I could watch our ghosts skinny-dipping and throwing green slime and celebrating birthdays. I looked around the playroom and watched us playing fort and watching TV and dressing up in costumes.

Mom's room was empty. Even the carpet was gone. I watched our ghosts play piano drunk and dab perfume for a date and snuggle in the bed.

Anne's door was closed but I saw us inside walking in her platform shoes and looking through her magazines and trying our hardest to be her.

Our ghosts ate and laughed and argued in the dining room. They had family meetings, read books, met weird people, battled snakes and ate marzipan in the living room. They sat in the trees out front, eating fruit from the branches and spitting the pits. I looked out the front window to the ghost of our barn and watched us playing in the mud and building a fence that could only fall down.

Then I joined everyone on the side patio where our ghosts were spitting watermelon seeds and calling for lost cats while we finished loading the last of the boxes.

Mom smiled too brightly. "Honey, go get your brother, sweetheart."

Montgomery was still in the tub. I didn't say anything, just extended my hand, which he took, and we walked out together. I turned off the light switch and heard that hollow sound they make in an empty house. We were really leaving.

Jay, Kay, Elle, and Em waved goodbye from their fence. We hugged Herbert and piled into cars and trucks and followed each other down the gravel drive and past the dead tree trunk, now in full bloom.

*   *   *

The farm is still there but its land has been cut up to add some suburban looking houses. I heard they redid the inside and modernized it.

The river still runs its course and the trains still cut the woods from it but the grocery is a thrift store and the town even has a restaurant now.

The remaining Lemons moved into side-by-side townhouses on Darkest Evening Way but never did get around to cutting a door connecting them internally.

Mr. Brant ended up being transferred to our new middle school, but the school had plenty of black kids and a black principal so he never puffed his chest.

When Kevin got out of jail, he came and found us at "our spot" on the lake for Fourth of July fireworks. He didn't say much but he stayed for hours. If souls do return, I believe Anne was there.

Isabelle and Merlin ended up getting married. Most of the Lemons showed up. Isabelle wore a Victorian dress like the one

Anne used to wear. The wedding was in an old barn that had been converted into a church. That felt right. Anne's school photo sat next to her grandfather's on the alter.

Carol lived with my Mom another ten years. She went back to being a teacher and even ended up teaching me sex ed. She was actually great at it.

We see Herbert now and again but he lived on the other side of town and got very busy with his new family. Tommy married a nice girl he met at the comic book store he managed. They had two boys and a girl so I figured he was well prepared for that. Cory became a Marine where treating the world like a jungle gym would fit right in. I lost track of Edwina.

Rayne moved north. I don't see her much anymore but she's still a sister to me.

Sammi got married and had a beautiful blonde child born with a halo and stars shooting around her. Her name is Anne. They live on a farm.

Montgomery's love for computers came in handy when he started working. He may not have followed in Dad's footsteps but he certainly followed the path Dad started for him. I still lose them to the computer room during holidays but now it makes me smile to see how that machine bonds them. Montgomery married one of the best women I've ever met. After stretching his heart to include all the Lemons, it was easy for him to love her tiny daughters as his own.

Mom built her own practice comforting others and helping them process pain and loss. She wrote books and meditative tapes. She showed me that you could "do what you love and the money will come." Mom had a lot of trouble finding her husband. She dated Arnold off and on for years, much to my irritation. They're still best friends, which doesn't bother me at all. In fact, it's kind of nice to have another person around who knows what Lemonade Farm was. Finally, Frank came along - yep, same name as Dad. He's a good man and he's good to Mom. It's easy to love him.

I ended up getting to live some of the things I used to picture. Despite my Amazonian height, I competed on my high school gymnastics team. I was great at playing hurt and even won some ribbons. Sammi almost always scored higher. Sometimes she'd get a red ribbon - I knew she loved those best.

I filled out and looked cute in halters and heels and, of course, I figured out what all that teenage-boy fumbling was about. I danced with boys I liked and even got to see Stevie Nicks twirling onstage with Fleetwood Mac - twice.

I modeled for thirteen years. Turns out there's one job perfect for too-tall girls. I was never the prettiest or the best or even the tallest, but it helped me pay for college and it beat the the heck out of shoveling horse shit. Plus, I got to meet "The Fonz" and David Cassidy.

Though I'll always remember my first kiss, I now know it's the last man I kiss that matters most. My husband has a very big family. They do everything together. If I'd never had that time at Lemonade Farm with such a large family, I'm sure I'd find the whole thing overwhelming. Every time someone new marries into our ever-expanding clan, I remember Carol moving in and becoming just another Lemon in our lemonade.

When we first left the farm, I saw Anne in every mall, every school, every room for years, but she disappeared slowly from them and haunts me less now. I plant blue morning glories everywhere I live to keep her around and I still cry when I hear her songs. They say time heals all wounds but I know now that the scars remain. I have no idea who I would have been if Anne hadn't been ripped from us so swiftly and violently. But the upside to knowing people can die unexpectedly, even young, is that I've endeavored to love well. I don't take for granted that I can apologize or thank someone tomorrow. I won't die with my mouth full of all the nice things I meant to say. I saw clearly that this is my one and only life, not the dress rehearsal so I was never afraid to follow my dreams into the unknown, to jump into abysses, to take what life dealt me and create something new from it.

I've lived a hundred lives since the farm. Different careers, different countries, different friends. But Lemonade Farm comes with me everywhere I go. It goes with all of us. We Lemons live thousands of miles apart now and we go about our lives. You might not even be able to guess if you met one of us, but we are indelibly marked by that time, by that place.

When I think of family, I think of lemonade.

Made in the USA
Middletown, DE
20 September 2018